About the Author

M.H. Baylis is a novelist, journalist and scriptwriter. He worked for the BBC as a storyliner on EastEnders (where he helped devise the ratings-grabbing Valentine's Day murder plot and made Dot Cotton consume cannabis), before moving to Kenya and Cambodia, where he trained local scriptwriters and created TV dramas for the BBC. After a spell living in a remote mountain village on the Pacific island of Tanna, he returned to Britain to take up his present role as television critic for the *Daily Express*. Baylis's first crime novel, *A Death at the Palace*, was published to much acclaim in 2013, followed by *The Tottenham Outrage* in 2014.

As Matthew Baylis, he is the author of *Man Belong Mrs Queen* (2013), which was a BBC Radio 4 'Book of the Week'.

Black Day at The Bosphorus Café

M.H. Baylis

First published in Great Britain in 2015 by Old Street Publishing Ltd
Yowlestone House, Tiverton, Devon EX16 8LN
www.oldstreetpublishing.co.uk

ISBN 978-1-910400-17-3

Typeset by JaM

Printed and bound by CPI Group (UK) Ltd, Croydon, CR0 4YY

To Mr and Mrs Brenard – Mazeltov!

CHAPTER ONE

Months later, when it was all over, Rex would recall neither the smell, nor the scream, nor the open mouths of the onlookers. Only the colours. The colours of a girl on fire. Flames like a dozen, separate little wings, dirty orange to ocean blue, seemed to speed the dark girl's flight as she tumbled screeching from the summit of the escalator, rolling twice before landing on the ground floor of Shopping City in a thrashing heap.

People threw coats over her quickly: partly to kill the flames, partly to hide the horror of her blistering, twitching body, and as they did so, Rex saw that one of her dirty, neon-pink-laced trainers was still alight. He came forward to stamp it out, then froze, shocked, as he realised he'd already forgotten that this was the foot of a person. The flames died away before he could decide what to do.

Noises then: alarms, screams, men shouting orders. In the confusion, he glanced up to the floor she'd fallen from. Just to the right of the escalator, peering over the safety rail, he thought he saw a face. Someone jostled him, and when he looked back, there was nothing to see. He wasn't sure there ever had been.

Someone went at the girl with a fire extinguisher and the flames disappeared, leaving just the appalling, summertime barbecue smell in the air. The girl stopped shaking and grunting, charred denim limbs coming to rest in a spray of indecent angles. A thin, young, suited black man – a doctor it seemed – approached and knelt at her side. His pose looked priestly, Rex thought, as he forced himself to look. She was a tall girl. He saw her long, straight black hair. A little jeans jacket with an unzipped, hooded top underneath. Small breasts under a political t-shirt: a fist, a star, a slogan. The doctor had two fingers pressed at the girl's throat. He shook his head, pulled one of the coats up to cover her face. It was a little girl's raincoat, covered in multi-coloured parrots.

Minutes before, Rex had been watching the mother of the child who owned that coat in conversation with Eve Reilly, newly selected Labour candidate for Harringay and Tottenham. A bye-election was on the way and Reilly had chosen today for her first lunchtime meet-and-greet. Whilst trooping round the ground floor of Wood Green's Shopping City, she had invited the tall African lady with the cropped mauve curls to tell her 'what issues really matter'.

The lady had obliged, and a few minutes in, the newly selected Labour candidate had begun to look as though she was regretting her question. Rex Tracey, who had arrived late after being sent to cover the walkabout for the local paper, was gleefully recording every stammered excuse in his notebook. He'd just caught a wink from Terry, the photographer, and had begun to enjoy what had promised to be merely the start of three months' worth of dull electioneering exercises, when

2

a scream like a vixen's cut the air. Everyone had stopped what they were doing and looked up to the mezzanine above, to see the awful, humanoid bale of flame as it tumbled screeching to the ground in its halo of heat and vapour.

In the aftermath Eve Reilly sprang into action, moving some people back from the charred bundle, berating others for filming the proceedings on their phones. She began to shout at Terry, who was, perhaps, the only person with an excuse to be taking pictures, but then turned and caught sight of the girl on the floor, whose gaudy face covering had slipped a few inches, revealing colours more disturbing. The young politician fell suddenly silent, then collapsed in racking sobs.

The photographer put an arm round her and ushered Reilly towards a set of fixed benches on the other side of the escalator. Music still played from somewhere, metallic and faint.

Rex stayed where he was. He recognised the words on the girl's t-shirt. Kurdish, the northern dialect called Kurmanji, which was written in Roman script. And today, a blustery Spring Friday, was the 21st of March, otherwise known as Newroz. Spring New Year across a swathe of the planet, from Eastern Turkey to Tajikistan – and in this region of north London, a giant hooley for the Kurdish community. Shopping City and the streets around it were full of Kurds, stocking up for a weekend of parties and, perhaps, if the weather brightened, picnics. That was why Eve Reilly had picked the day for her precinct tour. Was it why this tall, slim girl had picked today, too?

He spotted something on the floor by her left hand. He wondered if she had been holding it. He went as close as he dared to her body, trying to ignore the warmth it gave off. It was a little brooch, of coloured enamels, in the shape of a peacock. The sight reminded him, ridiculously, that he had an appointment with a man called Pocock, a Council Planning Officer, that afternoon. As the first wave of hi-vis-vested authority began to stream into the building with commands and crackling handsets, he remembered all the other things required of him. There was some Greek doctor who wanted to talk to him about the Cypriot community. His editor had an urgent, top-secret issue that she would only broach with him in a fifteen-minute window in a coffee bar in the early evening. In between: articles to finish, web pages to update, a shoe to be re-heeled. Pills to be swallowed. He suddenly felt anger towards the girl on the floor, for screwing up his day with her extreme protest. Then he looked back at her pretty peacock brooch on the floor and felt sorry.

He had an idea he'd seen something like it before. On whom? A girl? A colleague? His wife? He found it hard to think about Sybille. Soon, he knew, he would need to. He pushed the thought aside and looked around.

Shopping City was a two-headed retail leviathan, laying a turd – as one architectural historian had once put it – that became the A105. The section of the mall they stood in was quieter and emptier: there were probably no more than fifteen people standing around. They nonetheless conformed to the rules of all disaster crowds: there were those who hurried away at the first intimation of something horrid, and those who rushed towards it – often, nowadays, with their phone-cameras on record. A third, larger group consisted of people who felt it was their duty to hang around at a safe distance. Most of these had collected in the corridor behind the escalator, staring at the blinking, beckoning poker machines in the bookmaker's, uncomfortable, yet unable to leave. They needed to be told to go. Soon, the police would either start doing this, or else keep everyone inside to take statements. Rex wasn't sure which. In the years he'd spent tracking the vital signs of the borough, he'd witnessed hostage-takings, balcony-jumps, many ugly endings. He'd never seen anything like this.

He moved towards Eve Reilly, who had been surrounded by her own protective cordon. It consisted of Gil Agnew, the departing Member, moist, wheezing, a drinker approaching the true Last Orders, along with the broad, benevolent-looking local party chairman, and a chilly, priestly-looking figure from Millbank. Rex had shaken all of their hands (damp, rough, claw-like, respectively) at the start of the tour. Now they edged away from him, closer to their prize girl, as if he sought to do her harm.

'Eve won't be commenting on this,' said the Millbank man, adjusting his cuffs.

'I don't want her to,' Rex replied. He looked directly at her. She was still sitting with Terry on the bench, sucking a mint, staring into space. 'Are you all right?'

'What?' she asked, aggressively, as if the question had been an insult, and then added, less sharply, 'Sorry. Yes. I mean – I guess you have to expect the unexpected round here, don't you?'

He didn't imagine Eve Reilly, in her dark trouser-suit and her sharp hairdo, knew much about the borough. Until a couple of months back, he knew, she'd commuted in from High Wycombe, a typical modern, train-track politician, he thought, clattering along a set route from PPE at Oxford to the job in the think-tank to the safe seat. There were jokes about the gated mews flat she'd just rented, alone, at the very southernmost tip of Crouch End. Eve Reilly might have moved to her constituency, the wags said, but her kitchen was in Islington.

'I wouldn't blame the area. The last time a Kurdish girl set light to herself it was in Knightsbridge,' Rex said.

Terry frowned. 'Eh?'

'She was wearing a PKK shirt,' Rex said. 'And it's Newroz. Kurdish New Year.'

'I know that,' his Geordie colleague grunted. 'Doesn't mean *she's* set light to *herself*, does it?'

Terry was like this all the time now. He'd won a Press Award, a year back, for undercover reportage at a mosque that had been taken over by extremists. Now he challenged Rex at every turn, as if he thought he could do the job better. They were still friends. Friends who fell out all the time.

'I know there's a history of girls from the Kurdish community, here and in Germany, sympathetic to the PKK, setting themselves alight as a public protest. I also know the ceasefire in Turkey's been bollocksed by a PKK bomb in a college. I do catch the news every now and then,' he added, defensively.

'If you're referring to Trabzon, it was two months back, it was a barracks, and the PKK haven't claimed responsibility,' Eve Reilly said, staring blankly off towards the escalator. 'Given the number of Kurdish conscripts there were in that barracks, I'd call it a spectacular own goal if it was theirs. And the PKK haven't ended the ceasefire, just threatened to end it.'

'You're very well briefed on it,' Rex said. She didn't reply, just wiped a tear from her eye with a shaking hand. She still had a child's face, chubby and freckled.

'So if she was PKK,' Terry said, 'what was she protesting about?'

'I don't know. The threat to end the ceasefire? Or she could –'

'No, could you, actually, just shut up?' Eve's voice, tinny and harsh, cut through his own, silencing him. 'This gentleman's right. We don't know anything. And it's pretty disrespectful, actually, to be standing here arguing when there's a girl...' She stopped before she could say the word. She swallowed, a red flush climbing up her neck, then carried on more quietly. 'Look. It's my first day in my constituency and I've watched a... a girl burning to death.'

Rex thought about saying that it wasn't her constituency yet, that it might never be if the bye-election didn't go her way. He kept his mouth shut – the politician looked genuinely upset. As everyone was. The police arrived. They started herding people out – they were good at it.

'We'll talk,' the Millbank man said, catching Rex's eyes and making a phone gesture, as if this had been no more than a transport snarl-up.

'Lovely,' said Rex. He felt trembly and sick. He wanted his painkillers. As they trooped past the escalator and the awful, lingering smell, he asked Terry to take some pictures of the upstairs level, which he did, discreetly as ever, pretending to check something on his camera as he snapped away.

Outside, as a brief shower hit the High Street, a low, black ambulance parked at the kerb, and Rex looked through the pictures on the little viewfinder screen.

'What are you looking for?' Terry asked, wiping raindrops from the screen with a denim sleeve.

'I thought I saw someone else up there.'

'Up top? Who'd be up there?'

A fair point. Since the Primark on the other side of the road had expanded, all the other bargain clothes shops had struggled. The floor the girl had fallen from was full of empty units. Not that the ground floor was much better: a massive CashConverters and a bookies took up most of the functioning retail space. Eve Reilly had picked the sparsest part of the whole complex to conclude her walkabout. But maybe that had been deliberate.

'I can see like this shape of her,' Terry said. 'Every time I close my eyes. Like when you look at a flash.' He shuddered. 'That's probably what you saw.'

'Probably.'

Rex took deep breaths of Wood Green air: bus exhaust, rain and fag smoke, mostly, but still better than inside. He felt his heart slowing down. Terry was probably right. When he thought about it, all that remained was a thin flash of white. He could add details if he concentrated – it became a face, male, angular, skinny– but that's what he was doing, adding his own details to a flash of white. There'd been nobody there.

'Pretty shit, wasn't it?'

Rex looked at his colleague, bony and buzz-cut in his stonewash jacket-and-jeans combo, like an ageing hooligan. They'd seen a lot together, him and Terry, and they didn't discuss it much, but there was a comfort in knowing what they shared. 'Yeah, pretty shit.'

'Pint before we go back?'

There was a chain pub called The Seagull fifty yards up. At night, it ran a talent competition called Stars In Their Minds. In the daytime, the big screen showed live sporting action from Bucharest. The place had never looked so appealing. Rex was about to agree when his phone rang.

It was Mr Pocock, and he was waiting outside his house. Rex didn't much feel like meeting a Building Control Officer from Harringay and Tottenham Council. On the other hand, doing something so mundane might be good for him, take his mind off what he'd seen. And smelt. In any case, it had taken him weeks to fix this appointment, and he wanted to get his new windows put in before the summer.

But the fact was the girl was a scoop – that was an ugly reality of his job. He sent Terry back with the pictures, and ducked into the Boots to ring his editor, sitting on the row of seats by the pharmacy counter and dictating a few paragraphs for her to polish and post. That completed, he walked home, as he always did, fast, because it was less painful than walking slowly. Rex was a stocky man in his early forties, with a limp from an accident he'd had over a decade ago. People often looked at him twice – maybe because of his gait, or because he always wore a suit, or because his face reminded them of someone, or something. He was often deep in thought, as now.

He snapped out of it as he turned onto the lane where he lived, and saw the man from the council waiting for him. Ashley Pocock was a curly-haired, heavily freckled young man in a suit that looked too big for him. He was leaning against a car that didn't quite fit either: a brand new BMW, sleek and fuck-you crimson with a personalised number plate. AP 1985.

'I didn't know the council paid so well,' Rex said, nodding at the vehicle.

It was a meagre smile that came back. 'Something going on up at Shopping City? The road's jammed.'

'I think it's a fire,' Rex said shortly. 'Shall we?'

For the last decade, Rex Tracey had lived alone in an odd little detached house just east of the shopping centre. It had once been a garage, the bedrooms were right in the roof, and there were no windows at the back. The last two summers had been record-breakers, with nights so hot he'd ended up dozing uneasily in a plastic chair in the garden. Rex couldn't face another summer of that, hence his application to put in windows and skylights. A process which, he'd been assured by colleagues in the office, would be a piece of cake. He had a shock coming.

'The issue is, according to our records, there's no completion certificate for the conversion?' Pocock said, or rather queried, in the modern way, having let Rex take him over the house and show him where the intended adaptations would go.

'Meaning what?'

'Meaning,' the young man said, in his surprisingly deep voice, 'that it's not a legal dwelling until it gets one? You need an inspection.'

Rex nodded. They were standing on the tiny landing and he started to feel uneasy – the anxious knot that had been in his throat since Shopping City now spreading to his jaw.

'So can you do the inspection?'

'I could. The problem is, like, I have to tell you now, there's no way I could pass the place?' Pocock's accent was a manifesto for globalisation: local patois vowels with the 'Neighbours' question mark on the end.

'Why couldn't you pass it?'

'Because it's got no windows at the back?'

Rex laughed. Pocock, however, did not. He still had acne

on his chin, and he fingered a couple of spots with his nail, looking uneasy.

'So I can't apply to change it without a completion certificate. And I can't get a completion certificate...'

'Without changing it.'

Rex laughed again. This time, not because he found anything funny.

'There's people building all over the place. That Turkish social club on the corner's having skylights and solar panels and god-knows-what-else... Your boss is building a flipping zoo on the marshes, isn't he?'

Pocock shrugged. 'I don't make the rules.'

'So what can I do?'

Rex's phone rang. It was a mobile number. He'd had another call from it ten minutes ago. He went into the living room, took two deep breaths and answered.

'It's Dr Georgiadis,' said a woman's voice, sirens in the background. 'I can't find a way through to your office. They've blocked off the road.'

Georgiadis. The Greek doctor. He couldn't even remember what she wanted. Now his neck felt stiff. What was happening to him? 'Where are you?'

'At Turnpike Lane tube.'

'Stay at the station,' he said slowly, through lips that had started to feel numb. 'I'll meet you in five minutes.'

As Rex put his phone away with shaking hands, he could hear the same sirens in the distance. Pocock came into the room. 'I can drop you at the station, Mr Tracey. I have to get to another appointment.'

Rex grabbed a card of pills on his way out and instantly popped two. Feeling slightly better in Pocock's car, he

11

used the three-minute ride to the tube station to complain bitterly about the absurdity of council planning practices. They reached the parade, where the road turned into a pedestrianized zone in front of the toilets and the bus station. By the scaffolding outside the Trabzonspor Social Club, Rex saw a buxom, curly-haired woman in a raincoat, resting her briefcase on top of a bollard as she looked all around her. The mere fact of her standing still announced her to be a stranger. No one stood still there, if they had a choice.

She seemed to clock Rex as he clocked her. She gave a tentative smile. He assumed she was the Greek doctor, and smiled back. But he wasn't finished with Pocock.

'I can't leave it like that. There must be some way round this. Isn't there?'

'You need good advice, Mr Tracey. And that's costly, these days, isn't it?' Pocock gave him a long, blank look. One of the chin-spots he'd picked was bleeding. The man seemed to expect something else from him.

'You've got all my numbers,' Pocock said finally, springing open the locks. Dazed and frustrated by the whole encounter, Rex stepped out and watched him reverse away in his garish car.

'Rex?' said the woman. She sounded American. She held out a hand. He stared at it, wondering what he was supposed to do with it. His mouth felt dry and there was still the smell, that awful smell from the burned girl, in his nose. Singed cloth brought back older memories from childhood: standing too long in front of the fire in his pyjamas after his mother had left for work. Scalding his thighs.

'Are you okay?'

'No, I'm...' Before he could answer, he lurched towards her. She caught him, letting the briefcase drop.

'Whoa. You're not okay, are you?'

In the Bosphorus Café, over hot, sweet, sunset-coloured tea, Dr Georgiadis taught him something.

'Do the opposite of what you're telling yourself. Don't shut it out. Think about it – all of it – what you saw, what you heard, what you smelt, and while you're doing it, follow my finger with your eyes.'

He felt self-conscious, sitting there amid the fumes from the Enfield bus and the fried breakfasts, but he did what she said. He remembered the shriek and the colours of the burning girl and the smell and the odd, white streak that he'd thought was a face. And all the while, he focussed his eyes on the doctor's slim, honey-coloured finger as she moved it from left to right, first slowly, then with increasing speed.

'How do you feel?'

He hesitated. The appalling truth was that, alongside feeling no better, he had a hard-on. A great, unapologetic stalk. Perhaps because of the unfathomable connection between death and sex. Or more probably because it was the first time in ages that an attractive woman had been nice to him.

'Still anxious,' he said.

She had him do it again. This time, focusing carefully on his own inner state, he realised something had changed. The tight, nauseous ball that had been lodged inside him since the Shopping Mall, now seemed less obvious. In fact, after going through the process a third time, it seemed to have gone altogether, along with the smell, or its memory. He knew something bad had happened, something bad he'd witnessed. But he wasn't feeling it with his body any more. He took a tentative breath and smiled.

'Are you a hypnotist or a witch?'

Her eyes were brown and warm. 'EMDR,' she said. The accent wasn't American, he realised, just faintly foreign. Greek-Cypriot, he supposed. 'Eye Movement Desensitisation and Reprocessing. We use it with traumatised people in conflict zones.'

'You could call this place a conflict zone.'

'You could certainly call what you've just been through a very traumatic experience,' she said. 'You shouldn't be back at work.'

'If I wasn't, I'd just...' He stopped himself. 'I feel like I want to be busy and... well, at my age, you do know what's good for you, don't you?'

At this moment, the waitress put a toasted fried egg and halloumi sandwich on the table in front of him. Dr Georgiadis looked at it and gave a chuckle. It was a rather naughty sound, Rex thought, at odds with her composed exterior.

'Well, if you want to be busy, Mr Tracey, why don't we do the interview?'

'Good idea.' He got out his notebook. Then he looked at her, reddening. 'The problem is... I'm afraid I've completely forgotten why I'm interviewing you –'

She laughed again. She seemed to find him very funny. 'I work with a department of the United Nations which gathers medical and psychological information about war crimes, government-sanctioned torture and violence.'

Some of it came back to him. 'And you're here because of some missing people in Cyprus, right?'

'Over two thousand Greek Cypriot and Turkish Cypriot individuals remain missing after the events of 1962 to 1963 and 1974. We've been working with archaeologists, forensic scientists and the families of the missing to identify their whereabouts and their probable fates.' She spoke slowly, clearly, a much-practised speech. He was grateful for it – occupying him, without taxing him too much.

And he liked looking at her. He hadn't liked looking at a woman so much since Diana, an almost-girlfriend who'd gone away to South East Asia nearly two years ago. He liked this woman's eyes: the colour of figs and the deadly sweet-cakes in the Larnaca bakery. He liked the way she held her head. It was almost imperial, like a woman on an ancient coin.

'There have been a few discoveries. Mass graves found outside villages in both sectors of the island, also smaller finds on the Turkish mainland... So far, the remains of almost 400 Greek Cypriots and 125 Turkish have been returned to their families.'

'What happened to them?'

She frowned. Clearly this was a delicate point. 'The standard line on both sides tends to be: "We did what we had to do to defend ourselves, but the other lot, they were animals..." We can't do much about that. Our mission is to reunite bodies with families in the hope that, one day, for the children growing up now, there can be a peaceful future.'

'So you're saying each side committed murders?'

'Murders, abductions.' She ran a finger over her lips. 'And rapes. The main difference being that a number of the bodies of missing Greek-Cypriots have shown up in barracks and prisons – or places formerly barracks and prisons – on the

15

Turkish mainland, suggesting –' she paused, again rubbing her lips '– some more concerted form of state involvement. There was an explosion at an army base in northwest Turkey a month ago.'

He put the sandwich down. 'The Kurdish bomb thing. I think the girl this morning might have been making a point about that.'

She nodded. 'Whatever or whoever caused the explosion, there were more bones than bodies in the aftermath. An outer wall which collapsed shortly after the blast revealed a pit, containing up to 60 male skeletons, thought to date from the early 1980s.'

'Turkey has its own reasons to stuff people in mass graves, though, doesn't it? Couldn't they be Kurds? Or communists?'

'With crucifixes? Amulets of St Barnabas, the Patron Saint of Cyprus?'

'I hadn't heard anything about this grave. Where was it?'

'Trabzon, on the Black Sea coast. We're issuing the first statements this afternoon.'

'And you're telling my paper first?'

His boss, Susan Auerbach, was an old-school hack, a former Foreign Desk editor on the nationals. She'd get a kick from the scoop, even if they did nothing with it.

'Harringay-Tottenham and Enfield-Haringey have the largest Cypriot communities in Europe. We'll be hoping to match DNA from the remains with DNA from relatives of the missing. We've got a data-bank, a lot of people have co-operated, but we need more genetic information.'

'So, people can give you a DNA sample if they've lost someone, right?

'Right. But it's not that simple for everyone. Right from

when the data bank was launched, some people were nervous about the idea. There was even a crazy rumour that the information might be used for some kind of ethnic cleansing. And then some people died, some moved away, moved on, just didn't want to be reminded. But there's a new generation now, the tests are more sensitive. So the discoveries at the barracks in Trabzon are just the launch-point. We're visiting London, Munich, Montreal, Melbourne… everywhere with significant Greek and Greek Cypriot communities, to explain what we're doing, and invite people to come forward. The message is simple. If you have someone who went missing, give us a sample.'

'How?'

'I'll be giving test kits to the doctors at the local health centres. Each one comes with instructions for taking cheek cells from the side of the mouth, and a postage paid envelope. In addition, I'll be around, based here and visiting elsewhere in the UK, for the next few weeks, talking to community groups, interviewing people who might have significant information about '63 and '74.'

He finished his notes, took a card, gave her his.

'First time in London?'

'Actually, no. I spent a few months working here as a student. At the North Middlesex.'

'And you still came back? Wow. Where are you staying?'

She frowned. 'I think it's called The… Brunswick?'

'Christ. You need to move. Try the Royal in Muswell Hill. Or a bush in the woods. Seriously.'

She laughed again. 'Yes, the hotel breakfast was a little… unusual.' She looked at his plate. 'Come to think of it, I wouldn't mind a sandwich like yours.' She waved at the proprietor, a grizzled old Turk with thick glasses and a grey jumper, leaning unhappily at the counter. Rex tried too.

'Is he always like this?' she asked, after they'd both gestured in vain for some time.

'Actually, no,' Rex said, peering over. The Bosphorus – known to most, due to its location, as simply The Bus Place – had been one of his favourite spots for years. It was a plain, clean, functional place, livened by bright paintwork and consistently good food. The owner, one Keko Küçüktürk, did almost everything himself, assisted by a stream of Eastern European waitresses and a pretty daughter, whom Rex had watched growing up in the corner behind a pile of schoolbooks. He hadn't seen her for a while, he realised. Nor had he ever seen the owner looking so unhappy.

Rex caught the eye of the latest waitress, a beefy Hungarian girl who always gave the impression of not having understood, yet always did. They ordered another sandwich. It never came.

This was because, about a minute after the waitress had gone into the kitchen, two police officers entered the cafe. Rex recognised both: a slight, efficient Welshman named Detective Sergeant Brenard from the local CID, and with him, the black, motherly Yvonne Mackie from Family Liaison. If they saw Rex, they gave no sign of it. Their business was with the old man, who seemed in some indefinable way to have been expecting them. He slipped off his stool and went with them into the kitchen at the back, from where, after a few minutes, came a dry howl.

A builder, a pink man in a hi-vis vest, cracked a joke about the noise, but no one laughed. The Hungarian girl came out of the kitchen and told everyone they had to leave. They could get their money back later, she said. But now the café was closing.

'For how long?' asked the builder, who was halfway through a cheeseburger.

'For never,' said the waitress. She was crying. And Rex suddenly remembered, with a sickening lurch, where he'd seen that peacock brooch before.

CHAPTER TWO

By five o'clock, Rex was waiting for his boss, Susan Auerbach, to give him the ok on a short web version of what they knew so far. Mina Küçüktürk, a 19-year-old Law student, had set herself on fire at Shopping City, sustaining fatal burns. A law student at London Met, and a Union committee member, she had recently posted YouTube videos and made comments on blogs condemning both the PKK and the Turkish government over the stalemate their negotiations had reached. In the last of these, under the title, I Am Dying For Peace, she had written ominously of people bickering in their kitchens while flames were lapping at the front door. She'd also posted links to web pages about two girls who'd made similar protests before.

'Flames at the door... Sounds very poetic for a law student,' Susan commented. 'Is it a Kurdish proverb? Lawrence?'

Lawrence Berne, arts critic, 'Laureate of the Ladders' verse columnist and general know-it-all, peered over his half-moon glasses. 'Lord knows. But while we're on the subject of poetry, someone keeps sending in...'

Susan silenced him with a hand, swivelling back to Rex. 'Did you know the kid was political?'

'I didn't even know they were Kurdish. I'd have thought Küçüktürk was a Turkish name, wouldn't you?'

'Cypriots, Turks, Kurds – never understood the difference,' Terry opined, though a mouthful of kofteh. 'Food's all Greek, for starters.'

Susan cast one of her special chilly looks in the photographer's direction.

'The Kurds, Terry, are a distinct ethnic and linguistic group in the Middle East, scattered between Turkey, Syria, Iran, Iraq and Armenia.'

Terry shrugged. 'Fair dos. Where's Kurdistan meant to be, then?'

'It's a hope. Despite promises from Western powers and repeated attempts by the Kurds, an independent and united Kurdistan has yet to appear, although there is, currently, a Kurdish autonomous region in the north of Iraq, now under assault from fundamentalist groups as it once was from Saddam Hussein.'

Terry nodded vaguely and balled up his kebab wrapper, assuming the lecture was at an end. He was mistaken.

'The southern and eastern parts of Turkey are also mainly Kurdish,' she went on. 'And self-rule remains out of their reach in spite of a long, bloody guerrilla campaign by the PKK, the Kurdish communist party, whose graffiti you can see all across our borough. That's because the majority of the Kurds here in London are refugees from the conflicts in Turkey, who began arriving here in the 1980s, as well as setting up home in Sweden and Germany. Does that help, or is it still all Greek to you?'

'Yes – I mean, no.' Terry said, sheepishly. 'Thanks for explaining.'

Susan turned to Rex. 'What's the café called?'

'The official name's Bosphorus, but most people call it the Bus Place.'

'Bosphorus Caff! That's the magazines bloke isn't it?' Terry interrupted, wiping his mouth, eager to make up for his earlier gaffe. He started tapping away on his keyboard.

Seven years ago, Keko Küçüktürk had repainted the exterior of his café in black and yellow, causing people to complain that he'd made the place look like a wasp. He'd also put a cryptic sign which said, in English, Kurdish and Turkish, that he neither bought nor sold magazines. It had featured on the photos Terry had taken of the new, contentious exterior, which, when they appeared in the paper – under the headline Buzz About Bus Place – had prompted a few keen-eyed locals to write in and query the sign's meaning. An answer had never been found. When approached, Keko had seemed reluctant to comment. Eventually, the queries died away, and when the café was given a second, more modest makeover a couple of years later, the matter was forgotten. It remained a minor local mystery, like the Mauritian restaurant that had been promising it was 'opening soon' for the last eight years, or the well-dressed woman outside Halfords, who only ever asked passers-by for twenty-three pence.

'No magazines… I remember that. Is the sign still there?' Susan asked, skimming over the old photo on Terry's screen. Rex shrugged and she flashed him an exasperated look. 'You said you knew them.'

'Well, I do,' Rex said limply.

It was that curious, London way of knowing people, broad

and shallow. He had long known the girl who sat at the back of the café with the books was called Mina. It was Mina, in fact, who'd ushered him into the fellowship of the place as a whole, one stuffy June evening ten years ago. Crumpled and weary in a gingham school dress, she'd sat in her corner crying quietly over a piece of homework. He'd told her the right way to spell 'badger', that was all, but on the strength of that, become known to Mina and her father by name, earned the right to be served black tea in a tulip glass and to swap remarks about the weather, the rising costs of living and the many failings of the local borough, all of which put him on a different rung to most of the other punters.

In later years, he'd lent Mina some battered pass-notes for *Of Mice and Men* – a book that seemed to have bored her as much as it had him – and self-consciously, alert to the possibility of being misconstrued, given her, via her father, some freebie tickets to a pop concert in Finsbury Park on the occasion of her twelve, A-starred GCSE results. He'd never found out whether she'd been allowed to go. The last conversation he could remember had involved Mina trying to choose between Bristol University, or a London campus and staying at home. He hadn't seen her in the café for some time and had assumed she'd gone for Bristol. It seemed he'd been wrong. He remembered the brooch, though. The kid had worn it on everything – school blazers, kaghoules, disco tops. Had she said it was her mother's? He realised he knew nothing about the mother.

* * *

'Ok. Lock and load,' said Susan, who hailed from New York, and liked the odd Hollywood phrase. Rex turned to his screen and made the web article live. The phone almost immediately started ringing in the editor's office.

'That was quick,' said Susan, heading off to answer it. 'Did we spell the girl's name wrong?'

On his way back from the water-cooler, Lawrence peered at Rex's screen. 'Hmmm,' he said, at length.

Rex stopped himself from saying something rude. 'What, Lawrence?'

'Just thinking it's a bit rum, that's all.' He returned to his seat, waiting to be asked more.

Rex obliged, testily. 'What is?'

'I'm not intimately acquainted with the mind-set of the teenage self-immolator, but I'd have thought someone making a gesture like that would have chosen more carefully.'

'What's wrong with a shopping centre while a politician's doing a walkabout?'

'Quite a few things,' Lawrence said. 'Point the first being that she wasn't in a shopping *centre*, was she? Not the centre of the centre, anyway.'

'What?'

'The main event – the walkabout – had already happened over the road, hadn't it? Where the proper shops are. Q and A sitting in that little fake garden bit in the grand *hay-trium*. Big crowds.' Lawrence removed his glasses, jabbing the ear-ends towards Rex to underscore his point. 'If you were going to disrupt proceedings with an act of petroleum-based self-annihilation, you'd do it there, wouldn't you? Not at the arse-end of the tour over the road, when there's no one to watch except three alkies and a pit-bull.'

Rex was silent. Lawrence had a point. Although Shopping City's planners had doubtless never intended it that way, the place, these days, had partitioned itself, like some troubled country, into two distinct halves. In the west, a smart section, where high-end cargo like TVs, laptops and weddings rings was sold, alongside a cinema, coffee chains and a seating area around a water feature. The eastern chunk had become an emptier place, where rents were cheaper, businesses failed more quickly and the customers wore a harder, grimmer look.

'Maybe she meant to do it in the posh bit but she couldn't get there in time. Or there were more people in the posh end, so that meant more likelihood of being spotted and stopped.'

'It's about maximum impact, though, isn't it? No one sets light to themselves in their bedrooms. Not unless they've got their eighty-two thousand Twitbook followers watching on webcam. She'd have been thinking about where to do it for the best exposure. And if she was thinking that…'

'You're assuming reason. How rational is anyone prepared to set light to themselves?'

'Those Youth Tube videos and blogs seem pretty rational to me,' said Lawrence, signalling an end to the conversation with a fresh burst of typing.

Rex stared back at his screen. Annoying as Lawrence was, with his perma-tan and his golfing jumpers, he often made sense. Rex just didn't want, in this instance, to allow it in. Somehow, tragic and stupid and ghastly as it was, there was a way of processing Mina's suicidal protest – a label under which it could be filed and to some extent, held away. But if it was something else, he had to keep thinking about it, keep remembering the colours of the flames, the scream and the white face and that awful, mortal smell alongside the chatty little girl and the reserved teenager and the books and all the bright promise.

As a distraction, he wrote up his interview with Dr Georgiou. It was a piece that would garner a lot of local interest, perhaps do well beyond the borough too. It needed a picture, though, and he hadn't taken one. When he went onto the website of Dr Georgiou's particular UN department, the unhappily-titled UNWCAGRC, she was listed on a dozen or so documents, but there was no profile photo. He realised he'd need Terry to take a snap of her. He also realised he didn't want Terry to do that.

Susan emerged from her inner sanctum with an urgent look. 'Are you available for our...' she said, or rather mouthed the words in such a conspiratorial manner that everyone in the office made a note to gossip about it later.

The plan had changed, as plans often did with the editor. Instead of going for coffee, they now had to drive in Susan's car – a perky Mini smelling of leather and cherries – to an MOT Test Centre just off Philip Lane. She drove like the locals, many of whom had acquired their road-skills in Istanbul or Abuja: competitive, with liberal use of horn and hand gesture. He'd known Susan for a long time, worked with her, in another lifetime, on the nationals, and she'd always driven Minis which exuded the same, almost gentlemanly smell. But he couldn't remember whether she'd always driven that way. Back then he'd driven his own cars.

'Do you want to talk about it?' she asked, staring ahead as they let a formation of hijab-clad Somalis flap over the zebra crossing. 'The girl, I mean. I should probably send you and Terry for trauma counselling, but, well... I'm not going to be around to argue with you. I take it you'd rather spend the weekend drinking whisky in the dark, or something.'

'I hate whisky,' Rex said. 'But you're right. I don't fancy

lying on a couch and talking about it for a hundred quid an hour. Why aren't you going to be around?'

'Oh get an eye-test, fucko!' Susan roared, as a scaffolder's lorry executed some illegal move and caused her to slam the brakes on. A tattooed arm returned the compliment.

'Have you noticed all the building work?'

'Sure,' Susan said. 'Big question is, what's behind it? Easy loans, better times or the council that likes to say Yes?'

'Why would the council be doing that?'

'Because Eric is a shrewd operator.'

'I thought you were an admirer.'

'I am. Just look out of your window – the streets are clean for the first time in years. He got that TV chef from Highgate to make a *broighes* about the school dinners budget, and now our kids are eating organic. Ours is the only local authority in the UK to have *opened* libraries since 2010. Eric's only been in two years, and he's done great things. But he knows he's got to stay at the top to do them. Same in Montreal when I was there,' she said, executing the sort of three-point turn that wouldn't have disgraced a heist movie. Rex wondered when Susan had been in Montreal. 'Government says build more homes. So the Mayor has to build more homes. Only way to get that through is relax the zoning, let every Jack do what Jill wants. Five years on, place is groaning. Schools, hospitals, roads, buses, fucked. Full up. But all the people who pay taxes are happy, because now they've got their sauna rooms and their twenty-foot bird houses at the back. Eric knows what he's doing.'

She meant Eric Miles, head of Harringay and Tottenham's first, Independent-run council. He was the man who'd okayed the zoo project on the marshes – a move that had rather smudged the gleam on his popularity – but he was still more popular than any politician in recent memory.

'I wish Eric had had a word with the bloke who came to look at my house.'

Rex told Susan about the catch-22 situation surrounding his windows, and the even weirder response of Ashley Pocock, the young planning officer. Susan laughed.

'You've been a hack for, what, 23 years? You've lived here for nearly half of them, And you don't know what he meant?'

'No.'

'You couldn't pick up some clues from, for example, the German whip with the monogram plates?'

He was about to laugh at her use of the street vernacular for a BMW, but it died in his throat as he realised what she meant. What Ashley Pocock had meant.

'He was after a bung? No! He –'

'He what?'

'He didn't look the type,' Rex said lamely. Susan laughed.

'OK. Already I didn't like all this nesting you're doing. Now I think maybe you'd be better off on the *Methodist Times*,' Susan said, as she pulled in at the test centre. A neckless, Balkan-looking man in greasy blues approached. 'Talking of which. Please don't go to the *Methodist Times* in the next few months. The paper's going to need you. I've got to go to the States.'

'For a few months?'

'Maybe longer. The official reason is my health, but it's not actually my health, it's someone else's. I will be back, but I don't know when.'

He nodded. Susan's inner world was a mystery, closely

guarded, and although he joined his colleagues in speculating about it, he respected the distance.

'So you want me to be the boss?'

She leant her head back so that the bun of her dark, silvering hair touched the stitched headrest. 'Actually no. I mean – what I want doesn't come into it. Our publishing partners are sending someone else to keep a hand on the tiller. It's non-negotiable, and obviously no reflection on your abilities.'

'Funny you felt the need to say that, then.'

She frowned. 'Don't be a child about it, Rex. Look on the positive. Someone else will be taking the crap. Not you. How do you think you could helm up the paper and write it and get Sybille settled in France at the same time?'

Anger flashed through him. 'That's cheap, Susan, throwing her in.'

'What's cheap is you, making out this is your problem. If you considered me for a minute, you'd realise you are not the unlucky victim here.' Susan slid, with expert dignity, out of the car, handing the keys to the mechanic.

Rex stayed in the passenger seat for a second, jangled and awkward. It had been like a lovers' tiff, an exact replica, in fact, of the charges his wife used to lay at his door. That he was self-centred, made every problem about himself. He hated being reminded of it. And he hated how much his boss knew. But he wouldn't be here if she didn't. He'd be in a very bad place. And Susan Auerbach, and the trailblazing little local paper she ran and this teeming, ugly, lovely borough had rescued him. He couldn't forget that.

He got out of the car. 'Sorry,' he said, making a pacifying gesture. 'Sorry. It's a shock, and I don't want you to go. Who are they sending?'

'I don't want to go either. You'll find out who's coming on Monday morning.'

'That soon? Aren't you doing a handover?'

'No need.'

'Why not?'

'I'll be on a plane to JFK Sunday pm,' she said, not answering his question. 'Hence the last minute sorting-out of everything.' Her phone started to ring. She looked at it. 'I gotta take this. I'll see you back in the office.'

As dusk fell and the air turned cold, he trudged back past the grocers and tea-houses of Philip Lane, his foot beginning to throb, sweat on his brow chilling, a familiar thirst gathering in his throat as he went by the hand-written '7 cans for 5' beer ads in the shop windows.

Rex Tracey was not, by anyone's yardstick, a calm man. He ran on a fairly high throttle, ideas and notions and irrational summaries occurring to him constantly, needing to be acted upon, which he did, in the same, clumsy, charging fashion, like a bull in need of an eye-test. What with all that, and the painkillers he swallowed to ease the pain in his foot, and the other painkillers he swallowed to deal with the withdrawals from the first lot, he ended each day feeling as if he'd run a marathon. Feeling this way, he also felt entitled to sink a great deal of Polish lager, and more painkillers. He was a very fit man, in other words. He had to be, to survive himself.

And he might have been green when it came to opportunist planning officials, but his instincts were sharp where office politics were concerned. He was sure Susan hadn't been telling the truth. He doubted their parent paper had any sort of 'policy' when it came to caretaker editors; they were far too chaotic. Someone just didn't think he was up to the job.

31

That someone seemed to be Susan herself. And why had she said there was no need for a handover?

For a year now, Rex's newspaper and website had borne the unpalatable title of *s: Haringey*. Everyone hated it, but everyone knew it was better than no paper at all, which was what had nearly happened until the hefty, lefty national *The Sentinel* bought a controlling share, as it had done with dozens of sickly local titles around the southeast.

s: Haringey now shared stories with its mother ship, and on a Friday, alongside the local stuff, extolled in colour print the delights to be found in *The Sentinel's* weekend editions. For the most part, the job was the same. Most people, staff included, referred to both paper and website as the *Wood Green Gazette*, which it hadn't been for some years. Then again, most people still thought they lived in Haringey, a borough which, officially and constitutionally, had become either Harringay and Tottenham or Enfield-Haringey, depending on where you lived. So the new paper was either in step, or out of it. And whatever it was, people from its Head Office rarely made their presence felt. Which was exactly why Rex didn't believe this was their decision.

He crossed Philip Lane and headed south down Lawrence Road, a strange, near-barren landscape of dilapidated office blocks and textile manufacturers. Once, long before his arrival in the area, this place had been thriving, a hub for the garment trade now lost to China. The units still bore the names of their mostly Turkish and Cypriot founders, Kyprianou Brothers, Toprak and Co., Greeks and Turks now united in industrial despair. A few were still going: a military-looking hangar that made rubberised bedding, another low unit entitled Tents, Weatherproofs, Bags.

Toprak & Co., Textiles had been in operation, too, until a fire ripped through the place a couple of months back: there were hints that the insurance company was refusing to pay out, darker rumours of some long-running feud with Spyridonidis Sons next door. Now it was shrouded, save for one upper window, in sheets of ply. A light burnt in the window, though, and Rex had a picture of the boss, old man Toprak, sitting at some charred desk with his bald head in his huge, circus-strongman hands, hoping for an answer. Or calling his son, Bilal, who now had a top job on Eric Miles' council.

A siren wailed over on Green Lanes and he realised he could no longer tell the difference between ambulance, fire and police. At one point, he was sure, they'd all had their own sounds. Now, there was just a general clamour of trouble. That was how his life felt, too. Girls setting themselves on fire. Bosses lying. Officials after bribes. And his wife, about to leave or, more accurately, to be shipped three hundred miles away. Unless he could stop it.

A battery of fireworks in the still-light sky – Newroz celebrants, he guessed, too giddy to wait for dark. He wondered if they'd seen the news, or how much it mattered to all the people who would later be driving their cars slowly down Green Lanes with flags flying and horns blaring.

Everybody knew about the Kurds elsewhere, of course, the thousands pouring from the madness of Syria and Iraq into squalid camps, if they were lucky. The local Kurds, most of whom had come from Southern Turkey in the 1980s, raised money for their brethren, collected old clothes and canned food, marched and waved flags to advertise their plight. That image, of a woman shaking a tin for far-off relations, had at least replaced the older one, of the Bombacılar. The 'Bombers' were powerful Kurdish heroin gangs, who'd been shipping their powders through the back of the fruit and veg halls on Green Lanes since the early 1980s, occasionally conducting takeovers with cutlasses and guns. In between the tin-shakers and the gangsters, though, were a good few thousand other London Kurds, unnoticed, unrecognised, usually mistaken for Turks.

Had Mina Küçüktürk come from a line of agitators and protestors? Her father, with his lurid paintwork and his mysterious posters, perhaps had a touch of defiance about him. Principally, though, the old man in the ever-present grey jumper complained about the thugs around the bus station and the constant digging-up of the Lanes, the same issues plaguing most locals, whatever global fault-line they hailed from. But Mina? The little girl interested in badgers had turned, he remembered, into something of a green activist. She'd got her father into recycling, long before the council had made it mandatory. He was also fairly certain that she'd given up meat in her early teenage years. But lots of girls were like that, because they loved animals, or they wanted some cover story for losing weight. It was hardly a sign of imminent self-immolation.

There were other girls who'd set themselves on fire. At the office he'd followed Mina's links to the last two. Both refugees from Iraq, with lost family members and personal experience of being bombed and gassed and stateless. Their extreme protests were chapters, painful, undeserved end-chapters, of their already-extreme lives. He doubted they'd ever sat doing school projects about badgers, or braided their hair or been bored by their GCSE set texts. That was what made Mina's actions stand out, what made them so odd and upsetting. That, and the site of them, as Lawrence had pointed out – the quietest, least noticeable time and place for something that surely depended for its meaning on an audience.

He felt sick again and he sat down at a bus stop. He practised the eye and finger trick the doctor had taught him earlier on and immersed himself in the memories he wanted to forget. Most were fainter now. Except the white streak. The streak was now a face again – a skinny, pale, man's face, peering over the balcony. Irritated, he tried again and gradually felt some calm, or at least control, returning. Horns tooted somewhere. Life went on. There was a smell of blossom as the birds tweeted a bedtime song and the skies purpled.

He'd liked Dr Georgiadis, liked her dark, lively eyes and the frequency with which she smiled and laughed. That curious way of holding her head, high and slightly tilted back, a Queen at a Coronation, or a ballet dancer on stage. He hoped he'd see more of her.

He feared he'd be seeing more of Eve Reilly. The polar opposite of the doctor, with her pudgy Celtic face, eyes the colour of the Irish Sea and a shouty, school-teacher's voice. It would work in Parliament, he realised: all those jeering men would not like it, but they'd listen to it, because it was like the voice of their nannies and their teachers. He knew he should cut some slack in the direction of Eve Reilly, who must have slogged hard to get where she was, whose shoo-in seat was realistically no longer a shoo-in seat after the Independents' landslide in the council elections, and whose first proud walkabout had been upstaged by the one thing Millbank couldn't manage: a human fireball. Yet somehow he couldn't feel the compassion demanded. 'I think'... 'my first day'...

'I've watched' – every time Reilly had spoken, she'd made it about herself. He hadn't warmed to her at all.

A woman's figure appeared, from behind a parked van, walking quickly towards him. He thought for a moment that it was Dr Georgiadis, then dismissed as fantasy the idea that he could think about someone and have them appear. As the woman came closer, though, he realised he'd been right. It was the Greek doctor, approaching fast. He put up a hand in greeting. She didn't seem to see it at first, then, as she got nearer, recognition dawned. She didn't smile. She looked out of breath, troubled.

'Are you all right?'

'Yes, I'm good,' she said, then added. 'I am lost. I think.' She spun round, looking behind her, then back. 'Is this Lawrence Road?'

'It is. Where are you looking for?'

'The... Greek Cypriot Elders Centre?' she said doubtfully. 'Back in Cyprus we still call them old people. No one minds.'

'You're behind the times,' Rex said. 'Old people are elders. Violent is vibrant, and gang-bangers are young men with issues around stabbing.' He'd hoped for a laugh, but she wasn't listening. She was looking back up the road again. 'There isn't anything like your Elders centre down here,' Rex went on. 'I know there's one further up, towards Palmer's Green. Have you got a map, or something with the address?'

She stared at him blankly. Rex took out his phone and googled the place.

'There is a Cypriot Elders Centre on Lyndhurst Road,' he said. 'But that's a long way north. What made you think it was down here?'

'Lyndhurst!' she said. 'That's it. I got mixed up. I gave

the cab driver the wrong address.' She looked at her watch. 'They'll have finished now. Sugar!'

Rex didn't know anyone who still said 'sugar' instead of swearing. A bus came into view. It was a little one, a Hopper, which would weave south before joining up with St Ann's Road and ending by his beloved pub, The Salisbury. It was a Friday evening. The print edition had come out that morning. There were still things to do, but nothing that couldn't, equally, be done on Saturday. And if there was any day when he deserved to get drunk, then it was today.

'You might as well hop on this with me and take in some local landmarks.'

CHAPTER THREE

'Little Turk!'

'Sorry, Lawrence?' Rex placed his coffee down carefully on the desk. It was not quite the Monday morning greeting he'd expected.

'The girl's surname was 'Küçüktürk', which means Little Turk. The Ottoman Sultans forced the Kurds to take Turkish surnames, and that was one of the more delightful ones they came up with. So you could say being called 'Turk' is actually the hallmark of being a Kurd.' Lawrence grinned over his glasses.

'Unless you're called Atatürk. Or was he Kurdish too?'

The grin vanished, and Lawrence fingered his bowtie in silence. Rex, sore after a solo Sunday night attack on the raki bottle, regretted his words.

'Useful info, Lawrence, thanks,' he added, as he switched his monitor on. 'What the hell's this?'

'Oh. That,' Lawrence chuckled, with the satisfaction of a man who knows something other people are on the brink of finding out.

Susan had employed some electronic wizardry to ensure that, as each of her staff switched on their computers, a letter appeared on the screen, in a font that looked handwritten. In it, she explained that, due to health reasons, she was taking an extended break in her native USA, but had every intention of being back in her office before the autumn. She wished everyone 'a great spring and summer', and trusted they'd all 'welcome, assist and co-operate with' her temporary replacement.

'A.K.A. whoever's been in the Holy of Holies with the blinds down since the crack of doom,' Lawrence added, in a loud whisper, jerking his silvering curls in the direction of the editor's office.

'We've knocked and everything,' Terry said, returning from the toilets on the landing and wiping his hands on his jeans. 'But he won't answer. Definitely in there, though.'

'It doesn't have to be a man,' added Brenda, the receptionist, as she came in with the post. 'Susan was a woman.'

'*Was*, Brenda?' Rex queried.

'Maybe she's gone away for a sex change!' Terry said.

'Perhaps it *is* Susan in there,' Lawrence added. 'But now she's called Stephen.'

Brenda, a large lady who'd recently had her hair done like the Queen, touched the lacquered bun and looked about to say something stern. She never got the chance, however, because the door of the Editor's office opened, and the Whittaker Twins, Mark and Robert, walked out.

They were the paper's ad sales team, a faintly Dickensian pair with large, creamy faces and suits like school uniforms. No one found it easy to talk to them and yet, for reasons that remained a mystery, they were extremely good at conjuring advertising revenue out of the air. Susan had made all the staff create a Twitter profile and the Whittaker Twins had 9,400 followers. No one else had more than a few hundred.

Even so, even bearing in mind Susan's propensity for Zen-like management pranks, even remembering that she and the Twins had some unbroached, clandestine history, no one could believe this grey-eyed, charmless pair had been put in charge of *s: Haringey*.

They were right. As Mark and Robert Whittaker moved out into the room, another figure appeared in the doorway behind them. Slender but shapely, in black blouse and matching trousers.

'Ellie!'

'Hello, Bren,' said the new boss, striding across the room and launching a hug-kiss manoeuvre on the receptionist. Brenda Bond, mother to five grown-up children, was having none of it, and sat down heavily on the nearest swivel chair before Ellie could reach her. She went for Terry instead who, whatever his true feelings, never passed on a chance to press himself up against a pretty girl.

'It's good to be back,' Ellie said, reddening slightly as she removed Terry's hands from her waist.

'I remember someone being very keen to leave,' Brenda said.

Ellie Mehta had been the graduate trainee a couple of years back. Despite enthusiasm and brains, she'd been nigh-on impossible to train, had refused a pay cut when everyone else was swallowing one, then fled without notice to the nationals, promptly stiffing them on a big local story. Stiffed Rex, in particular, who was the last one to speak.

'So that's why Susan said there was no need for a handover.'

'Hang on. You knew the boss was leaving?' Terry's eyes narrowed.

'She told me she was going on Friday. She wouldn't tell me who was going to be in charge. She obviously knew how much flak she'd get,' Rex said wearily. He took a sip of his coffee, waiting for the painkillers to kick in. It hadn't been a bad weekend: pub with the pretty Greek doctor on Friday, an impromptu, blossom-sprinkled walk round Bruce Castle with her on the Saturday afternoon. On Sunday, he'd rung her up after doing a couple of hours in the office, but she hadn't answered. And then, somehow, there was nothing like being alone on Wood Green High Street on a chilly Sunday afternoon to make a person feel that their life had gone astray. He'd gone home and done a bottle in whilst Alan Yentob explored Islam on the TV.

'Rex,' Ellie said, settling for a chilly handshake with her former mentor. 'I know we've got the odd bumps to iron out and… well, what about lunch?' Sensing his reluctance, and other tensions in the room, she turned with a broad sweeping gesture. 'Everyone? A team chow-down? I've missed The Famous Manti Shop.'

'You always hated the place,' Rex was about to say – but the words didn't come out. Instead, he stood, smiled and said, 'Lunch would be good, Ellie. I'm in.' As he gave her a short, awkward hug, he was aware of his colleagues staring in amazement.

He knew they'd grill him about this later, but for now there was no time, as Ellie moved straight into morning conference. She began with a short, seemingly off-the-cuff speech, about how she was only there as back-up, a hand from Head Office, and in no way trying to be the boss.

She seemed to mean it. They ran through the stories of the day, discussing which were destined for the regularly updated website and which deserved longer treatment in the weekly print edition. At every stage, Ellie kept her gaze circulating around the small team, making it clear with her actions, as well as her words, that their views counted. She was trying too hard, Rex thought, but surely he'd been right to accept the olive branch. Why waste energy on a battle now when there would be dozens later? That had been part of his reasoning. The other part was fatigue, pure and simple, a heavy sorrow that had kept stealing up on him since seeing Mina die, making any fight impossible.

Terry was showing off some startling pictures of a fox, red and defiant, eating toast-crusts off his kitchen table. He thought they could link it to the unpopular zoo project on the marshes.

'You know... Tottenham's already got enough wildlife, thank you... sort of thing,' Terry said. 'I mean, everyone's complaining about the foxes these days. Well, and the zoo.'

Ellie tapped the desk with a mauve fingernail. 'A1, Terry. A1.' It was a perfectly pitched parody of Susan, and it worked. Everyone laughed, and the mood relaxed.

'I take it no one likes the zoo.'

'What zoo?' said Lawrence. It had become a local in-joke to say 'what zoo?' whenever the zoo cropped up. And whenever there was a joke to be worked to death, Lawrence was keen to oblige.

'It's still a wildlife and wetlands centre,' Brenda said, stiffly. 'That's what we voted for.'

Brenda and her husband Mike, a former policeman, spent a lot of time observing bird-life on the Lea marshlands that lay between Tottenham and Walthamstow. A decade ago, when the old council had first ring-fenced funds to improve the area's outdoor amenities, Brenda had been one of those arguing for a wetlands centre over running-tracks and football pitches. Her wish had been granted, a site was duly readied, but then no money was spent. There'd been a raft of local authority boundary changes in the meantime, deepening the inertia.

The zoo issue made Rex, for the first time in his decades as a journalist, feel true loyalty towards Miles and his council. The old Labour rulers had been a passionate, charismatic bunch, forever getting into spats and having unfortunate things found on their laptops: great news copy but actually, fairly rubbish at running the place.

The new Council was different. Its Scots leader, Eric James Miles, was a Spartan figure who ran 10 miles round the reservoir every morning. The most extravagant thing about him was his decision to quit the Lib Dems and stand as an Independent. That, and a lock of white hair that he kept too long, so that he had to keep sweeping it out of his eyes, like a schoolboy. His fellow travellers on the Council Cabinet gave off a similarly sober air: they never bad-mouthed the opposition, rarely made reference to creeds and ideologies. The Independents' dogma seemed to be mending the traffic lights on Westbury Avenue, their slogan something like 'let's put better lighting on the Harringay Passage'. In their spare time they all volunteered: helping primary kids to read, sitting with the elderly. They weren't what hacks like him called 'good copy', but they were good people doing their best for a place too long overlooked.

'It's all too easy to have a pop at the council...' Rex began.

'Oh I don't blame that lot,' Lawrence chipped in. 'I can't remember the last time we had a bunch in charge who were doing their honest-to-goodness. No, I blame the interweb,' he went on, adjusting his bow tie. 'If only the local population had laid off the iguanas.'

'Eh?' Ellie looked confused.

Lawrence was right, however obscurely he expressed himself. Thanks to the internet, some citizens of the borough had developed a taste for exotic pets, especially those which were dangerous, and therefore good for enhancing street-cred. Accordingly, the animal charities in the area had become overloaded with unwanted crocodiles, tarantulas and hyenas. When a child was bitten by a homeless cobra in a sandpit, the newly-formed Harringay and Tottenham council came up with a masterstroke: the surplus fauna would be housed, prior to placement in proper zoos, in an annexe of the wetlands centre, the former, it was hoped, drawing more punters to the latter.

Rex summarised for Ellie. 'They need specialist housing for the animals, heating ducts, extra ventilation, plumbing, drainage, staff – stuff they hadn't researched properly or prepared for. Now it's hit a stalemate, nothing's been built for months and it's not clear whether they can even afford to finish it. They won't release any information.'

'No one inside prepared to dish dirt?' Ellie asked. 'You'll have tried that, I know, of course,' she added.

'Eric seems to have brought in a uniquely loyal team,' Rex said.

'Actually, some of these letters I've been getting...' Lawrence began.

'He's not Eric, he's the Messiah,' Terry interrupted,

paraphrasing his favourite film, 'The Life Of Brian', to smiles all round. It was true that the atmosphere around Eric Miles was faintly cultic. The man himself was a lay-preacher at a big, new, enthusiastic type of church at Tottenham Hale, and a number of his staff were known to worship there too.

Ellie had either glazed over with disinterest, or else was mulling things over deeply. She was still pretty, Rex thought: an alpha-combination of the Indian goddess and the county gymkhana. After a while in repose, she made some stark, conclusive movements on her pad with her pen and then flicked her hair.

'I think the fox and the caption will work well on the web. Nice counterpoint to the grim stuff with the girl. What do you reckon, Rex?' Rex nodded. 'Talking of which,' continued Ellie, 'Interview with the girl's family. Where are we?'

'Mike says the Inquest will be today,' Rex said, referring to Brenda's husband, who now worked as a Coroner's Officer. 'Not expected to be anything more than a formality. I imagine they'll bury her over in Ilford tomorrow, seeing as they're Muslims.'

'They might not be,' Lawrence chimed in. 'Some Kurds are Sunnis, some are Alevis, that's a sort of Shi'a sect, then there's your Zaza, your Yarsani… that part of the world is full of…'

'So who is "they"?' Ellie interrupted.

'There's a father. I'm guessing there's a mum and siblings too, but I'm not getting in their faces today. I'll try at the college, and I'll get something before we update the page this afternoon.'

There was a pause. 'Sorry, my fault for not being clear. I don't want it for your webpage,' Ellie said. 'I want it for tomorrow's paper. And I want the family.' She clapped, a sudden report making everyone jump. 'Come on!' she said, leaning across the desk. 'It's not like this is just hours after. They've had a weekend for it to sink in. And it's what everyone wants to know. How do they feel? Did they bring her up to do this sort of thing? Are Mum and Dad proud of having a martyred daughter?'

'We don't bring out a paper tomorrow. It's on Friday.'

'*My* paper comes out six days a week,' Ellie said. 'And as you know, Rex, that's one of the conditions under which Sentinel Group News and Media keeps your paper going. If there's a story we want, we get first dibs.'

'So much for the helping hand from Head Office.'

'I thought a scoop in the nationals *would* help you, Rex.'

'I've had a few before,' replied Rex. who stopped himself from adding that he'd been on *The Times*' crime desk when Ellie was doing all her writing with crayons. 'And no, I don't like the idea of door-stepping a grieving father before he's even buried his child.'

'As you say, you don't need to bother the parents. There's bound to be half a dozen aunties and uncles and cousins who'll talk to you. You know what they're...' She stopped herself.

'Oh. What they're like? Lovely attitudes you picked up in Shoreditch.'

Silence. Rex heard Terry take a breath. 'Ellie, I don't mind going over to their house and...'

'Ok. I don't like it, Ellie, but you're right, and I'll do it,' Rex interrupted, suddenly. No way was he letting Terry seize the advantage. 'I'll do it. I'll find someone to talk to.'

Ellie nodded. 'Thanks.'

The meeting moved on.

As they discussed the plans for the old Surgery on Wightman Road, the new, aggressive wave of begging on the High Street, and the judging of the primary schools' RoadSafe poster competition, Rex barely spoke. He loathed himself for what he'd just done. It was cowardly, childish, spiteful. Agreeing to pursue Mina's family, not because it was right, but because he didn't want Terry to do it. He left the office as soon as the meeting finished, so he didn't have to look anyone in the eye.

He was relieved to see the Bosphorus Café was closed, blinds down, a handwritten sign in the door, simply saying 'Family Illness'. It looked like an old piece of paper, something they kept in a drawer.

He looked in the windows either side of the doorway, checking whether the proprietor's odd magazine-note was still there. He couldn't see it, but the salmon-coloured blinds moved as he was looking and he found himself eye-to-eye with the Hungarian waitress. She held up a finger, and went across to the door.

She let him in, the café strange and forlorn in the shadows, like a classroom at night. The girl looked like she'd been scrubbing the grills in the back: black smudges on her face and in her hairline.

'I didn't have what to do,' she said, wiping her forehead. 'You are the newspaper man?'

Rex confirmed that he was.

'I recognise you from picture. Boss is told me not to come in, but I thought… I tried to think of something I can do, and he does never like cleaning those… grills, so…'

Rex smiled. He hoped Keko would keep this girl on. 'Where is the boss?'

'At his house. Not house,' she corrected herself. 'Flat. Over his store. Same name, I think – *Boszprusz.*'

'Where is it?'

She shrugged, a very Eastern gesture, reminding him, with a sudden, unexpected shaft of pain, of an old girlfriend. 'I only here couple weeks.'

Rex wondered how many shops there were called 'Bosphorus' in the borough. A dozen? Probably hundreds.

'Must be near,' the girl added. 'Because was walking back there, five, six, seven times in a day for check.'

'To check what?'

'If she was there. Mina. His girl.' She lowered her voice and leant close, even though they were the only people there. Rex smelt chlorine and sweat. 'For all the last week, they didn't know where is she. Mina was missing.'

* * *

Bosphorus Continental Market was, as the girl said, close by: just east of the café on West Green Road, between another, identical-looking Turkish supermarket and a shuttered unit calling itself Alive & Descended Christ Fire Ministries. Rex couldn't remember whether he'd ever bought anything from Bosphorus or not, but they stocked his favourite brand of Polish lager, Okocim, along with the Levantine staples of white *peynir* cheese in cans, strings of red *sucuk* sausage and yard upon yard of sticky biscuit.

The sign outside was composed of red, green and yellow stripes, with the 'o' of Bosphorus formed by a little golden sun, and the same motif was visible throughout the interior. Over the tannoy, Rex heard the strains of Ibrahim Tatlises, bad boy of the Anatolian crooning scene. At the counter, surrounded by eye-talismans and other, less familiar dangling objects, sat a handsome, dreamy-looking young man in a denim shirt, flipping through a picture book.

Rex's phone rang then, and he ducked back out of the shop, under an awning fragrant with tomatoes and melons.

'What is it, Rex?'

En route, Rex had left a message for D.S. Brenard. To call this policeman a 'contact' would be an exaggeration. D.S. Brenard had arrested him on more than one occasion. But he also, grudgingly and irritably, traded the odd scrap of information.

'Mina Küçüktürk,' Rex said in a low voice. Two men passing by stared as they heard the name. 'Were you looking for her?'

'What do you mean?'

'Girl at her Dad's café says she was missing for a week before she... I wondered if anyone had reported her missing?'

'Definitely not. But she was a student, wasn't she? My eldest is at Bangor now, we never hear from the little horror until he's skint.'

'This was a Kurdish girl who lived at home.'

D.S. Brenard mulled it over. It was one of the reasons Rex liked D.S. Brenard. He always listened.

'Look. Politically active Kurdish girl makes a YouTube thing talking about the need for protest, writes a blog called 'Dying For Peace' and then sets light to herself. You can't be saying there's some big mystery over this, Rex. Because there isn't.'

'There might be a story, though. And I'm a journalist.'

A truck rumbled by, leaving in its wake a dirty smell, redolent of foreign cities. As the rumbling faded, Rex realised that cackling was coming from the other end of the phone. "'Ere, lads, Rex Tracey says he's a journalist,' Brenard said. Further, more distant laughs could be heard. 'No one reported her missing,' the detective said finally, and hung up. Putting his phone back in his pocket, Rex realised there was a 'no magazines' sign in the bottom left corner of the shop window. It looked forgotten, curling in the dirt and the ever-shifting temperatures. But what did it mean?

Rex approached the till, realising the young man's look wasn't, as he'd first thought, dreamy. It was the numb, staring look of someone who hadn't slept. He had thick, black, wavy hair, impeccably side-parted like some old matinee-idol. But he gave off an unwashed smell and his eyes were red. Rex introduced himself.

'I was there when Mina... When she fell,' Rex said. 'I'm very sorry.'

The young man gave a short, upward nod and murmured something indistinct. The picture book was all about birds. And it was birds, Rex realised, that hung all over the shop alongside the amulets: glass, metal, wood, paper, a whole handicraft aviary.

'I said where were you?' the young man asked softly. 'When she fell?' He had a local accent, like Mina.

'At Shopping City. I was going round the precinct with Eve O'Reilly.'

'Reilly,' the man said.

Ignoring this, Rex asked, 'Was she related to you?'

'Eve Reilly?' the man asked, staring.

This was getting weird now. 'Mina.'

'Brother,' said the man, in an even quieter voice. 'I'm Mina's brother,' he clarified. 'Aran.'

'I didn't know about you,' Rex said, and then, recognising how odd that sounded, he added, 'I go in the café a lot. I don't think I saw you there.'

'That's because I was here,' replied Aran blankly. 'Working in this place.' The way he said 'this place' didn't sound too happy. But then he had plenty of reasons to sound unhappy right now.

'I knew Mina,' Rex began and then, catching a shocked, almost hostile look from Aran, added, 'I mean, I talked to her in the café sometimes. To her and your father. We hadn't spoken since she went to university. How was she getting on there?'

Aran shrugged.

'Was she happy?'

'Sure,' Aran said. 'But that never stopped her being angry, too. You know. About lots of things. Prejudice. Things wrong in the world and that. You didn't want to argue with her.'

'Did you argue with her?'

He shook his head. 'I'm not, you know… I don't follow news much and that.'

'What do you follow?' Rex asked. He glanced at the book. 'Birds?'

Aran nodded. 'I like birds.'

'What about your dad? Did Mina argue with him?'

Aran frowned now, scratching his armpit. 'Are you interviewing me?'

'Sorry. I'm asking because I heard Mina went missing a week ago.'

'Who said?'

'The police,' Rex said. He didn't want the café girl to get into trouble.

'The police didn't know.'

'Why not?'

Aran came from behind the counter with such sudden determination that Rex steeled himself, squaring his shoulders, thinking he was about to be thrown out. Instead, Aran bolted the main door, then grabbed a black baseball cap from a stool at the edge of the counter. He was a slight man, Rex realised. His sister had been quite tall.

'Come on,' he said, beckoning Rex towards the back, where the chillers full of cheese and sausage hummed.

'Come where?'

'My dad says no one wants to talk,' Aran mumbled, not looking him in the eye, as he tugged the cap over his head. 'No one will talk about Mina – so you talk to him.'

Beyond the chillers was a double door. It led to a back yard with a metal staircase at the far end. They passed by a row of high metal cages, decked out with perches and tree branches and containing, as far as Rex could see, just one bird. He remembered Susan's comments about people building birdhouses and saunas in their back yards. Was this part of the boom? The only resident, in this case, was a huge peacock. It uttered a lost whine and strutted to the edge of its cage as Aran walked by. He let it peck at his fingers, turning to see Rex's reaction.

'You should work for Eric Miles,' Rex said.

Aran's face darkened. 'This isn't a zoo. He comes out,' he went on, poking a finger through the grille to stroke the peacock's breast. 'He's free, like he's meant to be.'

'Why's he in the cage, then?'

'He's been unwell.' Aran said aggressively. Rex was silent. He spoke again, though, as the man led him up the metal stairs.

'Mina had a peacock. I mean – a peacock brooch – didn't she?'

Aran looked at him in a more friendly way as he opened a white, plastic, panelled front door, complete with knocker and letter-flap and let him into a flat. 'Yeah. From our mother. The police haven't given it back yet.' He took his cap off the second he entered. Rex wondered why he'd bothered to put it on, for such a short trip.

'From your mother?'

'That was Melek,' Aran said, or at least, that was what Rex thought he'd said. He didn't have a chance to ask any more, though, because Aran showed him through a dark, damp hall – decorated with what looked like a picture of the former Prime Minister, John Major, but couldn't have been – into a stuffy, over-cushioned front room fronting the main road. In a brocaded, high-backed armchair, Keko was weeping. He was unshaven, and dressed in a white vest and dirty brown trousers. Another man was with him, standing up, smoking. Small like Aran, but somehow more dainty. He was dark-skinned, completely bald, in an elegant three-piece suit. Aran and the standing man exchanged words in Kurdish.

Keko gave Rex a nod, and waved him to the opposite armchair. As Rex sat, the old man nodded some more, as if to say he appreciated the visit, but then continued to weep to himself silently, twisting worry beads and a handkerchief round the fingers of his gnarled right hand. This was how they met death in some cultures: you sat with the bereaved. Simply sat with them, until the worst of the pain was over.

Being from another culture altogether, Rex felt uncomfortable. He sat looking around the room as two men chatted, another one wept, and everyone ignored him. He felt his phone buzzing, but he let it go. There was another phone, the latest iPhone, in fact, on the table next to him: an odd note in this room of faded Arabesque. The room also partly served as an adjunct of the store downstairs, with drums of oil and a dozen multi-packs of pink toilet roll stacked in one corner, a shipping crate of Rize tea in another. In between, some trappings of a normal family life: photos on an ornate, darkwood dresser. Mina grinning in pigtails. Aran, solemn in a mortarboard, rolled diploma in his left hand. And everywhere, in mugs, in vases and jam-jars, on every surface, fresh flowers, slowly curling in the warmth. The heating was on full-blast and the smell – bodies, grief, tobacco, pollen – was cloying.

'You've had lot of well-wishers,' Rex said to Keko. He didn't hear. He was leaking tears. Aran looked puzzled. Rex gestured towards the flowers.

'They're not to do with my sister,' he said. 'They were for Newroz. People bring them at New Year.'

A glass of black tea had somehow appeared at Rex's elbow, with a swollen cardamom bobbing on the surface. The man in the pretty suit held his own glass and raised it to Rex. Rex returned the gesture and sipped the tea.

'You want to ask some things?' Rex noted the man's deep voice. Small men always had these big voices. Was that something natural, or something they worked at?

'I wanted to tell Keko how sorry I was. But yes, I'm a reporter and I do have things to ask. People want to know how you all feel. Why you think she did it.'

'Mina was with me,' Keko interrupted, fixing a greasy, bulky pair of spectacles on, which magnified his sorrowful eyes to the size of eggs. His voice was hoarse. 'With me too much.

Keko is communist,' he added, making a fist with the hand containing the handkerchief and the beads and thumping it against his heart. 'I teach Mina, all day, BBC Radio 4, BBC World Service, Deutsche Welle, look, listen, politics. Mina makes Kurdistan politics because Mina...'

He paused, to make a dry swallow. Rex noticed how many times the man said 'Mina'. Not 'her'. Not 'she', or, like Aran, 'my sister'. He was keeping her alive. His loved girl. 'Mina was with me. No mother. Mother should be teach girls: make sew, make cooking, make house. But no mother.' He gave a dry heave. The other men watched calmly.

'Why no mother?'

'My sister died,' said the bald man, dabbing at his forehead with a silk handkerchief. A gold ring glinted, on a hand that looked somehow not right. 'In Germany.'

'It's where I come. First me,' explained Keko slowly. 'Turkey army make many bombings upon Kurdish peoples. Van. Diyarbakir. Move, move, many times. Come to Germany 1988. Many Kurdish peoples coming then, from Turkey, Iraq, Syria. Alevi, Yezidi peoples, to Germany, Sweden. After. Wife come 1991. Die 1997. 1997 coming to here.'

Rex hadn't understand all of what Keko told him – his English seemed to have deteriorated with his grief – but he concluded that Keko, like a lot of London's Kurds, had left Turkey when the conflict between the government and the Kurdish rebels, the PKK, had been at its most savage. He'd come to the borough via Germany, where Mina had been born, and she must have lost her mother when she'd been only two or three.

'So you all came to London then, in 1997?' he asked, looking at the bald uncle.

56

'I'm kind of all over,' he said vaguely. 'Germany, Sweden, here, North Kurdistan.'

'I thought there was no Kurdistan... Sorry,' Rex added. 'I don't think we've been introduced.'

The man smiled, as if Rex's turn of phrase amused him. He put his glass down and tapped his breast. 'I am Rostam. Rostam Sajadi.' He looked like an ancient Egyptian. A neat, mannequin-sized ancestor-figure. And were his eyebrows pencilled in? 'You thought wrong, Mr Tracey. About North Kurdistan.'

'He means the south of Turkey,' said Aran. 'Where the Kurds live.'

His uncle flashed him a look. Rex wondered what it meant.

'Mina could have explained all the geography and the history to you,' Sajadi added.

'Because she was... very passionate about Kurdistan?'

Keko rose abruptly and left the room. At first it seemed as if he objected to the conversation, but seconds later Rex heard a bathroom lock being slid across. Sajadi took the old man's place in the armchair. He looked almost child-like in it. A boy, with a three-grand suit and a three-thousand-year-old face.

'Listen, my friend, I'll tell you – Keko blames himself, of course, but he didn't have any influence on her, not since she was a teenager. It's the university. Full of trouble-makers. They got to Mina.' He tapped his forehead. 'Brainwashed her.'

'I didn't know her well,' Rex said. 'But she didn't seem like a girl who could be easily led. Who would be leading her, anyway?'

Keko called out something hoarse and indistinct from the bathroom. Aran caught a sigh in his throat, tore open a pack of toilet paper and headed out onto the landing with a roll. A quietly angry man.

Once his nephew was out of the room, Rostam lowered his voice and leaned closer, rotating the ring on his little finger. 'You don't know how they work. PKK, I mean. You know who I mean?'

'The Kurdish Workers' Party, right? Fighting Turkey for independence?'

Sajadi snorted. 'Workers' Party! Gangsters and terrorists. And they use children like her so people like you take notice.' He screwed up one hand tightly to underline his point.

'Mina was nineteen.'

'Exactly. A child. Not even married. This is who they use.'

'But what was she protesting about?' Rex asked, realising that this had been bothering him all weekend. 'No one knows who made the bomb in Trabzon. The ceasefire hasn't ended. So what point was she making?'

Rostam gazed at him coolly. 'Because I'm Kurdish I must know? I must be involved? I'm a businessman.'

'I thought you might understand more than me.'

Sajadi winced, as if he'd caught a bad smell on a breeze. 'That horse shit is for old men and teenagers. No one cares about that political horse shit any more. It's the same as religion…' Here, the man cast a hand towards the sky, dismissing the gods. 'It just makes everything difficult, gets in the way.' He fell silent, taking a lot of care to nip the glowing end of his cigarette off, and tamp it down in the ashtray. The atmosphere seemed to have soured quickly.

But two decades of interviewing had taught Rex a thing or two. When people were angry, when you'd annoyed them – then was the time to ask the awkward questions. Why not?

They were already annoyed. And their guard was down.

'Why didn't you tell the police Mina was missing?'

There was a pause, then Sajadi held a palm out. Now Rex realised what it was. His right index finger ended below the knuckle. 'What do police mean to a man like Keko? Do you know how the Turks treat the Kurdish people? The police are the ones who come for you at night.' He grabbed the lapel of his jacket. 'Police beat you on the soles of your feet,' he added, now making a beating gesture. 'You don't ask police for help. You ask them to stop killing you.' He'd spoken calmly, but his eyes flashed like searchlights as he acted everything out, made vivid every point with a gesture.

As Aran re-emerged onto the landing, Sajadi spoke more urgently, more or less in Rex's ear. 'Listen. It's like this. Mina was with a guy. There were texts. Gifts. In our community, that would be a massive dishonour.' The hand went over the face – a mask of shame. 'We were looking for her ourselves. Trying to sort it out quietly.'

'We?'

'Aran and myself. It would kill Keko if he knew. So if you care about him, you won't print that. Okay?'

'Okay. But why tell me?'

'Because I want you to understand why she did it.' The ring went round the little finger again, a compensation, perhaps, for that missing digit. 'It always happens like that. You know all those pictures of the *peshmerga* girls? Your newspapers love them, don't they? Our pretty girls who joined the guerrillas, with their pigtails and their AK's.' Tits were mimed now, and pigtails, and then guns. Was this what you did when you'd spent a life in exile, never being understood? 'That is horse shit. All those girls your newspapers printed

– they were just following their boyfriends. They had to run away to the mountains with their boyfriends because if the boys had fucked them, if the boys had even *kissed* them, you see, then they were ruined.' One, jabbing, phallic finger made the point here. 'Ruined in Kurdish culture. They didn't shoot AK's, those girls. Not *peshmerga* – not soldiers – just cooked rice. See? They were *used.*'

He spoke irritably, as if he was in pain. And there was something depressingly dismissive about what he said. As if Mina couldn't have had a mind of her own, a conscience, a will. She could only have been exploited by a man.

Sajadi sat back as Aran came into the room. The iPhone ran, with a snatch of German opera. He glanced over. A name flashed up on the screen. MILES. Rex passed the phone over. *Miles.* He had a sudden vision of a posh boy in tweeds and cords, an auctioneer. Or, more probably, judging by Rostam Sajadi's suit, a gifted accountant.

'Eric!' the Kurd said, jovially, like a man walking into a bar. Eric Miles, Rex thought. *The* Eric Miles?

Sajadi stalked into some deeper corner of the flat to have his phone call. When Aran returned, Rex asked if he could see Mina's bedroom. Partly, he wanted more clues as to what the grown-up, politically active and romantically entwined Mina might have been like. He also hoped he might overhear Rostam's conversation.

Both objectives failed. Mina's bedroom was a Spartan cube: desk, textbooks, bed, smart Venetian blind kept closed, a spectral whiff of roses. A solitary sheet tacked to the wall listed times for the Royal Marines Weekend Fitness Classes at Finsbury Park. Rostam, meanwhile, left the flat, still on the phone, slamming the plastic front door behind him with a bang.

Something caught Rex's eye as he was leaving Mina's room. A photoframe on the dressing table. A younger Mina, bad haircut and briefly tubby at twelve or thirteen, was sporting Mickey Mouse ears at the entrance to Disneyland Paris. She had something in her hands, small and red, oval like a tiny rugby ball. And with her, smiling sternly for the camera, an arm around her shoulder, was her Uncle Rostam.

Aran opened the front door to let him out. His face was blank, he seemed worn out by trying to be courteous. Rex understood that. True grief did these things: when you lost a person you loved, you lost the energy that came from loving. But he still had questions to ask.

'Do you really think someone put her up to it?'

Aran shook, as if the question required him to think of his sister and he'd somehow, briefly, been managing not to. 'Mina did what she wanted. Not what other people wanted. So I don't know. I don't...'

His uncle jogged back up the stairs at that point, a laptop under his arm. He barked some words at his nephew, and Aran threw him a set of keys. Sajadi caught them smartly in the damaged hand and headed back out again. The exchange was like a gear-shift for Aran.

'We want to be left alone to bury my sister's body, and to deal with it,' he said, firmly.

'Can I have a phone number?' Rex asked, staying put. 'In case I need to check anything.'

'The number's on the front of the shop. You can get out through the back gate. Goodbye, Mr Tracey.'

CHAPTER FOUR

Rex was still mulling over the encounter at Mina's house as the 43 bus deposited him outside the Metropolitan University building on Holloway Road. He hadn't been down here in years, recalled it as a place of fried chicken joints, pubs full of slowly dying Irishmen in mismatched suits. And it still was, strangely, aside from the spanking new university straddling the road, and half a dozen tiny Sainsbury's outlets, a region unchanged.

On the slow ride over, he'd written Aran's parting words down. Ellie would have her quotes, but what struck him – saddened him – were the less the words, more the ways in which the young man and his uncle had spoken. Aran had talked about Mina doing what she wanted, about himself being stuck at the shop, as if his obvious sorrow was really for himself. Uncle Rostam, on the other hand, had seemed irritable, almost dismissive, as if his niece's suicide was just another thing, like God and politics, that got in the way.

His niece who'd kept a single picture in her bedroom: of herself and her uncle at Disneyland. So they'd been close. Once. What had happened to change that?

He couldn't be sure it had changed, of course. Loss twisted things. One September day, he'd visited the parents of a five-year-old, mown down in traffic three days into her school career, who were almost hysterically upbeat. And his own wife's father had cracked a series of jokes, terrible jokes, as Sybille lay in a coma. The grieving put on shows, for sure – shows for themselves.

London Met, the site of the old North London Poly, was all hefty slabs and modernist horrorscapes, knifed up the middle by the A1. It was like Shopping City, so unapologetically grim that you had to admire its nerve. Rex walked down the pavement, past a building like a squashed battleship, towards the main entrance. A lecture must have just finished close by, and he found himself struggling against a flow of headscarved girls with folders, African boys in smart, church-going outfits, everyone wearing a pass on a lanyard. It was like the headquarters of a multinational, not somewhere girls were radicalised to death.

Then again, he thought, as he entered the main building and instantly came upon a steel turnstile and a guard behind a desk, Rostam Sajadi had a point. Time was, a local hack could have wandered over a city university campus at will. Terror, and the terror of terror, had made everything difficult.

'Can I help you?' the bored man in uniform asked him. Rex was studying the Students' Union board in the lobby. Mina's picture was still there.

'I'm here to see the Union President,' Rex said brusquely, flashing his card. He darted a look back at the board. 'Jan Navitsky.'

The Security Guard, a burly lad sporting one buzz-cut, one exquisitely sculpted line of beard and one black eye, frowned.

'You say it "Yan" yeah?' He picked up the desk-phone. 'Is he expecting you?'

'Should be,' Rex said carefully. He glanced back at the board. Navitsky's face caught his eye again. Was that because he was the only, strictly speaking, white person on the board? Or because he looked familiar? He took a deep breath.

'There's no one picking up,' said the guard, whose name-badge said Haluk. A Turkish name. 'What time was your meeting?'

'Five minutes ago,' Rex said. 'The traffic was mental.'

Haluk made a sympathetic noise. He picked up a walkie-talkie and stood up, extra-chunky in his ribbed sweater. 'I'll walk over to the Union building with you.'

Rex nodded gratefully. His first boss, Victor Eastwood, on the *Lincoln Daily Despatch*, had had an aphorism for moments such as this. *God loves a tryer.*

They crossed a precinct, with shops and seats and a cute little truck selling coffee. It looked like the sort of area that Holloway Road would have liked to have turned into, but hadn't – a VIP Holloway reserved for higher learning. They crossed the plain of students and into another building, down a bright corridor lined with computer terminals. It all seemed so alien, so modern, yet the notices fluttering on the walls might have been the ones a younger Rex had walked past, in Manchester, a quarter century before. *Bassist Needed. Women's Boxing – All Welcome. Auditions, Tuesday: Arthur Miller's 'All My Sons'.*

'You are now entering the Union State,' said Haluk with a grin. They were passing through double doors, emblazoned with flags and slogans. Hate Free Zone, said one. Another read: Les.Gay.Bi.Trans.3rdGender.NoGender.

The Students' Union office was reassuringly old-fashioned: filing cabinets, cast-off furniture, a grotty kettle on a tray and the distant smell of Instant Noodles. There were more posters on the walls, covering every topic from a new confidential harassment hotline to striking miners in Chile.

'Jan's usually in here if he's not in the…'

Haluk stopped talking. At a desk in the far corner, a black girl with braided hair was being helped into her coat by a grey-haired, outdoorsy-looking woman in a fleece.

'Right, Kye?' Haluk said. The girl cast him a disgusted look as she went past, her face glistening with tears.

'I'm getting her a taxi,' the woman said. 'She shouldn't have come in.' Rex thought for a moment that he recognised her, but she was gone with the crying girl too quickly for a second look. Some days, he thought he recognised everyone.

And then they were alone in the scruffy office. The Security Guard looked awkward.

'Er – Kyretia's the one who sorts out the appointments and that – she's like the receptionist? But she's the one that just…'

'Just went home. She looked very upset. Could that be anything to do with the girl who died?'

'Mina?' he said. 'Could be.'

'So you knew her?'

'She was on my course,' Haluk said. He twanged one of the epaulettes on his grey jumper. 'This is just what pays for it –' He looked around the empty office, suddenly awkward. 'Wait a minute, yeah?'

He went across the corridor, leaving Rex alone. He had just long enough to investigate the girl's desk and discover that Kyretia's surname was Pocock, like the man who'd been at his house, looking for a bung. There were coincidences like that all the time in his life. It was his job to ignore them.

Rex heard a door and voices further down. Haluk came back. His manner had changed. He barrelled right up close to Rex, challenging.

'What are you doing?'

Rex acted puzzled. 'Just looking out of the window.' He moved away from the desk. Haluk was uncomfortably close. Rex could smell his aftershave. Tommy Hilfiger. A Wood Green favourite.

'When did you say you made your appointment with Jan?'

'I didn't. It was this morning,' Rex bluffed.

A smile crossed Haluk's face, thin as his beard. 'Yeah? That's funny, 'cause on Friday afternoon, he cancelled all his appointments and flew home. Family emergency.'

Everyone's luck runs out some time, Rex thought, as he was gently frogmarched back out.

'I'm not trying to make trouble. I just wanted to talk to some people who knew Mina. People don't understand why she did it.'

Haluk stopped and took his hand off Rex's arm for a moment. He seemed about to say something, then rubbed the corner of his bruised eye. Rex wondered if he was going to cry.

'You'll have to go through the Press Office,' he said, his jaw setting. He walked on, through the coffee-drinking, texting, note-swapping gaggle of students, his hand no longer on Rex's arm. He almost seemed to have forgotten about him.

As he reached the pavement outside, the fleecy woman was waving Kyretia Pocock off in a cab. For some reason Rex thought of vicars. He caught her eye.

'Was she friends with Mina?' he asked.

'A lot of people have been affected by Mina's death,' said the woman carefully. She looked to be in her early sixties, with a northern accent, big teeth and thin, bob-cut, salt and pepper hair. 'And no, I don't mind you quoting that in your newspaper.'

Rex frowned. He hadn't mentioned his job.

'You were in one of my groups, Rex. At Highgate Hill.'

It came back to him. Maureen. She went on Youth Hostelling trips and took disabled kids sailing. She'd presided over a therapy group he'd been in, years back, after Sybille's accident. He ought to feel awkward, bumping into Maureen like this, in his new, reformed life, but he didn't. In an odd way he almost felt glad.

'Is this what you do now? You run therapy groups here?'

'Groups, individual counselling and psychotherapy. With supreme munificence, the university also permits me to treat private patients here as well.'

Patients. Maureen had insisted on the term. If you were in therapy, you were a patient, she said, because you needed to wait. Rex had hated that word as much as he had always hated waiting.

'Was Mina a client?'

'You know I wouldn't be able to tell you if she had been a patient.'

'*If* she had been...' Rex echoed. 'Did you know her, though?'

Maureen smiled. 'As Diversity Officer for the Students' Union, she had dealings with the Counselling Service. Referring students in need, that sort of thing. She was one of the Union officers who took the job seriously.'

'Meaning some don't?'

'For some, perhaps, it's more of a means to an end.'

'What end?' He shifted his weight to the other foot. Standing was hard.

'A job in politics in their home country. There's usually a home country, in the case of Union delegates. One that isn't this one.'

Rex remembered the panel of photographs – mainly African and Asian faces. Except for one, so incongruous it almost shone.

'Mina was different,' Maureen continued. 'She seemed to be doing it because she cared. I'm not saying some of the others don't, and I'm not saying it wouldn't have looked good on Mina's CV, as well. It's not easy for graduates, these days. Not unless your father's the Lord Mayor of Minsk.'

'Is that Jan Navitsky's background?'

She nodded. 'Most of the committee have an uncle who's a big cheese in Luganda or Dhaka or somewhere. Everyone except poor Mina.'

He thought about Mina's uncle. What variety of cheese was he? 'So she was out on a limb, a bit?'

'I don't think that affected her working relationships with most of them, no.'

'Most?'

'Gosh, you've got a way of pouncing on every word, haven't you?'

'Probably all that time I spent with therapists.'

Maureen made a wry face. 'It was common knowledge she didn't see eye to eye with Jan. I think there was a joke in the last issue of the student paper. When will those two cut the bickering and "get a room", that kind of thing.' Maureen made quote marks with her fingers as she spoke.

A thought struck him. 'When did that come out? The paper, I mean.'

'Just over a week ago.'

'Just before she vanished?'

Maureen looked startled. 'Did she vanish? I hadn't seen her for a while, but that doesn't mean anything with youngsters.'

'Do you think there was anything in the joke?'

She laughed. 'Sometimes a cigar is just a cigar. Weren't you fond of quoting that one? I think they hated each other's guts. Navitsky's a spoilt young... prat. Mina was a smashing young woman. Really. A fighter. You know – when they had that... doofus from the Foreign Office come here on a visit, she got right in there and shook a tin under his nose for the Kurdish refugees. Nearly got herself arrested.' She smiled at the memory. 'She had to bat off a few admiring young men after that.'

'Any young man in particular?'

Maureen shook her head straight away. 'She didn't have time for boyfriends.'

'Bit of a zealot, then?'

Maureen looked faintly rattled. 'A committed and eloquent activist.'

'Who suddenly abandoned eloquence for suicide. Doesn't that surprise you?'

'Must I be surprised? I can't say I was *au fait* with Mina's politics but I understand she was a passionate "blogger".' More finger quote marks adorned Maureen's point – like the *doofus*, her way of seeming modern was about a quarter-century out of date. 'If you're interested in being fair to her, I'd look at the blog.'

He thought Maureen was right. And, enduring Haluk's

steely stare, he nipped back in the foyer to grab a copy of the student paper, too.

* * *

The office was empty when he got in, just after midday. Ellie's desk-phone kept ringing, and the printer periodically gave out a noise to indicate that something was stuck, but apart from that, he was alone. He wondered if they'd all gone for lunch without him.

He stitched together a quick piece for Ellie, going off into the expected flights of fancy about the normally bustling supermarket, the shock hanging over the close-knit community and the emotional paralysis of the respected, café-owning father. It wasn't great. It wasn't what he wanted to say. It would do. He sent it to Ellie.

Then he started on the piece he wanted to write. Not in any form that could ever be published, just symbols and queries in amongst documents he cut and pasted from the web. It was how he'd always worked: free association meets print.

He started, not with Mina's assorted web-pages, but by returning to the two Kurdish girls who'd burned before. Neither case was very recent. In May 2011, a girl called Rojda had set light to herself outside the Turkish Consulate in Knightsbridge, part of a wave of protests in Turkey and across Europe. She'd survived for a few months, but her blog posts and her Facebook updates had all stopped on the Thursday of her solitary, extreme revolt.

Rojda had penned reams of bad poetry about sacrifice and martyrs, replete with references to seeds and soil, wombs and blood and tears. Alongside it, there were photographs of her in army fatigues, draped in a Kurdish flag. Before her, another girl had trodden the same path, at a rally in Dalston, in 2002. She'd written only in Kurdish, but her words were adorned with the same, artless kind of image. She had even photoshopped herself, like some eager groupie, into a picture of strapping, tousle-headed *peshmerga* fighters with a captured tank. She had not lived.

Both girls had come to London direct from conflict. Both girls had been protesting about distinct events: a fresh wave of anti-PKK action by the Turkish military in 2011, the abduction of the PKK's leader, Abdullah Öcalan, in 2002. Other girls across the Kurdish diaspora had been doing similar things: two in Stockholm in 2002, one in Berlin in 2011.

Yet Mina had acted alone. As Rex watched her YouTube address for the fourth time, he struggled to define what made him so uneasy. She had a style of delivery that was passionate; perhaps, like her uncle's, over-dramatic. But it didn't quite match the words. Apart from the title – 'Dying For Peace' – and her 'flames at the door' reference, the speech about the barracks bomb was without the gothic adornments of the others girls' outpourings. She'd posted links to them, it seemed, not to glorify their actions, but to point out that they'd been futile. Peace had not been won.

She'd made a handful of other posts in the past eight months, not draped in flags, not sporting combat gear, not even, in fact, concentrating exclusively on Kurdish affairs, but taking on a number of environmental issues, too. In her assorted blogs and her video-sermons, Mina seemed strikingly like her fellow Union committee-types: self-grooming for some sober, political future.

He realised he had a vague memory of seeing a teenage

Mina in the street at election time once, sporting someone's rosette, though the colour escaped him now. Keko had, as he said, made her in his own image. Political, but not revolutionary – they were all gone. A committee member. Which made her apparent suicide even harder to understand.

His phone rang.

'Where are you?'

Ellie. Somewhere loud. She and the rest of the newspaper staff were at the restaurant.

'I thought Terry told you what time to be here.'

'No.'

'You didn't see his message?'

'I didn't get one. Never mind, I'm coming.'

The Whittaker Twins came in to the office. They wore matching royal blue kaghouls, carried lunchboxes and thermoses under their arms. They never joined in. People, mostly, were glad. Rex hit 'print' on his long, pasted document of blogs and notes. Nothing happened. He looked back at the printer. It bleeped away underneath a sign Brenda had written. DO YOU REALLY NEED TO PRINT? Brenda, in her way, was political. And about as likely as Mina to set herself on fire.

Without bothering to unjam the printer, he put on his jacket and left.

CHAPTER FIVE

'Build an ark on water
And it will sail away
Build an ark on marshland
And everyone must pay.'

Lawrence passed the note across the table to Ellie. She sniffed it and grimaced. 'Lavender-scented. Granny's knicker drawer.'

Brenda bristled at the phrase, but took the note and looked at it with Rex. Spidery, copper-plate handwriting. Ellie was right: the most probable author was an elderly lady.

'And this is the second one of these notes you've had?' Rex asked, putting the note on the table. Brenda picked it up and brushed the crumbs off.

The Famous Manti Shop had transmogrified into The Gözleme Shop. The switch to baked patties from boiled dumplings could have worked in its favour except that, for some reason, Green Lanes had recently gone gözleme crazy. Every fourth business on the main drag had got itself a gleaming new shop-front, complete with a team of headscarved, gözleme-fashioning ladies in the window. It wasn't clear where all the money was coming from, but the whole area suddenly had a smarter, more confident sheen, and at the weekends, young, groovy types with beards and tight trousers were packing out the cafes in search of a new taste.

The Gözleme Shop had tuned into all this late, and done little more than swap its name and menu. The interior remained damp, its walls still festooned with the baleful eye-amulets and the frayed shepherd's bags. If the newspaper staff hadn't visited out of a semi-ironic sense of loyalty, it probably wouldn't have hosted any diners that day. They'd filled a table up with patties and olives, though, and four bottles of chilly red Buzbag were just about taking the edge off the place.

'That one about the ark and the marshes is obviously about the zoo,' Lawrence said, through a mouthful of spinach and cheese. 'But this one – I just can't fathom it.' He started to read as the proprietor collected a few plates:

> 'An 'A' for a penny
> A 'B' for ten.
> A 'Z' will cost you so dear
> You'll have to sell the hen.'

'Both addressed to you?' asked Terry, examining the second note, written in identical script.

'Both to me, care of the paper. Matching envelopes. N22 postmark. Second class.' Lawrence removed spinach from his teeth with a fingernail. 'And both arrived on a Monday.'

'Posted Thursday, then,' said Terry. 'Pension day.'

'How do you know that?' Ellie asked him, as he topped up her glass.

'I pick up me neighbour's sometimes,' Terry said. 'Mrs Christodolou.'

'Aw,' said Ellie. 'Isn't Terry nice?'

Brenda tutted. Rex caught her eye.

'Minx, isn't she?' Brenda said quietly, as Lawrence began a long analysis of what he thought 'A for a penny' might mean. Rex shrugged, reluctant to be drawn.

'Surprised at you, making your peace so quickly,' Brenda added.

'Big difference between peace and ceasefire, Bren.'

'Look at it, though,' Brenda said, refusing a top-up. They looked across the table to see Ellie taking a picture of herself and Terry on her phone. '*Selfies*,' she snorted. 'Says it all. They're only interested in themselves, these young ones, now.'

Rex filled his own glass, thinking. 'I don't think Mina was like that.' He told Brenda about the web material he'd been viewing back at the office: her earnest blogging, the pieces-to-camera. The stark contrast with the posturing of the other girls.

'It's no different,' Brenda said. 'Not in my view. If it's "look at me on a night out with my pals" or "look at me with my rocket launcher" or "listen to my opinion on Israel". It's all self-important, here-I-am. That's how they all are, putting it on the internet. If no one's looking, it's not happening.'

Perhaps Brenda was right. Even if Mina's obsession was with issues and causes, it could still be all self-serving, self-absorbed. Eve Reilly, with her 'I thinks' and her 'my constituencies' seemed proof of that. And if Mina was out there, on the campus, waving tins under people's noses, clashing with fellow committee members, then she wasn't at home, taking toilet paper to her father. As her clearly resentful brother had to.

'So you don't think it's that weird? A girl who writes an earnest political blog setting herself on fire?'

Brenda shrugged, her necklace clacking. 'I can see how one turns into the other. And with girls of nineteen, there's usually one reason.'

'What?'

She leant in. He could smell her face-cream. 'I kept a diary, every day, from when I was thirteen to when I was nineteen. Then I stopped for six months. And after that, I wrote the odd bit, but I never really went back to it. Do you know why I stopped?'

'No.'

'I met Mike.'

She inclined her head at him meaningfully. He took this in. 'They said there might have been a feller. Her uncle said it, anyway.'

He was about to say more when he felt a hand on his shoulder. It was Ellie. How long had she been there?

'Nipping out for a smoke. Get another bottle in?'

He nodded, relaxed a little. Perhaps this was going to work out.

'Just a bit of banter,' a flushed Terry was saying to Lawrence. 'But that one from before? With the curls and the big bazookas. I wouldn't mind.'

The proprietor re-appeared, and Rex asked for more wine. A sullen man with hawk-like features, he merely nodded as he gathered empty plates. Then he licked his lips and said:

'You like gözleme?'

Rex blinked. For this guy, it was practically an outpouring.

'We do. How come all the Turkish restaurants are doing them?'

'Not Turkish,' said the man. 'Kurdish. Gözleme are Kurdish.'

'But all the Turkish restaurants are doing them.'

The man almost smiled. 'Most of Turkish restaurants Green Lanes, boss... Kurdish.'

Rex stared at him.

'He's not joking,' Lawrence said. 'There are many, many more Kurds around this neck of the woods than Turks. Same in the supermarkets. You look for the colours. Red, green and yellow. Or those little tins, collecting for the Alevi Foundation or what-have-you. Dead giveaway. Kurdish.'

The proprietor, incredibly, winked at Lawrence and smiled. 'Kurdish.'

'Thought you'd have known that, Rex,' said Terry. Rex didn't much care for the way he said it.

He took a deep draft of the wine. 'Do you know Keko?' he asked the owner. 'The father of the girl who died?'

'Küçüktürk. Sure. No magazines guy.' The man shook his head, seemingly in admiration.

'You remember that? The 'no magazines' sign. Why did he say that?'

'He won't pay.'

'Pay for what?'

The man looked pained. 'The magazine. Because...' He frowned, trying to dredge up some words, but then shook his head. 'Sajadi is here now? I saw his car. German car. Rostam. Very high.'

'Very high?'

'Yes. High man. *Tawsi Melek*. Important.'

'What's *tawsi melek*?' Rex asked. He remembered he'd heard the phrase before, from Aran, though he'd misheard it as 'that was Melek'.

'Very high,' was all the proprietor would repeat. Slightly sheepish after so much revelation, he vanished into the back with a couple of plates and showed no eagerness to return.

'*Tawsi Melek* rings a bell-shaped object,' Lawrence said. 'I'll look it up. In the meantime, if I can change my dentist's, can I tag along to your Cypriot thing?'

'What Cypriot thing?'

'Oh – I...' Lawrence looked at Terry, who coughed.

'That doctor. Helena. She popped in this morning to tell us about something she's doing up at Sky City this afternoon. Kind of gathering war stories from the Turkish pensioners. She's invited us to take some photos. Maybe put a bit of video on the site, like. It's three until five.' He kept his eyes firmly on the glass in front of him.

'No one considered it worth telling me?' *Not even Helena*, came the private, sulky after-thought.

'I'm telling you now,' said Terry, finally looking at him. 'It's at the Sky City Community Centre. Three to five. With the Turkish Cypriot Pensioners' Group.'

'Play nicely, boys,' said Brenda into the silence. Rex stood up.

'Rex, man, don't strop off.'

'I'm just going to the khazi,' Rex said.

The toilet, situated opposite the vents of an adjacent Turkish, or more probably Kurdish eatery, smelled nicer than anywhere else in the place. Amid waves of roasting peppers and warm fresh bread, Rex washed his hands roughly at the sink. The soap was old and split, like a piece of driftwood. He'd been washing his hands on it for years. Years of being down here, getting companionably smashed with Susan, and Brenda, and Lawrence. And Terry.

There was guilt as well as anger. Last year, Terry had completed his award-winning undercover photo-essay whilst in the grips of a multiple sclerosis flare-up and on bail on a murder charge. Along with everyone else, Rex had thought him guilty, of the murder and worse, and had even told D.S. Brenard of his suspicions. He'd never confessed this to Terry. But at the back of his mind, always, especially now there were these sprouting tensions between them, was the fear that Terry might find out. Or know already.

But he was over-reacting, he told himself. Guilt was making him see phantoms. Terry was a wind-up merchant, always had been. He put a hand, warm, over his face and took a breath in. The soap smell reminded him of his wife, her embrace, after a shit day; forgiving, after a fight. He would see her tonight.

He glimpsed the white hand towel behind him in the mirror. It suddenly made him think of the flash-image, burnt into his optic nerve, from the Friday before. A pale face, peering over the balcony, just after Mina fell. Just an impression, he'd thought. But then, this morning, on the board at the university, he'd seen Navitsky's face. Whey coloured. Somehow lupine. And it had sparked something.

Where was Navitsky now? Gone. Suddenly. The same day Mina died.

His heart lurched as he headed out. He felt excited. But he might be over-excited. Sometimes, he knew, he saw connections between things, too many connections. It was a problem he'd had, ever since Sybille. He felt in his jacket pocket. Three left.

He was swallowing the last of the co-dydramol as he left the toilet. They were another problem he'd had since Sybille, since he'd torn apart his foot, and their life together, in the wreckage of their car. But the pills helped him to think clearly. If they made him see things as too significant, it was because they brought meaning to his life more generally. Ellie caught up with him by the stairs down. He stuffed the pill strip in his pocket.

'You okay?' she asked, as if he might not be.

'The proprietor doesn't seem keen to give us any more plonk, Rex said, waving her in front and heading down the stairs behind her. 'Perhaps it's for the best.'

At the bottom Ellie smiled and put an arm on his, staying his entrance into the room.

'I just want to say thanks. You know – thanks for being a ledge... A legend, grand-dad,' she clarified loudly. 'It makes a big difference, having you on board.' Rex nodded. She wrinkled up her nose and leant closer. 'I saw you sent me the family piece. Great stuff. And don't worry about Terry.'

'Sorry?'

'He's got ambitions these days. It's good that he's got ambitions. He's a great snapper. But he can't write. He just can't write. So there's no need to get wound up about him. Oh, and he hasn't got a hope with that doctor, believe me.'

She winked, then went ahead of him into the room, launching immediately into a funny story about a dog she'd seen outside. Rex hung back, watching her, and the reactions of everyone else around the table. How did Ellie know he *was* wound up about Terry? She had been out of the room for their most recent clash. Was she just guessing? And the doctor? Presumably Helena was the person whose 'bazookas' Terry had recently been slathering over.

They'd all shuffled, and the spare seat was next to Lawrence. He'd been reading the University newsletter that Rex had flipped through on the bus down.

'Laudably high standards of journalism,' Lawrence said. 'We should give the editor a work placement.'

This was a joke. Lawrence's tanned, manicured index finger was pointing to a 'Corrections and Apologies' column on page 7 of the publication. There were quite a few corrections. And one apology.

'In our February issue, contributor "Hollow Wayne" referred to Student Union President Jan Navitsky as 'our cheeky Czech Premier with the chequered past.' We accept that Mr Navitsky is from Belarus, not the Czech Republic, and that the reference to a 'chequered past' could have caused offence...'

It obviously had. To one Jan Navitsky, by the looks of it. So what kind of past did they mean?

*　*　*

The old woman had a face lined and scissored like a school desk. She sat on the chair in the circle, relating her experiences in Cyprus in one low, unbroken murmur. She looked down at the floor, throughout, as if there was something shameful to her words.

'Then we were with cousins of my husband, for several months, all of us, many cousins, in one house, in Famagusta. The wife of the house there, a woman called Emine, it's hard to explain. She looked down on us, because she thought we looked down on her. So if you were sad thinking about the village and you said, 'I wonder how our fruit trees are?' her face would be angry, and she'd say, 'I'm sorry we don't have a big orchard for you to take care of here.' You couldn't talk to the people in Famagusta about your old life in the south. Even though they were your family, your own people, they didn't want to know. It made them angry, and still you had to depend on them.'

Her daughter, a stout matron herself in a Marks and Spencer's uniform, interpreted in a high, melodic voice that seemed unique to Turkish women. Around the room, others – wiry old men in their navy caps, the black-wrapped grannies like Russian dolls – clicked and tutted in agreement, sympathy, shared recognition of the stateless state.

An old man spoke up now. He had sunken eyes and a reedy voice. He started in English but soon lapsed into Turkish, and, at a nod from the doctor, the shop assistant interpreted for him as well.

'He says you do everything looking back. Even now, in London, when he has coffee and bread in the morning, he can only think, what did the coffee and the bread taste like in Paphos? It's like your life stops. Even something new… you…' The woman pinched her nose, as if she could draw the words out. 'You see it from the eyes of there. Not here.' She shrugged.

Rex knew, and he found himself nodding in the silence that fell on the room. His was a life in the rear-view, too. Many things had happened in the past twelve years, but he felt sometimes as if he witnessed them all from a doorway.

Dr Georgiadis was looking right at him. He looked away, embarrassed, with the irrational idea that she'd read his thoughts. There was a school playground far below, and shrieks from the kids came through the one open window in the community centre. Nodding to the last two speakers, the doctor stood up, and switched off the video camera. She thanked everyone for their contributions so far, and suggested a short break. There was baklava in the kitchen, and hot coffee. Turkish, not Greek, she added, which got a loud, almost shocked laugh. Chairs scraped, and the old people argued softly over who was to fetch the coffee and who would stay put and rub their limbs.

She came over to Rex, who was sitting right at the back, by the window, his shirt undone. The Turkish Cypriot Pensioners group liked to keep warm.

'I looked for you this morning,' she said, sitting next to him. She smelt old-fashioned, he thought. Of coal tar soap and spray starch.

'I was out of the office. You should have rung.'

She rolled her eyes. 'They had a power cut at the Brunswick, and my phone didn't charge.'

'You have to pay for the VIP suite if you want electricity.'

She batted his arm. Terry, who'd been snapping participants with varying degrees of cooperation, came across.

'Great talk, Helena. Smashing. You really draw it out of them.'

'Thank you, Terry,' she said primly.

'Do you want to er – get a coffee?' He was like a puppy.

'Well,' she said. 'Seeing as you are the person on your feet, Terry, and I've been on mine all day, would you kindly get one for me? And for Rex?'

Terry looked from Rex to Helena and back to Rex, then nodded slowly. 'Slice of baklava and two forks is it?' he muttered, heading off to the milling kitchen.

'I think you disappointed him,' Rex said. He was glad Terry had gone. Even more glad Lawrence hadn't been able to move his dental appointment.

She frowned. 'I don't understand.' But then she looked out of the window and said 'What a place! Sky City! It sounds like it should be in China.'

Sky City was a little like the zoo: one of those bold flights of civic planning that seemed admirable in abstract, or even in Holland, but became a nightmare when translated into London stone. Conceived in the early 1980s as a housing estate on top of Shopping City, it was often compared to Palestine, and not solely because it resembled a thousand little box-houses on a hillside. Thanks to its numerous gangways and staircases, and its general isolation above the High Road, Sky City had become a haven for Wood Green's grimmer elements, and around a third of its flats now stood empty. On the council-house-swap noticeboards in the library, people had become so accustomed to writing 'Anywhere Except Sky City' that AESC was now an accepted acronym, like WLTM or ROFL.

'Is it a good idea for the old people?' she asked, after reapplying some earthy-red lipstick. 'Having to come up here for their community centre?'

'It's worse for the mother and baby group,' Rex said. 'You can only get one pushchair at a time in the lift. But until they start the renovations, there's nowhere else nearby.'

She'd put the lipstick away in her bag, and was rummaging through for something else. She glanced up, a rogue curl falling across her cheek. 'They should be building a new community centre then, instead of that zoo.'

'It has been suggested.'

She gave up on her search. Rex caught a glimpse inside the bag as she did it up. A knot of scarves and possibly tights and small, zip-up bags: Dr Georgiadis was slightly chaotic. He liked that, without knowing why. And he was relieved the phone had been on the blink. There was an awkward pause, where they both smiled at one another, but lacked anything to say.

Rex looked towards the posters on the wall. One had a council logo, and it announced 'ongoing maintenance' to the whole of Sky City. So it was happening at last. Another, in Turkish, Greek and Kurdish, was about the dangers of gambling. The new video poker machines seemed to be the direct focus: a young man doggedly played one while reams of cash flew, Disney-like, from the back of it and out of the window, over the heads of his unhappy wife and baby.

He saw Terry heading back with the coffees and a well-practised grin. It quickened his resolve. 'Look, er... Could I buy you a drink later? I enjoyed our walk on Saturday.'

She shook her head firmly.

'Oh,' he said, before he could stop himself.

'Dinner,' she said. 'You got me absolutely drunk on Friday, then on Saturday you walked me round until I was ready to drop and I kept thinking you were going to offer me something to eat. Don't people eat here?'

He smiled. 'What would you like to eat?'

'I don't care. But I am a Cypriot woman, Rex. I eat. Tonight. In Muswell Hill.'

'You're on. Why Muswell Hill?'

'Because this afternoon, I'm moving to that hotel you told me about.'

He felt a daft, teenage sort of pride as Terry returned and

continued, artlessly but with clear intent, to chat up the doctor. He'd started telling her about the extra functions on her video camera, and Helena was standing there with him, at the tripod, and giving Rex a precious, secret, wry look when the door opened. She looked away from him to see who had come in, then quickly back to her desk. She began to busy herself with her papers.

Rex looked over to the entrance. An old man in the company of a much younger one were standing just inside the room, coats glistening from the rain. There was nothing strange about that: many of the pensioners here had brought along a daughter or a son – to drive, to interpret, to protect them from the darker forces of Sky City. In this case, Rex recognised both members of the pair. Bilal Toprak was Development Officer at the new council, a tubby, prematurely grave man in his early thirties. The real surprise was his father, the factory-owner, Kemal, who'd always borne the look of a circus strongman with his naked head, tank-like frame and exuberant moustaches. Now he looked derelict like his factory: white and shrunken, a hesitant look as he held tightly on to his son's arm.

Rex went over. He'd known Bilal a long time: active in the Lib Dems, he'd quit the council's Media Office for an elected seat, lost it, and then returned to climb quietly through the ranks of local government. That wasn't an unusual story: serious, efficient people, imbued with sensible horizons and strong values by their immigrant parents, did well round here. They just rarely made the headlines.

'You here for the meeting?'

Bilal led his father to the nearest chair and helped him off with his thick, sheepskin coat.

'Dad wanted to come. He – he grew up in Cyprus. Place called Lapta. Is there somewhere I can…?' He motioned with the coat. Rex realised the old man hadn't said a word, and they were talking about him as if he'd disappeared long ago. He tried to make eye contact with Toprak Senior, but he just stared ahead, nervously rolling his jaw. His skin looked slack and lifeless.

Rex followed Bilal to the hooks at the side of the room. The Turks called a man's pot-belly his 'bread-basket', Rex recalled. Bilal's had become more of a skip.

'Is your father all right?'

Bilal frowned from behind his round, administrator spectacles. 'Not really. He had a stroke after the fire… Well, you know he did…'

Kemal had had the stroke whilst driving his van down Green Lanes, causing a tailback as far as the Palmer's Green roundabout. It had made the front page in a quiet week.

'He's been okay,' Bilal went on in a low voice, as they moved back to the seats. 'But he just stays at the factory all day. He's convinced the insurance are going to pay up any time. And then yesterday, he had a fright.'

'We all had a fright yesterday.'

'I heard about that. Mina, was she called…? Very sad.'

'Your boss was on the phone to her uncle this morning. Are they acquainted?'

Bilal stared at him. 'I don't know. I don't know who her uncle was. Is.'

'What happened to your dad then?' Rex changed the subject.

'Someone tried to break in while he was on his own at the factory. It'll only be squatters and that. But it's set him back.

His club's not so relaxing to go to anymore, so… that's why I thought I'd bring him over here.'

'He goes in Trabzonspor, doesn't he?' Rex was sure he had glimpsed Toprak Senior once or twice, gazing through his moustaches at an empty tea-glass in the Turkish social club opposite the bus station. Like everywhere else, it was currently undergoing a makeover. 'Trabzonspor is a football team, right? So why does he support Trabzon if he's from Cyprus?'

Bilal blinked, a proper man of offices and meetings, unready for personal chat. 'He left Lapta and went to the mainland, to Trabzon, on the coast. Lots of them did. Better life, you know, and there were grants, loans, things like that, to help. Mainly, that place is a club for Cypriots who ended up in Turkey. Well, it was.' He added. 'No one's sure what it's going to be when they're finished with the works.'

'Story of the area, isn't it?' Rex mused. 'Your planning blokes are obviously busy. I got about three minutes with one yesterday morning. Ashley Pocock.'

Something crossed Bilal's jowly face, before he nodded and rejoined his father. Was it concern? Irritation? Rex wasn't sure which. It made him want another word with Pocock, though.

The seats were filling up again, the smell of coffee mingling with unwashed wool and Deep Heat. Terry was standing next to the tripod, looking baffled.

'Is Helena starting again?' Rex asked.

Terry shrugged. 'I dunno. She just went.'

'What do you mean – went?'

'Grabbed her bag and legged it out the door.'

Rex went to the door and looked out. There was a long, wet

concrete walkway, leading to stairs. And no one to be seen. He looked back into the room. The woman in the Marks and Spencer's uniform seemed to be quizzing Terry, and he was shrugging and pointing towards the door.

He headed out into the wet breeze, down the walkway. They were about a hundred feet above the High Street. He leant over. From above, Wood Green looked just like anywhere else: just heads, shopping bags and cars and buggies and dogs. It wasn't just like anywhere else, though.

The walkway ended in a dark stairwell. You could go up, to higher levels of the 'city', or down, towards the street, in both cases accompanied by piss and gang graffiti and the mounting fear of encountering someone less scared than yourself. He assumed Helena must have gone downwards, but he didn't know why she'd gone anywhere at all. Had arranging a dinner date just been too much?

On the next level, a sign pointed two ways. 'Playground'. Playground? He doubted there'd ever been one of those. The other way said 'Shops'. He pictured the planners. In their 1970s suits, in some colourful office decked out with executive toys and dolly-bird typists, sketching it all, so sure this city in the sky would produce happy, productive citizens. So deluded.

He assumed the 'Shops' route would either intersect with the lift, or join up with some stairs that took him to the ground floor entrance by the back of the Market Hall. Instead, it took him on another zigzagged, sloping walkway, its walls lower, a green metal rail making some half-hearted gesture towards safety. He ran his hand along it as he walked towards the scuffed, steel-clad fire-doors up ahead.

There was a kind of gantry running just over these

doors – its rails done out in the same, council green and running around the side of the complex, level with the huge, illuminated signs that said CAR PARK and SHOPPING CITY. The gantry, he assumed, was for servicing the signs.

He smelled paint. A faint trace of it on his hands. Green, from the railings. With what was, perhaps, an old-fashioned sense of courtesy, he tucked a hand inside his jacket cuff to open the metal door.

Ahead of him was another doorway. A sign on the wall above it said 'Caution: This Door Is Alarmed', but there was no door, just a plywood frame, as if someone was in the process of rebuilding or replacing the important middle. There was a faint smudge of green paint on the wood.

Stepping through the wooden doorway, he suddenly realised where was he was. He took a couple of steps down. Then bright lights. Tinny music. On his left, an eerie shop in darkness, full of naked dummies, a bailiff's notice stuck to the window. And then, to his right, the balcony. The escalator. Where Mina had fallen.

The escalator was off, and the whole lower side of the arcade had been shuttered off with huge, sliding grilles. He dared a look over the balcony, afraid what might be down there. But there was nothing. Only a couple of the yellow cones they put out when someone spilled a milkshake.

Then he saw something else. Exactly where he stood, looking over, were two more green smudges on the rail that ran either side of the escalator. A couple of feet apart. Just as someone's hands would be, if they'd stood and looked over the rail.

He hadn't imagined it. He had seen someone else up there. Looking over. Someone who'd watched Mina fall.

He went back to the plywood doorway, looking at the handprint there, wondering who owned it. What they'd been doing up there.

And then he saw something else. On the wooden frame, around the height of his shoulder. A scorch mark, scimitar-shaped, dark brown at the edges, a nasty black at the centre. He pulled out his phone.

CHAPTER SIX

I t was only fitting, in this age of upheaval and upscaling, that the police should finally, after an eight-year wait, have moved to their new premises. Their former home, an ornately tiled Victorian building on St Ann's Road, was boarded up while developers prepared plans of ever-increasing extravagance. Meanwhile, D.S. Brenard and his cohorts had decamped, as grudgingly as teenagers on a family walk, to a trapezoid of glass and steel on Seven Sisters Road.

C.I.D. now occupied a middle floor, instead of their former, delightful wood-beamed attic, and very much gave off the air of people who hadn't settled. There were still piles of archive boxes in the windows, phone and computer cables snaked untethered across the carpet, and no one could ever quite get the temperature right. Whenever a big lorry passed, heading north towards the A10, the windowpane behind D.S. Brenard buzzed, and he glared round at it – a nuisance he refused to make peace with.

In spite of his frustrations, the neat, slight Welshman listened to what Rex had to say and looked at the photos he'd taken on his phone.

'We weren't sure which way she'd come into Shopping City, so that explains it,' Brenard said, nodding sagely. 'She must have come through the flats. I guess she knew that would be more private. Less chance of being seen before she...' Brenard paused. He was a decent man, Chapel-bred, who rarely even swore. '... She did what she did.'

'I didn't even know there was a way through from the flats.'

'Well there isn't now. There was. Until about 1993. But it just meant the shoplifters would run off into the flats and no one could catch them, so they locked it and alarmed it, and just left it there for emergency access. They've been putting a new one in now – that's why there's that plywood frame.'

'So Mina must have known she could get through.'

'Well... it's not a secret. They're doing up all the exteriors, aren't they? You even published the schedule of works in your paper the other week.'

'You think she had it all worked out in advance?'

'Maybe. Or maybe she tried to go through Shopping City but changed her mind and then ran round the flats and got lucky. If that's the word.'

'And this really doesn't change it for you?'

For a second time, he showed Brenard the picture he'd taken inside the wooden doorway between the Sky City flats and the mall. The scorch mark: sharp and curved, a thorn made of soot. He'd touched it with his fingers, even smelt the petrol. He felt as if the smell was still on them now, on his phone, from when he'd stood, and dialled the police station.

'I agree it changes the picture slightly, and I'll be sure to mention it at the Inquest this afternoon. It suggests Mina stood in that doorway and set light to herself there, before she headed through onto the mezzanine in the shopping centre.'

'But why would she do that?'

'So as not to be seen before her act was final? To collect her thoughts in private before she went out? Maybe she stood there for a bit, with the lighter in her hand, looking at it, trying to get up the neck to do it, then she just thought, 'Sod it' and sparked it? Or even sparked it too early, without meaning to.'

'What lighter? Did she have it in her hand?'

'On a cord round her neck. The kind that slots into a little leather pouch. They go for them, the young girls, so they can wear tight jeans. And their mums and dads don't catch on they're smoking,' he added. 'Except of course they do.'

'And you know she used that lighter?'

'There wouldn't be a way in heaven of proving that, no. But in the absence of a witness, it would seem so.'

'But the person I saw, the person who stood on that balcony by the escalator *was* a witness. They stood there, looking over, down to the ground floor, and they had their hands on the metal rail, and they left their prints there, didn't they?'

'You said you weren't sure you had seen someone else up there,' Brenard reminded him, patiently. 'Those marks on the rail are not prints, they're smudges and who's to say they're not Mina's? The Sky City railings were being painted yesterday as part of the on-going maintenance. If she came through into the shopping centre that way, as your photo suggests, then there's every chance she got the paint on her hands as she passed by.'

'And then for some reason – while she was on fire – she put both her hands on the rail at the side of the escalator?'

'Why not? Why wouldn't her hands touch the rails?

97

Doesn't have to have been deliberate, does it? I'm guessing someone on fire flaps around a hell of a lot. Unless they're Buddhist monks. You seen them on the news? They're the only ones I've ever seen, doing it, thank Heaven. But Mina was screaming, wasn't she? She wasn't calm.

Rex forced himself to remember. The scream. And the awful twisting dance. Almost like a dervish. He realised then that, in his mind, he'd made it seem like an accident. It looked like an accident, because Mina had screamed and writhed with such panic as she tumbled down. Because it wasn't like the eerie, meditative suicides of those Eastern monks he had, like D.S. Brenard, winced at occasionally on the TV news. But that didn't mean it wasn't deliberate.

It only meant Mina hadn't been prepared for the pain. The soft explosion as the air around her vanished and the space was filled with flame and horror and she realised there was no way back.

He shook himself. D.S. Brenard was looking sympathetic.

'Hard to forget, I know. I've had a few like that.'

Rex nodded. But something still wasn't right.

'What about the painter?'

'Eh?'

'Whoever was doing the painting outside in the housing estate would have had paint on their hands. Maybe that was who was up there. That was who I saw.'

'It's the council's own works department doing the painting and the door replacement. One of my team spoke to the bloke who was on it yesterday. Hang on…' Brenard shuffled papers, tugged at a drawer, gave up, asked a colleague. Nothing was in its right place, it seemed. 'A Mr Texo Chuba. Who was down at his van making some minor adjustments to the new door between 12.00 and around 1.30 pm. By the time he was ready to take it back up, the whole place was locked down.'

Rex took this in. The police had done their looking. They weren't going to look any more. But he still felt this doubt, this possibility that he'd seen someone else up there. 'But the door's still not there,' he said.

'What?'

'That's why I was able to take a picture of the scorch-marks on the plywood frame. That temporary doorway thing's still in place because they still haven't put the finished door in.'

Brenard considered this for a moment, then shrugged. 'Best take that up with Texo.'

He shuffled papers, signalling that Rex's time was up. Rex didn't move.

'Jan Navitsky.'

'What about him?'

'You know who he is, then.'

Rex wondered if there was a slight pause before Brenard said, 'Why? Should I?'

'I just wondered if the name meant anything to you. Apparently he and Mina had a beef, and there are references in the student newsletter to a chequered past. His, I mean.'

'Probably sleeps around a lot.'

'He also left the country, suddenly, on the day Mina died.'

'You're barking at shadows here, Rex. Seriously. We've never heard of him.'

'Your computer might have.'

Brenard sighed. 'What do you think I am? Google Rapsheets? Go home, Rex. Get some rest.'

* * *

Heading up the High Street towards the office, Rex tried the Council Works Department on his phone. As he waited to be connected, he noticed a large, beaming party of Chinese businesspeople in suits heading towards him. In the midst of them, making observations that seemed to be going down awfully well, was the council boss, Eric Miles.

Miles was a strange mix of parts. With his fondness for tweeds, his high forehead and his public school hairdo, he looked like the laird of the manor. In fact, he'd followed his father into the draughtsman's office at the shipyard, taken OU courses at night and turned himself, over ten years, into a teacher. God had become involved along the way, as had liberal politics and a spell of mission work somewhere poor and hot.

All these factors ought to have made Eric Miles an interesting man, but somehow they had failed to. Interviews with him always left Rex patting his pockets and checking his coat, thinking he'd lost something, until his conscious mind caught up with the unconscious, and he realised that the missing thing was Eric Miles. He was just a good bloke, Rex had concluded in the end. Jesus Christ had probably been the same – a bit dull. That was why people had made up stories about him.

He itched to ask the council boss what he was doing with the Chinese delegation. But after six rings, the ring-tone suddenly changed, then a woman answered.

'Works.'

'May I speak to Texo?'

'Sorry?'

'Texo,' Rex repeated, watching Miles and his entourage depart down the High Street. In the ensuing silence, he remembered there was a surname, but he'd forgotten it. 'Hang on,' he said, fumbling in his shoulder bag for his note-pad. Was his memory getting patchy? 'Chuba,' he said, returning to the phone. But the woman had gone. He rang back. Same as before, the tone changed after a couple of rings, but this time, no one answered. He gave up, puzzled.

A council road-sweeper he recognised was just coming out of the Ladbroke's. He'd recently won one of the paper's 'Community Champ' Awards for tripping up a bag-snatcher with his broom. It was worth a shot.

'Have you come across a bloke in the Works Department called Texo?'

The sweeper chuckled. 'Wait in there long enough, you'll see him.'

Rex went into the bookie's. It smelt of old newspapers, wet shoes and defeat. Men were shouting at a TV screen, not with hope, but with anger. They, at least, were animated – unlike the row of blokes at the video poker terminals, mute, staring, pressing buttons and pushing money in as though they themselves had become parts of the machines.

Rex, who rarely passed a day without at least four pints of strong lager and a dozen pills, couldn't understand gambling. Like a lot of addicts, he felt his was the one true path, everyone else's delusion.

With distaste, he picked his way through to a booth, where the only woman in the establishment sat, screened off from the grim maleness behind toughened glass. She looked Nigerian – fiercely painted, eyebrows stencilled into an expression of permanent alert, hair tinted to stop traffic.

'I'm doing some work with a man called Texo,' Rex lied. 'I was told he'd be in here.'

'Texo?' she echoed, with faint disbelief.

'Yes.'

'It's not his name,' she said, staring more or less up at the ceiling.

'What is his name?'

She sucked a gold tooth. This, Rex knew, could mean anything. He sensed a man at the poker machines, small, ruddy, shabby, looking over.

'What does he look like?'

She snorted. 'You like old movies?'

'Eh?'

She kept on gazing somewhere high over his head. African women often did this, he'd noticed. Respect? Indifference? A devotion to some Higher Power? He'd never worked it out.

'He's not in,' she said finally, each word on a different musical tone.

Nodding a wary thanks, he looked back at the poker machines. The little man who'd been staring over had vanished. His sudden absence, however, gave Rex a clear view of the man clamped to the adjacent terminal. Ashley Pocock.

He remembered the fleeting look that had passed over Bilal's face, like a squall at sea, when he'd mentioned the Planning Officer's visit. It was worth digging. With Ellie as his new boss, he needed his pockets full of pay-dirt.

'Winning?' he asked, peering over Pocock's shoulder. He had no idea what the configuration of cards and symbols on the screen signified.

'Nah,' said Pocock distractedly. Then, seeming to realise this wasn't one of his betting buddies, he looked up and stared, none-too-friendly.

'We met yesterday,' Rex said. 'The sky lights.'

Pocock nodded warily. Rex glanced briefly back at the screen. To his surprise, he saw that 'Poko The Magnificent' was two grand in credit. Rex tried to look as if he hadn't seen.

'I've been thinking about our chat,' Rex said, carefully. 'I think I understand the procedure you're talking about.'

Full House, Rex thought. Pocock relaxed, smiled, pressed some buttons and waited for the machine to print a slip of paper. Tucking it carefully into his wallet, he led Rex over the road to the Jerk Shack.

The Shack was an institution, tucked away unadvertised in between the cut-price pans and ersatz Tupperware at the back of the Market Hall. The sisters who ran the place knew Rex. They knew Pocock, too. As they waited for their drinks through the hiss of steam and the clatter of cups, Rex mused that it was an ideal place for secret business. Michaela and Linda, the joint proprietresses, could agree neither on the menu, the décor, the prices, nor even the choice of music. The only thing they shared was a conviction that the music needed to be loud. And so it was: old-school ska and reggae alternating with modern R&B and gospel. The people at the other tables, Pakistani pensioners on this Monday afternoon, mostly, accompanied by bags of halal chicken parts, couldn't catch a word anyone else said.

'So... if I was to go about getting the correct documentation,' Rex said, winging it. 'I assume I'd have to find a... consultant? To help me sort it all out?'

Pocock beamed. 'That sort of thing, yeah.'

'Would that be expensive?'

'Not necessarily,' Pocock shouted over the bass-line, as two mugs arrived. 'I could point you towards someone very good.'

'And they could guarantee a favourable outcome?'

Pocock had his mouth open to reply when a frown crossed his face and he stared behind Rex's shoulder. Rex followed the direction of his stare as Terry bounded in.

Terry. With his war correspondent's multi-pocketed vest on. And a camera round his neck. Everything short of a flashing neon PRESS sign.

'Where'd you get to?'

Rex kept eye-contact with Terry and said, 'Hey, Terry. Long time no see.'

Terry stared. 'What are you on about? We were just at the community centre thing. Anyhow, the boss wants you back at the paper.'

'I knew it!' hissed Pocock. 'You was trying to stitch me up!' He raised his voice just as the perky reggae track ended. 'I am a council officer and this journalist is offering me a bribe!'

A rustling of plastic bags came with the cricking of a dozen arthritic necks. Everyone in the place stared.

'What made you think I'd be up for it? 'Cos I'm black?' Pocock continued.

'You're white,' Rex said quietly. No new music came on. 'Aren't you?'

'Oh, like you can't tell I've got a black dad! Fuck's sake!'

Rex looked at the young man. Tight curls. A wide nose. Maybe a slight, caramel colour to the freckles. It hadn't occurred to him. It hadn't been important, anyway. Except…

'Have you got a sister? Called Kyretia?'

'What's she got to do with it?' Pocock kissed his teeth. '*Man a racisss!*'

He stalked out. The two sisters glared at him from the counter. Terry looked baffled.

'That went well, I thought,' said Rex.

* * *

'They were wrongly dubbed devil worshippers by the neighbouring Alevi and Sunni Kurds, you see, on account of a misidentification of their *Tawsi Melek* with Lucifer.'

'Who were, Lawrence?'

Rex wasn't in the mood. Still fuming at Terry, he'd necked a couple of pills from his desk drawer, but they were old, mail order from India, and they'd got him, irritatingly, just to the threshold of what he needed to feel and then no further. A chirpy, pungent IT technician had been called out to the printer, and was whistling, muttering and reeking just a ruler's length behind Rex's back. Meanwhile his keyboard was sticking, with random letters inexplicably needing to be whacked with great force in order for him to be able to finish the teatime update of the website, causing, in turn, a miniscule paper cut on his right index finger to smart. He felt certain he was going to blow.

'Yezidis,' Lawrence said. 'They're an ancient Middle Eastern sect.'

Rex sat back and took a deep breath.

'*Our* Lucifer, who was an angel, who got too big for his boots and was sent down to Hell, is *their* Tawsi Melek. Except for them, he didn't go to Hell. He wept for 7,000 years over his general big-headedness, filled seven buckets with his tears and extinguished the flames of Hell. As a reward, God forgave him and made him one of the seven angels who run things on earth. He takes the form of peacock. And also a rainbow.'

'A peacock.' Rex thought about the bird at the back of the

shop. He sat up. 'They own one. Mina's family, I mean. And she had a peacock brooch. Her brother told me it was from their mother, and he said… He said those words to me. Same as the guy in the gözleme shop. *Tawsi Melek*. So they must be these…Yezidis, then, don't you think? Not Kurds?'

Lawrence shook his head. 'Very unlikely. Anyway, they'd still be Kurds. In our way of looking at it, anyway. It depends who's talking. The Arabs say they're Kurds. The Turks say they're Kurds. Even the Kurds call the Yezidis Kurds, when it suits them. The Yezidis, on the other hand, well, some of them occasionally say they're Kurds, some of them say they're a completely different race to the Kurds. As, indeed, do the wider Kurds when the Yezidis aren't playing ball. I thought you'd got a degree in anthropology.'

'I did India. I think. I can't really remember.'

'Well this lot were all over the news a couple of years back.'

Yezidis. Rex did remember the name. Recalled some tribe of Iraqis, stuck up a mountain, being raped and massacred by rabid fundamentalists, forced over the borders into Southern Turkey. But then they'd been swallowed by the bigger, still-running tragedy of all the people, Kurds and Shia and Christians and those who just tied their shoelaces the wrong way, being butchered by the latest breed of monsters to crawl out of the faultlines. He didn't follow the world news very much these days. In any case, the world always came to Haringey. And two years ago, there'd been a lot going on, with the local elections and the boundary changes.

'Anyhow,' Lawrence was saying. 'Your peacocks must be just coincidence. There's no Yezidis in this country. The lucky ones got out of Turkey and Iraq in the 1980s and 1990s. And they're all in Germany. In the northern town of Celle, actually. Very nice place.' He adjusted his Rotary Club tie, the signal that a long segue was about to commence. 'Twinned with Tavistock in Devon...'

Rex interrupted him, more thinking aloud than responding. 'But they were in Germany. The uncle's got a German car. Mina's peacock brooch came from her mother. Who died in Germany. And anyway, two separate people said that name to me. Tawus Melek.'

Lawrence shrugged. 'Or something else that sounds like it. I really can't see a breakaway group moving to West Green Road, Rex. There's no inter-marriage. In fact there was a very creepy case in Germany some years back. Yezidi girl, caught hanging out with a non-Yezidi Kurd...'

'What was creepy about it?' Rex asked, then exclaimed, 'Shit!'

This wasn't in response to Lawrence, but to what Rex had just seen on the screen as he finally made the updates live. The piece he'd written about Mina's family – supposedly for Ellie's paper – was in front of him, on the local website.

But it wasn't the piece he'd written. Even though it had his name on it.

> 'Family members aired the possibility that Mina
> may have had a boyfriend, who had influenced
> or even encouraged her actions. Mina, who had
> publicly praised the self-immolation of other
> Kurdish activists...'

'What did you do?'

He bull-raged his way into Ellie's office, making her jump back in her chair.

'I didn't write that! That was confidential information that

I agreed to withhold! And what the hell is it doing on our website?'

'Could you stop shouting?'

She was still tensed up, expecting an attack. He knew he couldn't stop shouting. So he kept his mouth shut, breathing hard. Everyone else came to the doorway.

'I offered it to HQ, they decided not to use it. So I made some amendments and put it on the local site instead.'

'Amendments? You used information that you overheard, that you sodding well overheard me saying in a restaurant, and which may cause serious harm to that family. I didn't write that bollocks.'

'Well, you did, actually,' she said, pushing over a sheaf of printed papers. It was the notes he'd tried to print out earlier. 'And under the terms of our contract with us, we own it. Not you.'

'Take it down!'

'Since we're discussing your contract, Rex, I'm issuing you with a verbal warning.'

He lowered his voice. 'For what?'

'You're irrational, aggressive, your time-keeping is poor and several members of staff have raised concern about the amount of painkillers you take.'

He glanced round at his colleagues in the doorway. Terry. Lawrence. Brenda. Did they agree with her? He had to admit it – they looked like people who agreed.

'I've emailed you some contact details of organisations who can help, and I'd like you to consider going for some form of one-on-one...'

'Take it down and I'll go for one-on-one sumo training, whatever you like,' he snarled.

'I'm not going to be –'

'Take the page down, Ellie, and I'll do it.'

A stand-off. Then she nodded, turning the monitor towards her and she logged in. 'The warning still stands on your record,' she said, not looking up from her keyboard. She still hadn't learnt to touch-type, Rex noted. 'And if it goes unheeded, I will issue a written warning…'

He'd already pushed his way out. Lawrence caught him by the arm. Rex really hoped this wasn't the moment for a bit of Lawrence Berne wisdom.

'That German Yezidi girl going out with the wrong boy?' Lawrence said, in a low, solemn voice. 'You asked me what happened to her. Well, they set light to her. She died of 80% burns.'

CHAPTER SEVEN

The Sisters of St Veronica of Jumièges were not a secluded order. They dwelt in world cities like Toronto and Sydney, tended to their most sick citizens in the midst of the well and strong. The nuns left the premises often, and the distinctive, pigeon-grey dresses of the London chapter could be spotted all round Muswell Hill, from the Sainsbury's to the Pound Shop and even, on certain saints' days, the O'Neill's. The nuns' choice of location, however, suggested a wish for distance from the temporal plane. To reach their dwelling-house, it was necessary to leave the already secluded path from Muswell Hill to Alexandra Palace, in favour of descent down a dim track that wound through thick trees. At night-time, the only lighting was provided by an unreliable lamp on the nuns' porch at one end, the 144 bus-stop far back above and, if you were lucky, the moon.

It was easy to think you were being watched and followed as you went down through the wooded parkland, and, in fact, Rex had experienced both in the past. Tonight, despite being preoccupied with the events of the day, he had a strong sense of someone, or something, out there, amongst the moving darkness of the trees, just watching, and somehow keeping him in its sights whichever way the path led. An unpleasant feeling – like an uninvited finger in his collar.

He was glad that the door opened almost as soon as he'd rung the bell. Sister Florence, the tiny Belgian nun who admitted him, would normally clap her hands in delight, and immediately begin discussing her current, favourite TV viewing in tones that other nuns reserved for the Sacred Heart. Tonight, her greeting was as subdued as it had been over the phone for the last couple of weeks. And Rex knew why.

'Still not from Aurelie one word of the hour and the day,' she whispered, leading Rex down the damp, ancient-smelling corridor lined with nuns' needlework and childrens' drawings.

The hour and the day. For a year now, his wife's sister, Aurelie, had been pressing to have Sybille moved to her house on the outskirts of Paris. Aurelie didn't drink any more, she was married to a high-ranking policeman and in this new, sober form had become determined to improve her sister's care – after several decades of only caring about vodka.

Rex did not dislike Aurelie. He'd felt sympathy for the old, self-loathing one, and been as fond of her intermittent bursts of irony, insight and song as he'd been amused by the stories Sybille told him about her sister's wild childhood. There was one he particularly enjoyed, about a convent boarding school on the outskirts of Nantes, so pious, so regimented, that the girls sent to it by their top-drawer families were often just one step away from jail. The nuns of Nantes had sent Aurelie back home after a fortnight. They'd even refunded the fees.

But he didn't know this new version of Aurelie, and he found he couldn't trust it. He didn't trust that the new phase, or the policeman, or the grand, renovated house would last. He accepted that there were places where his wife might be more comfortable, eat better food, be less exposed to the cave-like damp of an old nunnery and to the low-quality TV crime dramas obsessively watched by her main carer, Sister Florence. He wasn't convinced those things mattered to Sybille, though. He wasn't, except in odd, painful moments when she would pat his hand or use a phrase from the old-time, convinced that he mattered to her either. But he was not prepared to let go.

A gear-shift had occurred one damp and foggy Friday, four months back, when Aurelie had arrived, in triumph, accompanied by the policeman husband and a brace of fine lawyers from both sides of the Channel. Invited to prove, with binding effect, that she understood the proceedings and their consequences, Sybille had done so brilliantly, promptly handed power of attorney to her sister and declared her wish to move to Paris. Just a few short moments later, as witnessed by both Rex and Sister Florence, and possibly the French policeman too, Sybille had started talking, incoherently, about her dead father being in the next room and her equally dead mother finding a hammer in a meadow, both of which were garbled references to a recent episode of 'Midsomer Murders'. But Aurelie and the lawyers had had the twenty seconds of clarity they'd sought. And Sybille was going to be moved.

Dates had come and gone. There was trouble finishing the downstairs room she'd be in, then a snarl-up with the specialist transport. Sybille's belongings had been packed and unpacked again. And now there was a new date, set for a fortnight hence. Rex and the nuns were supposed to start re-assembling the dozen cardboard boxes they'd got, for free, from the devout Brazilian girls who staffed the StoreSpace down the hill. They were waiting for a final go-ahead from Aurelie. But now she had become hard to reach.

'She told as well that she would pay all the expenses for the last quarter,' said Sister Florence. 'So I add them up, I write them, I email. *Rien.*'

'I'll pay them,' Rex said. 'Don't send me the bill, just… you know…'

Sister Florence understood: she would only tell him the figure owed. Another of the nuns, Sister Mary Sulpice, always sent the itemised account when it was her turn to compile it, and it pained Rex to see it, like seeing his wife laid bare, next to the quarterly total for her sanitary towels and suppositories. It wasn't his delicacy, but a respect for her, for the corners of her life she'd kept discreet. He'd had to buy her tampons once, just once, when she'd been pole-axed with flu. And Sybille, mortified, had dragged herself from bed to leave the money, penny for penny, silently, on the table. That was just the way she was.

'You are sure you can pay?' Sister Florence asked, as they went in to the TV room where Sybille spent her days. 'I thought that you were making the grand renovations to your own chateau now.'

'I'll get hold of Aurelie,' Rex said, avoiding the topic of his house. 'But all the while we're here, I pay.'

A brief nod and then Sister Florence was back in joyful nun mode, clapping her hands and exclaiming in a bright, sing-song voice about the handsome man who had come to call.

Sybille stared sightlessly at the television screen. 'Midsomer Murders' again.

He kissed her. Sometimes he tried hard not to breathe in the smell of her, the Mitsouko perfume she'd worn, every day of her adult life – with him and then in this after-world. He took her hand, with its long cool fingers, unchanged, so perfectly unchanged that if he only looked at that, it could be as if the accident had never happened. Sometimes she squeezed his fingers, sometimes she did nothing. Today was a nothing day.

'A mess to clear up,' she said. 'A terrible mess. Ran and hid. From the mess. A mistake.'

'*Alors, Sybie, tu sais que L'Inspector Barnaby va le trouver!*' exclaimed Sister Florence brightly, patting the TV set fondly, like a relative. '*Comme toujours!*'

'Yes, found. Always found out,' said Sybille indistinctly. The pins holding parts of her jaw together were eroding, and another operation was due. Still, sometimes, a word or a whole sentence would come out with shocking clarity, as if recorded long ago. As now, when she suddenly said, 'Rex.' When she had his attention, she asked, 'Will you go, or shall I?' and laughed like a docker.

Sister Florence left them, and he stayed for about another ten minutes. When he let himself out he felt, as he so often did, drained and slightly spooked. He knew that he imagined things sometimes, but he also knew that there was some eerie part of his wife still there, trapped in a dark room and angry with him for it. Comments like that one – *will you go or shall I* – were her dream-like way of telling him he was not forgiven.

As he headed back up the gloomy, whispering pathway in

what was now driving rain, he knew he was not mistaken this time. A figure moved in the trees to his right. He stopped still, in the middle of the track. It seemed, at first, to be hideously deformed, and he almost laughed aloud with relief when he realised it was Sister Florence, wearing a navy kaghoul over her habit.

But what was she doing there? It seemed to be some sort of pagan, or at least, non-Vatican-approved ritual. As the downpour continued, she laid out a glass on a tray at the base of a tree, and filled it with some clear liquid from a flask. Next to the glass, she placed a saucer, and on it, something flat and round, like rusks or wafers. Having laid these offerings out, she waited in contemplation for a moment, crossed herself and turned to scurry back through the mud and mist. Rex darted behind a bush and watched her go into the house. He wanted to look at the tree, but he felt as if he'd intruded on something private, a rite he hadn't been meant to see. Puzzled, he hurried on to the lights of Muswell Hill.

He was even more puzzled, when, checking his phone in the orangey light of the bus-stop, he saw a text from Helena Georgiou. He'd left her a couple of messages during the afternoon and early evening, all unanswered.

Sorry. At hotel now. Call me. Helena.

He rang. She didn't sound overjoyed to hear from him.

'I'm sorry. I had a migraine. I could feel it getting worse and I knew I was going to be sick, so I just ran out. It's ok. I told the group lady. And your friend Terry is looking after my camera.'

I bet he is, Rex thought. He also thought how strange it was, that she'd seemed so lively just before the migraine had forced her to leave the Community Centre. But he'd known many women do that – his mother, Sybille, Susan – carry great, regular lorry-loads of pain without making it that obvious.

'How are you feeling now?' he asked. 'I'm actually up in Muswell Hill if you –'

She interrupted, as if she'd been waiting for it. 'Not tonight. Okay, Rex? I'm sorry. I'm feeling better but I'm not at my best. Okay?'

He felt startled by her tone of voice. It was as if she was backing out of an agreement, and expected him to argue.

'It's fine. Another time,' he said coolly, and waited for her to reply. When she didn't, he added, 'Let me know what you're up to.' And left it at that.

It was just after eight – that oddly deserted hour in the outer city, when everyone was in the pubs or on their sofas. He sailed down the hill on a bus, all steamed-up windows and sticky floors. His only companions were a pair of pre-pubescent lovers, and an old Irishman saying over and over, into his mobile, 'Hackney Wick? Hackney *fooken* Wick?' as if he'd been asked to go to Baghdad.

The teenie-snoggers troubled him, with their school bags at their feet and their ink-stained fingers in each other's hair. He thought about Mina, and how these kids, not so much younger than her really, would live, and she wouldn't. And then, as he'd known it would, his mind turned to his wife's words.

The terrible mess. She referred to it with increasing regularity now. And to hiding it. As she had done. Leaving it for him to find. As he did, in the bins outside their house, a week after the accident that changed everything.

'Do you want to film us or sum'n, bruv?'

'Perv!'

117

The kids had stopped grappling with each other and were glaring at him – angel-faces with scowls copied from the TV. They thought he was staring at them. He looked out of the window. The traffic was heavy and the bus was crawling through the rain towards the Turnpike Lane crossroads. There was a Greek-owned off-licence – the only one shut on Sundays in this neck of the woods. Outside it, a thick-set man was hitting a black girl, a clutch of people enjoying the spectacle. Mobile phones started to appear. People disgusted him sometimes. He wiped the window with his sleeve. Then he saw: it wasn't a man hitting a woman at all. She was beating the shit out of him.

She, in this case, was Kyretia – the receptionist at the Students Union, who'd been overcome with grief at Mina's death. And he was Haluk, the beefy Security Guard.

A police car appeared. Rex rang the bell, but the driver was new, a stickler, and wouldn't let him off before the stop. Rex had to watch uselessly from his rain-spattered window as the response team, stiff with assorted weapons and policing gadgets, lumbered out of their vehicle to bring peace to the street.

By the time he'd been permitted to leave the bus, of course, and worked his way back, through the rain, to the off-licence, everyone had gone save for a local notable called Bird, a scrawny, elderly black man who spent his time on the streets, drinking strong lager and shouting. He seemed to be replaying match highlights from the fight in his mind, in between dainty sips from a can of 11% Navigator.

'Black girl give 'im *licks*,' he enthused yeastily. 'Proper *licks*!'

Realising that the night was, to all intents and purposes, over, Rex went into the off-licence. He irritated the man in there by forgetting to ask for *ouzo* instead of *raki*, added some weak-looking Cypriot lagers to the haul by way of apology and was just having them wrapped in paper when his phone rang.

Helena. 'I'm sorry, Rex. I'd just woken up. Is it too late to change my mind? You've probably gone back down the hill now, haven't you?'

Rex eyed the off-licence man warily, wondering if it was worth asking for a refund. He decided against it. After all, Helena might like a nightcap.

*　*　*

Rain hammered on the window as the tiny kettle came to a cheerful boil. Down the corridor: sounds of trolleys, smells of bacon. They'd woken early – both, it seemed, a little unused to having another life-form in the bed. Talked softly for a while, made love again, fallen asleep again. Now it was nearer the business end of the morning. Helena had showered and was sitting on the end of the bed, applying some herby-smelling solution to her hair.

'Lunch?' he asked.

'I told you, I'm driving to Bristol today. I showed you that horrible pink car the hire people gave me… Do you actually remember anything from last night?'

'Yeah. You're… Francesca, right?'

A cushion hit him in the face. He threw it back. He remembered a great deal. From before they took their clothes off. They'd talked about their childhoods – of hers with a vanished father, in a house deserted by Turks. Of his life, too, in a Lincolnshire council house, with a similar father-shaped hole in it. There, perhaps, the similarities had ended.

'It's bleeping,' she said, tossing his phone at him. 'If it's

Francesca, tell her she's welcome to you.'

It was emails: the first of the morning police, fire and ambulance updates. A woman had assaulted a man on Turnpike Lane last night. That had to be the fight he'd witnessed, between Mina's friends – Kyretia and Haluk. He wondered if anyone had been charged, and if D.S. Brenard would volunteer any information.

Further east towards Tottenham Hale, a mother taking her child to the school's Breakfast Club at 6 am had been struck by an entire windowpane falling out of a new build. The kid was unharmed. The mum was in the North Middlesex hospital, injured but all right. He shuddered. Helena, zipping up her skirt, asked what the matter was.

'I'm not sure if it's the thought of a kid nearly being orphaned by dodgy building work, or the thought of a kid being dropped at school at 6 am. When did that start?' He looked at her as she buttoned her blouse. He liked to see a woman get dressed. As much a privilege, he thought, as the opposite.

'My mum left the house at 5 every morning to go to the hospital. It's what she had to do. We got ourselves up.' Her face darkened as she clipped earrings on. 'Actually I got my brothers up, even though they were older.'

She wasn't close to her brothers, he'd gathered that much over the course of the preceding evening. For her mother, effectively widowed overnight, forced by the conflicts of 1974 to leave an idyllic farm village for a stranger's tiny house in the city, she seemed to have more sympathy. But not necessarily more affection. He found he didn't mind that. They were both alone.

'It's sweet that you think about the kids,' she said, bending over to kiss him. 'Perhaps you really want to be a daddy?'

'Maybe,' he said. He found he couldn't say anything else. Luckily, she'd disappeared back into the bathroom, to do whatever women do.

He got up, rubbed his bad foot, hunted around for his pills and some fluid to knock them back with: these were his morning prayers. He spilled a little water from the glass as he put it back on the desk at the window, splashed some drops on a buff folder. Papers shifted out as he picked it up and dabbed it. She'd done a lot of research into the borough's Cypriots: printed up articles from the web, even recent articles from his own paper – about the fire at Toprak's factory, the old man suffering a stroke in his van.

'What are you doing?'

She was in the bathroom doorway. She'd put her make-up on. He'd never known a woman do it in private before. He stepped away from the desk, as if he'd been caught doing something wrong. As, in a sense, he had.

'Sorry, I spilt something.'

She crossed to the desk, stuffed the folder and a couple of other items in her open briefcase, her back to him.

'Sorry,' he said again lamely. She turned round, serious.

'You've ruined it. Years of research. A lifetime. Destroyed.'

'Sod off,' he said, grabbing her as she laughed. They kissed. Fell back together on the unmade bed. His hand crept up her thigh.

'Oh all right then,' she said.

He was first in the office, before even the Whittaker Twins. He found himself wanting to look up Cyprus, to understand more of what she'd been talking about, to know more of her. She'd grown up, he knew, in the divided city of Nicosia, but the family had fled from a village in the northern part of the island when it was invaded by Turkey in 1974, the year of her birth. At some point in this flight, it seemed, Helena's father had either been killed or disappeared, and she'd been born without ever knowing him.

'So I understand the hope,' she'd said last night, solemn and seriously beautiful in the candlelight of a near-deserted pizza restaurant. 'I understand the hope of these people when some more bones appear, when they take the test and they get the slip of paper. And the flat feeling that comes afterwards. No. Because you were stupid to hope. You feel stupid. And they tell other people, so even if they've got someone missing, they won't take the test, because they don't want to hope and feel stupid either. That's what we're up against. Except I'm not against it. I understand it.'

She wasn't stupid. Anything but. He knew she wouldn't be here long. And he didn't like casual flings, never had. But it felt good, being with Helena, like something he'd been missing for a long time. He didn't want to forgo it, just because he knew it would end.

He shook himself, and got down to making some notes of potential stories to discuss at the conference. Then he looked up the two men who'd been occupying his thoughts much of late.

He still possessed enough 'O' level German to work out that Rostam Sajadi was much as he'd described himself. A businessman based in Hanover, which wasn't a million miles from Celle, the Yezidi enclave Lawrence had mentioned. Sajadi owned a sweep of dry cleaning outlets from Rostock to Bonn, and also in Stockholm, and was a member of a charitable business-people's association in both countries.

His presence on a Turkish website was harder to interpret: from the assorted maps and cgi-cityscapes, it looked like he was involved in building a new town, called Yenişakir, somewhere in the predominantly Kurdish southeast of the country. There was a picture of Sajadi, and several others, beaming proudly in hard hats and clutching ceremonial trowels. Was he financing the place, Rex wondered? Or just doing the dry cleaning? The point was, Sajadi was a man of influence – very different from his brother-in-law, Keko, a communist with a shop and a caff in Tottenham.

A search for illuminating details on the Student Union President, he of the chequered past, Jan Navitsky, yielded nothing. About his father, though, also called Jan Navitsky, there were some surprises. Navitksy Senior wasn't, as Maureen had said, the Mayor of Minsk, but of a town to the south called Salihorsk. Far from being of the mouth-breathing, leather-coated *kriminalny* type, Navitsky Senior was an earnest-looking, suited bureaucrat, up to his elbows in the country's pro-democracy movement. The BBC World Service loved him; the Poles, the Germans and the US State Department hoped he was the future. There was, certainly as far as Rex could divine, with no knowledge of Belarussian and five spare minutes' web-time, no indication of any crisis or emergency, either in the man's private or political life, that might have required the son to fly off home at a moment's notice. So perhaps Jan the Younger wasn't a chip off the old block. Perhaps Jan was rotten for his own reasons.

He remembered the note in the university newsletter and hauled it out of the mess on his desk again for a look. In an earlier issue, it seemed, a contributor calling themselves

"Hollow Wayne" had dubbed Navitsky a 'Czech with a chequered past' and been forced to apologise. Rex wondered what other things "Hollow Wayne" might have said, and flipped through to the back.

Wayne, it seemed, fancied him- or herself as a gossip columnist, and the column was essentially a series of semi-cryptic lines concerning events and people in the goldfish-bowl world of a campus university.

> *Which buff-lookin' rapstar beefcake in the Sports*
> *Psychology Department swallowed so many*
> *'study aids' that his heart-rate broke Olympic*
> *Records and he had to leave his lec-cha on a*
> *stret-cha?*

Underneath that was the reference Maureen had mentioned:

> *At the Union Committee meeting on Wednesday:*
> *the usual sparks flew between a certain*
> *toothsome two-some, a.k.a., in the red corner,*
> *the girl who's redder than the Red Flag, and in*
> *the white, well, who ordered the White Russian?*
> *Who you trying to kid, kids? Travelodge are*
> *doing a special. Get. A. Room.*

It gave little away, except that, based on two weeks' worth of references, Jan Navitsky seemed to crop up a lot in the gossip column. But that was because he was the President. For much the same reasons, Eric Miles was always in *s: Haringey*, despite being as dull as he was decent.

He wondered what else Hollow Wayne might have said

about Navitsky, and thought about getting hold of more back editions of the student paper. But there ought to be a more direct way to find out.

Rex rang the number listed for Navitsky on the university directory. Straight to answerphone. He was leaving a message as Lawrence came in.

'Now then,' he said meaningfully. 'I needn't ask if *your* day got better towards the evening.'

'Sorry, Lawrence?'

'How was your pizza?' Lawrence asked. Then, before Rex could reply, went on: 'The Venerable Mrs Berne and myself passed by The Napoli after a talk at Muswell Hill library. You looked very cosy in there. The pair of you.'

A couple of years ago, Rex had had a fling with Lawrence's niece, Diana, a doctor. It hadn't worked out – Diana had gone to Cambodia to minister to the sick – but for some reason Lawrence still felt involved in Rex's private life.

'I had a good evening, thank you, Lawrence,' Rex replied stiffly as Terry and Ellie came in with matching coffee cups.

Lawrence put a wad of printed papers down on Rex's desk, making him feel guilty about his unfriendliness.

'Mrs B and I worked it all out using *The Joys of Yiddish* and Google Translate,' he said. Rex stared down at the papers blankly. They appeared to be from German newspapers in the late 1990s. He spotted words he felt he should know. *Schreckliches. Verkehrsunfall.* Then some he definitely did know. *Küçüktürk. Kurdisch. Alkohol.*

'No suggestion of any of that, what d'you call it, "honour killing". Mina's mother, Meda, died in a traffic accident crossing the road. Van heading north towards Hamburg. Didn't stop. Remains one of the roughly twenty-seven fatal hit and runs that go unprosecuted in Germany every year. Compared to our nineteen, so they're less efficient than us at something...'

'Everybody! Circle up! Meeting! Let's go!'

With another neat impersonation of Susan and a brace of hand-claps, Ellie started the meeting. It was a subdued, business-like affair, with everyone trying so hard not to seem affected by the row of yesterday that it hung around them like a bad curry. Ellie approved of going big on the falling window. She liked the idea of a sideline discussion topic too, about Breakfast Clubs, and whether family life was suffering because of people's long working hours. She was so supportive of a piece on the video poker machines that Rex suspected she'd gone home last night and taken advice from someone on high. Or just some Prozac.

She was not, however, going to let him forget his promises, and as he headed out to start his research into the poker machines, she called him into her office and shut the door.

'I shouldn't have done that yesterday. I don't mean the story. I mean what I said to you in front of everyone else, about... about your problems and... finding a therapist. I'm sorry.'

'It's okay. A lot of what you said was true.'

She nodded. 'Based on your response, Rex, and what I've seen, I am obliged as your line manager to recommend that you seek some counselling. I don't know if you know but our main office has a Men's Group that meets...'

'I've got a therapist,' he lied quickly. The thought of a Men's Group at the head office in Shoreditch drove him to it. What would go on down there? Drumming? Hugging?

She looked surprised. 'You've got one? Can you give me the details? It's not to be nosey. I think I can get you some money towards it if it's the right sort of...'

Backed into a corner now, he said, 'Maureen Beddoes. She's based at Metropolitan University.'

'And you're seeing her... when?'

He forced a smile. 'Today.'

Ellie nodded. 'Beddoes. Met U. Great. If you get me a letter or an invoice from her, I'll talk to Finance about the money.'

Rex sighed loudly as he went down the stairs, so loudly that Brenda, on the receptionist desk, pointedly stopped speaking into her telephone and waited until the interruption had passed. The sun was shining on the puddles outside, though, and as he walked down the high road towards his first assignment, he thought that seeing Maureen might have some benefits. If he was clever, he might find out some more about Jan Navitsky's chequered past, and whether it had involved Mina. Before that, though, it was poker-time.

CHAPTER EIGHT

Self-satisfied Crouch End, bookish Highgate, hard Seven Sisters: to ensure an even spread, he'd picked bookmakers all over the borough, and talked to two or three poker-players in each. He was still none the wiser.

He could see why the big companies wanted the machines in their shops, because they were highly addictive, required no manpower and sucked up cash in a way that betting on horses and football never could. He could see, in at least two out of the three cases, that the individual managers were less keen, if not on moral grounds then because they feared being replaced by machines themselves.

As for the sort of punters locked onto the terminals between nine and eleven on a Tuesday morning, Rex admitted to being blinded by his own prejudices. He'd never really got games: the idea of trying to win something for the sake of winning, rather than the reward, was to him as alien as Clapham, or performance art, or sushi. And that seemed to be the real drive for the worst addicts. Not winning cash, because they knew they'd never really win cash in a form they could hang onto, but simply beating a machine. Was it powerlessness, then, the true drive – the simulated thrill of taking on the system?

One of the people he'd talked to, a gaunt, uncertain man in an Argos uniform, described it as a 'buzz'. Rex wondered if pulling the power lead out of the machine and sticking it in his mouth would have provided something similar.

In a bid to understand more – and to get on with his own, private queries about the Shopping City repairs – he headed to another shop, the one just over the High Road from his office. Track betting had begun now, and the place was full of hi-vis and durable trousers. Poring over the papers with scholarly concentration, there was another man, a huge, wide, leather-black African in a checked shirt and a Stetson, who looked up when Rex asked the counter-lady if Texo had been in.

'That's me,' said the big man. 'What do you want?'

He stood with his legs apart, a fancy belt buckle glinting in the lights from the poker consoles. Vast, ebony fingers hovered over his jeans pockets, as if itching to draw out six-guns.

'Texo Chuba?'

People chuckled. The man bristled. 'Tex. Ochuba.'

The twitching trigger-fingers brought out a council pass from one of the pockets. Most people wore them round their necks. Tex kept his hidden.

'I just wondered,' Rex said, slipping onto a stool. 'If you'd seen anything up at Shopping City on Friday? You know, when the girl fell?'

'I tol' the police,' Tex said emphatically, displaying a dazzling set of white and gold teeth. 'I had the door down at the van. Trying to fix it. I didn't see anything until I took it back up at about half past one and then there was a policeman there and he said area was shut off.'

'Is that why you couldn't put the door back in?'

Tex frowned, repeating Rex's words to himself silently before saying: 'The door is back.'

'The entrance door from Sky City to the shops? It wasn't yesterday.'

'What?'

Tex grabbed a diadem of different-shaped keys from the slim formica bar next to him and, without a backward glance, fled. Rex was intending to head after him but a hand stopped him. It was the small man he'd noticed on his last visit. He had a face like a disused car-park: cracked and sprouting.

'He was in the Coral's at the bottom from twelve till gone three,' said the man in a low voice. He smelt of frying oil, loneliness and regret. 'I was in there, and I lost in all the same races he lost in. Dogs. Wimbledon. Then he was up here, four 'til late, telling everyone how much money he'd won before.'

Rex frowned. 'Why would he do that?'

The man laughed bitterly. 'Because he's a cunt. I used to work with him. At the Council Works. And he's a cunt.'

Rex made to head off, but the hand shot out again.

'That's worth a drink, isn't it, boss?'

All Rex had on him was a pair of two-pound coins. The man accepted them and fed them, worshipful, into the nearest poker machine.

He hoped Tex and his Stetson might still be visible on the high street, but as he was going through the doorway, he encountered another obstacle. A man who refused to move.

Ashley Pocock kissed his teeth at him. 'What are you doing?'

'I'm fond of poker,' Rex said. 'Like you.'

The eyes narrowed to vanishing point. 'You've got the wrong idea.'

'About what? About you taking bungs to feed your love of Texas Hold 'Em?'

Pocock snorted. 'Yeah. That'll do for starters.' He then muttered something rude but indistinct and pushed past Rex into the shop.

There was no sign of a ten-gallon hat on either side of the street. Rex wondered about crossing over, and going through the Market Hall to the entrance to the Sky City flats. Someone would be bound to come in or out, at some point, someone who couldn't give a flying one about security, and would let him up to see if Tex Ochuba was there, frantically doing something about the mysterious missing door. Then his phone rang. Maureen, returning the call he'd made to her as he left the office. She could see him in an hour's time. Or not at all for another week.

* * *

'I'm noticing that there does seem to be a lot of loss around, Rex.'

'Around?' he echoed cynically. Rex knew he sounded like a surly teenager. But he couldn't help himself. He resented the language. The *around*. The *there does seem* and the *I'm noticing*. Resented the studiedly restful counselling room, with its beige linens and its one, tasteful poster advertising a long-gone Kandinsky Exhibition in Bruges. *You are in a place of thought*, the poster said. While the box of tissues on the hexagonal table said: *Go on, cry*. He was determined not to. He'd done it before, spilled his guts to order in precise, fifty-minute intervals. And that was over. His therapy was finding things out now, his medicine cold Okocim Mocne, 7.1%.

'Yes,' Maureen said, unflapped by his sarcasm. 'Your mum. Your wife. The – was she Lithuanian – the artist girl who died? Diana, the doctor you were seeing, who left. And now Mina. So many lost girls you're trying to find.'

An awful image came to his mind. As he'd feared it would. Returning to the flat in Camden, half-crazy, stinking after the accident and a week-long vigil at the bedside of his unseeing, unresponding, destroyed wife. Doing crazy tasks that weren't important: paying a water bill, emptying the bathroom waste-bin into the big bins by the gateway. *Most men think it's their job to empty the bins* – she'd said, more than once. *Why do you never do it?* But this time, he did. Flies everywhere – in December.

'What are you thinking about, Rex?'

'I –' He swallowed. An odd thought occurred to him. That he could just say it. Jump in. Then his phone rang. 'I have to take this, I'm sorry.'

Maureen sat in disapproving silence, hands clasped on her lap, as he answered. The voice on the other end reminded Rex of tv commercials. Clear diction, perfect English, vowels copied from Hollywood.

'I'm sorry for not replying to your messages. I just got back to the Union office today. I'm Jan Navitsky,' the voice added.

'Wait there,' Rex said.

Five minutes later, he was in the scruffy office that smelt of Pot Noodles. Jan Navitsky, his Brasso-blond hair swept back, all gleaming in a white rugby shirt, was not a Pot Noodle man. He had a tropical fruit salad from Waitrose.

'My step-mom had a small operation in Berlin and my dad was unfortunately at the last minute not able to see her safely back home, so…' He shrugged. As if he felt under suspicion, Navitsky showed him an image on his iPad – of himself and a very beautiful, Slavic-looking woman not much older than him in a wheelchair.

'Your stepmother?'

'My third,' Navitsky replied, still smiling. His eyes glittered like frost. 'I got the call from my dad around midday, I cancelled my arrangements for the afternoon, went by my apartment and told my flatmate and then I was on a plane at 3.40 from London City to Tegel. I think I picked up my step-mom at about 7.45.'

'So your dad calls you, and you drop everything to fly 1,000 miles in an afternoon?'

'When my dad asks people, they do it,' Navitsky said, more proud than resentful. 'Anyway, I have a Lufthansa Platinum Card. I just walk on.'

'You seem fond of your… stepmother,' Rex said, nodding towards the image on the iPad.

The smile didn't move. 'And?'

'I heard that wasn't the case with Mina.'

'We argued. I never make any secret of my background, you know, we're a wealthy family, I went to boarding school in the States… Some people here believe that makes me less qualified to do my job.'

'People like Mina?'

'And I would say the same thing back to her. You know – why do you know more, Mina, why are you a better person because you went to the rubbish state school and your dad runs a diner? It would go like that a lot. At meetings. In the

134

bar. Everywhere.' He laughed a little. It seemed almost fond.

'Leading people to suggest that you two should get a room?'

He shook his head, good-naturedly. 'Opposites attract? I don't believe it. But I did respect Mina. And I was very upset to hear the news. I couldn't believe she'd do something like that.'

'You couldn't?'

'It didn't make sense. I was here, in this office, when she got the news about next year's funding. That was only just under a month ago. She was… to me she seemed overjoyed.' Navitsky frowned. Rex was reminded again of that face on the balcony. A thin, hungry face. Could it have been him? 'Is that the right word?'

'I don't know. Overjoyed about what?'

'She got a Brady Institute Scholarship to spend next year working in a… I suppose a Refugee Law Centre. For Kurdish refugees. In Turkey. It was like her dream. When the news came, Mina and Kyretia were making so much noise in the office that the psychiatrist lady came in from next door to ask them to be quiet.'

'So Kyretia was pleased for her.'

'Pleased for herself. They were both going.'

'Two women from the same university. They must be a talented pair.'

'A talented pair together, sure,' Navitsky said, implying something Rex couldn't divine. 'I don't know if Kyretia will go now. I heard she'd dropped out of the course. She's not coming back to man – I mean – *take charge of* our Reception Desk, anyway, I know that.'

He made a face. If Navitksy wasn't actually sorry for the

135

girl, Rex thought, he did a fairly good version of it. 'It was a big thing for both of them to go. They were learning Turkish. Going to the gym to get fit, eating a special diet. I think Kyretia grew up on top of a cake-baker's shop in Tottenham, you know. For her, the east is Chingford.' Navitsky grinned at his joke.

Rex found he was still thinking about Jan Navitsky's grin five minutes later as he left the compound through the reception area. As a basically anxious being, he instinctively mistrusted anyone who was that self-assured. And yet, it seemed to him, there had been genuine affection in the man's clear, grey eyes when he spoke about Mina, genuine bewilderment at what had happened.

The photos on the iPad seemed to back up his story, too. But he'd seemed slightly too eager to display them. And how hard would it be, for a young man with his connections, to hook an alibi together? The whole string of events: the call at midday, the back-up conversation with the flatmate, the plane times, had slipped out like something rehearsed. No, he didn't believe Jan Navitsky, even if he didn't know why he'd been lying.

He glanced at the Security Desk on his way out, wondering if he'd see Haluk, but today, a rangy-looking Somali boy with crazy hair was wearing the uniform, lost in the music being piped noisily through vast, baby-blue headphones.

Haluk turned out to be just a short distance away, though, on his way in to lectures in a grey hooded top, clutching a brown paper bag from McDonalds. The burly man didn't look overjoyed to see Rex.

'I wondered if she'd matched the other eye up.'

'What?'

Haluk pulled the hood off. The original black eye was fading to yellow. The shaped-stubble beard was getting out of hand, too. Apart from that, Rex thought, he looked surprisingly unscathed.

'I saw you last night. At Turnpike Lane. You and Kyretia were…. Having a bit of a set-to.'

Haluk squinted at him. 'Set-to? Aah, that? That was nothing, man. Play-fighting.'

'The police didn't seem to think so.'

'They got the wrong idea. It was just… you know… a lovers' tiff.'

'A lovers' tiff? So, not a play-fight, then?'

Haluk was silent for a moment. 'Started out as a joke, then it sort of got out of hand. No biggie. Kye's got a temper, isn't it?'

'Has she? How long have you two been together?'

'We liked each other at school a bit and that, but nothing happened. Then we kinda clicked when we seen each other here. It's a bit of a on-and-off fing? Like we break up and get it back on all the time? But in the break-times, man has to see ovver gels, isn't it?' Haluk winked at him. 'And Kye don't like it.'

'What did you think about her going to Turkey?'

He shrugged, and rather studiedly eyed-up a pair of tiny, chic Asian girls clopping by with book-laden bags. 'Why not go? Gyal spend her whole life on top of her dad's shop, innit? And I ain't gonna be lonely, *naam'sain* bruv?' His manner changed, suddenly provocative. 'Can I go now, please?'

'One more question. Nothing to do with you. Who's Hollow Wayne?'

He snorted. 'Fuck knows. Made-up name, innit?'

'It would be a pretty shit real name,' Rex conceded.

Haluk laughed. 'Nobody knows who it is. Serious. Even the guy edits the paper, man, dun-know, seen?

Haluk – enough patois, seen? Rex thought that, but didn't say it. Instead, he said: 'So even the person who edits the newsletter doesn't know who "Hollow Wayne" is?'

'Emails it in,' Haluk said. 'Every week, different address.' He started to walk off, chuckling to himself. 'Pretty shit real name…'

Rex called after him. 'Why would Wayne say Jan Navitsky had a chequered past?'

Haluk turned. 'You gonna stop buzzin' me?'

'If I must.'

He gave a hard man's nod – all neck and muscle. 'Few fings. Few fings few gels mighta said. Man tries a bit hard, *naam'sain*. Don't like it when they say No.'

* * *

It was exactly as he'd hoped. He'd only had to wait two minutes at the door up to Sky City before a beleaguered-looking Latina mum had appeared with a buggy and a brace of kids. You held the door for her, you bowed until she laughed, you smiled, you bypassed the cruddy security. *Bingo*, as Victor Eastwood would have said.

The wind had picked up and was funnelling crisp packets and sturdy bits of wet cardboard down the walkways at considerable speed. He took a wrong turn at one point and came upon two squat men, doing something furtive by a stairwell. He gave them a kind of 'no problems here, pal' wave and scooted off in the opposite direction, hearing mocking laughter above the clatterings of an occasionally airborne Kestrel can.

Then he reached the sign he'd laughed at before: *playground/shops*. And soon he was by the door that connected the housing estate with Shopping City. The brand new, gleaming steel security door, with a digital entry pad on the side. Whatever he'd said to Tex Ochuba, or whatever Tex Ochuba had said to somebody else, things had moved fast. Maybe the modern council was really that efficient.

Or maybe not. He took a picture of the door, thinking fast. If Tex Ochuba wasn't lying about where he'd been on Monday afternoon, he'd certainly been lying about mending the door. Why? Because he had been there, after all, and seen something, something he didn't want to talk about? Or because he hadn't been there, because he was, as the little man in the bookies had said, someone who did nothing, apart from lay bets up and down Wood Green High Road all day? That would explain the bewilderment and the panic: someone else was meant to do Tex's job on that day. But they had left it undone.

Rain came at him, briefly, like a spray at sea. He headed back into the estate. This high place had clearly been designed with Mediterranean and Levantine villages in mind: tiered rows of little box-shaped maisonettes, reached by short, steep staircases. The place wasn't as abandoned as everyone said: there were ply-boards and tin shutters, for sure, but there were also curtains in other windows, untarnished satellite dishes with new names – *Romani-Sat, BieloTel* – pointing towards the homelands of the poorest, freshest arrivals.

Something struck him then. If Mina had been absent for a week before her death, could she have been here – right next to where she'd died? Sky City was a good place to hide out, if you were hiding: huge, confusing, high above the streets, and full of folks minding their own business. So what had Mina's business been?

The answer, surely, was going to lie with a person. Mina had been close to Kyretia Pocock. They'd been going to Turkey together. Kyretia had been away from university and her place of work ever since Mina's death – sick, apparently, with grief. So where was she? He needed to find her. Could she be close by?

He turned a corner to find a group of Roma boys: four or five of them, the youngest with a runny nose, the eldest with peach fuzz on his lip. They approached him as he approached them.

'You live up here?' he asked. 'In Sky City?'

They stood around him, rather like kids with a teacher. 'Yes, Sky City,' said the eldest, obligingly. They moved in closer, smiling.

'You know a black girl?' Rex pulled at his hair. 'Braids?' It was worth a try.

'Black girl!' came the reply, as they huddled in closer. He caught an odd whiff from them – sweet, chemical – had a memory of Airfix kits.

'Kyretia?' He tried to step back, but they were all around him. 'Kyretia Pocock.'

'Suck your cock!' said the littlest one. The boys all laughed but the eldest cuffed the child hard, and the child began to cry.

'Hey don't –' Rex began, but then there were suddenly hands all over him, pulling lightly at his coat, inside his coat, fingers in the back pocket of his jeans. He had a sudden, absurd vision of nature documentaries: the kill.

'Kakhilia ma pe tutte!' he shouted. *I'll shit down your throat.*

A helpful man from the Roma Gypsy Traveller Network had taught him that, years back. The boys halted for an instant, shocked to hear a curse in their language. It gave him just enough time to barge through them and down towards the stairwell. He didn't know if they'd stolen anything from his pockets, and he didn't care, he just knew they were behind him, shouting, running, a lot quicker than him. The Roma weren't into random nastiness. The few who were into crime – and it was fewer than people thought – were mainly into stealing things and legging it. But there'd been a distinct smell of glue around this crew; the eldest one had definitely looked high. If he had a blade, and a point to prove to his little brothers...

Shafts of sheer agony went up his leg as he landed on the bad foot at the bottom of the last stairs. He fell on the metal release button, rather than pressing it, sure he would pass out and the boys a few feet behind would overwhelm him on the ground.

He was out in the street as they were coming through the door. A big, black car sounded its horn as he ran towards it. Someone leant across and flung open the passenger door.

'Rex!'

He didn't know who it was. If they knew his name and they had a car, then they'd do for now. He dived in, and the car screeched off with expert ease as the Roma boys spilled off the kerb, gesturing and flinging cans from the overflowing bins.

Rostam Sajadi grinned at him as he deftly steered his hundred-large hunk of Vorsprung through the double-parked clutter of Caxton Road towards the Morrison's car park. An egg-shaped object rolled across the dashboard.

'You annoy people, I think.'

Rex, who was struggling to catch his breath, managed to say, 'I've had complaints,' before a coughing fit seized him. Sajadi said nothing, merely manoeuvred his car into a space, while the on-board computer made assorted, tasteful dings and bleeps.

'Your office,' he said, resting his hands on the steering wheel and pointing with the blunted finger towards the unit in the far corner. *s: Haringey* shared its entrance with a call centre and a mysterious outfit called Limassol Forwarding.

'So you know where I work,' Rex said, as sweat bloomed on his brow. Sajadi was neat and cool, as usual, the faint tang of cologne amid the new upholstery. He'd ditched the suit for a black granddad cap and a bomber jacket.

'You've been asking questions about me,' Sajadi said. 'So I asked about you.'

'What did you find out?'

'You're a journalist. My brother-in-law says a good one.' He looked at Rex. 'I say there is no good journalist. You make decisions about people, like judges.' Here Sajadi mimed a hammer, a judge's gavel. Rex wondered if he'd ever been in court. 'But you have no evidence. All the horse-shit you are saying about Mina. All those articles, in the newspapers, calling her a head-scarved activist. She was wearing a hairband! A hair-band to keep the hair from her eyes when she made that... film for the website, but to you it becomes the headscarf of a fanatic!'

'Other papers have said that. Mine didn't,' he said. He knew though, that for a few minutes at least, there'd been something just as bad on *s: Haringey's* website. Long enough for a few dozen hits – although, so far, no feedback, no backlash.

'Come with me,' Sajadi said.

It wasn't an invitation. The vehicle swung out of the car park, sailed over the lights and onto Lordship Lane, the plastic egg hurtling back and forth across the dashboard like a pinball. Sajadi's driving wasn't aggressive, but Rex had the strange sense of the traffic parting as they swept along, east towards Tottenham, of vehicles trying their damnedest not to get in the way.

He was uneasy. Not because of Sajadi's manner, or even because he was effectively a captive. But because he'd been driven this way before, a year ago, by a woman called Rescha Schild, who'd deliberately ploughed the vehicle over the Angel Road roundabout in an attempt to kill them both. She had been fifty percent successful. Rex had only sat in the front of a car four times since.

'Were you waiting for me?' Rex asked. Sajadi jerked to a stop at the lights and the plastic egg shot into Rex's lap.

'No, I wasn't waiting for you,' Sajadi growled. 'I was sitting. Like I've been sitting there every day since Friday, for hours, trying to understand what happened to my niece!'

The egg in Rex's hands was a copy of the Disneyland picture he'd seen in Mina's bedroom. A photograph of Mina, with her uncle, clutching an egg. Printed, for reasons unclear, onto a further, plastic egg and stored in Sajadi's car. Sajadi pressed a button, and something resembling a glove compartment flipped open in front of Rex. He got the idea that the egg was meant to go in.

'She gave it to me last New Year,' Sajadi said, as the lights changed. 'Mina. Our joke.'

'Is it a Kurdish New Year thing?' Rex asked. 'The egg?'

'Yezidi,' came the gruff reply. 'Different. God made the

world like an egg. Then he sent his angel down. Tawsi Melek.'

'The peacock?'

Sajadi snorted, seemingly unimpressed. 'Tawsi Melek pecked the egg and cracked it. Then the flowers and the trees could come. So, every New Year, eggs.'

'I was given to believe the Yezidis all live in Germany.'

'They do.'

'Except the ones who live round the back of the Bosphorus Continental Supermarket.'

'It's my tradition. Not theirs.'

'I thought there was no kind of intermingling, though, so how did your sister…?'

Sajadi turned and gave Rex a stare so long, so pained that his words simply dried up. Then the man turned back to the road, saying nothing. After a while, Rex dared to ask where they were going, but Sajadi just said he'd soon see. He felt reassured, slightly, by the man's comments about Mina and the egg, so he sat back for a while, trying to get some control over the pain in his foot and leg. At least, he thought, as yet another white van waited respectfully for them to pass before pulling out, there was no chance of an accident in this car. It was a battle cruiser.

They turned onto the A1. It was too early to know whether the destination was the motorway, or the marshes. Neither prospect filled him with joy. The doubts had not taken long to resurface and now Rex was racking his brains to think who he'd asked questions of, how Sajadi could have heard that he'd been digging. The man in the Gözleme Shop? Serious, fat Bilal from the council?

They pulled over. The marshes. A very familiar bit of them, screened off behind a wire fence. Half a building. It

144

looked almost as if it had been suddenly abandoned – stray gloves and thermos flasks lay about the site, amongst rain-filled wheelbarrows. Some wags had walked a long way to write *What Fucking Zoo?* on the sign that hung on the wire. The sign itself announced that there was 24-hour security on the site. But there was nothing to secure.

Or so Rex thought. Sajadi beckoned him out, marching determinedly over the wet soil in his loafers and pointing towards a dark red shipping container resting just to the west of the site. Sajadi refused to admit the finger had gone, Rex realised. He'd been like that himself, too, at the start, with his mangled foot, forcing it into old shoes that almost made him faint, jumping off the old Routemaster buses, damage-first. In a way, he admired the stand.

'Want to see inside?' Sajadi asked, zipping up his bomber jacket. 'Come.'

'I don't want to see inside it,' Rex said.

'Why not?' asked Sajadi with pantomime bafflement. 'Oh? You think there's something bad in there? Full of heroin maybe, because I'm a Kurdish businessman with a nice car?'

'No, I –'

'This is what's in there,' Sajadi said, curtly, pulling out a wad of papers and shoving them at Rex. They amounted to some sort of Bill of Lading for the stuff inside the container. Heating ducts. Pipes. Energy condensers. Misters, coolers, fans, boilers, solar cells. All from Hamburg.

'All the things they need to finish the job,' Sajadi barked. 'See? I am giving it to them. Me. I want them to call it Mina's Place. On account of she loved animals so much. That's who I am, Mr Tracey. Okay?'

Eric Miles. That's why Sajadi had been talking to Eric

Miles. To make a donation to the zoo.

'I never thought anything different,' Rex said. 'You're big in German dry-cleaning circles. I know.'

'You thought something else.' The collar of Sajadi's jacket rose up in the breeze, like a photoshoot from a catalogue: a mannequin-sized man. He leaned in, eyebrows raised, always acting. 'Didn't you? Admit it.'

'I don't think. I look. That's what good journalists do.'

Sajadi looked at him sceptically. Then he turned on his heel to look at the shipping container. *Hanseatic League*. He remembered the name from his history 'A' level: a 14th-century German trading cartel. Was it really still going?

Sajadi swivelled back again. 'You were right. If you are Yazidi, and your sister goes with someone outside the group, it's bad blood. You are supposed to seek revenge.'

Rex didn't like the quietly threatening way Rostam had spoken. He wondered what the man was about to confess to. 'It's not just the Yezidi who do that,' he said.

'Sure. Kurds. Turks. Iranians. Pakistanis.' He chopped a hand sharply in the air, delineating tribe after tribe, like those colonial bureaucrats who'd divvied up the East with rulers and string. 'Yezidis don't even mix with others, though. Live in their own villages. Lots of… restrictions. Special numbers. Colours. Can't wear blue. Can't eat lettuce.'

'Lettuce?' Rex blinked. 'Seriously?'

'Blue is the peacock colour, so a man can't wear the colours of God. Lettuce, it's… something to do with the word Shaitan… you know, the devil, and trying to make the Muslims people understand we don't follow the devil.' Sajadi gave Rex a long look. 'You're nodding like you understand. Don't pretend to understand. It's horse shit, Mister Tracey.

It's all horse shit. Everything somebody asks you to believe
– equality, God, miracles, lettuce – horse shit. This is real.'
He pointed at the shipping container. 'That's real.' Back at
the big German car. Suddenly there were tears in the man's
eyes. His moods shifted like Wood Green weather. 'Forty-
two days. Forty-two days it took us, in 1991, to walk, through
the mountains, to escape Saddam. Another eighty-one days,
on the border, between Iraq and Turkey, waiting. My mother
died there. Of cold. Your government dropped blankets.
Sometimes 1,000 Kurdish people dying in that camp every
day. Babies, grandmothers, from hunger and sickness. Even
still, in the camps, they were fighting amongst themselves.
"You – you are Yezidi, you must go over there." Sunni Kurd
won't eat with Alevi Kurd. You think God was there? That
anybody's God was with us, in those places? Stupid. And
the ones who didn't believe in their Gods, they believed in
Britain and the USA. Like me. I believed you. ' He tapped his
breast fiercely. 'And you know what you did? You dropped
blankets. And the Turks stole them. Six months later, I saw
them selling British army blankets at the market in Mardin.
Because that was real. Not the promises of your government.
The market, the money.'

'So you're actually Iraqi, then, not Turkish like Keko?'

Sajadi squinted at him, disparaging. 'You never understand.
Your people decided these things. Not us. Your people, who
knew nothing about Kurds and Turks, nothing about Alevi
and Sunni and Yezidi. Same as now. Why is my brother-
in-law's café called Bosphorus? Because he is a Turk? No.
Because if he called it Murat, if he called it River Zab, you
wouldn't understand! On the way back, I'll show you, just by
Tottenham Hale, a café called Bodrum. No one inside there

has been to Bodrum. They're Kurds, from Diyarbakir, in the east! They call it Bodrum because their customers have all been to Bodrum on package holidays. Diyarbakir you don't understand!'

'I understand, Mr Sajadi. You came from the south. The part that people here call Iraq.'

'Yes. We came from Iraq because the British and the Americans said that all the Kurdish people should unite together and rise up against Saddam. Every night, on their radio station, in Kurmanji language, in Sorani, in Arabic. More promises. More belief. Trust in us, they said. They promised our leaders, at secret meetings in Geneva and London, of your support. So we did. It was our intifada.' He smiled – a proud memory. 'They took Ranya. Suleimanya, Arbil... Our fighters took all these towns from Saddam. On Newroz that year, they took Kirkuk. They expected you were coming to help, because you had promised, and they believed – but no one came. Then Saddam came back – Kirkuk was his prize, no one could take the oil and gas from his Kirkuk and get away with it. So everyone had to run. And you didn't help. You sent us your old blankets.

'We tried to run north, over the mountains, into Turkey, Saddam's planes dropping bombs on the lines of people. The Turks wouldn't let anyone in. No more Kurdish troublemakers, see? But I had connections. I got us across: Meda, my father, my brothers. Some soldiers caught us on the Turkish side, a river near to Kantar. We had gold. They didn't want gold. Or money. It's not the only real thing, you see. Just wanted Meda. Who was sixteen. And green-eyed. For one night. My sister was raped, Mister Tracey. Again and again, by Turkish soldiers. Then they left her by the side of the road, with the bottle they had emptied and the tins of fish they had eaten. Like rubbish.

'So I picked my little sister up and I got her to a hospital, and I got them all to a safe place. And then I went away, to get money, find a proper place to live. I went to Mardin, where I saw the blankets. And when I was away, you know what they tried to do – my father and my brothers and my uncle, after all we had been through, what they tried to do because of their belief? They tried to hang Meda. For the dishonour, you see. To them. *To them*!'

Rostam swallowed, as if he felt sick. 'I got her out. To Germany. She was in a hostel for the refugee people and she met Keko. He had lost his first wife. He wasn't Yezidi. His family religion was Muslim, but he was communist. And he looked after Meda. So I trust Keko. Not Yezidis. My *people*.' He spat the word.

'And when she had a daughter with Keko, you were close to her.'

He nodded. 'Especially after... after Meda died.'

Rex remembered what Lawrence had told him. The road to Hamburg. The van that didn't stop. He wondered if Sajadi had looked for his sister's killer, if he was still looking.

'I didn't keep Meda safe. Or Mina either.'

'I wonder how you can keep someone safe from themselves.'

'You think she needed to be?' Sajadi asked, turning out of the breeze to light a cigarette. Same bad hand. He dared people to look.

'I don't know,' Rex said. 'I don't understand any of it. And I particularly don't understand why someone who was overjoyed about going to Turkey for a year would suddenly do that.'

Sajadi peered closely at him, the leather collar flapping in the breeze. A soldier on guard: under the peak of the cap, his dark, smooth face gave nothing away. But there'd been a flicker of something. Rex couldn't decide whether the news about Mina was a surprise, or if Sajadi was just surprised the third-rate local hack had found out by himself.

'Can you understand it, Mr Sajadi?' Rex dared.

Sajadi threw the cigarette on the ground, carefully making sure it was not just out, but buried under the soil. 'It… adds to my feeling that something is not right. That there is something we don't know. And we need to know. I ask you – please – not to give up. Please. The police have their answer, and they're not going to look. Continue to look for an answer.' The truncated finger tapped a cheekbone. 'People say you are good at this kind of thing. So please.'

To Rex's astonishment, Sajadi held out a hand. He proffered his, and allowed it to be squeezed vigorously, and almost pleadingly as Sajadi went on. 'Whatever you can find, Rex, please, tell me.'

CHAPTER NINE

He sat at the prow of a 123 bus, sailing through the cranes and pile drivers that seemed to be refashioning Tottenham Hale in the image of some new, Dutch or Danish industrial town. After pleading for his help, Sajadi had, with typical abruptness, ordered him into the car, ignored him whilst barking at some underling on speaker-phone, and finally turfed him out at a bus-stop in the rain. Rex didn't mind. The bus was often his office. And the ride gave him a chance to write up some notes on the poker machines. It was how he often worked – slotting one task into another, fitting the day's proper agenda around the seams he was privately mining.

When he'd finished there were still a couple of stops to go, so he made a call. D.S. Brenard was in high spirits, having just nicked a wife-beater who'd forgotten the sixteen rocks of crack in his coat pocket until they were processing him at the Police Station. In a helpful mood, he confirmed that he knew about the assault at Turnpike Lane last night.

'Did it involve a bloke called Haluk and a girl called Kyretia?'

'I won't deny it,' he said good-naturedly. 'She was beating the shibboleths out of him.'

'That's what I thought. Any reason given?'

'He said it was a lovers' tiff. She said nothing. Legal expert, our Kyretia – refused to speak.'

'Pressing charges?'

'The Turkish lad didn't want to, but it's out of his hands.'

'Why?'

'Because Kyretia smashed up WPC Akamba's police radio while she was being restrained. So she's going to be up before the beak. Prob'ly get away with 40 hours' Naughty Step. Might not even put a brake on her glittering legal career, these days.'

'And no indication of any reason for it, apart from the two of them apparently being the Taylor and Burton of the Turnpike Lane area?'

Brenard chuckled. 'Well that was one funny thing. Lizzie Akamba was the one picked it up. Sharp lass, that… The girl wouldn't tell us anything, not even her name at first, so we asked the lad for her phone number. And he didn't have it. We went through his phone menu, and he didn't have a home number for Kye-re-tia, or a mobile number. And she didn't have any for him, either. Bit peculiar for a pair of modern lovers, isn't it?'

Wasn't it? He wanted to think about this some more, but they'd just gone past the Castle, and it wouldn't be long before he reached his destination. There was another call he needed to make, away from all the listening ears in the office. He dialled a new number.

Even the telephones in France sounded sophisticated, he thought, just before Aurelie's husband picked up.

Rex exchanged pleasantries and asked if he could speak to his sister-in-law. There was a pause.

'She isn't here today, Rex. She's gone into Paris. Gone into the centre to get some more things for Sybille's room… Curtains!'

The classic lying pattern, he thought, as they flew past the Crown Court. Victor Eastwood had taught him that. A liar elaborated on the hop, adding more details as he went along, to firm up the essential untruth he'd begun with.

'We're concerned because she hasn't been in touch for a while,' Rex said, aware that his own voice had taken on a ridiculous French twang. 'And the date for the move is getting closer.'

'I know, Rex.' said the husband, quietly. There was another pause. Rex sensed he wanted to say something else. In fact, he'd sensed some time back that Aurelie's husband was unconvinced of the wisdom of his wife's plan. 'I don't know what I can tell to you. Everything is booked for the… Aurelie will come on that date. I don't know about myself because of the shifts at my job, but she will come. The room, it's ready.'

Rex hadn't said the date. The husband hadn't said it either. Because he didn't know it. He didn't even know if his wife knew it.

'Is Aurelie all right?'

'*Mais oui*, all right, of course, of course,' the husband said cheerily, before claiming that his work-phone was ringing. Rex couldn't hear any work-phone. But that was okay. He didn't blame the man for covering for his wife.

Back in the office, a new poem had arrived in the post for Lawrence.

> *Jee, they like to claim*
> *Religion carries the blame*

> **Islam** *has nothing though*
>   *On seven eight double o*
> **Crimes** *that shame*

Same neat writing, same second-class stamp, same lavender notelet set, Woolies, probably, circa 1986. But this time, arriving on a Tuesday. Something new about the writing, too: the first words of the first, third and fifth lines had been etched in heavily, so they looked darker and bolder, a stress the reader was meant to mark.

'Seven-eight-double-oh,' Terry murmured, tapping the letter lightly on the desk as if some further truth might fall off it. 'An amount? How much was your council bloke asking for his bung, Rex?'

'We didn't get that far, did we?' Rex said stonily and then, regretting it, added, 'Could be a point though, Tel. I heard today that the Yezidis consider some numbers very important. Mina's mother and uncle are Yezidis,' he clarified, to his puzzled colleagues. 'A Kurdish kind of sect, from Iraq.'

Lawrence instantly started typing something. Ellie sat on the edge of Rex's desk. 'Jee Islam Crimes,' she repeated. 'J.I.C?'

'Semirc Masli Eej,' added Brenda.

'Who's he? Bloke who runs the phone shop opposite?' asked Terry.

'It's Jee Islam Crimes backwards. I won a prize once on holiday for reciting the whole of 'Rule Brittania' in reverse,' Brenda added.

'Must have been a fun holiday,' Rex said. Brenda pretended to be annoyed and everyone laughed. It suddenly felt like old times, everyone together, joking, working out a problem.

'Yezidis like the number seven,' Lawrence said, looking up from his screen. 'Because they believe God sent down seven angels. Nothing about eight or zeros, or seven thousand eight hundred... Why would my anonymous poems have anything to do with the Kurdish girl's uncle, anyway?'

Rex shrugged. 'It was just a thought.'

There was an awkward clearing of the throat from behind the group and they turned to see Mark Whittaker fiddling with the end of his tie, a sixth-former forced to address the parents. 'We, erm, have to deal with the council a lot because they take out big notices most weeks and erm, 7800 is the last bit of their number. The main... main sort of general, erm, number... it's 0208 112 7800.'

He melted away as he had appeared, blushing at the edge of his collar, leaving everyone wondering how he'd ever flogged a single ad. But Lawrence was nodding happily.

'We had that rhyme about the ark – obviously the zoo. And then the second one...' He produced it from his desk drawer and recited. 'An A for a penny, a B for ten...'

'Someone suggesting there's corruption in the council?' Rex said. 'Like Planning Officers asking for bungs?'

'Not yet proven,' Ellie added.

'So who'd be sending letters like this?' Terry asked.

'Someone with a grudge? Someone who's recently left the council? Or been chucked out?'

Half an hour later, Rex was back over the now-sunny High Street to the bookie's where he'd met Tex. He wasn't looking for Tex, but the little, unfortunate-looking man who'd helped him, for a fee, before. He wasn't there. Nor was he in the bookmaker's inside Shopping City, Rex discovered, after a journey which required him to go past the spot where he'd stood only four days ago watching Mina fall to earth. The escalator had been boarded off, but it had been out of order for months anyway. A bunch of flowers had been left at the side of them, with a plain card, and one word written on it. *Tatlım*. A Turkish word, one he heard all over the borough, but very specific nonetheless. He took a photo of the message and left.

Then, further down towards Turnpike Lane, he spotted the grim little man, as mesmerised by a glowing poker console as some medieval denizen of *Toteham* might have been by the nearest chunk of stained glass. As Rex went in, he saw to his dismay that the person at the adjacent machine was, once again, a glowering Ashley Pocock.

'We have to stop meeting like this, Ashley.'

'This is harassment,' said Pocock.

'I came to see him,' Rex said, gesturing to the man who had, a couple of seconds before, slapped the screen in disgust at his recent loss. 'But now you're here – where can I find your sister?'

Pocock sucked his teeth at him and barged out.

'Thought not,' said Rex. He held out a fiver to the little man at the other machine. 'Care to expand on your recent comments about Tex Ochuba?'

The man frowned. 'Care to what?'

'You said Tex was a cunt. I wondered why. And I wondered if Tex's alleged cuntiness was why you no longer worked at the council.'

The man stared at the note. He still wore his Council Works jacket. A name over the breast pocket, US army style, a change Eric Miles had brought in, Rex remembered, to give the council 'a face'. *McKenzie*.

McKenzie finally took the note and stowed it fast. 'The place changed when the new lot got in. I don't mean just the – wassit – councillors and that. The rest. Works, engineering, secretaries and that. They're all in it.'

'In what?'

'Up each other's arses. They all go up that hippy church, and when a job comes up, it goes to one of their mates. That's what it was like in Works. You're not in, you're out. So I was out. Just in time, I heard.'

'Why?'

The man glanced round, as if about to tell Rex something important. But then he said, 'Try and go up the Works Department. That's my advice. Try and go up there.' Mr McKenzie ostentatiously busied himself with the racing pages of 'The Star' and a biro, signalling an end to their dealings.

'Try' was the right word. The council was a place that attracted angry people to its doors. They were angry about housing benefit and dog mess and stained mattresses on the street and getting sent the wrong bills, and if they weren't the sort to write cross emails to the newspaper, then they were the sort to come down to the big hulking fortress on Station Road, to thump the answer out of someone.

Hence: protecting the officers of the council from attack, three of the Congo's finest prop-forwards beefily stacked behind a desk in paramilitary garb, themselves behind locked, glass doors. If you wanted to get even that far, you had to go into a little booth just by the entrance, pick up a phone and state your business. Rex stated his. They gave him a number for the Works Department and told him, unceremoniously, to ring it.

He tried another tack. He rang Bilal Toprak instead, inventing some ponderous zoning query that might appeal. Bilal said he could see him in an hour.

He had a feeling he was wasting his time. Even just standing here for a few minutes outside the council offices, he could see proof of what he already knew to be true. There were women in full hijab working at the council, and men in turbans. The idea that everyone went 'up that hippy Church' as the disgruntled McKenzie had put it, was rubbish. No doubt there was some cronyism, as in every large organisation, but there might be plenty of other valid reasons to get rid of a glum, charmless Works employee with a gambling habit. So why was he bothering? Just that last look of McKenzie's – and those words, 'just in time', and the glance over the shoulder, as if he'd been about to say something important. Rex couldn't ignore that.

He had some time to kill before the meeting with Bilal, and so, as another spring shower sprinkled upon on Wood Green, he sat at a bus-stop googling for bakers and cake shops in Tottenham. There were a lot: the Turks and Greeks and Serbs, in particular, had a dangerous weakness for layered things dripping in honey and nuts. But they, along with a more recent crop of Brazilian and Portuguese outfits, were easy to discount on the grounds of their names. That left three others in the zone, all within about ten minutes of the Seven Sisters Road – where, irritatingly, he'd been earlier in the day. He caught an inexplicably slow, inexplicably crowded bus, and got off, like everyone else, in a foul temper.

The first on his list, at the end of Philip Lane, called itself a Traditional West Indian Bakery. It turned out to be a thriving, single storey unit, between a gospel music shop and a halal butcher. If Kyretia had literally grown up on top of a cake shop, as both Navitsky and Haluk had said, it couldn't have been here. Unless someone had lopped the top off.

Nor the second, on the Seven Sisters Road just by the new Police Station, recently opened on the site of a former dress shop, and, calling itself a patisserie. Oversized coppers, bulked out with their stab vests and pepper sprays, were bursting out of the place onto the pavement.

The third, however, at which he arrived with just twenty minutes spare before his appointment back in Wood Green, offered some hope. Humming Bird Caribbean Bakers was shut, and gave off the impression of having been shut for some time. It also had a flat over it, a buzzer on a door at the side. No name.

A man answered. 'I know Kyretia was a good friend of Mina's,' Rex said. 'And I wondered if she could tell our readers more about the sort of girl she was.' Click. He wondered if the man had not believed him. Then a buzz, and the door opened.

Like the clay beneath the pavements, there was a core population in the area, unchanging in dimensions or in nature. People moved in and out of it, yet it endured, and it was distinguished by a kind of poverty that involved owning more or less nothing. Eryl Pocock belonged to this stratum: existing in a pair of cold, damp rooms, with one sofa, one table and three folding chairs.

There was a radio but no TV. A camping stove, no fridge. The things Mr Pocock wanted to keep cool, like milk and cheese, hung out of the window, student-style, in a thin, candy-striped carrier bag. Mr Pocock had a sherry-glass of rum in front of him on the table, and from the way he kept looking at it, it was meant to last him all day.

'Kyretia comes back sometimes,' Eryl said, in a soft, lilting Bajan accent. 'She has her room here still. But mostly she prefers to stay with friends from university. Well...' He gestured at the shabby, chilly room. It smelt of yeast and mould. There was a newspaper cutting on the woodchip wall, nothing else.

'Has she been staying recently?'

Eryl frowned, thinking hard. 'For the last couple of weeks, yes,' he said, finally permitting himself a minute sip of the rum. He was a man bewildered, Rex thought, a man who'd seemingly woken up one morning to find everything gone. 'I don't think she likes being around people from the university right now, you know. Too painful. She doesn't like being here, either. Goes for big, long walks on her own, she says.' He scratched his neck, the cactus-bobbles of Afro-stubble. 'I don't know if she's telling the truth. I don't know where she goes. I don't want to push her, you know? But I don't want the girl to drop out. She's worked so hard. We all did.'

'You said she'd been staying a couple of weeks. So she was here before Friday? I mean before the day Mina died?'

'For maybe a week before that she was here. And there was already something wrong. I thought so, anyway, but she wouldn't talk.'

'What made you think there was something wrong?'

'Anxious. She wasn't going out all the time before Mina died. Went to the gym once, I think. Rest of the time she was just here, nowhere else, not going out, y'know, constantly checking her phone. Kept going down to the street because she was worried the signal wasn't strong enough, back up here. Took the thing into the toilet with her. Very, very hard to be around, you know. I'm a calm man. You have to be, in my line of work.'

There didn't seem to be much work going on. Rex looked at the newspaper article. It was from one of the London-Caribbean papers, dated December 2010. *Buck House Boost For Bajan Baker*. A taller, stronger-looking Eryl was beaming next to an elaborate, tiered confection. He'd been selected, the article said, from hundreds of independent bakers in the country, to bake the cake for Prince William and Kate Middleton's wedding the following year.

'That was a major honour,' Rex said. 'Did they like their cake?'

'Seven tiers, ten sections each,' Eryl said, with a cloudy look in his eyes. 'For the seventy nations of the Commonwealth. First tier was going to be a Tottenham cake. You know Tot'nam cake? You have to use real mulberries...' He stopped himself, mid-reverie. 'I never made it. By the time it was due, I was going under. I asked the Palace for a loan, you know... Got Kyretia to write a letter to them, proper-style.' He snorted at his own naiveté. 'I'm getting back on top now. Serious. It's a new age for baking. Like that programme on the TV? Celebrities are into it. My son's helping me.'

'Ashley?'

'A good head for business. Studied hard. I made sure they both study hard, my two. Ashley's taken charge of the books, the company bank account. We're going to be back up, baking, very soon.'

He'd straightened in his chair as he spoke, the rum forgotten. Mr Pocock looked so full of hope that Rex tried hard to look as if he shared it.

'Could I see Kyretia's room? We might see something, you know, that explains where she's been going.'

The appeal to his fatherly concern worked. Pocock showed him to a small, cluttered box-room, barely larger than a bed. It was the opposite of Mina's: a trove, stratified into life-layers of early adulthood, adolescence and primary school. Swimming certificates down low, flyers for club nights high. A photograph caught his eye. Mina and Kyretia at an outdoor pop concert, a gang of friends around them, wide-eyed, all a little high. Mina was waving something, a flag or a pennant. Was anyone else from the university in there – anyone who might know something? There were two boys. Was one of them the alleged lover? Using Terry's favoured covert technique, Rex snapped a picture while pretending to check his phone.

Soon after, he thanked Mr Pocock and left. The shutters outside were rusted and clearly hadn't been opened for a long time. Was Ashley Pocock seriously intending to get this place running again?

He was ten minutes late for Bilal. Happily, once you got beyond the UN peacekeeping force at the gates, you encountered more reasonable officials, one of whom gave Rex a pass and directed him upstairs.

He'd been in the Cabinet Office before, of course. Under the old lot, in the Haringey days. It seemed different now – emptier, quieter. Rex could hear phones ringing in distant parts of the building, a loo flushing somewhere below. Where was everyone?

Then he reached the main meeting room. Everyone seemed to be in there – twenty-odd people, all races and ages. All staring hard at the mahogany meeting table. Hands clasped. In silence. He remembered McKenzie's words.

Eric Miles looked up and saw him at the door. Flustered, he swept the lock of hair from his eyes, made some sort of verbal signal, and everyone broke from their concentrations as the boss strode towards the door.

'Can I help?'

People often said that, Rex thought. When they meant fuck off.

'Were you just praying?'

Miles again wiped the long flick of white hair irritably out of his eyes. 'No we were not,' he said. 'We take a little time out, every day, together, to think, in silence. We don't pray. Now what do you want? You're the gentleman from the paper, aren't you?'

Bilal had appeared at Miles' shoulder. 'He's here for me, Eric. Sorry.'

With what seemed like a guilty air, Bilal ushered Rex away down the corridor to his own office, a cluttered cell smelling of bad breath and tuna-sandwich. As Rex entered, he turned back to see Miles still at the door of the meeting room, watching them, a hovering, headmasterly presence.

'You wanted to know more about the new zoning regulations around Duckett's Common?'

Not really, thought Rex – but he let Bilal explain and took a few notes, while he scanned the room. There was little of personal note: some jokes along the lines of 'You Don't Have To Be Mad To Work Here But It Helps', at least four bottles of pills. And a medal in a frame.

'You a military man?' Rex asked, once Bilal had stopped his ponderous explanation. Bilal followed his gaze to the medal.

'That's my dad's.'

'Kemal? Who did he serve with? The Brits?'

Bilal shook his head. 'His dad, my grandfather served in the police under the British, in the 1950s. But my father was later. *Siyah Tilki* – a Black Fox.'

'Sounds glamorous.'

'They were a special unit of the TMT – *Turk Mukavemet Teskilati*.' He pronounced the Turkish words with such sudden, unexpected fluency that it was as if he'd become a different person. Perhaps that was what it was like, Rex thought, being here, one person in Wood Green, another heritage at home. 'They were the resistance movement that campaigned for the north of Cyprus to separate.'

From what Rex had gleaned from conversations with Helena, there'd been another group, called EOKA, doing similar on the Greek side, seeking union with Athens by means both political and explosive. Then there'd been all the people who wanted a state that was Greek-Cypriot, but nothing to do with Greece. And those who wanted to be a fair mix of the two, or simply to get on with their lives. A mess. And still going on, like Israel, like Iraq and Syria and all the other ancient messes in which Britain had, usually, had a hand.

'And then he moved to Turkey after the war?' Rex asked, remembering their earlier talk in the Sky City community centre.

'They looked after the people who'd been in the TMT. He was in the police,' Bilal said. 'For a while. Then he got a job at a... something like a zoo, I think. Not with the animals, just...' He shrugged. 'Then here.' He shuffled printouts. 'Is there anything about the zoning regs I can email you, or...'

'I'm fine. Thank you. I see our own zoo is finally happening,' Rex ploughed on, as he closed up his notebook. 'Thanks to Mina.'

Bilal blinked slowly – a ponderous bird. 'Not exactly because of her. Mr Sajadi was intending to make a donation before the events last week.'

And you made out you'd never heard of the man, Rex thought.

'I'll see you out,' Bilal said.

Rex cursed inwardly. The whole point of this meeting had been to get inside and wander about.

'No need,' said Rex. 'I've kept you long enough.'

'I'm going out anyway,' Bilal said. 'Aisha in HR is going off on maternity leave, and I'm buying the goodbye cake.'

'Haven't you had a lot of people leaving lately?'

Bilal made a puzzled look, his jaw vanishing into his collar. Here was a lad who needed no more cake, Rex thought. And what were all those pills for? 'No one's left this office. Apart from Jean in Admin Support. But she was only six months off retiring anyway.'

'Why would anyone leave sa job six months before they retire?'

'She'd had enough. Never got to grips with new database software. Wouldn't go on a course.'

Jean had been disgruntled then, Rex thought. They went past a loo on the landing. Never before had the smell of Glade 'Fruits of the Forest' represented a life raft.

'Bilal, I'm going to pay a visit,' Rex said. 'Thanks for everything.'

It wasn't quite the pissy, functional unit he'd expected. The sinks were bowls on dark-wood plinths. Like something up west, a nightclub loo. Nightclubs splashed money on their khazis. And so, clearly, did Eric's council. He counted to ten, then opened the door. Making sure Bilal was gone, he stepped out into the corridor.

Victor Eastwood had had a good line about snooping: 'It's the quietly closed door people notice.' Years after leaving the *Lincoln Daily Despatch*, years after Victor Eastwood had himself been dispatched to the great newsroom in the sky, Rex had come across the line again in a spy thriller. It was possible the author had nicked it from Victor Eastwood, rather than the other way round.

Well-schooled, Rex knew not to creep around the place, and when he came upon a tall, frazzled-looking rasta-lady hefting a tower of files, he merely pointed down the corridor like someone every bit as pressed as her and said, 'Works Department, love?'

'Not sure any more, darlin',' she said. 'Used to be downstairs, turn left at the staircase.'

And it still was. The door was locked, though. The greyness of the stippled glass panel suggested no lights were on inside. He took out his phone and rang the number. No phone rang on the other side of the door. A woman answered.

'Works?'

Wherever she was, she wasn't on the other side of the door. Rex thought quickly.

'My name's Yas Khan? Maintenance team at Shopping City?' he began. Silence invited him to continue. 'It's about that new door you installed, between the mall and the flats? The entry codes don't work and there's an alarm going off constantly. Someone needs to come, yeah?'

Ten minutes later, damp and breathless, he burst into the

s: Haringey office, so excited he barely felt the savage ache in his foot.

'Can anyone ferry me about for an hour or so? I've got a feeling I'm going to be following a van.'

He expected groans, queries, grudging compliance. Instead he got a shocked, silent room.

'What's going on?'

'Rex.' Ellie spoke from behind him, in the doorway to the inner office. 'There's been a serious allegation against you.'

His mind raced. What had he done lately? Snuck around the council building? Impersonated a member of the Shopping City maintenance team? All part of an average day.

'Ashley Pocock? Says you're continually following and harassing him, making libellous allegations against him, and you racially abused him at a bookmakers on the High Street this morning.'

'I didn't racially abuse him!'

'You admit to the harassment and the allegations, though?'

'Get knotted, of course I don't. He's lying. I never said anything abusive to him.'

'He's got a witness. Someone right next to you in the bookmakers.'

McKenzie, the grim little gambler. Who would say anything for a few quid. Who'd hinted to him, very cleverly, in fact, that the Council Works department was missing. *You try and go up there.*

'He's lawyered up and he's making a stink. I've just spoken to Head Office and they're very clear on things like this. I'm sorry. I have to suspend you without pay until it's resolved.'

'Bollocks! I'm not going anywhere!' he shouted.

He felt a hand on his arm. 'Rex, come on man.'

'Oh, fuck off Terry!' he snapped, pushing him away. In the process, his arm, or perhaps Terry's, knocked a cup of steaming coffee over a laptop keyboard. Everyone paused, to watch, in a kind of fascination, as things fizzed and the screen turned a deep, dark blue.

CHAPTER TEN

'Don't!' she said. 'Don't do it!' She slapped at him. 'If you spray that thing in my car, you're getting out and you can do this… thing on your own.'

Rex put the can of RightGuard back in the Boots bag. He'd only just bought it, conscious that the day's exertions had made him smell like a pack of out-of-date bacon.

'I like the way men smell,' she said. 'I had a teacher at primary school, and I used to volunteer to clean the board at the end of every day so I could smell his jacket. Everybody said I loved him. Actually I only loved the smell of his jacket on the chair. Cigarettes… Hair… I guess because there was no Dad at home.'

'You had two smelly brothers, I imagine.'

She scowled, briefly. 'Boys. They are still boys, my brothers.' She sighed, looking out of the window. 'That's what it's like in Cyprus. All the men are still boys, looking for their mummies. All the women looking for fathers. Nobody finding what they are looking for.'

The rain had given way to hot sunshine, the puddles turning to vapour all around as they waited, in Helena's absurd prawn-pink hire car, at the back of Shopping City. No one noticed them; the kerbs always seemed to be lined with cars with people inside them. Helena, who'd never done anything like this before, had accepted the mission with enthusiasm, perhaps not realising how tedious it might be. She didn't seem to mind though, seemed happy to sit with him, talking and waiting.

'I don't understand why you're doing this if your newspaper suspended you.'

'Because they're going to un-suspend me, and when they do, I'm going to have a story for them, that's going to make them very sorry they ever thought about suspending me.'

'Turk's words,' she said.

'What?'

'Something my mother says. If someone is being, you know...' She put her fists up. 'Probably the Turks say 'Greek words'. I don't know.'

'You were speaking Turkish at the community thing.'

'Sure. Lots of people speak both. It's not what everyone thinks. The house we lived in, in Nicosia, it had been a Turkish house, that the people had left very suddenly. And we put all the things they'd left in one room at the top. We looked after them. In case they came back. We weren't supposed to touch the things in there, but sometimes I went in.'

'What was in there?'

She shrugged. 'Same things we'd left behind. Cushions. Records. Pictures.' She smiled. 'There was a photograph of a Turkish man with a big moustache. I used to go and look at it. I don't know why. A kind of crush, almost!'

'So what happened to all the things in the room?'

She shrugged. 'No one came for them. My brother, Yiannis, he broke the picture and hid it.'

'Why did he do that?'

'I don't know. Well, I do. He took it and then he shut me in the room and he said I was a dirty Turk so I should stay with the Turks' things, and he shut me in there for a day and a night. There!' She smiled uncertainly. 'I never told anyone that!'

'Why did he do that to you?'

'He hated me,' Helena said simply. 'My younger brother, Alex, not so much, not when we were alone together, but Yiannis and the cousins...' She shook her head. 'It was my cousins, my mother's sister's family, who bought us to Nicosia. They were the ones who found us the house. A Turk's house. Most of those places were looted, straight away – the people either took everything, took them over, or just burnt them down. But this one... nobody touched it, so we went there. And so the cousins said it was haunted, that was why nobody else wanted it. And they called me a dirty Turk, a Turk's bastard.'

'Nasty kids.'

She shook her head. 'They were just children! They only said it because they heard their parents saying it.'

'But... I don't understand... Why would their parents say that?'

She seemed to be wrestling with something heavy, but before she could master it, a scruffy yellow van pulled up outside the entrance to the Sky City flats. Three men got out, all young, scrawny, a trio of nationalities: Somali, Chinese and someone from the vodka-drinking lands. A paint-spattered toolbox followed them out of the van. The

Chinese man had a council digi-pass on a lanyard and they got straight in.

'Do we go after them?' Helena asked. 'How do we get in?'

'We don't,' Rex said. 'We wait.'

They waited. She checked her phone, sent a text, squeezed his hand. It was the first time she'd shown him any affection since they'd left the hotel bed. He leant in and kissed her.

She smiled, in the midst of their lips. 'So you still like me?'

'I thought maybe you didn't like me,' he said.

'It should get easier, being older,' she said. 'It just gets worse.'

'More at stake, maybe,' he said. They just sat for a while, close, holding hands. 'What were you going to tell me – about the things your relatives said?'

She looked straight ahead. 'I wasn't there, but you know, my job is speaking to the people who lived through that time, and… they didn't just pack and catch a bus. You know? It was a bad time. Bad things happening. My mother was… She wasn't well. Growing up, I always knew that. I thought she was just sad, because we'd lived in a lovely village and we'd owned three thousand fruit trees and now we had just this old, rotten house in the city that wasn't ours and she had to go out to work. And she was sad because of those things, but also because of…'

Now she looked at him. 'Bad things happened. On all sides. Everybody has a way of separating themselves from what happened. Everyone admits, now, that their own side did things wrong. But in Nicosia and Limassol, in the cities, the people say it was only the Greeks who came from the mainland, the army officers from Athens. Or it was only the poor Greeks from inland, from the mountains. Same for the

Turks. *Yes, there were bad things,* they'll say to me, *but that was those Turks over there, the ones we never liked, not us...* And yet everyone agrees on one thing. Everybody. All the Greeks and all the Turks, the army officers from Istanbul and Athens, the guerrillas in the mountains, everyone says there was one group of Turks, who everyone feared. Monsters. Like those fighters in Iraq and Syria beheading people. But not even with the excuse of God.' She fell quiet, lost in fog, then spoke again, very quietly, hardly even to him. 'So they said she was lucky.'

'Who was?'

She never got to answer, because the three workmen re-emerged with the toolbox, looking puzzled. The Chinese man, the youngest, the shortest, but the one with the authority, was making a call. Then they all got back in the van.

'What now?'

'My first guess was that the Works Department, or whoever's claiming to be the Works Department would send a crew out. And I was right, so I'm on a roll. My second guess is that, having found nothing to fix, the likely lads are going to go back to base.'

'Which is where?'

'We don't know. So follow that van,' Rex said.

'Wow. Cool.'

The van drove slowly, super carefully, as if the man at the wheel was new to it, or trying to stay out of trouble. They went along all the delicate tendrils of the borough, which were seeming to unfurl in the sudden, unexpected good weather. Down Lordship Lane, in amongst the gleaming, ship-shaped hulks of all the new-builds, Turkish shopkeepers were clicking out striped garden chairs to sit in the warm fumes. Tottenham boys, more image-obsessed than the girls, had stripped hurriedly to vests to air their steroid-pumped six-packs and their faux-prison markings.

The van halted outside a Tool Hire outfit on an overlooked spur of the Great Cambridge Roundabout. The men got out, and filed into one of the legion of nondescript, shabby-looking offices that dotted the area. Supermarket boxes in the window, dying yucca in the corner: such places fought deportations, shipped crates, sold airline tickets with one laptop, one knackered woman and a microwave.

This one, according to the name and a quick search on Helena's phone, housed a charity, handsomely endowed by government and several leading TV celebrity business figures, for helping the long-term unemployed back into work.

'So that man in the council is using these people?' Helena mused. 'Maybe for free?'

'They don't look like the long-term jobless,' Rex said, observing as the Chinese foreman-type spoke to a doughy, grumpy-looking woman at a desk. 'More like recent arrivals doing every job going. So what does this place do?'

'Let me find out,' said Helena. 'Not you,' she added, getting out of the car. She'd gone in before he could stop her.

He wound the window down and watched. It looked like the fat woman was making Helena wait. It could have been a scene from a Sumerian wall-carving: well-fed scribe, desperate petitioner.

He looked at his phone and then, since there was still nothing happening inside the office, he had another look at the picture he'd taken in Kyretia's room. He enlarged it slightly, which made it more blurry, but he was able to work out that it wasn't a pop concert she'd attended with Mina and a small group of male friends. Not unless they allowed pop concerts outside Big Ben. Mina had a flag in her hand -- and it was a bright, multi-coloured affair, also reflected in the banners all around them. They told him something, so did the body language of the group. He flipped to the other photograph he'd snapped that day: the flowers left at Shopping City. That word *tatlım*: it was really only kids who used it. Kids in love. Mina's uncle had been right: there was a lover.

'Drive,' Helena said, out of the side of her mouth as she slid in. 'She's looking.'

'I would,' Rex said. 'But I haven't got a license. And you've got the steering wheel.'

She did a double-take, then burst out laughing. They drove onto the roundabout, picked another spur at random and stopped some way down in a residential street full of skips and scaffolding. They were building even here.

'I worked out what was going while she ignored me,' Helena said, flushed with excitement. 'They get work for people with no papers. Then when she finally gave me her attention, I told her I was Greek and I needed work.'

He tried hard not to show his annoyance. 'What was the point of that? Greeks can work here. It's part of the EU.'

She looked at him coolly. 'Number one, I told her I was Greek because she is obviously Greek.'

'Why obviously Greek?'

'There was a Twelve Apostles Church sticker on the bumper of the car outside. That's the place we're having all our meetings for the Greek and Greek Cypriot groups. I've even got one there this afternoon. And she was speaking

Greek when I went in. Not exactly disguising her identity, Rex.' She grinned.

He smiled back, pleased, and yet something about what she'd just said seemed wrong – somewhere in his unconscious, he felt a ticket was being filed, a request to wonder. He ignored it and asked, 'Number Two?'

'Number two, there are some very poor Greek communities outside Greece. Like in Albania, and the Pontic Greeks in Kazakhstan and Southern Russia.' She smiled. 'A job in the UN teaches you all sorts of things.'

'Wow. So you're a Kazakh Greek who'll do anything. Did she take you up on the offer? What *is* the offer? It's not massage, is it?'

'Cleaning, she said. Tonight, from midnight. I go there, do six hours, and in the morning, she says I go back and I get twenty-five pounds cash. If I do good, she says, maybe she can get me something else. A government job, she said, looking after old people, or maybe in a school.'

'A council job,' he said.

She handed him a slip of paper, a Spurs F.C. Post-It with some biro scrawls. The job tonight was for a firm who imported cooked and smoked meats from Southern Europe. They had premises on the White Hart Lane Business Park, a complex of storage units and light industry.

'What are you thinking?'

'We need more evidence. Anyone could have written this.'

'Like a recording, you mean?'

He nodded, distractedly, before he realised she was holding her phone out to him. 'What? You got it?'

She beamed, proudly. 'I got some video, too. I did that trick you told me – pretended to be putting her number in

176

my phone. Shall I go, tonight, to the meat place, as well?'

He shook his head, pulled her close. 'I've got better uses for you.'

* * *

By tea-time, he was back on the streets again. All the premature heat of the day was drifting upwards, the sky was streaking and the muscle boys in their vests were looking sheepish as they shivered home. Rex wasn't feeling the cold, though – he had the glazed, soppy grin of a lotus-eater plastered across his face. They'd stolen a three-hour honeymoon in her hotel room before finally parting company. Now he was heading back down the hill, a cracking good story in his pocket, a date to meet up with Helena later on. Everything looked good.

He loved the view from the top of Muswell Hill: the marsh plains of north-east London spread out before him like a huge runway. Tower blocks and one church spire, jutting up like a thorn. He took it all in for a moment, before he checked his phone. There were four messages. Maureen, 'double checking', as she tactfully put it, the details for their next appointment. Helena: a mix of semi-colons and dashes and brackets, that he was meant to read sideways. Lawrence: ignoring or forgetting the earlier contretemps, wondering if he'd found out anything useful about disgruntled council employees. And finally one from Ellie, ridiculously, checking he was 'okay'.

He replied to the middle two. Maureen, as he saw it, was just bullying him. And Ellie? He'd promised, in the car earlier on, that he'd find out something, something to make her regret suspending him. He now wondered if that was a waste of a good story. She and her bosses had shown no faith in him, suspending him on the say-so of one, disgruntled loudmouth. Why should he show faith in them?

Changing his mind about heading into the office, he veered off left into the wooded slopes where the nuns' house sat. Something seemed odd about the undulating path, but it was only when he reached the convent's doorway that he realised what it was. The one, inefficient bulb had been replaced by a new, gleaming searchlight, adding its own, powerful glare to the retreating daylight.

'Isn't it wonderful, Rex?' said Sister Florence as she bustled him in.

'Your bills won't be if you keep the thing on all day.'

'Peter says he must to adjust the... sensor? Such a clever man! He also has mended most wonderfully the car of Sister Anna-Claire, which did not work without the smoke of plumes for a year!'

'Who's Peter?'

'We don't know,' said the tiny nun with a delighted shrug. 'God has sent him to our door, asking one day for some food.' She lowered her voice. 'Sister Anna-Claire believes he is staying at a hostel, Rex, and we allow to her to believe that, because, you know, she would worry. Actually, you know, he lives out there, in the woods! A true hermit!'

It made sense of what he'd seen. Not Sister Florence conducting some secret ritual. Just leaving out a drink for a tramp in the woods. A mechanically-gifted one, by the sounds of it. Rex liked that the nuns were so trusting; they were the opposite of just about every other institution in today's world, which greeted you with latex gloves, a checklist and a terror of being sued. But he wondered if they should be more careful. Who was this Peter?

'I don't know!' repeated the nun, cherishing this tiny Tolstoyan mystery in her ordered life. 'He will speak very little. *Alors!*'

She clapped her hands, snapped modes as they went in. The TV wasn't on. Sybille seemed to be just sitting. Rex cast a concerned glance to Sister Florence.

'She says enough of the detectives. I said okay – then the Gardening World, please? The Great British Bakers? She says no. No TV.'

'I'm bored of it,' Sybille said. 'Hello Rex. You smell tired.'

He sat next to her. It was one of the clear days. He took her cool, slim hand and she squeezed it as Sister Florence discreetly slipped out.

'I need a bath,' he said. 'I've been working too hard.'

'You always did. That's why Aurelie wants me to go to her. She doesn't have to work.'

'Have you heard from her?'

She didn't answer. A dog barked outside.

'Aah, there she is,' Sybille said. They both smiled. Her face was still smooth – the scar tissue didn't wrinkle.

'Do you want to go to Paris, Syb?'

'Didn't mean any of it,' she said.

He sat up. 'What you told the lawyers, you mean? You didn't mean it?'

'An accident. Will you find it? It was careless, he said. One little sin. There has to be forgiveness.'

He felt his chest locking tight again, the hope ebbing away between their touching fingers. His love had gone. In her place, the Sibylline Sybille of the elliptical phrase and the shrouded hint. A mixture of dark allusions to their shared, unutterable past and sheer gibberish. The nuns, soppy and unworldly, mistook his visits for devotion. Something else, more often, drove him up the hill, though. Fear.

'She is talking so clearly, no?' Sister Florence said, as she let him out into the stadium-glare of the porch. 'And sleeping well at the moment, as well, none of the *cauchemars*... nightmares.' A hand, light and almost ethereal, on his arm. 'Ever since Peter. He fix the window catch in her bedroom. And now...' Beaming serenely, Sister Florence glanced to the sky. Rex was angry.

'Hang on, you're saying he's been in her room? Listen – I don't want you to let men, from the woods into Sybille's room, Sister Florence. Please.'

She withdrew, disappointed, the sliding of the bolts a rebuke to his lack of faith. On the way back up the path, on top of the noise from the buses and cars, he felt sure he could hear a man, sobbing somewhere, among the trees. He thought about ringing Sybille's sister, who, if she was contactable, would surely talk a more fiery brand of sense into the nuns, but that would only make Aurelie come quicker with her van and her plans.

He stood at the bus-stop. Took stock of the day and the hours left of it. Rang Helena, who was just finishing her meeting at the Church.

'I was just wondering if you wanted to go out somewhere in Muswell Hill instead?'

There was a long, unexpected silence. 'Why?'

He pondered the reasons. He'd suggested, whilst cruising high on a tide of achievements and endorphins, dinner at his place. Now Rex realised he'd have go back and clean. Change the duvet. Tackle the High Street and not only buy food, but cook it. The hour with Sybille had taken some of the shine off the day already; he didn't want to lose any more.

'Is there some reason why you don't want me to come to your house?' she asked sharply, before he'd had a chance to reply. 'Like you're not being honest with me?'

'No,' he said, keeping his tone neutral. 'It was just an idea. Come to my house.'

Rammed between pushchairs on a 144, he wondered why she'd been so cold, instantly suspected him of wrong-doing. He hadn't kept anything from her – he'd told her, on their first evening in The Salisbury, about the wife he'd lost but stayed with. Sybille had never been one of those paranoid wives herself. Her doubts and suspicions had all been focussed inwards.

One little sin. As the bus lurched, he couldn't help smiling. At university, still picking off the suckers of her Catholic education, his wife had seriously believed each, individual cigarette and drink was a sin. She was coughing to around fifty venials a day at St Pat's, and the priests didn't know what to do with her. He'd teased her for it. And maybe, when she'd said those three words this afternoon, she'd been referring to that, happier part of their life together. Or to a different sin altogether.

Careless, he said. But who was *he*? Anyone? Someone? No one? Or the person he'd been wondering about for twelve years.

CHAPTER ELEVEN

'I wish we were walking to the real Bosphorus for breakfast.'
'You've been?'

He nodded, squeezing her hand. 'You haven't?'

'For work, to a couple of places, yes. Antalya, Adana... but just in, and then out. It's not easy.'

'You mean, visas and suchlike?'

She shook her head. 'No, I mean... I speak Turkish and I have Turkish colleagues and...' She pursed her lips. 'I don't think I can make you understand.'

They left it there, walking hand in hand to the café in the morning sun. He knew there were parts of her he couldn't understand. He didn't mind; everyone was like that, really. She'd visited, as planned, last night, and not objected to eating takeaway lahmacun from the Pamukkale, nor to the hastily spruced interior of his home. She'd been in no rush to leave, at any rate. And wasn't that enough, for now?

They were walking down the short parade of shops, opposite the bus-station, past the Trabzonspor Social Club with its obligatory skip and scaffolding. Inside, a couple of old men were staring at the tv. Normally, there were football matches showing but today, it seemed to be some kind of newsflash, with ticker-tape going across the bottom of the screen, a vividly made-up reporter by an ambulance. Outside the club, another pair, in classic OAP Turk-garb – vintage suit, cable knit v-neck, flat cap – were staring up at the scaffolding, muttering.

'Not happy,' Helena said, as they walked by.

'About what?'

She shrugged. 'I couldn't catch it.'

Rex remembered Bilal talking about his father: unhappy at his usual watering hole, taken to brooding alone at the factory. 'Would you be happy if they turned your favourite club into a building site?'

They waited at the lights. 'They could always spend time with their wives.'

'You've clearly never been married,' he said.

She poked him playfully as they crossed over. Then they went into the Bosphorus café, where Keko was lecturing the Hungarian girl about the extractor fan.

He spotted them and came over – the same old man, yet somehow, lesser. 'Thank you,' he said, solemnly shaking their hands after they'd ordered. It was as if they'd shown him a kindness by coming in. There weren't many who had, to be fair. People still seemed to fear death – thought it was catching.

'It's a good thing to be at work,' Rex said. He meant that. It had saved him, after Sybille, although his career on the nationals had been part of the wreckage. An old colleague of his from *The Times* had rung him, while he was still having five times a week therapy up at Highgate Hill, to tell him about this local title she'd just bought, in a hard, scruffy, little

184

borough where they'd never be getting a Waitrose. Was he really not planning to go back to it now?

Keko nodded his agreement, slowly. 'Same when Mina's mother die. I stay working, just working – baby in corner. In corner,' he repeated, his dull gaze pulled over to the corner where Mina would never again sit.

'Nobody was ever caught,' Rex began. 'For the accident your wife had?'

Keko sat down with them – an unprecedented honour. 'Germany Police. You –' He mimed an uncouth unofficial finger, pointing at Rex. '*Gastarbeiter*. *Turk*. Not interest. Not look.'

'You should have told them you were Kurdish,' Rex said.

Keko shrugged. 'Same as here. Most people don't understand that Kurds is not Turk. Anyway... I am communist. Man first, father number two, communist number three ...

'And Kurdish?' Helena asked.

Keko paused, thinking, as two mugs of tea arrived at the table. 'Kurdish number ten!' He leant over, intent, a brightness briefly returning to his eyes. 'You know, before, hundreds of years before, only the high... er, chiefs? Only high chiefs, the *aghas* are call themself Kurd. Everyone else – Christian, Muslim, Yezidi – just...' He mimed something tiny with his gnarled fingers – little people. 'Nothing. No Kurdish nation. And all the tribes of Kurdistan – you got Aruk peoples, Bejani, Kucher, Zerzan peoples – it means nothing! If one people get war, go join another tribe. One tribe get good rich, okay, more tribes are joining in them. See? Tribe is meaning nothing. Kurd – nothing. Just a name.'

He shook his head, and fell quiet, the gleam in his eyes

fading again as the grief returned. Rex wondered if Keko had always felt this – if he'd hardened towards Kurdish nationalism after Mina's death. Or someone else had changed his mind. 'You sound like Rostam.'

Keko frowned. 'What?'

'I've talked to your brother-in-law. Rostam. He says the same kind of thing.'

Keko flinched slightly, as if slapped. 'Rostam? Rostam is very high *peshmerga*! He is a soldier who faces death. In Iraq... at Kore... 1991... Rostam, one hundred fifty *peshmerga* fight to Saddam. Whole Iraqi army beat by one hundred fifty *peshmerga*. A lot of Yezidi peoples, they won't fight. Won't join with other peoples. Rostam? Rostam broke with his people to join *peshmerga*. He is very high. Hero of Kore. Loving Kurdish people very much.'

It explained, perhaps, the timid reverence of the man in the gözleme shop, who'd repeated over and over that Mina's uncle was 'very high'. It explained, considerably less well, the things Rostam had said to Rex. A man who had professed to loathe politics, to despise the Turkish Kurds' resistance group, the PKK, and even his own family, was a hero of the Kurdish rebellion in Iraq. Why would he cover that up?

Rex wanted to ask more about Rostam, but just then, there was a small crash and a shout from the street opposite. It looked at first as if some minor piece of masonry had fallen onto the car of one of the dandies having patterns shaved into his hair in the Kutz Karib Barbershop. As the vehicle's aggrieved owner, still swathed in a gown, came out to remonstrate, and a stooped, hairless Turkish elder emerged simultaneously from Trabzonspor, there came another, greater crash, as the scaffolding collapsed, bringing much of the upper floor of the building with it. Over the road, people darted into the Bosphorus for safety and stayed there, watching through the windows in fascinated horror as a plaster-cloud swirled amid car alarms and human cries and a timpani symphony of hollow poles hitting others on the way down.

Helena was already on the phone to the emergency services. Rex switched his camera on to video and rushed out. People were steaming in already, some to gawp, some to help, the odd one to grab what he could find and run. Rex shouted at them to get back.

'It's not safe. The whole thing could collapse! Get back!'

'Why don't *you* get back then?' shouted one of the barbers from Kutz. Pure Haringey: macho ball-busting, even while a building collapsed.

He'd never seen so far inside a Turkish social club. The back, where they served tea and coffee from a counter, was intact, although covered in glass and dust and smaller pieces of masonry. The TV had crashed off its bracket onto the floor, but it was still on: the Mata Hari-like reporter interviewing some schoolkids now, words he recognised on the ticker-tape. *Polis. Fanatik.*

Fortunately, the club had had few customers at 10.30 on a Wednesday morning, and the majority had made their way, dust-frosted and bewildered, to the opposite side of the road. One man had what seemed to be quite a bad head wound, and Helena stopped him from wandering dizzily in the road and made him sit down. Then, as the dust cleared further, it became apparent that there had been one, serious casualty.

The bald man who'd come to the front when the first piece of stone had fallen was lying under a huge chunk of wall. He was white with shock, groaning faintly, blood on his lips. He was Bilal's father, Kemal Toprak.

'Help me get it off him!' Rex shouted. No one moved.

Rex grunted as he tried to shift the slab which had scraps of some old, floral wallpaper still attached. The old man was no longer groaning, only making a husky whirr, like a knackered clock, while he breathed in and out.

'Here, Rex!'

He looked up. Terry was opposite, levering a scaffolding pole under the slab. He pulled down, Rex dragged and the thing began to shift. Others had joined them now, mostly the barbers and customers from the next-door shop and it came away – leaving the old man broken beneath on a bed of milky rubble, staining slowly carmine with his blood. Helena knelt beside him, checking his vital signs as the first of the emergency vehicles pulled in.

'It was waiting to happen,' one of the patrons kept saying, to anyone who caught his eye. He was an unhealthy-looking man, a mouth permanently open, a face the colour of greaseproof paper. 'I was in the building trade. And I kept telling them. Don't care who's signed off on it. Not safe.'

Terry paused, mid-snap, to wink at Rex, any quarrel of theirs long buried. 'You gonna take some notes, big man?'

He had just started to do that as Kemal Toprak went into a shuddering series of convulsions. Helena was no longer anywhere near him. Looking round in confusion, Rex saw her a little way further in, staring at a picture on the wall of the café.

'He's having a fit!' Rex shouted. 'Helena!'

She glanced back at the man as the ambulance crew arrived. Then, briefly, at the photo on the wall again, before she rushed over to join to the paramedics. Kemal seemed to have relaxed again. His eyes were wide open.

Rex stared at the picture, wondering what had caused Helena to leave a man on the floor on the verge of death. The image offered no clues – it was just a bunch of young men in army gear. One had an award-winning moustache, and from the foppish hair and the exuberant sideburns on all the participants, Rex guessed, they must have assembled for it sometime in the mid-1970s. In Turkey? In Cyprus?

He turned round, still filming, then abruptly switched his phone off. The ambulance crew were pronouncing Kemal Toprak dead. His son, Bilal, who'd arrived wheezing with exertion on the scene himself only a few minutes before, collapsed with shock, cut his head, and had to go to hospital with the others – a tragic sort of gate-crasher. Helena seemed to have vanished into thin air.

Across the road, as Rex was preparing to leave, Keko was pulling the café blinds down. He had been ordered by the police to vacate for safety reasons. 'Black days,' he muttered to himself. 'Too much black days.'

* * *

In the office: the silent, ordered frenzy, peculiar to newsrooms. The smell, too, was one associated with deadlines: coffee on the breath; deodorant and perfume hastily sprayed onto shirts no longer fresh; hot paper and ink. Ellie and Terry sifted through images from the Trabzonspor collapse – for the website, for the Friday print edition, for the nationals.

Behind them, Rex wrote up what they had, chased quotes and verifications, updated the earlier pieces about the falling window at Tottenham Hale to link with the newer, bigger possibilities. New buildings were going up everywhere. How many of them were safe? Despite, or because of the seriousness of the events, it felt exciting. It always had: a drug-like tingle, to be against the clock, thinking clearly, reacting quickly, part of something. And to be back on board. He'd brought the scoop straight to Ellie. A peace-offering. A bribe. Whatever it was, she'd been unable to refuse it.

Behind the questions he was asking publicly, others were pooling. How many buildings might be unsafe because the planning office was bent? In how many other places, in the nursing homes and the schools and the housing blocks, were the checks not being made, the borough's residents being sold short, because the work was being farmed out to the gang-masters? There was one thing he no longer doubted: he belonged here, doing this.

Ellie took a call in her office. There was a hiatus, nothing more to be done until she gave her verdict on the web copy he'd just drafted. Rex fetched a cup of water. It was the first thing to pass his lips since a few sips of tea that morning in the Bosphorus. He was wearing jeans – the only unfamiliar element to the situation. His suit trousers had been knackered in the building collapse. His spare suit trousers were at the dry cleaners. No one had ever seen him in jeans before; everyone kept mentioning it.

Lawrence, standing by the water-cooler, in his black slacks and slip-ons, made the obligatory denim-related comment but then added, 'Good to have you back.' Which was Lawrence all over – annoying, but all right.

'Thanks. It was a short retirement.'

'Talking of which, thank you for your text about Jean in

190

the council. A Mrs Jeanette Crosby, in fact. And you're quite right – she left the council four weeks ago, after 26 years' dedicated service. And guess what else? Was a runner-up in our poetry competition two years on the trot.'

'A disgruntled poet. Of course. Good work. We should talk to her.'

'I tried. Knocked on her door. She lives on the Ladder. Lord, it's noisy down there. Every third house is having something done. Anyway, Jean isn't. She's spent her money on a cruise. Which she is now on, according to Vonda, who lives next door.'

'Ah.'

'She could have written them all in advance, of course, and got someone else to post them. Could even have got the neighbour to do it. Our Vonda had a shifty air, if you ask me. Trying to get me off the scent with cake.'

'Cake?'

'Hot fresh parkin. She gave me a wedge once she'd made sure I wasn't the mafia. And once she'd recognised me from the newspaper...'

Rex let Lawrence chunter on, feeling that his efforts at the council had been in vain. An ocean-cruising poet sending her Delphic missives in via a third party sounded improbable. It was a dead-end. But who was sending them?

Ellie had finished her call, but before Rex could ask for her input, she'd summoned him in.

'Head Office are making an exception due to your valued contribution on the Trabzon collapse. While the suspension remains in place, you can work for us, freelance, on an agreed story-by-story basis. But you won't get a byline. It's all going in under my name. Or Terry's.'

'Can I choose?'

'Do you want this job?'

He chose to ignore this. 'It goes deeper,' he said, closing the door and sitting down. 'There are rotten elements in the council lining their own pockets while the safety standards go to hell. That's why Kemal Toprak died today.'

She opened her mouth to argue, but he got in first.

'Council services are being farmed out through an agency that pays slave wages, cash in hand, no questions asked. I've got proof of that here,' he said, putting his phone on the desk between them. 'But who's to say it stops there? Someone in the council seems to be trying to warn us about it. If I can find them…'

'And you can actually prove what you're saying…'

'That guy Pocock – he's involved. I know he is. This whole complaint thing is a bluff, he thinks I'll back off. I'll prove he's involved. I'll prove all of it. And it'll be on your watch, Ellie. All glory, honour, credit, Shining Star stickers and c.v. points going to you.'

She smiled, not quite able to hide the hunger. Seizing the advantage, he played her the recording Helena had made. After a few seconds, she paused it, frowning.

'Is it all in Greek?'

'Well… yes,' he said, kicking himself for his oversight. 'But translated, it'll prove what I'm saying.'

'It'll need more than that.'

'I can *get* more than that. I can get everything. I just need a week.

'A week?'

'A week.'

He didn't know why he'd said that. He didn't know for sure

if he could prove it in a year. The point was, Ellie, at length, nodded.

'A week. And you promise to go back to Maureen. You've stopped, haven't you?'

He frowned.

'She rang here. Very discreet. Left a number. I looked it up. I am a journalist as well, you know.'

He went straight out and booked another appointment for the afternoon. Given the promise he'd just made, he had a feeling he might be needing Maureen.

He'd intended to head directly to her consulting room during the afternoon lull, but the arrival of a bill, hand-delivered, from the nuns, pricked his conscience. He had it all worked out, a new route. Quick handover of cheque at the door, back up the path to catch a 43 in Muswell Hill, which would take him round the wooded flank of the North London mountain ranges, descending through the suicide viaducts of Archway onto the Holloway Road, just in time for some gut-spilling *chez* Maureen.

It worked well until the end of stage one, when Sister Florence insisted on him coming inside for a moment to see Sybille. Reluctantly, he complied, passing through the earthy warren to a sort of breakfast room he'd only seen once, on the day his wife moved in a decade before. It was sunny and bright, with a view of the tiny boating lake. Sybille was sitting in a wicker chair by the opened sliding glass doors, clearly enjoying her surroundings.

Sister Florence fingered the olive-wood cross she wore around her neck. 'Yesterday, just, she asks to sit. And she stays.'

'It's a nice room, Syb,' he said.

'It's a beautiful room,' she replied. 'There's a bird. It's a... Listen!' She held a finger aloft, cocked her head as a deep, hollow-sounding tattoo sounded outside. 'A woodpecker!'

Sybille had never shown any interest in nature. They'd had no garden at their flat in Camden, but she had managed to kill cut flowers and houseplants, even cacti, with great speed and skill. Now, here was his eminently metropolitan wife, in raptures over a woodpecker. But this was something real – outside the narrow tracks of the nuns' routines and the TV crime dramas. Sybille wasn't, as he often suspected and feared, indifferent to her surroundings. She cared.

That made him care, too. She couldn't go to Paris. No way would he allow it.

'Maybe you could visit this room every day,' he said.

'Hmm,' she replied, dreamily. Then she began to sing. Hoarse, off-key – as ever. It was a song he'd never heard before, from her, or anyone else.

> 'Drobna, drabnitsa, drobna, drabnitsa
> Drobni dozhdzhik lye...'

He looked at Sister Florence.

'Peter?'

'Peter,' the little nun affirmed, guilty, eyes cast down to her stout, lace-up shoes. 'He was here for mending yesterday the slide-door.'

The song sounded Russian, or perhaps Polish. It continued, with words Sybille had trouble pronouncing, but tried nonetheless. *Byedna basota... Di garyelki...* Then she began again. He recorded it this time. He could play it to Aurelie, he thought, and prove to her that Sybille was thriving here, where she was, even if she was doing it in Slavic verse.

'Rex, don't be angry,' the nun said, mistaking his determination for disapproval. 'Peter is not a bad man – look!'

Before he could reply, the song ended. But Sybille launched straight into something else. The same language, or kind of language, but not a song. Something serious, urgent.

> *Bo'ya milastsi khachu a nye akhvyari, i*
> *bogavedanya baly'ey, chim usespalennya'u*

It sounded like an oath or a threat. Only one person could tell him which.

'Is he here today?'

Sister Florence shook her head. 'He comes. He goes.'

'When he next *comes*, tell him I want to talk to him before he *goes*. I want to know what he's saying to my wife.'

He gave her one of his cards. Sister Florence made a face, as if the notion was ridiculous, and Peter could only be contacted through prayer.

'Where's he from?'

'I think Russia. Sister Mary Sulpice says Poland. Sister Anna-Claire thinks Greek.'

'Greek?'

Sister Florence rolled her eyes. Sister Anna-Claire was known to be seized by odd notions. But then what was odder than the reality: some tramp blowing in from the woods and inducing Sybille to swap 'Ironside' for Slavonic choruses?

Heading down the Archway Road on the top deck of his next bus-ride, Rex felt as if the 43 was about to sail off the edge of the world. London sat below, like a bauble in a bowl. If you lived up here, he thought, you'd feel like you'd conquered the city. Down on the marsh-plains where Rex lived, it was the reverse. The place owned you. It bred hard people, fighters, who felt they had to punch their way out.

He tried Aurelie again. Once again, he got the husband.

'I'm going to send you something. It's a recording. Sybille singing. She's got this new room. It's like she's waking up. And she doesn't want to go. Really. She mustn't go.'

He stopped, aware that he'd done a lot of breathless, loosely connected rambling and the person on the other end had said nothing.

'Rex. I am pleased about those changes. Really, I am. But I have to tell you now, Aurelie has booked the transportation. It is for Saturday the six April.'

'Why don't the nuns know about it, then?'

'They do know. It's why Sybille is staying in that front room in the daytime. So that they can pack up her room.'

Between the lines was the point that Rex didn't know much about the daily business of the convent. Because he wasn't that involved. And yet the man wasn't point-scoring. He spoke like a policeman, experienced at delivering bad news but still human.

'So why am I finding this out from you?' Rex demanded, clinging onto the last scrap of indignation to which he had any right.

A pause. 'The view of my wife was that it should be better to tell you closer to the date. She ask this of the nuns, and, I am sorry, that they agree with her.' The view of the husband, quite clearly, was otherwise. But even so, it was his ear, two hundred miles away in a Parisian suburb, that got the blast-back.

'You tell your pisshead wife it would be better if she dropped dead. Sybille is NOT going!'

* * *

Later, in an armchair at Maureen's – still scorning the cliché of the couch – he mentioned the incident.

'Did you still send him the recording of your wife?'

'No.' Rex touched the phone in his jacket pocket. He'd toyed with fulfilling the promise, but realised that no one, neither Aurelie nor her husband, would now be in a mood to take him seriously. Restless in the latter stages of the bus journey, he'd ended up setting Sybille's weird song as his ring-tone.

'I've never told anyone to drop dead before.'

'People have dropped dead all around you,' Maureen observed quietly.

A point she'd made before, but no less true. His wife wasn't dead, but she had been snatched from him. His mother had, more literally, dropped dead: they'd parted at Lincoln bus station one blowy October morn, her to her job in the hospital shop, him to his second year at University. By the time Rex had reached Manchester on the coach, he had been orphaned by an embolism. Maureen kept trying to make him talk about it – to make him cry, as he saw it. And people had always done that to him: the WPC who broke the news, his tutor, the priest at home. The only one who hadn't was the poised, auburn-headed French girl who'd always seemed to be nursing some private joke, always seemed to be sitting opposite him in the University Library, long before they even spoke. Sybille.

'I'm wondering if that's why deaths bother you so much,' Maureen was saying. 'And why you spend so much time investigating them. You want to heal them. But really, perhaps, it's you who needs healing.'

Rex wondered briefly what Terry would say, if he was sat in here in Maureen's armchair. *Haddaway an' shite, woman, man.*

Maureen noted his sceptical expression. 'Your last girlfriend… Remind me how you met her?'

'I don't see why we need to discuss someone who's been six and a half thousand miles away for the past two years.'

'Isn't it more like eight thousand?'

'No, it's six thousand, two-twenty.'

Maureen's look of surprise managed to express just how unsurprised she was. She'd laid a trap, and she'd been right. He knew exactly how many miles away Diana was, because he cared that she wasn't near.

He sighed. This, he thought, was ultimately why the talking cure was never going to work. Therapists were like confidence tricksters, who hung around after they'd scammed you to point out how they'd done it. Having one of them lead him by the nose to sip from some well of truth only annoyed him. He should have been able to get there himself.

He was happy to agree with Maureen about something, he thought, as he headed out over an empty concourse. Whatever the reason for it, it was true that he was driven to find things out. And Mina's death still posed a lot of questions, questions still clamouring for an answer. That was why he zoomed in on an immaculately-clad Jan Navitsky, striding the other way with laptop and folder. He looked like they'd taught him to walk that way at his swanky international boarding school: the stride of success.

'The man with the chequered past,' Rex said, approaching

him across the concrete flags.

Navitsky slowed down and smiled, as if flattered by the reference. 'You read widely.'

'Only when something bothers me. Was Mina the only girl you had a problem with, Mr Navitsky?'

The smile vanished, a fly swallowed by a frog. 'What do you mean?'

'Have you got a girlfriend?'

He knew he was pushing his luck now. He wasn't a policeman. He just wanted to see the young President's reaction. It was hard to gauge, though, because the strains of Peter's song suddenly came out of Rex's pocket. Someone was calling him. The dentist. He remembered sticking a note on the fridge: *Don't Forget*. He'd forgotten. Hearing the song, Navitsky's expression seemed to change like an autumn day: anger, bewilderment, then amazement.

'*Drobna drabnitsa!*' he said. 'Who is the girl?'

'Someone I met. What's the song?'

'A Belorussian song. Like a kind of old drinking song.'

'A folk song? What does it mean?' Rex asked, as the messaging service now made an automatic call, and Sybille's recital began again.

'Not a proper folk song, just kind of old peasant thing,' Navitsky said, an almost pained look forming in his eyes. 'Like, "from a Monday to a Monday, we rascals getting drunk in the rain, if you laugh at us, we knock you down." Why have you got this?' He asked the question as if Rex might have been playing the song as an insult.

Had someone else laughed too loud at Navitsky, Rex suddenly wondered? A girl. Who had to be knocked down?

The young man's expression changed again, to intent

focus, as the second repetition of the song gave way to the odd bit, at the end, where Sybille suddenly sounded as if she was reading the news. Navitsky's mouth seemed to be shaping the words.

'Another folk song?'

Navitsky shook his head. 'The Bible. *Khassiy…* one of the prophets. You call the book Hosea, I think.' He made a wry face. 'In Belorussian Sunday school, you don't just listen to a few stories about Jesus. You sit and you learn the whole Bible. Can I…?'

Rex played it again. Like a wave suddenly hitting, doors opened all around the compound and students surged out. Navitsky stood, oblivious to them, like some Old Testament figure banishing the seas, reciting from his childhood.

'I wish for mercy, not sacrifice. And for knowing of God, not burnt offerings.'

Rex stood marooned, too, unnnoticed by the hordes with their modern student kits of lanyards and smart-phones. *Not burnt offerings*. Why would someone have taught his wife to say that?

* * *

Back at his desk, he had more than enough to occupy him before the tea-time update. Periodically, throughout the afternoon, Ellie would leave her desk and peer through the slatted blinds at him. Reminding him, as he saw it, of the rash assurances he'd made earlier on. But before he could continue digging, there was today's mess to report. There were reactions, official and otherwise, to the Trabzonspor club collapse to write up, cross-borough traffic chaos caused by the cordoning-off of the adjacent bus station to be reported on, some mention – without names at this stage – of an old man's ugly, unnecessary death. He remembered the two fellow club-members who'd stood on the pavement opposite by the Bosphorus café, and the unhealthy-looking man, a former builder, who'd said it had been waiting to happen. Rex should have got a name – that would be a useful line to pursue. But there was no point calling the club for a members list. Was there some Turkish-Cypriot tradesmen's directory, he wondered – like the kosher Yellow Pages that circulated in the Hasidic areas of Stamford Hill, for when only a Yiddish-speaking plumber would do? He decided this would all have to wait for tomorrow.

Meanwhile, the mother hit by the window at Tottenham Hale had emerged as a rare treat in a hard day.

'I just feel lucky that it hit me, yeah?' she'd said when he rang her for a quote. Her name was Ms Marquetta Driscoll, she was 29, and she worked as a cleaner in a local authority nursing home. "Cos I've got a very hard head. Serious. I'm lucky. The nurses and doctors all spoiled my little boy, so he got sweets and his mum just got stitches. And now I'm back at work, so. It worked out all right.'

She hadn't mentioned suing anyone, compensation, making heads roll. Her view seemed to be that life occasionally hurled heavy objects from the sky, and if you dodged them, it was to be celebrated. He wondered whether Ms Marqueta Driscoll, Tottenham-born and with a quick-fire delivery suggesting some West Indian heritage, was a churchgoer.

Someone clearly was – someone whose words had kept nudging at him during the pauses in the day's activity, like a dog begging for a walk. Belarus, the origin of Sybille's Old Testament lines – and presumably whoever had taught them to her – was a religious country: mostly Eastern Orthodox, some Roman Catholic, even the odd Muslim Tartar. Belarus was also, as he'd discovered from a glancing search on the internet, a troubled economy, a tuberculosis disaster-zone and, until the party championed by Jan Navitsky's father had gained some sway, as unfriendly towards protest and the general speaking of minds as Turkmenistan. On a website of UK census statistics, he read that some 1,500 Belarussians had declared themselves resident in 2001, but that there were thought to be at least four times that number living and working here now.

Rex wondered what they found when they arrived. Since they weren't EU citizens, it could only be low-paid work, like the stuff on offer via that shabby office off the roundabout. No training, no tax, no insurance, no questions, no rights. And if you lost your job, what then? Perhaps only the woods. Like Peter. Who spoke of sacrifices and burnt offerings. And why?

As he celebrated the passing of the day's mini-deadline with fresh baklava and a mug of Brenda's Special-Brew-strength tea, he heard the 'pop' of a new email.

It was another one from the UN address. It was from the account of the Scandinavian-sounding colleague, Kristian Lund, and Rex's first thought was that it had come from Helena, whom he'd tried to contact a couple of times since the morning.

> Hello, it said, *I am Dr Kristian Lund, Chief Consultant of the United Nations' War Crimes, Atrocities and Genocide Research Commission, based in Nicosia, Cyprus. I am writing*

because I will shortly be travelling to the UK,
to visit, interview, make archive recordings
with and, where invited, obtain DNA samples
from members of your area's sizeable Greek,
Greek-Cypriot, Turkish and Turkish-Cypriot
communities. I wonder if your publication would
be interested in running an article...

At first he thought the original email must have somehow got itself re-sent. But this wasn't the original email. This one was signed Kristian Lund, and it had a different phone number at the bottom. He rang it.

He heard that long, low tone again – pictured a phone ringing on a desk by a shuttered window: through the slats outside, things like heat, dust, date palms... He laughed at himself – he didn't have a clue what Nicosia was like. Helena hadn't really told him. And whatever exotic view Dr Kristian Lund's phone had, it wasn't being answered, and it didn't allow for the leaving of a message. Rex was glad. As soon as he'd thought about Helena, he'd realised the proper thing was to talk to her.

She answered her phone, pleased to hear from him, but she couldn't speak. An organisation of prominent Greek-Cypriot businesswomen was giving her tea. From the tone of her voice, and the alacrity with which she agreed to meet him later in The Salisbury, it sounded a long and painful tea.

She confirmed as much, with a shudder, as they met and kissed over cold, amber glasses of Czech lager that evening. She took a long, long draft from her drink, and he watched it, with pleasure, going down her neck.

'Better?'

'Ask in three glasses' time.'

Life offered many more intense experiences, of course, but whenever it happened, he couldn't think of one finer than sitting here, amid the dependable dark oaks of his favourite pub, with a beautiful woman, just talking, laughing, being. He was reluctant to spoil it with questions.

Helena didn't mind, though. 'That's the U.N. all over. We're a very small office, and while Dr Lund has been away in Rwanda, I got the ok to come over here from our parent unit in New York. If he got back last weekend, as I think he was due to, he won't have seen anyone to tell him what has happened. Sorry. I'll talk to him tomorrow.' She took another drink, almost polishing the pint off. 'There was just as much of a mix-up when he vanished to Rwanda.'

'And where did you vanish to this morning?' Rex asked, after fetching over a couple of fresh ones. 'The ambulance came, but I couldn't see you anywhere.'

'I told the paramedics I was a doctor and I'd been trying to help. They said to get out.'

'Nice of them.'

She shook her head. 'They said it for my own good. I don't have a license to be a doctor here. If it turned out there was something I should have done, or something I did wrong... I mean, I know there wasn't, but... People could make things difficult. I'm afraid that's how it is now. Doctors don't rush in and try to save lives. A lot of the time they rush away.' She smiled. 'Kind of the opposite of your job.'

'Maybe I should run away sometimes. Might make for an easier life.'

He told her what he'd said to Ellie that afternoon – the promise he'd made. She listened, watching him carefully.

'Well – I'm glad you went back to your job. But be careful. Sometimes, you are looking for one thing, and you find something else completely. It's not always good.'

'Has that happened to you?'

She looked reflective for a short while, then shrugged. 'The strange thing is, in my country, all this wouldn't even be a story for the back page. Everyone expects the government to be corrupt. Same in most places. Look at that thing from Turkey today.'

'What thing?'

She showed him via her phone a page on the BBC's news site. One of those strange slipstreams of global randomness whereby, as Haringey's Trabzonspor social club was collapsing, the real Trabzon had been, too. A former chief of police in the Black Sea town had been gunned down in the market: a clean, professional hit. The blogosphere was teeming with theories, from a clash with Georgian mobsters to some sort of government cover-up stretching decades back. Rex nodded as he read – remembering the images on the little portable tv in the club: the ambulance, the words *Polis*, *fanatik*. It explained why his web report about this insignificant Turnpike Lane social club had been getting an extraordinary number of hits from abroad.

'People here have reasons to be cynical, too. But they've had two years of getting used to Eric Miles, doing what he says he'll do, clearing the rubbish, opening the libraries up again. If this is true, and it comes out, it won't just kill people's trust, it will kill him. I feel sorry for the guy.' He took a drink. 'I feel even sorrier for Bilal, if I'm right, and it turns out some bent bastards in the council he worked and fought for basically caused his father's death.'

She was silent at that, as if she'd suddenly had enough of the subject. He remembered, then, how distracted she had seemed inside the half-open social club, as the emergency unfolded. He mentioned it. It didn't seem to ring a bell.

'Before you legged it, you were staring at a picture,' he said. 'A group of Turkish guys. Army shirts. Lot of hair.'

She smiled. 'Was I?'

He showed her the picture on his phone. She took another drink.

'It reminded me of the Atrocity Museum.' She shuddered. 'It's a place in Cyprus. You go on a school trip there – everyone has to go. The Turks have one, too. The bodies. The graves. The soldiers, before and after. The burnt-out villages.'

'They make children see that?'

'*Den Ksechno.*' Like Bilal, she almost seemed to become someone else as she spoke her mother-tongue. '*I do not forget.* It's written everywhere. Signs. The side of mountains. Like they need to say it. Who do they think is going to forget?'

'I thought things had got better – people going across the borders and things?'

'Turks don't go back much. Mostly just Greeks do it, to look at their old houses, and feel worse.'

'Did your mum do that?'

She shook her head, took another drink. 'After they opened the Green Line in 2003, an old neighbour, a friend of hers, went to Lapithos, to the village. And when she came back, she brought my mother a bag of white plums, it's a very special kind, from the trees that had been ours. My mother threw them at her. Chased her down the street, throwing the plums after her. *I will eat the fruit when the trees are mine!*'

'I guess they're not friends any more.'

She made a face. 'They never really were. She was just someone who tried to do something kind. Everyone knows how my mum is. In the bakers, they understand she will always accuse them of selling a light loaf because she's ashamed, she's been ashamed for 41 years that she has to buy her bread from shops now, not make it, like before. She's not the only person like that, who is never going to be all right. Just maybe the worst in our street.'

'You don't live with her, though, do you?'

She shook her head. 'It's still the street I grew up in. She could be okay – sometimes – but you knew she was only okay because she was trying very hard. Like at school, going to see the teachers. Or at Church, at Easter. And you'd also know she could... explode, at nothing. A dropped spoon. A schoolbook not put back in your bag. And then slap you, slap you so hard and keep on doing it, so you knew the only thing you could do – to save her, really, as much as yourself – was to get away, get right away.'

She'd coloured as she dredged up these memories, as if they stained her, and her eyes had become wet, but she seemed to want to tell him.

'But you could never know. Which one you were going to get. Like the time Yiannis locked me in the room... the room at the top we called the Turk's room. It was a day and a night he kept me in there. I had to, I had to wet on the floor.' Her soft brown eyes flicked to his face and down, embarrassed. 'I thought we would all be in trouble. But she did nothing. Not to Yiannis. Not Alex. Not me. She gave me this ring the next day. She left it on my bedside table.' She showed him a simple trio of garnets on her middle finger. 'Like she was sorry. Sorry because –'

Her voice died away, as if something too heavy was blocking it. He wanted to say something. He didn't get the chance.

'Rex? I thought it was you!'

He glanced up. His heart thudded. Browner and thinner than before, and sporting the sort of awful trousers that young girls buy on their gap years in far-off climes, was a woman he'd last walked away from, cursing, in a beer garden in South East Asia. It was Diana Berne, his former GP, former... what? He wondered for a second, ridiculously, if Maureen could be behind this.

'You look well, Rex.' Diana's eyes darted from him to his companion. 'And jeans? I didn't know you owned a pair of jeans.'

Maureen had called her a girlfriend. But what had it actually been? A couple of dates; an interrupted shag; a tearful break-up as she'd departed to work in a Cambodian hospital; a joyous, filmic reunion, as he'd flown out to visit her among the coconut palms. Then what? Boat trips, close tuk-tuk rides, shared looks, brushed limbs, clear promises, the betrayal of discovering another man in the wings. All without a relationship in the middle.

He rose from his stool and kissed Diana clumsily, forgetting which side to go, his lips making an unfortunate smack on her soft cheek. 'How long are you back?'

She sat on the spare stool, revealing further ill-advised purchases in the exotic jewellery department: a bracelet of coconut shell. Rex sensed, rather than saw, a bristling of feathers from Helena.

'A couple of days.'

'Long way for a couple of days.'

Diana frowned. 'Sorry. I've spent so long surrounded by weird Norwegian doctors I don't speak proper English anymore. I mean I've been *back* a couple of days. I'm staying. I'm doing some locumming at the surgery for Dr Shah while he's in Lahore and then – well, who knows?'

She smiled, and he smiled back rather more broadly than he'd meant to. Catching Helena's eye, or again, perhaps only feeling it, he introduced the two women to one another and they greeted one another in a certain bright, tight way. Then there was a pause, while everyone took big sips of their drinks, and everyone, in their own, separate ways, took stock of the same truth.

In Rex's case, it was truth spoken in the chirpy, toothy, Harrogate tones of Maureen – a Maureen vindicated. He hadn't merely gone from one doctor to another. They weren't simply named after matching goddesses. Mother of God, they even looked alike.

CHAPTER TWELVE

Thursday was a traditional heads-down day – the day they went to print. Like a weekly version of Christmas Eve, with its own special scents and baubles and songs: the wassail of the battered keyboard, the mid-time baklava box, the gift of coming in an hour later on Friday morning and diving into the deep , crisp and even snow-plains of a new edition. Rex hated weekends; he loved the ends of the week.

He was liking this one slightly less, because he'd drunk too much the night before. It wasn't the physical hangover – he lived his life with them – but the spiritual one, a result of having been annoyed when Helena abruptly declared her preference for an early end to the night, alone.

As he tried to keep pace with her up a windy Green Lanes to the 144 bus stop, Rex had rashly suggested this move had something to do with Dr Diana Berne. Helena, inscrutable as the Sphinx, had stood listening to Rex's accusation with curls blowing about her face, then denied even noticing 'that fat girl with the trousers' and hailed a passing black cab. Later, there came a text. *What a silly reaction.* (Hers, or his, he wondered.) *I have to go to Cambridge all day tomorrow. I'll call when I am back.*

He noted the absence of x's, endearments, or even a name. Helena was cross. Cross, he thought, because she had been jealous, had sensed some bat-squeak of a history between the other two people at the table, and worst of all, had had this jealousy pointed out to her. Women didn't mind you knowing what they were up to. They minded you telling them you knew.

He tried, and for the most part, succeeded in keeping it out of his mind as he got on with readying the paper for the final lock-down. But text messages had always bothered him. People complained that they were an incomplete method of communicating, too easily misread. He thought the opposite: they gave everything away.

He'd thought that, ever since a November night thirteen years ago, just before the accident, when his wife had been away at a conference, and she'd sent him a text. *Wot u up to? Xxx.* 16 characters, including spaces. Almost every one indicating that she had intended this message for someone else.

Sybille never wrote 'wot', never used 'u'. Neither was 'up to' a term that had ever graced their walls. And although Sybille did use three x's as a sign-off, the convent-schooled lawyer in her pedantically, unfailingly, insisted they all be lower-case.

He'd meant to raise it with her, but then he'd had a weird, embarrassing night during which his sister-in-law had drunkenly got into his bed and so, instead of being aired in a sensible, adult fashion upon his wife's return, the text had added to the bootful of doubts and resentments which the pair had jointly driven, at speed, into a central London wall a couple of weeks later. Destroying everything. Although it turned out the shocks were not to stop there.

After lunch – lamb-shin stew in a clattering room of hip, successful young Turks – he returned to the office to note the tang of Lawrence Berne's aftershave on the stairs. The Laureate of the Ladders always showed his face on deadline-day, principally to hold things up with tiny, niggling queries, and make legions of irrelevant changes to his own pieces, right up to the eleventh hour, so that the whole layout ended up off-cock.

Today, though, Lawrence had other business: a new missive from the lavender whistle-blower, this time hand-delivered. Brenda hadn't seen the deliverer: she'd been 'attending to something'.

'See, that's another reason we need CCTV in the foyer,' Terry said. 'Brenda spends hours on the cludgie.'

Brenda left the room in protest. No one paid this much attention, though; they were too busy watching as Lawrence opened the purple envelope.

> *Morecambe to Clapton*
> *Andaman Port*
> *He thought*
> *He could stay un-caught*

'Port Blair,' said Lawrence, veteran of the Finchley and Barnet Pub Quiz League. 'Administrative capital of the Andaman Islands.'

'Meaning?'

Lawrence shrugged.

'They're all on the coast then,' Terry mused. 'Andamans.

Morecambe. Clapton. Oh no, that's Clacton…'

Rex picked up the envelope. Ellie, used to the more psychotic deadline atmosphere on the nationals, was getting itchy.

'Can we do the mystery letter trail in the pub later, guys? Rex – I've had an email from Police Press Liaison. Some old bird with Alzheimer's has wandered off from her home on Morley Ave. I know you're under the cosh, but she's 90, and it's going to rain like fuck tonight. Can you get something on the website asap?'

'Sure,' he said. But he didn't get on with it. He was sniffing the purple envelope as he headed down to the Reception area, where Brenda was enthroned in queenly indignation with *Take-a-Break* magazine and a tin of her home-made lemon thins.

'Brenda–' He handed over the envelope. 'What does this smell of to you? I mean, apart from the lavender?'

She took it and sniffed it. 'Allspice,' she said.

'That 1970s aftershave?'

'Not Old Spice. Allspice. I use it in gingerbread, things like that. It's a kind of Jamaican pepper, I think…' She pointed to her immaculate counter, where a packet of antiseptic wipes lay open. 'If anybody had been listening up there, I would have told them there was flour on my counter, too.'

Lawrence clipped down the stairs in his tasselled shoes. 'Are you coming back up? Ellie's going doo-dah up there.'

'I think I've worked out who our letter-writer is,' Rex said, heading up the stairs. 'But it's going to have to wait. By the way,' he added, on the threshold of the office. 'I bumped into your niece last night.'

Lawrence rubbed the back of his neck, looking

214

uncomfortable. 'Yes, she's er gone back to the surgery, moved right back in to her flat… Trying to move on.'

'Move on from what?'

A look of alarm flashed over the top of Lawrence's gold-rimmed, half-moon spectacles, their owner having obviously said too much. 'Not my business to say,' he blustered, and fled back to his desk.

Rex added this vague news about Diana to the list of things he had to put out of his mind, and got back to work. The day turned out to be a long one: gremlins on the website, gremlins with some new update to the layout software, the promise of a quote from the investigations team who'd been picking over the Trabzonspor site all day, but who'd then buggered off back to Welwyn Garden City without remembering. The day wound up so late, in the end, that after lock-off no one had the energy for the pub, so Rex drifted homewards, alone, just after nine thirty.

At the crossroads, ancient as all the city's crossroads were, he felt a primal tug toward the pubs where everyone else seemed bound. There were nights, now, when he felt as if he didn't belong out, like a salmon, stuck on a rock while the rest of the species headed off to spawn. Many of the pubs Rex loved best had gone earnest in the recent boom: brewing their own ales, which came with tasting notes and a six quid price tag. And filled with kids, all pierced and inked up to their eyeballs, who were peaceable but looked askance at the man who was not young, yet not quite fully old and still there, among them. Sometimes, Rex just wanted to be at home on the sofa with a cold Okocim. And that troubled him. He'd always felt he belonged on the streets, on the top deck of the buses and in the bars, watching, asking, writing it all down. And now? Susan had talked about his 'nesting'. But didn't nesting involve pairs, pairs of creatures producing many more? Maybe this was closer to what followed when an animal crept off to be alone. It died.

Upon his return, he found to his sorrow that the four black cans of Okocim he'd pictured chilling in the fridge had all been emptied the night before. It was raining heavily now, as all the reports had predicted, so he took the hoover out of the cupboard to fill the time until the shower stopped.

It was an old hoover, a remnant of his marriage, and it gave off an acrid, burning smell, growing stronger the longer it was used. Thoughts of Mina came up again – Mina on fire, the petrol smell in the doorway. He realised he'd never truly stopped remembering it all, however busy he was, however much he focussed on other things. She was still with him. And the rest of it. The doorway she'd gone through – left open by the slipshod maintenance crew. The agency farming out the jobs. The officials pouring their bakshish into the poker machines. Where did it stop? And could he really hope to stop it? He had to try. And he would. Tomorrow. Thanks to today's letter, he knew where to start.

He kept glancing at his phone, resting on an arm of the sofa, as he hoovered around the sitting room. There'd been no message from Helena all day, and he hadn't sent anything to her. He had a sense that he wouldn't hear from her now until Friday, when they would pick up where they'd left off, point made, his sentence served.

He couldn't help looking, though. And not just because of Helena. He had Diana's home number still. Before she left, she'd said something about a free-floating, arty friend being happy to sit the place and pay the bills while she was gone.

He wouldn't mind betting the phone number had stayed the same. And he wouldn't mind finding out what had happened. Why Diana was back.

It felt wrong. It felt misguided. He did it anyway. 'It's me,' he said, when she answered.

'Hello you,' she said. It was that easy, he thought. She sounded happy, slightly drunk. There was soft music in the background. Or was it the boyfriend? What was his name – the Norwegian, Harley-riding, baby-saving doctor in the cut-off denims? *Kjell.*

'Are you having a party?'

'No. Annie, the girl who's been living in the flat, she painted my kitchen orange! So we're painting it un-orange again. With the aid of a box of wine.'

The pronoun hadn't gone unnoticed. 'We?'

'Annie and me! She's still here.'

'Oh.'

'But she's about to go to some actors' party in Tufnell Park. Without me, of course.'

He was in the hallway, buttoning up his coat when he realised he hadn't put the hoover away. Did it matter? The only thing that mattered was the quickest way to her flat in Archway, a rather thornier question since they'd shut down the bus station.

He had one hand on the door-handle, one hand on his phone when, from the other side of the frame, there came an assault of hard knocks. He jumped in shock, dropping the phone. The battery fell out.

'Who is it?'

More knocks. He put the chain back on and opened the door a crack.

'Do you like champagne? At Trinity Hall they've got their own label!'

She had a bottle in each hand, a long, green scarf thrown fetchingly round her neck, earrings glinting in the lamplights of a Wood Green night, like some goddess of high-end booze.

She frowned. 'Are you going somewhere?'

'I just got back,' Rex said, letting Helena Georgiou in, loathing how easy it was to lie.

* * *

'Let me get this straight, man. You feel like a twat for cheating. But you didn't shag Diana. And you didn't do the honours with Helena either?'

Rex sighed as Terry drove them south, in his ancient Chevette, down through the rainy, carbon monoxide circus of Shopping City. Terry had a way of summing things up.

'I did. I mean – I have. *We* have… But not last night. She came over – she seemed a bit – I don't know, manic. She had these two bottles of odd-tasting champagne and she just seemed to want to get shit-faced. So I obliged, naturally. Then she fell asleep. This morning she had a terrible hangover. So she's still in my bed. Sleeping it off before she goes up to Glasgow.'

'So Helena's going to be out of the picture for a few days now,' Terry said, meaningfully.

'Terry, I don't want this. I don't enjoy it. I sent Diana this shitty little text saying "sorry, something's cropped up at work". And I hated myself, because I…'

'Because you're a one-bird bloke,' Terry pronounced expertly.

'Or maybe a no-bird bloke. Or – I don't know. Seeing Diana again just made me...' He sighed.

'What fookin' pod did ye come outa?' Terry exclaimed quietly, watching in a kind of angry wonder as a pair of young hipsters in skinny jeans and rabbi-beards pecked across the road in front of them. Like many immigrants, Terry didn't approve of the people who'd come in after him. He turned his attention back to Rex.

'You want my opinion, bonny lad – that doctor's a nightmare.'

'Which doctor?'

'The old one. Diana. Starts getting it together with you then fucks off to Shangri la to save lepers. Right? She tells you to come see her, so you fly out there – just been fucking stabbed, hadn't you? So you still go out there, ten thousand miles, whatever, she spends a week cock-teasing in the back of a fucking rickshaw then up pops the boyfriend an she goes, 'Ooh can't we all be friends?' Y'knaa? Now she's back, on her tod, sees you with a fit bird and thinks I'm going to bollocks that up for him. Again. Whatever she's prescribing, man, it's poison.'

'Wow.' It was touching, in a way, that Terry felt so protective towards him. Unsettling, on the other hand, that he had such a dim view of Diana. Rex wasn't even sure they'd ever met.

'Now Helena... Well, you know what I think about her,' Terry said, making vague, curving gestures with his left hand, an aerial tribute to womanhood. 'I want to kick your shins, man, but I'm delighted for you. Seriously. She's class.'

'She lives in Nicosia.'

'Good for holidays. And hummus. It is hummus, there, isn't it?'

'But I want…' He stopped. Terry wasn't thick, though. The Geordie shook his head and laughed.

'You want to settle down? Is that what all this… doing up your house is all about – so you can stick a missus in there, and have dinner parties and spend Saturdays at IKEA having a barney about the pelmets? You?'

Rex said nothing. Terry looked at him.

'Hey, sorry – I wasn't saying, like, you couldn't have all that, if you wanted it, like, just… It doesn't…'

Rex let him off the hook. 'Doesn't sound like me. It isn't. I'm all over the place, you know.' He sighed, finally owning up to his feelings. 'Ever since Mina. I've been trying to forget about it. About her and… the whole thing. But it's still there. I walk past the caff every day and it doesn't go away, any of it. What she was like then. What she was like on that last… when we saw her on the floor. You can't see things like that and not be… not be affected, can you?'

Terry trawled hard for a response and finally shrugged. Rex laughed.

'Unless you're made out of stotty cake and Newcastle Brown.'

'Never touched broon in me life, man,' Terry said, as he swung right onto Falkland Road, one of the higher rungs of the famous Haringey Ladder. Rex thanked him for the lift, and got out, checking the number Lawrence had given him. Vonda Paul lived in a neat terrace with hanging baskets and a fake wishing well in the front garden. The knocker was shaped like a little hand. Lawrence had been right – everyone was building. In a year's time, Cap Ferrat would be crammed with retired scaffolders.

A door opened, but it was the one next door. A stout

Jamaican grandma stood on her step, a floral apron over a velour tracksuit.

'She's away. On a cruise.'

'And is that what you both say, when someone knocks at your neighbour's door?'

Jeanette Crosby, for it was she, cast an eye over him, seemed to find some traces of respectability there, and nodded. Assorted, yeasty, toasty smells came from behind her.

'It stops those boys pestering – Sky Sports, gas company, electric, there's always someone. Vonda says it for me, and I say for it her.'

'You realise that if it's someone with an interest in house-breaking, that's like giving them a floor-plan. They'll think it's someone rich living in there – and someone who's away.'

Jean took this in. 'You're right. It's a very stupid lie. We need a new one.' She chuckled. 'Are you from the police?'

'Newspaper,' he said, showing her the card. 'You've sent us some poems.'

'Aah!' she said, beaming. 'Heavens! Come in!'

As the kettle boiled, in a kitchen covered with Christian homilies and ceramic trolls, it emerged that Jean Crosby had sent a number of poems to the old *Wood Green Gazette*, but years ago, in response, as Lawrence had said, to two competitions. She denied having sent any more recently – or even writing any poetry. She'd joined a writing group up at the Big Green Bookshop, she said, and had been advised to try historical fiction. She was clearly telling the truth.

So who was the baker-poet?

'Your neighbour, Vonda… she never worked at the council, did she?'

'Vonda? Ha!' Jean chuckled, although she didn't explain why the idea was so absurd. 'No, just me. But what's the council got to do with it?'

'I'll be honest with you. I can't say in full. But there seems to be someone at the council sending us peculiar poems. Sort of… gossip, you know, but disguised. I'm trying to find out who. And I heard you'd left not long ago.'

The frank approach worked with women like Jean, as it had always worked with Rex's mother. They'd outlasted husbands, raised, banished and welcomed back wayward sons; they expected lies. Especially from men. Honesty tended to knock them off their slippers. Jean cut him a huge wedge of fruit loaf and sat down with a sigh.

'Well, it's not me. If I've got a problem, I say. And I did say.' She smoothed the apron down. 'I didn't like the new… thing… database. I said I was happy with the old way. Eric says to me, there's only the new way now, Jean. Actually he called me June. He always called me June. I went to see… that girl in… what do they call it now? Human Resources? No – the "People Team". People Team, ha! Of course. And she's one of Eric's… people, too.'

'How do you mean – Eric's people?'

Jean rolled her eyes. 'He invited me to his Church. I go to Zion Baptist in Hornsey usually, but I went. I'm not, you know, a limited kind of person. Afterwards I told him, I said, Mr Miles, it's just not for me – big television screens up there. People fainting all over the place. That was what did it, I think. He made up his mind. But it's fine. If I'd hung on another six months, I'd be getting two pounds and twelve pence more a week pension, so. Ha!'

Rex finished his cake and said his thank yous. Jean saw

him to the door, taking her apron off in honour.

'But Eric's "people" don't all go to his Church, do they?' asked Rex in the doorway. 'What about Bilal? He'll go to the mosque, won't he?'

'It's more about whether you worship Eric Miles. I'm not sure Billy's one, anyway.'

'Not a Muslim?'

She frowned at him, as if he was being especially stupid. 'On the day I had my little leaving... party there, I left my brolly upstairs. I knew I'd have trouble getting it back once I handed my pass in, so I went back up. I thought there was no one there, but when I was on my way out it sounded like crying. A man crying. It was Billy...' She corrected herself. 'Bileeli. The man just sitting at his desk, crying like a boy. And I asked him what's up and he just said. 'It's a mess, Jean. A mess.' I asked him what he meant but he just said it again and then he walked out. A mess. So.'

Outside, sitting amid the building noise in the little hidden, lawn-sized park that Falkland Road and Frobisher Road shared, he took out his phone to ring the council. He saw he'd had a text, from Ellie: *Spotted something. Call.*

Intrigued as he was, he didn't call. He rang the council. A woman with a South African accent said Bilal was working from home. In some senses that was even better. Bilal lived just two roads down the ladder. Rex didn't remember the number, but he did remember it was very close to the top end, and that it had a gate with a *Cave Canem* mosaic sign on it, despite the owner's lack of pets or Latin. He set off.

So Jean hadn't sent the cryptic poems. But she'd been revealing, in her solid, matriarchal way. Painting a picture of an increasingly cliquey council where the old, or those who resisted the 'new way', were squeezed out. And where, in the midst of the enthusiasm and the good works, somewhere, something had begun to go wrong.

As Rex turned into Effingham Road, he was instantly confronted with a clot of hi-vis and flashing vehicles. There were the ubiquitous skips and steel-poles and Krakow lads in hard hats down here, too, but they'd all stopped working and were standing about in clutches, smoking, all staring in the one direction.

Turkish pop was blaring at tooth-shaking volume from a house two down from the top. The front door was open, and Tesco bags full of shopping sat clumsily poised on the lip of the porch. An ambulance door was being shut, and close by, a suited detective was handing a pale, sobbing, rosette-sporting woman into the care of a black WPC. He wondered, in the absurd way trifles strike us in the midst of bigger things, if this was P.C. Lizzie Akamba.

He knew who the detective was: it was D.S. Brenard. He recognised the sobbing woman, too, with the red rosette dwarfing her little grey jacket: prospective Labour MP, Eve Reilly. And as a uniformed policeman emerged from the house and shut the gate, he had a good idea who was in the ambulance.

'I don't want to call you an ambulance chaser, Rex, but…' said Brenard.

'Either that or they chase me. What happened?'

The detective cast a morose eye towards the front door as the music was finally switched off. 'Missy here was doing a spot of canvassing. Comes to this one. Sees shopping bags on the porch, like. Door's open. Loud music. Thinks she'd better go in.'

'Really? I wouldn't.'

'Me neither, but she's a black belt and all that, isn't she? Haven't you read her leaflets? Anyway, she clocks there's water pouring down through the ceiling. Goes up – whatshisname's in there – the council feller, Bilal Toprak, in his bathroom. Fully clothed. Half of him in the still-running bath and a cracked head.'

'Unconscious?'

Brenard cast his eyes down, old-school, reverent. 'Dead as the double LP, Rex.'

CHAPTER THIRTEEN

Until the Toprak family was informed of the latest tragedy, Bilal's death had to remain off the news radar. At first Ellie had been keen on an unspecific piece about the prospective Labour MP finding a body whilst out canvassing, but this idea was blocked by her own boss at head office. In the meantime, there was plenty of background to be written in, and plenty of speculation to be indulged around the office. This ranged from Brenda's mutterings about 'a curse' on the Toprak family, to Lawrence's theory of delayed shock killing Bilal after his having witnessed Kemal's death, to Terry's off-colour suggestion that Bilal and the Trabzonspor club might just have employed the same shite builder. Everyone had a view. So much psychic energy was expended on this that Rex only recalled Ellie's text message several hours later. And when he asked her about it, she was at first unable to recall why she'd written *Spotted something. Call.*

Then, at a nudge from Brenda, it came back. The copy of MetLife, the student rag Rex lifted from the University, had ended up on Ellie's desk. Flipping through, and coming across a slot called @FashionFails, she'd found an old photograph of Mina.

@FashionFails was a regular column in which students, and the occasional, eager-to-please staff member underwent ritual humiliation by supplying photographs of their former, misguided selves in unfortunate, now-dated clothing.

'I don't see what's wrong with most of these outfits,' Brenda said, as the magazine was now displayed to Rex.

'You need to be young, I guess,' Terry said.

'I don't get it, and I *am* young,' Ellie said.

Nobody commented. The point, in any case, was not the outfit being worn by the twiggy, awkward sixteen-year-old girl in the blurry photograph, but the fact that she was in the old offices of the Liberal Democrat party in Crouch End. There, stuffing envelopes in the company of Eric Miles and Bilal Toprak, was the younger Mina. She'd been political at a young age. Rex had remembered the rosette, just not the colour.

'And two of those people are now dead,' Brenda said portentously.

'And Bilal made out he didn't know her,' Rex recalled.

'Well, there's a whiff of Billingsgate,' Lawrence said. He whistled through his teeth. 'The deaths, the letters, the council… Could they really all be connected?'

They used the white board in Ellie's office to sum up everything they knew so far.

'Mina dies, in what looks like a political protest. She is highly political, confirmed by friends and relatives as well as her web presence. But it's not clear what she was protesting about, and her internet posts imply she thinks suicide pointless.'

'Plus the when and the where,' Lawrence added. 'Remember? Why do it at the scrag end of the shopping precinct at the scrag end of Eve Reilly's tour?'

Rex added it to the board. 'Most importantly, she was excited about going to work in Turkey, with Kyretia Pocock, whose brother is…'

'Ashley Pocock, who's still thinking about suing us,' Ellie concluded.

'Who was fishing for a bung,' Rex reminded her. 'Who is lying about my abuse of him, and spends his days putting huge wedges into the poker machines. As does one Tex Ochuba, whose Works Department doesn't do any work, but seemingly dishes it out, via an agency, to people straight off the bus. One of whom, since we know there was a maintenance worker up there that day, and we know it wasn't Tex Ochuba, might be the person I saw on the balcony at Shopping City just after Mina fell.'

'The person you perhaps saw,' Terry added.

'I know I saw paint handprints. I don't believe they're Mina's, and we know where Tex was getting his staff from. Meanwhile, higher up the council, we've got a cryptic whistle-blowing poet with a fondness for lavender and baking; Bilal, sitting in tears about the 'mess' and lying to me about knowing Mina and her uncle. Two buildings crumbling, one with fatal consequences for Bilal's father, Kemal, followed two days later by Bilal's own very peculiar death – fully clothed, drowned in his bath with the front door open and the radio on.'

'Didn't you say Mina was in love with someone?' Brenda added. 'You forgot that.'

'I think she was,' Rex said, remembering the flowers and

the endearment on the card. 'But I'm not putting that up here until I prove it.'

'So what about the uncle?' Lawrence said, jabbing the ear-ends of his spectacles towards the board and clearly rather enjoying himself. 'Rostam.'

'Her lover was her uncle?' Terry said. There were groans.

'What was it you told me?' Lawrence went on. 'He claims to hate the PKK, Kurdish activism, and so on, to be just a successful businessman, but turns out he's a decorated hero of some legendary Kurd versus Arab battle in Iraq.'

'Lies about his past…' Rex mused. 'So what else could he have lied about? But on the other hand he begged me to find out what I could. He adored Mina. Keeps a present from her in his car. Same goes for the brother – just a bird-nerd. More interesting, in my view,' he went on, taking up the marker pen again, 'is the Students' Union President, Jan Navitsky, with whom Mina regularly clashed, who flew out of the country on the day Mina died, and is said to be funny around girls.'

Ellie frowned. 'So what are you saying – this guy's been missing ever since?'

'No, he came back a few days later – claims he jetted off to accompany his step-mum back from hospital – even showed me the photographic proof.'

'So why are you suspicious? Actually, look, it's not important,' Ellie said, folding her arms and sitting down. Rex sensed he was losing her. 'I agree there are question marks. But that's all we have. Yes, it looks as if there might be something dodgy going on at the council, which Bilal knew about, and someone else out there clearly wants us to know about, too. Maybe that has something to do with Bilal's death, maybe not. The only links between all that' – she pointed the board – 'and all this stuff about Mina, are just coincidences. She worked with Bilal – well, she was a political sort of girl, and before he was tempted away from the Lib Dems by Eric Miles, he was a political boy. Bilal denied knowing her – well, she was the 16-year-old, probably painfully shy envelope-stuffer who came into the office a few times while Bilal was forging ahead in local politics, so why would he remember her? As for your man at the top of the escalator, Rex – *if* he was there, *if* you saw him, *if* he was one of these illegals employed to do the maintenance works, *if* he saw Mina's death, then, ultimately, so what? He saw her death. You're not going to find him.'

'So?'

'So, sorry. I think you've got all these doubts because you knew Mina, you cared about her, you were horrified by what you saw, you felt a bit paternal towards her…'

'I didn't.'

'Well, whatever you felt.' She put both her hands together on the desk and leant forward, like Susan did in her Eisenhower moments. 'I don't want any more time or money wasted in this office, on this story. Got it? Sort out whatever's been going on at the council. Bust it. But accept Mina's death for what it is.'

She'd addressed it to the whole room, but everyone knew she only meant one person, and they were all waiting for his response. He gave it – a sober, chastened nod. But he kept his fingers crossed behind his back.

And the next day, a Saturday morning, in his own time, he went, with the newsletter photo, to a modest but smart little house in the Noel Park area. A sub-district of orderly Victorian villas to the east of Green Lanes, Noel Park had been London's first Garden Suburb, although these days it boasted fewer celebrity residents than the one in Hampstead. There was one well-known Noel-Parker, though. Down Morley Avenue, a dainty, tree-lined street of speed-bumps, red bricks and gabled porches, dwelt Eric Miles.

A workman – shaven-headed, shy, Slavonic – was fitting some sort of complicated lock to the front door. He motioned to Rex to walk in. Rex called out, 'Hello?' but no one replied. Encouraged by further nods and gestures from the workman, he went uneasily a little way down a bright painted, tiled hallway until he came to a kitchen where a tall, thin, stooped and white-haired old lady ran at him with a vegetable knife, aiming for the artery that ran up his neck.

There was no hate in the old lady's pale eyes, no fury or coldness. Rex saw something worse: nothing. Instinctively, he put a hand upto protect himself.

Fortunately a fat, cheery, Tamil lady in a green nurse's dress appeared at that moment, heading in via the back door from the garden, herbs in a colander.

'Ena!' she said firmly. 'No!'

At a few further, peremptory words, the old lady allowed herself to be disarmed and seated at a chair. Rex rubbed his neck, his heart thudding as he explained who he was.

'Sorry,' the nurse said. 'She's nervous of strangers. DON'T LIKE OUTSIDE ISN'T IT?' she shouted at the old lady. 'BUT YOU STILL TRY AND GET OUT, ENA? NAUGHTY ISN'T IT?' She looked apologetically back to Rex. 'Got out yesterday. Had police, everybody, looking for her.'

Rex remembered Ellie's request for the website. A woman down Morley Avenue. Had it been Mrs Miles?

The nurse looked at him expectantly. 'So, *s: Haringey*? Is that social services, police, what is it?'

'It's a newspaper. I wanted to see Eric.'

'Ah. I thought it was about Ena. He's not here. Gone church. Only Ena's here. Eric's Mum. Sit – it's ok – sit.'

She motioned to the table where the old lady was sitting, with an open book of crosswords. Nervously, Rex sat. She had a big, brainy-looking forehead, he realised, like her son.

'LOVES THE PUZZLES DON'T YOU ENA?' bellowed the nurse. 'Crosswords,' she added, for Rex's benefit. 'Used to be librarian.'

'I was a *library assistant*,' said Ena Miles, quietly and precisely, looking up from her puzzles to meet Rex keenly in the eye. She was telling him that she could hear perfectly clearly. 'First in Glasgow, then down here. Forty-two years. Now it's just crosswords.'

'Not just that,' the nurse said softly. 'Come on.'

'I've always liked libraries,' Rex said.

'Eric never reads,' Ena said flatly.

'Good talker though, innit, Eric is, Mrs M?' said the nurse, putting a hand on Ena's bony shoulder. 'Has to be. For Church and council and that.' She hadn't bellowed this, but spoken like a friend. In response, Ena Miles had briefly put a veined, bird-like claw on top of the Tamil nurse's fingers. Things often weren't quite what they seemed. These women liked each other.

'Yes, good at that,' said Ena. She started crying. 'Oh my Jackie. Where's Jackie now?'

Rex didn't know what to say. He took in the kitchen – new and immaculate, a gleaming mixer on the worktop, next to a nippy little digital radio, next to the sort of big, chipped brown pudding bowl his own mum had used. A space shared between a middle-aged man and an elderly woman. Could he have ended up like this, too, if his mum had lived? Rex declined biscuits, left a message for Eric Miles, said goodbye, and went. The pale workman smiled broadly, as if it was safe to do so, now that Rex was leaving.

He took a long walk back, through blossomy, sunny streets down to Lordship Lane, and then headed back along Westbury Avenue towards his home. The route took him past Bosphorus Continental, the odd, ancient, handwritten notice about the magazines still fading slowly in the window. He went in. A headscarved girl with glittering eyes and loud earphones was sitting at the counter. He asked after Aran. She gave him twenty Marlboro. He asked again. Reluctantly she let one, tiny, hissing earbud out of the folds just long enough for him to state his business a third time. 'He's not on today?' she said, or rather queried. Then she frowned. 'Was you the guy what was…?' A look of alarm flashed across her face, then she shuddered, shook her head. 'No, course you're not.' She looked all set to restore her live-feed to Miley Cyrus, but Rex stopped her.

'The guy what was what?'

'This other guy was asking after him, few days back. But I…' She blinked, the toughness fading for an instant. 'I realised it couldn't be you because then you'd be dead.'

This was bizarre. 'Why am I dead?'

'I'm not saying you're dead. I'm saying that guy's dead. The one that came here looking for Aran. Fat bloke, glasses. He came here, then like, a day or two later, I was reading about him on the news? That Turkish guy. Worked for the council.'

As she withdrew into her music, Rex went round the

shelves, filling a basket, only half-aware of what he was putting into it. So Bilal had been here, looking for Aran. It was a long way off the council-man's turf, though not far from his father's textile factory. What business could they have had together?

Still deep in thought, he took sucuk, pastirma, olives and a wad of the stippled, mattress-like Kurdish bread up to the counter. The girl stowed them wordlessly in a carrier bag. It wasn't the usual flimsy affair you got in local supermarkets, but something hefty they'd had printed themselves. Bosphorus Continental Market, a yellow sun, a peacock.

'Nice bags,' he said to the girl.

She flashed him a disgusted look, snatching one of the headphones out again. 'What?'

'It doesn't matter. Actually...' He jumped in before the headphone went back. 'Seeing as I'm not dead, can I ask you a question?'

A faint smile came his way.

'Do you know what he wanted? The fat man?'

She shook her head. 'He said he kept trying to call. He said to tell Aran... he was too late.'

'Too late?'

'He said he was too late, and he wanted to know what happened,' she said, nodding. 'That was it. No. There was something else. When he was going out, he said... I don't know why he said this... I thought he was a bit off his head... he said, "People like you don't need that sign in the window no more, do you?"'

'What sign? The magazines sign?'

She nodded, warily.

'What does it mean?'

235

She gave him a long hard look and took the other earphone out. 'It's meant to be how they raise money.'

'Who?'

A long pause. She went on, eyes downcast. 'They go round Kurdish businesses and that, saying it's raising money for *peshmerga*. For the PKK. They do where I'm from, anyway.'

'Where are you from?'

'Edmonton,' was the unexotic answer.

'So why doesn't this shop want to stock them?'

She frowned at him. 'Stock them? They don't exist. There aren't any magazines. They just say it.'

'Who's "they"? And why did Bilal say you don't need it anymore?'

She shot him a withering look and put the ear-bud back in. As he lugged the shopping back to his house, he wondered about the conversation. He could remember his mother telling him about a Catholic Social Club in Lincoln, where they used to pass a hat round at the end of the night. Everyone said it was for the band, even when there wasn't a band, because the money was going over the Irish Sea, to the I.R.A. You weren't forced to give, of course, but it took some nerve to pass the hat on without putting something in it. Perhaps the PKK raised its funds in the same way. And old Keko, with his own brand of Marxist internationalism, didn't want to play along.

What did any of that have to do with Bilal, though? Perhaps nothing. But Bilal knew Mina. He'd forgotten that. The photo in the student magazine had shown her working with Bilal, and Eric Miles. Could Bilal's trip to the supermarket have been connected to that?

At home, still mulling it over, he ate a small snack and

cleared up. Most of the time he felt as if he'd forgotten all ways of living, other than alone. Occasionally, though, doing the most mundane things, he had a sense of peering down a little hole into another, older life. Putting a new duvet cover on. Scrubbing the bath. And now, as he washed a plate and a cup – something he might once have done with his wife next to him, her putting the food away, or niggling him, half-jokingly, about how much he'd eaten – he felt briefly, intensely incomplete.

OK. See you. That had been Diana's response to his hurried, lying, bail-out message on Thursday night. Since then, nothing. He remembered Terry's forceful comments in the car and thought he had a point. Then he thought, uncharitably, that a man in his early fifties who still went trawling Tottenham night-spots for one-night-stands, was bound to have a cynical view of womankind. But perhaps Rex did, too. Otherwise, why do this? Why bugger two people about?

He looked at his phone. It rang. His spirits lifted – it was Helena.

'How are Scotland's Cypriots?'

'Cold,' she said. 'Cold and fat. Do you know, they've invented a new dish? It's deep-fried halloumi. In batter. But this is the best bit. They put the battered halloumi into a pie. With curried macaroni. You would probably like it. I am going to bring you one.'

'One? I want six.'

'You can have one, and me. That should be enough for you.'

He paused, more surprised than embarrassed by her sudden switch into phone-vamp. She seemed to sense the pause.

'Are you okay, sweetie? I sent you a lot of messages.'

It was true, she had. On Friday, making her slow, hungover way to Scotland, Helena had sent him a slew of photos: the train indicators at Tottenham Hale all saying cancelled, her big, frosted, hair-of-the-dog G&T in the Stansted Airport bar, an entire family dressed in tartan. He'd replied to the first two, had meant to reply to the rest, then given up. The frantic messaging didn't bother him, exactly, but nor did it seem quite like her. Or quite like he'd thought she was.

'I'm fine,' he said. 'Sorry I didn't reply. It was another frantic day.'

'I thought Fridays were your easy day.'

'They are when no bodies show up.'

She laughed, but then realised he was serious. 'Really a body?'

'Bilal Toprak. The guy whose dad died in the social club.' The club right opposite the Bosphorus Cafe, Rex suddenly thought. Keko's place. Bilal had told the shop-girl he was 'too late'. As, indeed he had been, arriving at the scene of the accident to find his father breathing his last. He wanted to know 'what happened'. That, surely, was why Bilal had gone round to the supermarket. The café had been shut, ordered to close by the police. So he'd gone, agitated, upset, to the supermarket, hoping Aran could tell him.

'Are you still there?'

'Sorry, yes.'

'I said what happened? To Bil – to that man?'

'I don't know. I don't think anyone knows what happened.'

'But they're trying to find out, right?'

'Of course.'

She said something indistinct. He asked her to repeat it.

'I miss you, honey,' she said. 'I'll see you on Tuesday night, yes?'

'With the pies.'

'With one pie. Unless I've eaten it for insulation.'

'Cold in those churches?'

'I haven't even seen inside a church. That's the main difference. Everything I've done in London – with Greeks, I mean – it's in a church. That one in Palmer's Green, Twelve Apostles...they even sent me a link, to a website, about their church, before I came. In Glasgow, no. Everything in this one, horrible old library.'

He suggested that perhaps Glasgow's Greek Cypriots were all communists. She said that was unlikely. They said their good byes, and hung up.

He realised, as he finished the washing-up, that something was bugging him, like an item of shopping he knew he needed, but wasn't on the list. It was Helena, or to do with Helena. Not just her behaving in ways he didn't expect. Something else. A feeling he was sure he'd felt before, but equally, couldn't recall when. Had she said something? Something that didn't make sense?

At the same time he was looking forward to her return on Tuesday night. And he couldn't remember the last time he'd looked forward to seeing someone. Terry was right. Why mess that up?

His hopeful mood lasted as long as it took him to wring out the dishcloth and drape it over the taps. There was a knock at the door. Ellie was standing on the porch with a copy of yesterday's *s: Haringey*.

'Thanks, but I've already read it.'

'Let me in, Rex.'

As she went past him down the hallway, her smell made him feel a brief tug of desire, not for Ellie, but for the situation. Of a woman coming in, from the outside: a unique mix of the rain and the streets, perfume and hair. The musk of assignations, lovers coming back.

On Rex's kitchen table, Ellie spread the paper out. Flipped past the news, the diary, the arts round-up, Lawrence's page of witticisms, the teaser section for the parent paper's weekend edition. To the Announcements. An *In Memoriam*.

> *Tarcey, Rex (30.9.1973-5.4.2015). Beloved friend.*
> *A sad loss.*

'Well they got my birthdate right.'

'Let's hope that's the only thing,' Ellie said, glancing up.

The death date was the 5th of April. Next Thursday.

'I might just stay in bed on Thursday if it's all right with you,' Rex said.

She ignored him. 'I did the final check before lock-off. I guess 'cause of the typo it just didn't register. Any ideas who might be behind it?'

'Thousands. Ranging from Ashley Pocock to a girl whose vintage scarf I ruined at a dance in Louth Scout Hall in 1990. Can't we trace the payment?'

'It's not that simple. The classifieds are all handled centrally now, and they can be placed via the web. Like this one. They used a Hotmail account and a top-up debit card. The police could find out more, and as your *de facto* line manager, I am...'

Ellie was slipping before his eyes into the check-sheet, tick-box, brain-off droid persona she'd learnt on her grown-up, modern paper. He dived in before her.

'It's a joke, Ellie. A prank. When I was at university, I said I'd be dead by the time I was 44. Every now and then, a few of my old chums like to remind me. Nothing to worry about.'

Her eyes narrowed. 'That's bullshit. If you thought that, why ask me if the payment could be traced?'

'I just wondered which of my old chums had done it.'

'You haven't got any old chums, Rex. You don't want the police involved because you think it's got something to do with the council, or your Mina-obsession, and if they go charging in now, you'll lose your scoop. Rex, this is a death threat!'

'It's a joke.'

'You've lost your grip.'

'I've never felt in more control in my life.'

'You're such a dickhead. Am I going to have to sack you to keep you safe?'

She left soon after that. Later, he couldn't recall if she'd gone before he necked the three Codilex with the mug of neat raki, or while he was doing it. He wasn't sure it mattered. The end point was the same, after all. Someone, apparently, planned to kill him on Thursday.

* * *

Another Miles-masterstroke had been the flogging off and conversion of the Borough's two handsome Magistrates' Courts into a mix of private flats and social housing. This meant that the Petty Sessions now took place within the same impressive, 1950s-built complex housing as the Crown Court and the Town Hall. *s:Haringey* had benefitted, not just from having less mileage to cover, but also from the occasional, comedy snarl-ups engendered by the close clustering of so many civic offices. A blushing bride had been nicked on her way out of the registry office, for failing to appear before the Crown on fraud charges. One morning, a magistrate sent a man to prison, for failing to pay child maintenance, unconcerned that the same man was due in Crown Court in the afternoon to give key testimony in a murder trial.

The Coroner's Inquest into the death of Bilal Toprak was unlikely to deliver comedy gold, but the press section was packed out. It usually was when the North London District Coroner, Peter Duncan, was doing the honours. A sparse, nimble-looking man in his mid-sixties, Duncan cycled between his appointments on a folding bike, and spoke like someone from the pages of *Little Dorrit*.

'The unfortunate gentleman's constitution was assailed, not merely by the sudden loss of his father, but by high blood pressure and a recent but persistent history of fainting and occasioning unto himself significant injuries thereby.'

Rex glanced around him. Many of the kids sent by the nationals weren't even bothering to take notes. At this Monday morning inquest, they were just waiting for the verdict, and hoping in the interim that Duncan might say something antiquated and quotable.

The cub-hacks' inactivity might also, in fairness, have been because they were as baffled as everyone else at the way things were heading. Eve Reilly, wan and black-suited, had just given her evidence, describing how she'd been canvassing and leafleting in the area when she'd come across an open door, two bags of untended shopping, and a great deal of noise from the stereo. Noticing that water was dripping through the ceiling, she had gone upstairs to the bathroom, to find the bath overflowing, and the body of Bilal, fully dressed, with a head-wound, half-in, and half-out of the full bath.

A cool, cocky young pathologist had then taken the stand to explain his findings. Bilal, it seemed, had sustained more than minor injuries when he fainted and fell at the Trabzonspor collapse. The fall had caused some swelling on the brain; he had also had two long-term conditions: diabetes, and high blood pressure, and the combination of these things had led to him, in a confused and debilitated state, forgetting his shopping, going upstairs to run a bath before suffering a stroke, knocking himself unconscious as he fell and then drowning in his bath.

'My arse,' said Terry. The coroner had given him a sharp look through his tiny round glasses, but it was what many in the room clearly felt. And Duncan paid some recognition to that in his final summing-up:

'Many elements of this regrettable case seem unusual – the shopping bags in the doorway, the stereogram at high volume – yet they are clearly indicative in themselves of a man in the state of diminished cognitive capacity that can precede a stroke. This is confirmed by the subsequent misfortunes with which Mr Bilal Toprak met upstairs in his bathroom, as well as by what the autopsy was able to conclude, with acceptable levels of scientific certainty, after examining a body that had rested in running water for a number of hours. My verdict is inadequate and imprecise, given the complexities of the matter, but it is the only one permissible in the circumstances. Since we cannot determine whether Bilal Toprak would have survived his stroke had he not banged his head and fallen into the bath, it would be agreeable if we could give a verdict

243

of accidental death *and* natural causes. Since such a capacity does not exist in English Law, we must instead declare a narrative verdict. Thank you.'

Amid the ensuing chatter, Mike Bond, Brenda's husband who now worked as a Coroner's Officer, stood and asked people to leave quickly and to refrain from discussing it in the corridors. Another inquest, he explained, was taking place straight away – the sudden death of a three-year-old girl in her bed. Out of consideration for the family, he urged people to let it start with speed and dignity.

Everyone complied, shuffling out of the court-room in one subdued group, eyes down, trying to avoid looking at the pale, red-eyed, ruined people waiting their turn. Rex found himself next to Eve Reilly as they emerged onto the street.

'Christ, I could murder a smoke,' she said.

He sensed a touch of the matey gambit. 'Not one my vices,' he said, with a smile. 'Sorry. Been to the Bosphorus, I see,' he added, pointing at her carrier bag.

'They're my constituents,' she said.

'You mean they might be.'

She made a brief sideways gesture with her head, as if deflecting a blow. 'Was that you loudly expressing your doubts in there?'

'That was me,' said Terry, joining them. 'I dunno, though. The pathologist bloke's probably right. Just looks weird, because Bilal was acting weird. I definitely saw him whack his head when he fell at that club place.'

'What do you think?' Eve Reilly asked, looking at Rex.

'Why do you want to know?'

'Jesus – is he always like this?' she asked Terry. Eve Reilly strode off, stowing the carrier bag inside her voluminous handbag. Rex watched her go. He could have been more pleasant, acted a little less awkward. But something about her seemed to bring it out. He also hadn't known what to say to the woman. The truth was: he couldn't decide what to feel about the verdict. The circumstances around Bilal's death seemed to involve so many events and factors: long-standing illness, a shock, a blow to the head, a bereavement, a radio on, shopping on the door-step, a slip in the bath. It was like all the deaths he'd ever reported on, rolled into one, yet pronounced, bizarrely, an act of chance. That was, of course, what Peter Duncan's 'narrative verdict' meant: you had to know the whole story. And when you did, it made sense. It made sense, too, of what the headscarved girl in the Bosphorus supermarket had told him: Bilal, going round there in search of answers, agitated, out of sorts. What term had she used about him – *a bit off his head*?

He turned to Terry.

'Going back?'

'Going to Soho,' Terry said. 'Might have something for ye. See ye after.'

Rex turned back to the young crowd milling about around the entrance. They reminded him of the uneasy gatherings he'd seen, and taken part in, outside the university exam halls, nervous about what was to come, shitting it over what had just happened, comparing notes without any joy. In the midst of them, a genuine student appeared, a constellation of multi-coloured beads sewn into her braids. Kyretia Pocock.

He thought about approaching her, but then saw who she was with. Ashley Pocock, dressed down for the day in chinos and a bright, sporting sort of shirt, gave his sister a hug and then ran across Lordship Lane, car-keys in hand, dodging buses. Kyretia continued walking, a hefty string bag slung over the shoulder of her grey, suede jacket.

Rex caught up with her, flashed his card, introduced himself. She stopped, eyeing him like a racehorse abruptly prevented from winning.

'Why were you and your brother at Bilal's inquest, Miss Pocock?'

She fixed him with a teenager's beam of contempt. 'I wasn't at the inquest, *Mister* Tracey. I was in the Magistrates' being bound over to keep the peace. Ashley was there to support me.'

He remembered Brenard saying she'd get the Naughty Step after the fight. 'You were lucky. I hear the last person to break a police radio got life.'

'I thought that was going to be me,' Kyretia said, patting the heavy bag. 'I even showed up with a toothbrush.'

He smiled – unwisely, as it turned out, since this evoked another, regal look of scorn from the tall black girl.

'If Ashley sees you bugging me…'

'Tell him I was asking you about a word, Miss Pocock. *Tatlım.*'

She looked shocked. He'd meant her to be.

'The best translation would be "sweetie", wouldn't it, but that doesn't sound as good. Doesn't get across how loving it is. And I could tell how much you loved Mina from the photograph of the two of you at the Gay Pride rally.'

She might have a hard outer shell, but now Kyretia's top lip began to quiver. Rex made a silent, secret nod to the wisdom and discretion of Maureen, who'd said that Mina didn't have time for boyfriends, and clearly meant much more.

He pressed on, more gently. 'I might not be your brother's

favourite person, Miss Pocock, but I do know something's not right with what happened to Mina, and I'm trying to find out what it is. It's unfortunate that you're the person I've got to come to. But I won't stop coming. Because I knew Mina for a long time, and I cared about her, just like you.'

They went to the Jerk Shack. He'd avoided the place ever since the row with Ashley, but the sisters didn't seem to remember. It was possible that people were always accusing one another of being racist in the Jerk Shack. They certainly did it a lot to each other in traffic, and in the aisles of the supermarkets. In Wood Green, where everyone was a racist in one sense, and no one was in another, the term was just another way of saying 'fuck off'.

Kyretia asked for an ice-cream shake, an order that seemed to take up a lot of the sisters' concentration. Rex had coffee which, along with the ice-cream shake, didn't come. He took out his pad in the clattering steaminess of the cafe, hoping none of his colleagues came in and interrupted.

'You came in to talk to Jan. I saw you that time.'

'I think Navitsky knows more than he's letting on.'

Kyretia licked lipstick thoughtfully off one, dazzling white tooth. 'Well, he definitely saw them arguing a few times, in the office.'

'Sorry – saw who arguing?'

'Mina and Haluk. It's his fault. It's all his fault. Stupid Turkish dickhead. Mina went out with him once. Before she… You know. She wasn't sure about herself. Not like me. She went out with the guy one time and he took her to Chicken Cottage. Dick.' This time, Rex's smile met with one back. 'But he wouldn't give up. Hassling her. Calling her. So what happens? Mina's uncle gets the idea he's her boyfriend and has him beaten up. That's why she ran away.'

'And why you beat up Haluk.'

'Dick,' she said again.

'Yet when the police came, Haluk stuck to some story about you and him being lovers. Why did he do that?'

She shrugged. 'Because he's a dick? I don't know. Maybe he thought if he kept the Feds away, I'd be like grateful to him or something?'

'I don't understand. Why did Mina have to run away in the first place?'

Her eyes widened. 'You ain't heard of honour killings? You think they're all nice gentlemen, you fell for that? Mina's dad with his nice BBC World Service on the speakers in the caff and that. Uncle Rostam and his generous donations. *Truss me*, yeah, these guys are old school. For real. Whatever they come across like. Mina was afraid they was going to murder her for having a boyfriend. And the only way to convince them she didn't have one, would've been to tell them about us. Which would have probably got both of us done in. That's why she ran.'

Rex took this in. He felt slightly unwell. The coffee and the shake arrived, but neither he nor Kyretia touched them.

'So what do you think happened to her?'

Kyretia shrugged, her great hooped earrings moving with her. 'She was alive. I know that, because she sent me texts. But she wouldn't tell me where. Said it wasn't safe for me to know. Then she died. So someone musta found her.'

'Her family?'

'Her dad, maybe. Or her uncle.'

'Not her brother?'

She snorted. 'He's a birdwatcher.'

'So you attacked Haluk because you blamed him. But why didn't you just tell the police all this when they arrested you? Tell them what happened to Mina?'

Back to the polar looks. 'My dad went to the police nine times when those players started in on him. When they threatened to break his knees. When they put a dead dog in the back yard and called the Environmental Health. Nine times, and the police? The police gave him a diary, some skanky little notebook from W.H. Smith's so's he could note everything down in it.'

'What "players"?'

She frowned. 'I don't know their names, do I? Started in on the shop for money. He couldn't pay. They broke him. And the police did nothing. They said he was just making it up because he'd drunk away the money and now he couldn't make that stupid Royal wedding cake. And of course, all the police knew how much he drank, because he was always being thrown out of The Swan.'

She sipped her shake. Made a face. 'Something stronger?' Rex suggested.

They decamped to 'The Seagull', where the burly Baltic lads were coming on like gangsters with their big coats and their multiple mobiles. Few of them were anything of the sort, Rex knew, as he fetched two large brandies from the bar. The real villains slipped in between, like wraiths. So that even the police failed to see them.

She scribbled her phone number on a beermat and he took it, thanking her. 'Did Jan Navitsky do anything with this information – that Haluk was hassling Mina?'

She laughed. 'Jan? No. Why are you so bothered about him?'

'Because he left very suddenly on the day Mina died. And there were rumours about him and Mina.'

'What rumours? Oh what – you mean Hollow Wayne?' Kyretia let out a great, delightful laugh, which temporarily silenced the pub. 'That's him! Jan Navitsky writes that thing.' She shook her head. 'Man, trust me. He sends them in to the newsletter guy from a tempmail. Last time one went in, I was first in the office the next day. My computer's down. I go and try Jan's. He hasn't deleted his history. What's his last site? Tempmail. He writes them about himself to try and look interesting. He's a dick. All men are dicks.'

Rex sipped his brandy, letting the warmth seep through him along with the realisation. He'd got a lot of things wrong. He'd forgotten, it seemed, that a lot of the people in his sights were just big children. They loved like children, were spiteful and furious when the love didn't work out. And they pretended like children, too. Navitsky's posturing in the gossip column wasn't, really, that much different from a lad Rex had known at Manchester, who'd sailed into town, every weekend, dressed like Lord Byron, only to have the shit beaten out of him. Or the brash, orphaned boy from the Lincolnshire village. In the library, telling the pretty French girl he'd been all over Africa. When he'd never been south of Spalding.

He looked at Kyretia, now hewing away at her phone keypad with long, neon talons, and he was sure, 100%, that she believed what she'd told him. She'd had time with it, of course. It was new to him. He feared the moment when it sank in. He took another drink.

'You've no idea where Mina was hiding?'

'Tower block?' Kyretia said. 'I don't know. I went round all the ones I could get to.'

'Why a tower block?'

'A couple of her texts said "up here". "It's all right up here". "Whatever people say about this place, the views are lush."'

Rex was silent, thinking. There was one obvious place to look. He wasn't going to go alone, though. He glanced up. Kyretia had drained her drink and was shouldering the huge bag.

'I notice things like that, Mister Tracey, the words people say, because I'm training to be a lawyer. I'm a good lawyer. I won a Junior Bar bursary. I chose to go to Turkey next year. I could have chosen to do a placement at South Square – you heard of them, right? The Chambers in Gray's Inn? I was offered. Four places, eleven thousand applicants. And the reason my brother said he knew someone who could help you with your pathetic skylight thing? It's because he thought of me. He's actually my half-brother, but he's all brother to me. And he was going to recommend me. To help you.'

'Would you have been able to help me much with a planning dispute?'

'No. Ashley doesn't know that, though, does he? Man's just trying to look out for me, help me make some money for my trip.' She sucked a tooth. 'And I did help you as it turned out. I got him to drop that stupid complaint about you. You'll be getting a letter about it.'

Kyretia Pocock gave him an almost pitying look and walked out. As she passed the bar, a plastic gangster thought about making a cheeky comment. And then, clearly, thought better of it.

CHAPTER FOURTEEN

Predictably, Lawrence Berne knew a lot about Sky City and the shopping centre next to it. In the 1970s he had commuted to his job in a Wood Green accountancy firm via the railway station that had taken up the site before. He had been present at the very first, tempestuous public planning forums, held in 'The Railway' pub on account of asbestos having been discovered in the old council building. In the company of an assortment of local worthies, Lawrence had looked around the first of the new flats, with their fitted kitchens, and unique vistas over the shopping centre air vents. He knew the history behind Sky City's advertised but absent 'playground', thought unnecessary because the Shopping Centre had included in its atrium one huge wooden, and ultimately unsafe climbing frame in the shape of a frog. If they should be pounced upon, Rex thought, by some pack of Romani mudlarks, high on Bostik, then Lawrence could probably lecture them all to death.

He had, however, answered the call, as he always did, because, in his belted raincoat and his slip-on shoes, Lawrence Berne was a hero. Remarkably, he had held onto a copy of the original plans for the Sky City estate, making him a damn sight more useful than Terry, who'd disappeared to Soho on some unspecified, mysterious errand involving an old mate. Together Lawrence and Rex worked their way through the 201 housing units, arranged in tiers of five on sloped walkways, knocking on doors where they dared, peering through windows where they didn't.

After an hour and a half of this, up and down steep stairways, whipped by an odd, dust-carrying wind that made them feel as if they were wandering round an empty desert fortress, they'd got nowhere. At one door, a ramrod-backed Somali granddad had invited them in, taking them for representatives of the council, and more or less refusing to believe otherwise.

Finally, though, as they were on the verge of quitting, a ghostly, paranoid-looking woman, with dyed black hair, and sporting more gold than Rex had ever seen outside a national vault, hovered at the crack long enough to whisper that she knew of one flat to which all sorts of people came and went, very quickly. 'The one next up', she said, trembling from cold, or nerves or something more serious. 'It's empty now, but there was people up there until last Friday. Lots of argy-bargy before they left.'

They were now outside the unit above her on the tier, which had a lime green door and a matching knocker.

'Someone, once, cared about this door,' Rex said. 'Even though they had rotten taste in colours.'

'They didn't care enough to lock it when they left,' Lawrence said, pushing the door open. They came upon a laminate-floored hallway, awash with envelopes.

Like all the flats, this was a small, simple means of storing humans: bedroom and bathroom one side of the short hall, kitchen and living room the other. Apart from one wooden chair, it was empty and clean. Very clean. In the kitchen, Lawrence sniffed the air demonstratively, as he ran a finger along the draining board.

'No dust. Everything honks of that fizzy stuff Mrs B uses. Cilitt Bang. I'm not Quincey, but I'd say someone's been here recently and left it very clean.'

'But not bothered with their letters,' Rex said. He said it to an echoing space, though, because Lawrence had already gone into the hallway.

Rex found him out there, on his neatly-creased navy knees, rummaging through the envelopes like someone searching for a lost ring in a wood. Rex picked up an envelope. It was from the council. Addressed to a Mr Emicer Majlises. He went for another. It was also from the council. For a Sree C Amji Selim.

'Odd names,' Lawrence said. Rex opened an envelope. It was a receipt of sorts, informing the tenant that the housing benefit for that month had been paid to the landlord. He opened another one, and it said the same thing. Judging by the size and colour of the envelopes, over half of them were benefit receipts for Messrs Selim and Majlises.

'Selim!' Lawrence suddenly shouted. 'Good Lord in Harpenden, why didn't I see it? Miles – Selim. They're all anagrams of Eric James Miles. Look!'

Rex looked. 'What about that letter you got? Not the last one – the one before. What did it say? Jee Islam Crimes...'

'Those were the words that were highlighted. Another anagram of Eric James Miles.'

They rose to their feet. It was a moot point who found it

harder' to do so: 64-year-old Lawrence, or 42-year-old Rex. Both were slightly giddy with what they'd found.

'What exactly did the other three poems say?'

'I can't recall every word. They're back at the office.' Lawrence winked at him. 'Madam can't complain that you're following the wrong trail now. Besides, she's off at HQ all afternoon.'

Brenda made no comment on the bulging carrier-bag of letters they carried past her reception area. She did, however, opine that someone who'd had death threats ought not to be running around the place so freely.

Rex, who had been managing to forget the nasty little message in the classified column, batted the comment back. 'I've never run anywhere, Brenda,' he said. 'What are you doing with that?' he added, spotting the bottle of champagne on the desk. A label he remembered, for a reason he couldn't.

'Some sort of promotional freebie. No one here else wanted it,' Brenda said defensively. 'It's not real champagne. It's British.'

Upstairs, in the office, they put the three poems together. The first two had confined themselves to making cryptic comments about the council: wasting public money and, perhaps, selling its services. The third had taken a more blunt tone: not only including an anagram of Eric Miles, but openly including the council's phone number. And the final, hand-delivered poem, they now realised, carried almost a note of desperation.

'*Morecambe to Clapton*.' Rex read aloud. 'Eric Morecambe. Eric Clapton. They'd kind of abandoned the subtlety, hadn't they?'

'Well, it was too subtle for us until just now,' Lawrence

said. 'Andaman Port meaning Port Blair... Eric Blair – real name of George Orwell. This is someone who reads a lot.'

'Or does crosswords,' Rex said, as the answer leapt into the light. Ena Miles had gone missing on the day the last letter was hand-delivered. A faint dusting of flour and allspice on the envelope because crosswords were not the only thing the former library assistant got up to in her kitchen, with its pudding bowl and its mixer.

He remembered the flat way the old lady had spoken about Eric and his lack of ability. Most mothers did the opposite. Unless they'd been shocked out of the maternal fugue. Badly disappointed by the boys they'd borne and adored. Could that be it?

'I think Eric Miles was in it. I think he was involved in the corruption. And he's been shopped by his own mother.'

'What are you going to do?' Lawrence asked.

'Bring it all down.'

Rex sat down at his desk and started making notes. He wanted it all fixed in his head, but he still didn't know the ending. He didn't even know the next act.

He'd barely started to get his thoughts in order when Terry came back, looking flushed and slightly twitchy.

'This you've got to see.' He sniffed loudly. 'This is...' He sniffed again as he went over to his laptop and fired it up. Rex wondered if the old mate in Soho had sold Terry a cheeky line or two.

More publicly, what the mate had given him was a little grey memory stick, which went into the laptop and eventually led to the menu page of some kind of video editing suite. Terry clicked. Mina's last YouTube pronouncement appeared. Terry moved a time-slider over to halfway through her speech.

257

Meanwhile, outside, an emergency vehicle could be heard. It seemed to be stuck in the traffic.

'My mate works for a post-production place,' Terry shouted, over the sound of the sirens. 'I asked him if he'd have a look at Mina's thing, kind of frame by frame, like, in case there was something we'd missed. Look –'

As the siren mercifully moved on, Terry let the piece play at its normal pace. It was footage Rex had watched many times before. Mina was sitting in front of a slatted white screen or blind, wearing a long-sleeved, wine-coloured top, no make-up, that wide, so publicly misconstrued hairband pushed up high on her forehead.

'People are justified in saying that their sacrifice has been futile,' she was saying, in the over-blown fashion of a person acting up to a role. 'Justified in saying that two more burned girls have changed nothing. Blame the parents. Blame the schools…'

Terry paused it. 'See it?'

'See what?' Lawrence peered at the screen. Terry reversed the footage and put it on a slower function, so that every movement and gesture of the speech bore the portentous quality of ritual.

'Look at the back-drop.'

Another siren-bearing vehicle drove by outside, its progress a little smoother. They waited for the noise to fade, then watched. Brenda joined them, wheezing from the stairs. The slowed-down footage revealed a minute interval, where the slatted blind parted, as if in a breeze, and a distant, glowing yellow peeped briefly through the gap.

'The NCP sign on the shopping centre,' Lawrence said. 'She recorded this at Sky City. I'm afraid we got there already, Terence.'

'I didn't mean that,' said Terry. 'Not the window. These bits.'

He rewound again and let it play. As Mina's lips began to form the initial 'B' of 'Blame the parents', there seemed to be a minute jump. Terry's bitten thumbnail jabbed at the screen.

'It's a different blind,' Brenda said. 'Nice pine toggles on the second half. Knotty bits of string before.'

Terry played it all again. Even the Whittaker Twins watched this time.

'The wooden one looks like the one in her bedroom,' Rex said.

'Someone's stitched two bits of film together, haven't they?'

'Why would anyone blame the parents for a girl setting light to themselves?' Brenda asked. 'Or the schools? It sounded like it made sense when I heard it the first time, but it doesn't really.'

'Because whatever Mina really said in the last video before she died,' Rex said, 'Someone got rid of it.'

Before he could say anything else, his phone rang.

'Rex, you must to come,' said a hoarse, urgent voice. It was just recognisable as Sister Florence. 'Please. There is a fire.'

Terry drove him. Fast. 'I'm hoping some sarky bastard copper will pull us over and ask us "where's the fire?"' Rex tried to smile. He leant his forehead against the cold glass of the passenger window, trying to calm the inferno of visions. Smoke, screams, shattering windows. Sybille, unable to move, to escape the flames. Was this all just coincidence? Mina dies in flames. Someone threatens his life. A nunnery, a hospice, full of the weak and the sick, including his wife, starts to burn.

Fate always finds a way to cheat us. We think we can prepare for the worst, by picturing the worst. But then what happens is the un-pictured worst, the thing we never envisaged.

There was a fire engine sitting in silence at the top of Muswell Hill. No smoke. No ladders. No crowds. No one to ask what was going on – only his imaginings in the void. Across the road, an ambulance, also eerily at rest. As he walked through the trees down the blossom-covered pathway, Rex saw only what he'd seen on every visit to his wife, for more than a decade. The low porch. The word PAX in wonky, crafty letters over the door. There was an unfamiliar smell – something chemical and unpleasant – but there was nothing else. He rang the bell, as he always did.

The fire, Sister Florence explained, as she led him through, had started in the back lounge. The sliding doors had been open, but for reasons unknown, the ancient curtains, made to 1970s standards of combustibility, had begun to burn. They'd caught, and spread to an equally unsafe pair of armchairs before someone had seen the flames and the smoke.

That someone, Sister Florence explained, as they stood in the damp, black, reeking lounge while two firemen took readings and samples, was Peter. Unconcerned for himself, the man had picked the unconscious Sybille from her armchair and borne her out into the safety of the back garden before heading back in to alert the rest of the house. Without him, the whole place might now be gone.

Sybille had been taken to the Whittington in the first ambulance, but was thought to be recovering from smoke inhalation. Peter, the nun told him, rolling her eyes, had refused medical attention, saying doctors were for the body, not the soul, but accepted the offer of a bed upstairs for a lie-down.

'How does a pair of curtains just burst into flame?' Rex asked.

'I don't know. But there is near to one side the electric socket. *Regarde – là!*'

Sister Florence pointed to a plug socket, scorched at the side of the sliding door. One of the Fire Investigators, white haired and stocky, caught Rex's eye and shook his head conspiratorially, one bloke to another.

'That wouldn't have done it. There must have been a heat source right up close. Lighter. Ciggie. Candle.'

'Nobody smokes!' retorted the nun hotly. 'And candles? Inside here at the daytime?'

The fireman shrugged, looking out to the trees and the park beyond. 'Easy for some numpty to get over that fence.'

The police were on their way. Rex knew he had to talk to them. An ad in the Personals, he could ignore. An attempt on his wife's life was something else. Someone meant genuine, permanent harm, someone trying to get at him, through the people he loved. But a pair of goons in a squad car would do him no good. He had to take this higher.

Before he talked to the police, he had to see Sybille. Before that, though, he wanted to see Peter. Sister Florence looked doubtful.

'He saved my wife's life,' Rex insisted. 'I want to see him.'

Reluctantly, dodging firemen and frowning at the thick, almost shitty smell of the extinguisher foam, Sister Florence led him upstairs to a small room where relatives sometimes stayed, close to the end. She opened the door gingerly, a priestess tending a mystery. Peter was snoring. The room smelt awful – not the downstairs odour of smoke and wet cloth, but the ripe, cheesy one of a long-unwashed man.

Peter stank. His nails, fastening a rough blanket around his thin body, were yellow, dirty clasps. He had his back to them.

'*Il dort*,' said Sister Florence, trying to close the door. Rex pushed it open.

'I know he's asleep. I just want to see him.'

He crossed to the other side of the room, from where he looked at Peter's bony face, with its sunken eyes and its slightly parted lips. The light from the window cast shadows and he thought for a moment that the man was like that famous, phoney imprint of Christ on the Turin Shroud.

But that wasn't where he'd seen him before.

* * *

By the time he got back to Wood Green, the sky was turning purple. He was trying not to see things in the gathering shadows, not to feel unsafe on the manor he'd come to view as a part of himself. He'd spent an hour holding his wife's hand in a stifling hot room at The Whittington, wondering how she could feel so cold when the place was like an orchid house. The doctor he'd spoken to – bouncy, cheerful, fresh out of Pony Club – said she'd be fine.

Outside, among the smokers in their dressing gowns, he'd done the right thing and rung Sybille's sister. He knew he couldn't hide this from her. And if his wife was in danger then maybe, with leaden heart, he had to admit that she needed to be somewhere else. Aurelie had answered this time – bright, clear, sharp. She hadn't gone off the rails. That was just something he'd hoped – an awful, selfish hope.

'I understand, I understand,' she'd said, feeling but not over-emotional. 'It's not good. But I cannot come before Saturday, Rex. You must ask the hospital to keep her safe there.'

He sighed. You couldn't ask for a loo roll with any confidence in the beleaguered Whittington. Rich Parisians like Aurelie just didn't understand.

'Well, if not that, then the police will arrange a guard, yes? You have told them already, of course? Now tell them that they must.' There was a whispered background conversation in French, and then she returned. 'My husband will make some calls to an associate of his in the Scotland Yard, okay?'

Rex bit his tongue. One of the reasons Aurelie had crashed so spectacularly, he had often thought, was because life failed to meet her expectations. She'd grown up to assume, as the women of her swanky *arrondissement* did, that some money, or a word to a well-connected friend was bound to solve everything. But they'd been unable to do anything about the cheating husband, the sister in a coma, the parents withering suddenly to nothing, the son in prison for drug dealing. The husband's friend in Scotland Yard would do nothing.

He had to, though, so he'd moved on from the hospital to an awkward, two-hour session, sweating for his painkillers, in the bowels of the Police Station. He'd been bolstered by messages of concern from his colleagues – from Terry, from Brenda, from Brenda's husband at the Coroner's Office, Mike. A later one from Ellie: *I heard. I'm worried for you. Let me know Syb's ok. E x* 'I', 'I'm', 'me' – Brenda was right about the self-obsession. But Ellie had texted, nonetheless.

In the cop shop he'd reminded himself that coppers, even the good ones like D.S. Brenard, preferred fewer details, not more. Accordingly, in his short run-down to the detective, he kept Mina out of it, Mina, and her uncle, and the doctored YouTube speech, his worries about Bilal's death, other things, too, although he sensed them all still there at the edges of his mind, a voiceless chorus gesturing for his attention. He said he might, perhaps, have trodden on some toes while researching a spot of standard Rotten Borough stuff at the council, but otherwise, had no idea who could be trying to kill him, or his wife, or why.

Brenard, sharp as drill bits, wasn't having any of it. 'You are not a man, Rex, who has ever come to my nick because he doesn't have a clue who might have done this or that. You come here, because you've got at least half a dozen barmpot theories, about who did this and that – the odd one, granted, very, very rarely, turning out to have some truth to it, despite all the pills and booze. So leave out the babes-in-the-woods act. Who have you pissed off?'

Rex was silent. He remembered Maureen saying something about talking, and how it could be a relief, a joy, almost a liberation. Rex took a deep breath. But what could he say? There were only feelings, half-formed, doubts that existed more in his bowels than his brain. Brenard would listen, as he always did. And then dismiss them, which he also pretty much always did.

'Look. I'm not bothered about myself,' he said, finally. 'My concern is Sybille. The nuns have a rather different idea of what vigilant means. Can't you at least keep an eye out?'

Brenard scratched his ear. 'You know the answer to that. What we can do, in an expedited fashion, is run a trace on the IP address of whoever placed the advert in your paper, and have a look on the CCTV-feeds from Alexandra Park. But until we know more, watch yourself. Don't get so drunk. Think about what you do. Don't sleep next to your windows. Do sleep with a phone next to you – one that works.'

* * *

That phone, Rex noticed, as he now headed away from the bustling safety of the High Street and into the loneliness of Morley Avenue, was nearly out of juice. And it still had work to do.

Eric Miles was wearing his smart, front-pleated suit trousers with a frayed, old tennis shirt. It had a faint pink bloom – something white that had been washed with red socks – and in an odd way it worked well with the man's current complexion, which had turned full-on puce.

The radio was playing gospel in the kitchen. Ena Miles was busily doing something with sugar and butter and the mixing bowl, and didn't even turn round. Eric Miles, who seemed to have been expecting a visit, if not this one, offered Rex a drink from the bottle of Bell's he was slugging his way through. Rex, who desperately wanted a drink, but gagged at the smell of Scotch, was forced to make do with lemon squash.

They were about to speak when Ena suddenly murmured, 'Vanilla Essence', and darted off to a little pantry area behind. Miles brushed the famous lock from his eyes and smiled sadly.

'She told me about the poems. I'm glad.'

'Glad she told you, or glad she shopped you?'

'Both. I'm glad it's out there and that it can stop. The funny thing is, she wouldn't even have been writing them if...' Miles shook his head, took another drink, winced. Rex couldn't help smiling at the face he made – like a baby trying a slice of lemon. Miles noticed and grinned.

'I don't like the stuff much, either. Jackie – my father... it was his drink. He always got it down with ginger ale. Masses of it. And you know what? When he died, the doctor said, if he'd drank it neat, he'd probably still be here.' He looked at Rex through rheumy eyes, waiting for a response. 'You don't think that's remarkable? I do. Things are designed. That's how I know God exists. Some things come together so cleverly. It's like a snowflake. Something that clever, it couldn't be chance. But it's not just nature. The things that destroy us, too. Like the ginger ale.'

The man was sweating, Rex noticed, although the back door was open and the room was cool.

'That was how it all came together and I started...' He frowned. 'I went onto a wicked path, Mr Tracey, but it started in such a simple, innocent kind of way. An ordinary weekend, eighteen months ago. Shilpa – the carer you met – I'd promised to pay her two weeks in advance because she was buying a new car. But my bank cards had got eaten up. I hadn't got to the NatWest to get her her money. And then Naji, from three doors down – he used to live three doors down, I mean, he's in St Albans now – tells me his whole property chain is about to collapse because he never got planning permission for his shed. It's a tiny wee thing, I mean... Here's a man, a decent man, needs a bigger place because his daughter's had to come to live with them and her baby... And it all comes down to one piece of paper. Just a letter, so the solicitor could say he'd seen it, and that would be it. I'll always remember what he said – "If I was back in my country," he said, "I could pay someone for that bit of paper and we'd be all right." And I started thinking, well. This was why I left the Party, stood as an Independent, got voted in. Promising people I'd cut through all the crap, use common-sense, just look after their interests. This man needs help. You see? It all started fitting in, like someone putting these little bits of a model together. Then he just comes out with it, and says it. "Come on, Eric – what if I gave you five hundred quid?" How did he know I needed exactly five hundred quid to give Shilpa? He didn't know, of course. Someone… something, that's the only way I can see it, it was arranged, to fall into place like that. He gave me the five hundred quid. Shilpa got her car. Naji got his house. And how was that any different, really, to him paying a solicitor or an architect or a planning consultancy fee?'

He looked up, seeming to seek approval as his mother came back with the vanilla essence. She paid him no attention and he gazed sadly back into his glass. His hand shook as he took another sip. Just as Miles blended the shipyards with Highland tweeds, Rex thought, he made a strange mix of a man calmly facing his future whilst falling apart. He had turned, at last, in his downfall, quite interesting.

'I meant that to be an end of it, but then Naji mentioned it to someone he knew. And Mum was getting worse back then. Alzheimer's. Shilpa was saying she couldn't cope with her, she'd have to leave. But they'd tried her on this drug, at the North Middlesex, for a few weeks, and it was brilliant. She was baking again. Doing the crosswords. Then they said, well, thanks for taking part in our trial, but it'll be ten years or so before you can get this from your doctor. So I tried to get hold of it. It's no' that hard, actually, there's the internet and… well, other ways now to get something much the same, but it costs. So I had to sell another letter. Sign-off on conversion of a carport into a garage. Nothing. See? No one harmed. Set up for me, Mister Tracey, wisnit, beautifully?' Miles asked, swilling the whisky around his glass, Glasgow roots coming up like the vapour. 'Waiting for me to make my choice.'

'I'm glad you think free will played a part.'

'Of course! I just hadn't reckoned on the free will of others. I tried to make up for doing the drugs-thing by selling another one – late-night license for a nightclub up near Ally Pally, nae bother tae anyone – and with the money I bought a new minibus for the Church. I said that was it. But it just went on from there.'

'I can't believe it was that easy.'

'Nor me. But that's still how a bureaucracy works, Mr Tracey. Pieces of paper. People, with the authority to issue them, and other people, with the authority to say they've seen them. That's it. Hasnae changed since… the Pharaohs in Egypt, probably.' A dreamy look passed across the man's sweating face: an administrator, dazzled by what administration could achieve.

'I didn't mean easy to do it. I meant – easy for you, Mr Miles. An apparent man of conscience.'

Miles nodded, the dreamy look abruptly gone. 'I wonder how many more times I'd a done it if had been just me. But secrets are like water, aren't they? Always find a way out. Always.'

'So someone found out? Who? Bilal?'

'I'd have been lucky if it was him, or the police, or someone like that, but it wasnae. It was a very bad person. He was the real owner of the club I'd got the license for. And he said he'd ruin me if I didnae work with him. He owns a lot of flats. Masses of them. Bought too many when they were still super-cheap. More than he could get the tenants for.'

'Up at Sky City?'

'There, and elsewhere. So we worked out a way of renting out all the empty properties to people who didn't exist, and claiming housing benefit for them. We got mother to come up with the names. Do you know – she remembers thousands of names – literally – old novels in the library, ticket-holders....' He tapped the side of his head. 'It's all still in there. I didn't realise she knew what I was up to, though, and she'd stopped using the names from her memory. Started making them all out of my name.' They both glanced at the apron-clad Mrs Miles, as she switched the oven on.

'Bilal found out,' Miles went on. 'I don't know how. He found out there were other things going on, things I didn't even know about. I'm still responsible, though. Evil is like that. It only takes one person to give in.' He shook violently, spilling some of his drink.

'Maybe you've had enough, Mr Miles,' Rex said. He didn't like the way the man's left eyelid kept quivering. And yet he did, to his surprise, find that he liked listening to Eric Miles. He was a good talker, even-voiced, but honest and expressive. Rex could imagine the sermons going down well in that spruced-up Gorbals accent. There wouldn't be any more of them, he guessed, except in the prison chapel.

'I taught for a long while. You knew that, I imagine. Later on, I went to Kenya, with the church I was involved with at the time, to build a school, in a very, very hard place. We joined up with some brothers from New Zealand, who'd been there for a while. I'll never forget one of them. Young man. Knew his Bible backwards. One night, in the drink, telling me it was fine to have sex with the girls out there, because sex didn't mean to them what it meant for us. And everyone was doing it. And it was a way for them to earn money. For school. So... so he was helping, he said.' Miles swallowed, with difficulty, and wiped his face.

'See, that disgusted me at the time. But I was no better, because that's what happened in my council, too. People saw the evil going on around them, and took it for good. Or at least, for normal. And if everyone was doing it...' He shrugged.

'People like Tex Ochuba?'

'Ah, well Tex isn't the only cowboy in Dodge City.' He laughed. 'Bilal found out about all of it. He got together this – a dossier, I suppose, listing everything. Names, dates, figures. He showed me. It was very thorough. You know, if more documents, in local government, could be like that...' Miles closed his eyes, once again, seemingly in rapture over a well-executed bit of paperwork. 'Bilal was always a capable person, but he'd had some help with this one, I could tell.'

'From who? Someone else on the council?'

'I don't know. Someone with some legal background. For all its conciseness, there was a wee bit of the 'notwithstanding the heretomentioned' sort of thing and... Well, you know. I suppose he could have made it up himself. But he's no like that, Bilal... he wisnae, I mean. Not the sort to try it on. So when he said, you know, he'd get rid of his dossier if I put a stop to it all, straight away, I believed he meant it. But how could I? How could I stop all those people?'

Miles had changed colour in the course of their talk – faded from pink to fish grey. He was shaking all the time now, like someone intensely nervous. He was making Rex nervous, too. He was nervous for other reasons, in any case, having heard a tiny bleep from his pocket, indicating that the battery was about to fail. He prayed it would stay recording a few minutes more.

'He must have been preparing to drop his bombshell any

time. But in the meantime, well… Mother was making her own efforts.'

Ena Miles put a cake tin in the oven and set a timer. She seemed far more on the ball than her son.

'I didn't do anything to Bilal, if that's what you're imagining,' Miles said. 'I'm a weak man. That's it. A weak man.'

'What about Mina?'

He looked shocked. 'Mina?'

'Mina Küçüktürk. She worked for you once, when you and Bilal were still with the Lib Dems. Then she died. I wondered if she'd found something out.'

'No, but…' Another painful swallow, while Mrs Miles sponged the work surfaces. 'I guess it coulda worked either way, couldn't it? Bilal told Mina, and she took the news to him. Or she found out from him, and told Bilal she knew.'

'I'm not with you. Who's him?'

'Rostam Sajadi. Her uncle. He's the one with the club and the flats. He's a dangerous man.' He looked Rex in the eye, a tough undertaking, since he was sweating and shaking so much. 'I had no choice about accepting the stuff for the zoo. I didn't want to go near him, but he told me he was doing it …'

Rex was silent, the truth of it washing over him. Sajadi: a dangerous man. Had Mina been right, then, to fear her uncle, to run from him? Was it time he began to fear Sajadi, too?

'What are you going to do?' Miles asked. 'I– I don't mind. I mean, I won't be stopping you.'

Rex sat back. 'Tell the cops. Print.'

Miles nodded. 'And I go to face justice.'

'You'll do two-and-a-half tending tomatoes with some disgraced MPs, Mr Miles. I wouldn't worry.'

'I'm not worrying,' he said blankly. 'I don't mean that kind of justice.' He let out a sudden noise, somewhere between a shout, a sigh and a retch. Even Mrs Miles, rinsing out her jay-cloth, reacted to it. 'I get mum's pills cheaper if I buy them in hundreds,' he wheezed. Then he shuddered.

It seemed an odd thing to say. Rex was about to ask Eric Miles what he meant, when the man suddenly grimaced, lifted up a hand as if warding something off, shook violently and slipped from his chair onto the floor. It was suddenly obvious why he'd mentioned the pills. Rex leapt up.

Miles was twitching on the varnished floor. Ena Miles turned from adjusting the dial on her oven and looked down at her son, curious. Then she looked at Rex.

'It isn't right, is it?'

'No,' he said, dialling 999. 'It isn't.'

A short while later, as the ambulance drove away with Eric Miles and his mother in the back, he used the phone in the hallway.

'I've got something. It's big. I'll be in the office. How soon can you get there?'

'I spent the afternoon being hairdryer-ed by the Managing Editor. He says if you've had death threats, you shouldn't even be allowed in the building.'

'What do you say, Ellie?'

A long pause. 'I've got a career too, you know! This isn't fair. I knew you were going to be a fucking nightmare.'

'Ten minutes. Give me ten minutes and if you're not impressed, I'll take the whole problem off your hands. I'll resign.'

A sigh. He thought he heard her talking to someone. 'I'd just pulled.'

'Bring him along, he can do a bit of colouring in the corner.'

'Twat.'

CHAPTER FIFTEEN

Brenard rang the next morning, just after ten, as Rex was approaching the Bosphorus Café with fried eggs in mind. From a distance the place appeared to be shut, but before he could be certain, he felt his phone buzzing in his pocket.

'What do you think?' he asked.

In the small hours of the morning, he'd emailed Brenard a file from the office. A recording of his interview with Eric Miles. Scans of the Housing Benefit letters. He and Ellie – in half-hourly contact with a frazzled *Sentinel* deputy, working from home and dashing between laptop, knackered wife and teething twins – had cooked up a strategy. Hand the story to the local cops and the Serious Fraud Office in return for privileged access to the arrests and the office-ransacks, then run it big before anyone else got wind. Terry was expecting so many photo-worthy moments over the next 48 hours that he'd got a mate haring down the M1 from Consett to help.

'I always thought they were too good to be true, that lot. I've passed it up to Borough Command – there's a strategy meeting at eleven.'

273

'So you'll be letting me know what comes next.'

'That's not a given,' Brenard said tersely. 'I was actually calling to discuss your other problem. There's news. Don't panic,' he added, hastily. 'Your wife's fine, the nuns are fine.'

'I knew that,' Rex said. 'I've checked already. Twice. What's your news?'

'CCTV on the park showed up nothing. Just mums, kids, canned lager enthusiasts, dogs. No one heading in the direction of the fence between the park and the convent. The IP address of whoever who put your death notice in the paper is an internet caff in Finsbury Park. They've started keeping a customer log, because of… well, you know, various agencies telling them to keep a customer log – who's been skyping their mates in Mogadishu and all that. There's a name. John Major.'

'Great. Have you arrested him? Did Norma put up a fight?'

Brenard ignored him. 'Does the name John Major mean anything to you?'

'Apart from the big specs and the unlikely shag revelations, no.'

'No one else has used that ID over the past six months and the owner doesn't remember what the person looked like. We'll just have to keep an eye on things. Have you had any more threats?'

'Nothing. How's Eric Miles?'

'Recovering. Look after yourself, Rex,' Brenard said. Rex wished he hadn't said that. As he looked over at the shuttered-up Bosphorus, he remembered the last time John Major had interfered with his consciousness. The photo in Keko's flat. Of another bland, grey man in big specs. Some noted Kurd? A beloved relation? He wished he'd asked.

He certainly wouldn't be finding out today. Despite the blinds being down, the door of the Bosphorus was open, and everything inside was being covered in brown dust-sheets. The Hungarian girl spotted him, and came over to the doorway.

'Sad, huh?'

'I don't know – is it?'

'Boss is decided to retire. Place finished. He gone to Germany for bit. Just kept me on to clean up it.'

'Too many memories, maybe.' Looking in at the forlorn room, he remembered Kyretia yesterday, although it seemed a lifetime ago, telling him that Mina had hid from her uncle and her father. He knew, as he'd known then, that she was mistaken about Keko. When the kid was in the corner doing her homework, her dad was always coming over, interrupting her with milkshakes and little snacks. Devoted, besotted, proud.

That was when she'd been a child, of course. There were cultures – cultures who shopped at the Morrison's, sunned themselves on Duckett's Common, just like everyone else – where girls seemed to become something 'other' as they grew into women. Something dangerous, to be contained, wrapped up and feared. Not in Mina's household, though. She'd been encouraged to go to school, to university, to be involved in the world. Keko could never have threatened his daughter, let alone harmed her.

Sajadi was a different matter, though. Rex couldn't see the man perpetrating one of those so-called 'honour killings' on his niece when he'd once saved his beloved sister from one. But perhaps business, to Rostam Sajadi, was a different sphere to blood. If Mina had found out about the flats, and the council corruption, and told Bilal, then her uncle might have wanted her silenced.

And what else was he capable of? Rex remembered how he'd gladly been scooped into Sajadi's car, outside Sky City, blindly believing that the man had just been parked there, thinking about his dead niece. Wasn't it more likely that he'd been following Rex? He'd known where he worked. Found out, from somewhere, that Rex had been asking questions about him. Like an idiot, Rex had shook Sajadi's hand and agreed to help him – never guessing that this was just a ploy to keep him on-side. There was no mystery behind the death threat in the newspaper. It was obvious who was behind the fire at the convent, too. Could he have also started the fire that claimed Mina?

He was so lost in these grim musings that he barely registered the Hungarian girl flitting back into the café and rummaging for something behind the shrouded counter. She re-emerged, with a couple of sheets of paper in her hand.

'There was a shelf in the back they called always Mina's Shelf.'

Rex nodded. The younger Mina had probably kept her schoolbooks on it, since the café was where she'd sat every evening.

'Boss cleared up it. But I think these were fell behind. I am going straight this afternoon to Hungary, so…'

She handed him the papers. They seemed of little importance. One was from London Metropolitan university: Getting Here For Your Interview. It made him sad to think of that – the girl with so much promise, heading excitedly to her new life, directions in hand, then taking a wrong turn. Or being pushed down one, by those she'd loved. He put the piece of paper in his pocket.

The second was a brochure for some sort of military-based weekend course. He remembered the army-run Fitness Classes for which Mina had had a schedule on her wall. The 'training' Navitsky had referred to, in preparation for her year in Turkey. This was a more serious version: it involved assault courses, target practice, evasive driving, hostile environments. Had Mina paid money to learn things like that? Because she'd been trying to protect herself? Perhaps he should be doing more to protect himself.

It was hard getting up the street, as always: double buggies, a bus-stop every ten yards, someone blocking the flow by having a chat or tying their shoelaces every twenty. If someone wanted to do him harm, they had ample opportunity here: a knife to the guts, a gunman on a motorbike, a car that didn't stop. Then again, such opportunities were available all the time, and so far no one had taken them. Was it just a warning, then, the death notice in the paper? It was possible, but what about the fire at the convent? That could so easily have claimed lives.

He forced himself to keep moving, keep focussing on the positives. He'd cracked a big story. No one would try anything at the moment, too obvious, too visible. The cops were looking. And Helena was due back at tea-time.

In her last message she'd expressed a longing for traditional food, so he'd booked a table at Kytherea, a Cypriot place in the unlikely suburban dinge of Winchmore Hill. It was considered so authentic that the Cyprus High Commission ran a monthly staff shuttle-bus up from their headquarters in SW1. He felt hungry at the thought of it. And of her.

At the reception desk Brenda appeared to be hosting a coffee morning. There were flapjacks out, mugs from the kitchen, and Lawrence was making a pair of unidentified stout old ladies roar with laughter. They all went quiet when Rex came in. One of the pair, he realised, was Jean, lately of the council.

'Vonda and I wanted to see you,' Jean said, delicately wiping crumbs from her mouth with an embroidered hanky. 'So we thought, while we're in town…'

They sat on the awkward foam blocks, next to a plant that looked artificial, but apparently wasn't.

'We read your piece about the Inquest into Bilal's death,' said Vonda, who was taller and a little younger than her neighbour, with a Bohemian look comprised of long scarves, craft jewellery and vivid nails. 'And it's wrong.'

Jean nudged her. 'What we mean is, we spotted a few things.' She removed a little notebook from her handbag, polished her glasses, and began. 'The second time you mention Eve Reilly, you call her Eva.'

'Oh. I'm sorry. That's the kind of thing our sub-editor is usually good at rooting out,' said Rex, looking directly at Brenda. 'I'll make sure it's corrected before the print edition's out on Friday.'

'Also, she's not 33,' Vonda said. 'You got that off the Labour Party website. She's 36. I know that because of that *Guardian* profile where she said she was "born in the year of Blair Peach, Maggie and the Iranian Revolution".' She snorted. 'Looks 45 with that new hair anyway.'

'She won't be getting your vote, I take it.'

'I'm an anarchist,' Vonda said, adjusting her bright green cardie. 'Ever since the '68 sit-in at Hornsey Art School. I was there, darling. And Jean's Conservative.' She returned to the subject of Eve Reilly. '*And* she was rude to Jean on that walkabout thing in Shopping City. Wasn't she, Jean, rude to you in the Costa?' She looked at Rex. 'Before you got there, that was.'

'Quite the different lady when the world's press aren't around,' confirmed Jean. Rex thought he detected a touch of irony.

He thanked them for dropping by, and they, for their part, thanked Brenda for the flapjacks. But a certain troubled look remained on Vonda's face, and just as she was leaving, she added: 'Can you settle an argument? When it's a thing like an Inquest, do you copy down every word, in shorthand or something, or record it?'

'A mixture of the two. I make sure any quotes or direct references are accurate.'

'So she did say she'd been going "up" the road then. How odd.' She smiled. 'I suppose it depends on what your "up" and your "down" are, doesn't it? My… sort of chap – Wilf – lives in Effingham Road. And he says he cycles *up* into Islington. I'd call it down, wouldn't you?'

'Well, erm…'

Fortunately Vonda didn't seem interested in a reply; she headed off towards the delights of Wood Green, arm-in-arm with Jean, her unlikely friend. Rex went upstairs, bothered by the encounter without quite knowing why. Was it what they'd said about Eve Reilly being rude on her walkabout? He hadn't been there, of course, when that had happened. But had there been other things about that day that he'd missed?

Until the police made their intentions plain over the council revelations, there wasn't much to be written up. For a while he concentrated on the print version of Bilal's death, discovery and inquest, sourcing, with a private nod to

Vonda, a particularly unflattering photo of Eve Reilly in her new hairdo.

After a short briefing with Ellie, he then went out to cover a lighter, local tale, involving an artisan bakery near Priory Park, at the middle-class end of his turf. Someone had painted YUPPIES OUT on their windows, the third such assault on themselves and the trendy beer shop next door. The police maintained it was the work of bored local kids. Rex's view, expressed to vigorous agreement from the tattooed, baffled young baker, was that no one under 40 even knew what a yuppie was. He left, with a warm, delicious-smelling loaf in a paper bag, and headed up the hill to visit his wife.

Sybille seemed flushed, and dry mouthed, although Rex wasn't sure if that was from the effects of the smoke, or just from being in the Whittington hospital for 24 hours. She was in one piece, at any rate, but it was sad to see her stuck in her bedroom, surrounded by cardboard boxes, when she'd been enjoying the garden room so much. The fire and water damage, Sister Florence had said sadly, meant it was unlikely Sybille would get to spend more time in her favourite room before she left. And that point was now approaching with inexorable speed. Aurelie had rung that morning to say she'd managed to change the bookings. She was coming two days earlier now. On Thursday.

When they were alone, he broke the news to Sybille. For a moment it seemed as if she hadn't heard. And then she sighed and said, 'It worked for her. It didn't work for me.'

What worked? The timing? Was Sybille saying that Aurelie was happy with the arrangement, but she wasn't? He didn't know what she meant. Ineffectually, he wrapped a couple of her favourite ornaments in newspaper: a china frog she'd had since she was a girl; a Murano owl he'd bought her on a trip to Venice; a slim bottle, seemingly made of bone, with Chinese writing on it. He didn't remember that. He glanced back at his wife, propped up on the bed, unsightly woolly green socks on over her tights. She was clutching something in her left hand.

'What's in your hand, Syb?'

'Nothing,' she said, transparent as a caught-out child. She kept her hand round it, but she let him gently open her fingers. He wondered if she, like him, felt any pulsar echo of desire when their hands touched, a memory of what those fingers had once felt like, elsewhere.

'Christ, Syb. Where did you get it?'

'Sister Anna-Claire smokes,' she said, in her child's voice again, telling tales with barely concealed delight. 'Hid it down the side of the chair I sat in.'

'So you set fire to the curtains with her lighter, Syb? Why?'

'When Aurelie came home...' she said hoarsely, a woman again, 'When she got sent home from the convent, that was because she'd set light to the music room. She made a fire. She came home to her room. She got to stay where she wanted.'

He stayed longer than he'd stayed in months, lying there with her, on the bed, his head on her shoulder, his hand in hers, breathing in the smell of her, hoping she couldn't feel his tears. From the way she patted him, occasionally, though, he knew she could. He hoped she understood, at least, or sensed, that in amongst his grieving there was relief. His life might still be in danger, but hers was not.

There was a certain look in Sister Florence's eye as she showed him out, a glint that spoke of expectation, anticipation: she knew he knew something, and assumed he would share it. She seemed deflated when he just asked where Peter was.

'Away once more. Into the trees,' she said, bluntly.

'But you gave him my message? You told him I wanted to talk to him.'

Sister Florence nodded vaguely, then suddenly gripped his arm. 'You will be here, on Thursday?'

'Of course. And before.' There was a silence between them as she opened the main door, which had now been festooned with extra bolts and locks. He assumed the nun was thinking of the same things as himself – of all the nights they'd stood here, the tiny, truncated intimacies these two, entirely different people had shared at the edges of a great sorrow, without ever wading in deeper. Would he ever see Sister Florence again after this week?

'I can't believe it's really happening,' he said.

'I cannot believe that it will,' she replied, or rather recited, as if her words were the second half of some elaborate, foreign greeting. Like a prayer, Rex thought, as he walked through the trees. Trying to make something true by saying it.

Maybe that was what he needed to do with Peter, he thought, after twenty minutes of fruitless looking for the man among the trees. There was a kilometre of parkland around the palace, and the mysterious, pale hermit could have chosen any bush or hollow of it to shelter in. If he was even there at all. He needed to find the man, needed to know for certain if his suspicions about him were true. But maybe the nuns were right – trying to find Peter, or to make him appear, was like trying to make it rain. One could only really trust. And he knew he'd be back before long.

As he stood on the hill waiting for a bus to take him back

down, he went to the brink of ringing Aurelie. Sure, he could tell her there was no threat. But if he told her why, told her what his wife had done, what would it achieve? The one consistent part of Sybille's sister, from the wild child to the dypso-Sloane to the current clean and serene version, was stubbornness. Aurelie wouldn't change her mind. She'd change everything else to fit it. She'd still cart Sybille back with her and install her under 24-hour supervision in some flame-retardant, match-free annexe; persuade the priests at St. Eustache to celebrate a special, candle-free Mass. He wanted to ring, he knew, because he wanted to feel as if he was doing something. But what was there to do?

A phone call shook him out of his worries. Brenard, following protocol, had rung Ellie rather than Rex with an update on the Borough Command meeting. Ellie was now marshalling her troops for the afternoon of news-scooping ahead. She was excited, and he quickly got caught up in it, as the 144 carried him down to battle on the plains.

* * *

It was a long afternoon – his only breaks buying cartons of mango juice from newsagents, so that he could swallow pills as he went along. He exchanged a couple of texts with Helena, but apart from that, he belonged to the story, and he was everywhere with it. In its high, historic moments it seemed like a wall frieze or a tapestry: outside the Town Hall as the bagged-up computers and the box-files were carried silently into custody. Watching the Stetson-less Tex Ochuba filling out the back of a tiny police car, the fat Greek lady from the labour agency feigning some sort of hysterical collapse. By tea-time he was sharing pavements with faces he recognised: *The Times*, the *Evening Standard*, the BBC, there was even a UK-based Polish TV station with someone on the case. But *s: Haringey* and *The Sentinel* had got there first. He had broken the story. When the glamorous lady from ITN asked him for an interview, and he felt himself tempted, he realised it was time to leave the scene.

He had a lot to do in the office, of course, and he wanted a wash and brush-up before he met Helena, so he barely paid any attention to the small, blonde family yawning in Reception as he went up. It was nothing unusual to see motley people in the building's foyer: the call centre spat out employees like a saw-mill.

Seconds after he'd arranged himself at his desk, Brenda rang him to come back down. He swore. He was still swearing as he came down the stairs to find a mum, a dad and their earnest twin daughters with neon rucksacks.

'If you've quite finished with that talk,' Brenda said coldly. 'The Lund family are over here on holiday.'

Apologising, Rex shook hands with them all, not at all clear why the Lund family should be over here on holiday in his office.

'I wrote to you about my plans to come and visit, Mr Tracey, connected to the work of the UNWCAGRC,' Dr Kristian Lund said, with the rising-falling, slightly irritated intonation of the Nordic peoples. 'My family and myself are having a short holiday here in London beforehand, and as I had not heard back from you, and my daughter here was interested to see the palace named after herself, we decided to come.'

The young Alexandra Lund was nudged forward, teeth, freckles and all, polite jokes were made, grins exchanged, international accord repaired. At any rate, Rex seemed to have been forgiven for shouting 'Who the pissing bloody fuck is it?' down the stairs. But Dr Lund's eyes, behind the exquisitely minimal Danish frames, preserved a chilly look, and he soon asked Rex if they could speak privately.

Brenda cracked open the cake-tin for mother and children, while Ellie let Rex and Lund have her office. 'After I wrote to you, I researched, Mr Tracey, and I saw your name on an article about the work of our unit in Nicosia, and the programme of awareness-raising going on here. Apparently being undertaken by Dr Helena Georgiou.'

'She's been here a week or so. I did see your email, but I thought it was a mistake.'

Lund looked affronted. 'Why?'

'Because Hel – Dr Georgiou told me it was. She said there'd been a mix-up, and she would talk to you.' Even as he spoke, Rex began to hear the dawn chorus of panic, those first, tiny, almost innocent cheeps of impending trouble. 'She does work with you, doesn't she?'

'She did,' said Dr Kristian Lund. 'But she was fired. She hacked into my email account in order to make contact with you.'

* * *

He slept on Terry's floor, rat-faced on raki, Okocim and, eventually, some appalling chestnut liqueur the photographer's sister had brought back from a holiday in Corsica. The mate from Consett was there, too, in and out with joints and powders and some impenetrable business of his own. Rex never quite learned his name. The mate from Consett never quite learned his. It seemed not to get in the way.

One of the benefits of being friends with a real bloke's bloke like Terry, Rex thought – in those early stages when thought was still possible – was that no one needed to talk that much. In very few words it had been communicated that Rex had a problem with a woman. In just as few the message came back that it was no problem, he could stay here, listen to Led Zeppelin, find oblivion unpestered.

He was not unpestered, though, because he could see the texts and the voice messages hitting his phone like rockets, shoals of desperation, bewilderment and anger surging through the troubled sea that was Dr Helena Georgiou. Rex could have switched the phone off. He did turn the volume down. But he could still see it. And he kept it in sight, because he wanted to see it.

It was a sad tale, told without anger or pleasure by Dr Lund, a colleague who until recently had obviously had professional respect for Helena, as well as personal sympathy for her problems. Now he was approaching those problems like the scientist he was.

'She was an able member of the team until around six months ago, when she got some news. It wasn't news intended for her, I gather, but a report from a nurse, who lived in Nicosia but had been working in the UK, looking after old people. I don't know what the report was, but I believe it was some information concerning Dr Georgiou's father, whom she did not know. It had a dramatic effect on Dr Georgiou. She became depressed. She asked for time off and, of course, our organisation recognises the stresses people in this field are under, so that was no problem. She returned to work after six weeks' break. But it was clear that Dr Georgiou wasn't better, only in fact worse. Very erratic, argumentative, emotional – quite different from the way she had been. It had been indicated to her, before she became unwell, that this job – coming here to the UK – would be hers. Afterwards, of course, there was no way we could permit someone in her state to represent our work so we told Dr Georgiou that there had been a change of plan. At this point, she crashed into the ceiling.'

'Hit the roof,' Rex said absently.

'Exactly. She refused to accept that decision and became difficult. She insisted there was nobody else who could do this job. We offered her a year's sabbatical, but she refused. Then she said she would take it, actually, provided we let her come to the UK to do the job first. She was fixated upon this. In the end we had to terminate her contract. It was very sad.'

'I'm supposed to be seeing her for dinner,' Rex said, ridiculously. Dr Lund looked embarrassed.

'Today I see from my researches on the internet that she has now travelled all over the country – claiming to be representative of the UNWCAGR. I haven't reported it to my superiors yet, but I will have to. And I will need to talk to your police.'

Rex had begged Dr Lund for a stay of execution – 24 hours, so he could speak to Helena himself. Lund, who had promised his family a day-trip to Brighton, had agreed, and given him until 7 pm tomorrow.

But the more he drank in the evening that ensued, the less Rex knew what he could say to Helena. The night, a night that should have been spent in celebration, became a race to get to the point where no words, or thoughts, or memories were possible. And he hit the finishing line fast.

Chapter Sixteen

Even a bloke's bloke like Terry couldn't help being curious, and as they stepped out, queasy and raw eyed into the cool morning, he asked, 'What happened then? She got a hubby and four kids back in Larnaca?'

People, smart, hurried, businessy people were charging past all around them towards the Tube, a breed who slept in the area but had little to do with it. Rex, bleary and confused, almost collided with a cross man in navy before he could reply.

'Something like that,' he said. 'But not that.'

It was enough for Terry. They parted where the road split, and Rex headed home for a change of clothes before work. In the enclosed courtyard that served as a garden, there was a petrol can. It wasn't his – he'd never run a lawn mower engine or lit a barbecue in his life. Someone had put it there. Someone with another message for him.

In his exhausted brain, the connections fizzed. In all the victories and the defeats of yesterday, he'd overlooked something. Eric Miles had named Sajadi in his confession – purchaser of the nightclub license, owner of a legion of falsely-rented flats. Those details hadn't been published of course, they would compromise the investigation, but the police, surely, would now have the Kurdish businessman in their sights, would possibly have hauled him in already. Was that the reason behind this, latest, nasty symbol? A sign, direct from the man to him: *You know. And I know you know.*

He moved the can warily, and found it to be empty. There was no smell of petrol around, or inside the house, which he checked, inch by inch, in sort of fever. Carefully, with a rubber glove he used for clearing the drains, he stowed the petrol can in a couple of Lidl bags, doubting this would satisfy anyone's evidence-preservation criteria, but feeling marginally better for doing something. He rang Brenard, told him about the can, trying to sound casual, popped the question.

'Rostam Sajadi?' A dry laugh. 'The flats, the nightclub – all owned by a shell company that's owned by another shell company that's owned by a fishing tackle shop in the Caymans. Never dealt with Miles or the council, he says, except to donate the stuff for the zoo.'

'And you believe that?'

'Not about that, is it? Given the set-up he's got, given the sort of lawyers he can afford, he's safe as houses. Why? You think he's the one doing all this stuff to you? I don't reckon he'd go near it, to be honest.'

'He wouldn't have to, would he?' Rex said, looking at the can. 'Someone else would do it for him.'

'Why though? He's teflon and he knows it.'

He showered and changed, shivering, and not from cold. Brenard could be right. Threats, in general, were the stuff of street-hoods. The only real power they had was intimidation, so they used it, inefficiently, risking detection and capture, in the hope that it would work. Big league villains didn't bother with threats. If you were in their way, they just wiped you out. But if Sajadi wasn't behind it, who was?

* * *

On his office desk, crisp and still warm from the printer, was a new contract. He was back on board, exonerated, rehired by Sentinel Group News and Media, on a full-time basis, with a raise that amounted to an extra twenty quid a month, after tax. Or 21 cans of Okocim, he thought, if he went for one of the 7 for 5 deals on Philip Lane.

He understood, from the way Ellie was hovering in the doorway to her office, that he was meant to say something grateful and humble about the contract. But the petrol can had got to him. So, too, had the sight of Helena, on a 144 bus, just as he'd been approaching the Turnpike Lane crossroad. She was standing by the doors, waiting with the others to get off, and he'd dived into the nasty newsagents to avoid her. Under the glare of the aged proprietor – who specialised in giving short change and accusing everyone of stealing from her – he had a word with himself. This was crazy. He had enough people to hide from – he couldn't do it to her. He'd asked her colleague, Dr Lund, for time to sort it out. And whatever deceits she'd wrought, she was a person in need of help. A person he'd grown to like.

The messages had stopped around one am, and there'd been no more since. He wondered what she was planning to do with her day. Would she carry on going through the motions of being Dr Helena Georgiou from the UN unit with the ridiculous acronym? Or had his silence made her realise it was all over? He had to talk to her.

In the office, he signed the contract, half-heartedly murmured his thanks, tried Helena's phone. It was switched off. Ellie continued to hover.

'Had a call from the editor. He's had a call from Millbank – they're wondering why Eve Reilly hasn't been asked for a view on all this. I know, I know...' She went on, as Rex began to show signs of rumbling. 'It sounds like they're trying to use it to get some extra PR for their candidate, it absolutely stinks. On the other hand, it's an angle. And the Big Boss agrees.'

'I wouldn't want to lose my twenty quid bonus,' Rex said, standing up and gathering his things. 'I had such big plans for it.'

* * *

Reilly's office was in the local Labour Party HQ, a flat shack of a place formerly a Minicab Office in Crouch End. It was the one seedy note in an area dominated by wide-aisled, mum-friendly coffee shops and places with tiny, expensive wellies in the windows. Crouch End had become a temple to child-rearing, Rex thought. People here seemed to have children, not in the way humans had been having them for 65,000 years, but in a loud, self-conscious, zealous way, like teenagers in a pub who thought they were the first people to discover booze. Rex used to look at them askance, all these lifestyle-parents and their wittily-named kids. These days, he just looked. He wondered what it was like to have a hall filled with small wellington boots. He knew what an empty hall looked like, after all.

Even though she was only the party's candidate in the forthcoming bye-election – the incumbent MP, the heavy-

292

drinking, depressive Gil Agnew, had three full months left to serve – the party office was already Eve's office. There were berry-bearing twigs in glass vases, personal photos amongst the party posters, soft, breathy songs playing through the computer speakers.

Eve wore a purple, wide collared blouse and grey trousers, and a garnet on a silver chain around her neck, which she fingered as she spoke. Or recited. 'I'm confident the police and the relevant agencies will get to the bottom of what has been going on, and I'm confident that, when the time comes, Harringay and Tottenham's hard-working people will choose how best to go forward.'

'Your mate in Millbank could have texted me that,' Rex said.

Eve Reilly shrugged. 'Take it or leave it. I'm busy campaigning, Mr Tracey, not crowing over the opposition's misfortunes.'

'Fair point.' He remembered her recent efforts at campaigning, and how they'd turned out. It can't have been a high point, finding a body – and not long after witnessing Mina's death. He put his pen away. Something else struck him – something odd that Vonda had said.

'Did you say you'd been working your way *up* Effingham Road when you found Bilal Toprak?'

She frowned. 'What's this got to do with the council?'

'Nothing at all. Off the record. I just wondered.'

'Yes,' she said, staring at him. 'Up.'

'So 'up', as in, from the Green Lanes end towards Wightman Road?'

'What other "up" is there?'

He shrugged. 'I don't know. People have odd ideas about that sort of thing.'

'Some seem to,' she replied drily. He laughed at that, and

she smiled faintly back. 'Is there anything else?'

'No,' he said, standing up. A framed photo stood on a shelf right by his head. Young people in huge, padded parkas, binoculars, somewhere rocky and desolate. A flag flew on a low, white building. 'Norway?' he asked, as he pulled his coat on.

'Vardo. A university expedition.'

'Funny place for the PPE undergrads.'

'I didn't study Politics, Philosophy and Economics, Mr Tracey,' she said, holding the door open for him. 'I didn't go to Oxford. Or Cambridge. I'm the only child of a single mum who worked nights in a sweet factory so she could afford the rent. It's been covered in a lot of interviews. Maybe you should read one. Maybe you should interview me, properly, about why I believe in what I do, why I want to work for the people of this area, instead of just chucking my name in your paper whenever someone dies.'

'We should run a profile,' he said. 'You're right. And I'm sorry about... the way I was at the Inquest. It must have been a grim experience for you.'

'It's nothing to do with me. What made me angry was all these people making out the verdict was some sort of scandal. It's disrespectful. Whatever it looked like, the science gave us the answers. Bilal Toprak was overweight, he had diabetes, high blood pressure, a recent bang on the head. I don't know what else people wanted to make of it.'

He held up his hands. 'You're preaching to the choir. I saw him when the club collapsed, remember? I heard he was pretty agitated afterwards, as well.'

She nodded, distractedly, then seemed to tune in, frowned. 'Who from?'

'Sorry?'

'You said – just before – you said you'd heard he was agitated.'

'Oh. He seems to have gone into the Bosphorus supermarket, not long before he died. The girl serving there recognised him. Perhaps he was looking for answers.'

'Answers about what?' she asked sharply.

'I'm guessing he wanted to know more about what happened when the building fell down. He couldn't ask in the café, because it was...' He trailed off. She was staring at him, but at the same time, seemed to be somewhere else. He waved a finger at her. She snapped out of it.

'Sorry. Yes.' She rubbed her forehead. 'I was just thinking that would have been helpful at the Inquest. Anyway. It's over. We know what happened. I just wish people would shut up about it now. I mean – if it had been some kind of robbery, they'd have stolen his laptop, wouldn't they? Or his phone?'

'You saw them there?'

She nodded. 'I didn't notice them at the time but... I did yesterday.'

'Yesterday?'

She bit her lip. 'I'm afraid I went back and looked through the front window. I don't know why. Pay my respects, I guess.' She shook her head, briskly. 'Anyway, it was all there. I guess the family haven't got round to clearing it up yet.

* * *

The bus that took him back towards Green Lanes was a regularly-threatened, ferociously-defended hopper called the W5, manned by motherly ladies who dished out lollipops to the younger travellers once a month. The rest of the time, as the little back-street buses soared up and down the hills like some Hebridean community outreach service, the drivers helped people on with their pushchairs, went extra-slow for the old people, and generally set about restoring people's faith in humanity, in the city, and particularly in the city's bus drivers.

It was a pleasant journey back, with the little ones whooping on the steeper descents, and the odd, unexpected, dramatic view of Ally Pally gleaming on the hill like a fake Montmartre. He got off at the Arena retail park, normally a soul-sucking experience, with a certain glow. Then again, his pills had just kicked in.

Effingham Road, guarded at its eastern end by a Greek baker's and a Turkish jewellers, snaked from the Lanes back up the hills he'd just ridden down. There was, as Eve Reilly had said, no way to describe that route, other than 'up'. He wondered what Vonda had been getting at. Perhaps she'd swallowed something during the 1968 Hornsey Art College Revolution, and never truly returned to earth.

He had the idea of copying Eve Reilly and peering through Bilal's window, just to see what was there. He wasn't sure why he wanted to do it: a mawkish trace in him, perhaps, or else a sense of something still not quite right about the affair.

Today, a wiry lady with short hair and a thick gold necklace was moving around the front room with a bin-bag. She looked up – he waved – she frowned and shook her head, turned her back. He rang the doorbell. Eventually, on the third ring, she answered it, chain on, wary. She relaxed a little when he showed her his press card.

She was Cemile, she said, Bilal's oldest sister. Her mum, who'd lost a son and a husband in one week, wasn't getting out of bed. Nor was her own husband, but that was nothing new, she added darkly.

'How did Bilal seem to you?' he asked. 'Before he died?'

She shrugged. 'He was upset. We were all upset because of our dad. That was normal.'

'Of course. And he wanted answers, I guess.'

'Answers?'

'He went to some lengths to talk to the people who own the café opposite the club. They said he seemed quite troubled.'

Cemile considered this, then nodded, slowly. 'I didn't know that. But yes, he would have seemed quite troubled. He was.'

She started to take the chain off the door. Rex felt a tiny stirring of hope. Or perhaps dread. Was there something she wanted to share?

'While you're here, would you mind helping me get his desk out? If I leave it out the front there's some boys on Freecycle who'll take it away.'

He went in behind Cemile. The place festooned with bin bags and cardboard boxes, reminding him of Sybille's packed-up room and then, inevitably of death. Bilal had a desk in his living room and a tiny, joyless sofa. A man who always seemed to be working, even when he wasn't working.

The desk was solid, as Bilal had been. Despite the difference in physique, Cemile had the same manner as her brother, too: a kind of melancholy heaviness, like a piece of Ottoman furniture in a museum. Like the thing they were trying to shift, in fact, and couldn't. They needed to take the drawers out. On doing so, they realised they were still stuffed with papers.

'More binbags,' she said, with a heavy sigh, wiping her

hands on her sparkly black t-shirt. She looked around, tutted. 'The roll's upstairs.' She went out.

At the top of a box of things balanced on the sofa, was Bilal's laptop. Eve Reilly had been right, Rex thought – if the man's death had been motivated by robbery or political skulduggery, the laptop would surely have gone. While Cemile moved about upstairs, and then shouted in Turkish at someone, presumably the absent husband, on her phone, he had, and dismissed, the idea of firing up the lap-top. Then he saw the phone, slipped down the side of the box. He pulled it out. He switched it on. It came to life with agonising slowness, while Cemile's harangue continued upstairs. The battery was low.

With the feeling that he was doing something very wrong indeed, he looked at the call menu. It revealed little: Mum, Cemile, Dentist, Eric Work, Eric Mobile, Eric Home, a couple of mobile numbers not attached to names. Rex moved on to the texts.

There was a conversation between Bilal and Mina. Initiated by her, dated around six weeks back.

Gf's bro wx in Plan Off. Heard some things. U OK?

With a thumping heart, he decoded it. Mina had found out about the corruption in the council via her girlfriend, Kyretia Pocock, sister of Ashley.

There were too many back and forth messages to read, but as Rex scrolled inefficiently upwards, a few more struck him as important.

Mina to Bilal: *Cant act as lawyr. Nor K. Not qfd. But can read and advise.*

Mina to Bilal, again, 12th of March – just before she'd vanished. *Now need yr help. Need swhre to stay. Safe. PLEASE.*

And another transmission, from Wednesday the 19th of March, two days before she died. *OK. Sitting tight. Have you done it yet?*

And the last, on the day of her death; not a message, just a shortened URL. He clicked on it, unwisely, just as Cemile began to come down the stairs.

He dithered, as the speech Mina had posted on YouTube began to run on the little screen. He pushed buttons, clicked away, trying frantically to turn the thing off. Just in time, he realised the obvious course of action.

Noisily, he helped Bilal's sister empty the drawers into bin bags, and to haul the great oak desk down the hall, all the while trusting that the phone he'd just stolen wouldn't fall out of his back pocket, and that Cemile wouldn't hear the tinny little voice seemingly coming from his backside. Then as they were up-ending the desk in the doorway, the phone died.

By way of the area's most obliging phone accessories vendor, he headed home to plug the thing in. It didn't fire up immediately, just got stuck on a cheery, blue logo, forever saying 'Welcome' but never letting him in. He took deep breaths, trying not to lose his temper. He had knackered dozens of laptops and phones himself, merely from losing patience with them.

Could this phone hold the key to Mina's death? It seemed to imply that she'd helped Bilal – as Eric Miles had guessed – providing legal advice while he compiled his explosive dossier. Then, as she came under threat – from her uncle, it seemed – Mina had called the favour back. Bilal had found her somewhere safe to stay. But someone had found out. Or betrayed her. Who was that? Could it have been Bilal himself?

At last the phone came to life, re-starting on the recording it had crashed on: Mina, in front of the shabby blind in her Sky City refuge. It was still in the opening seconds of her speech, before she got into her stride, hesitantly but with gathering force discussing the dashed hopes for a ceasefire in Turkey, the tragically vain sacrifices of her Kurdish sisters.

He was so used to hearing the speech, had played it so many times, on screens and in his head, that he almost stopped listening. It was only when Mina coughed that his attention returned to the words she was speaking, when he realised that the speech – this section of it, at any rate – was different from the version he'd heard before.

'I've been involved in the political process since an early age. I went round leafleting when I was 14. More recently, I've been heavily involved in student politics as Diversity Officer for the Union. But I'm abandoning the political process now, I'm saying goodbye to democracy. Those of you who ask why may find at least some of the answers in Harringay and Tottenham Council, and the events that I know are about to take place there, the shockwaves that will follow. They, and my experiences on a Student Union dominated by people only preparing for high office in the countries of their birth, have led me, as a woman and a Kurd, to realise that the only true, honest struggle is one achieved by…'

Although the counter said there were two more minutes, the frame stuttered, vanished, returned to the main menu of the cloud server site. He cursed, jabbed at a few buttons in irritation. Nothing happened. He pressed a few more. Instead of returning to the website, the phone took him back to the texts. Where, for the first time, he noticed a conversation between Bilal and someone not named, just a number. It was a number he knew very well. Just a string of digits, that kicked him in the chest.

Suddenly, his urgent desire to see the final minutes of Mina's true, hidden internet speech, vanished. It – and the questions it raised, such as who had edited it, and why – could all wait. And one thing could not. Because, he realised as he leaned back on his kitchen chair totting up all the question marks of the past few days, he had found Bilal Toprak's killer.

Did the truth, as Maureen and St Paul promised, set him free? It depressed him immeasurably, he knew that. He went back to work, mainly because he couldn't stand to be alone with it.

* * *

Half an hour later he was penning an advertorial about the fabulous new dining and socialising opportunities opening up on the west side of Shopping City. Someone was clearing out the vacant units and replacing them with the 'Tokyo Quarter': a floorful of raw fish, karaoke, computer-gaming arcades and a 'traditional Izakaya', whatever that was.

He sighed as he got stuck in to the briefing notes. Had he been in one of the nuns' endless TV shows, he'd have segued straight from his kitchen to an assignation down some alleyway. Instead, he was back at the *s: Haringey* offices, listening to Lawrence nosily wolfing down a prawn baguette and neurotically checking his phone every few seconds.

And if you fancy sake, instead of the same old Sauvignon…

His phone rang while he cringed at the sentence he'd just penned. He closed his eyes.

'Helena.'

'Sorry. I missed your call. I didn't hear the phone. Where

are you? Are you all right, Rex? What's happened? You didn't come last night, I couldn't get hold of you, I was worried...'

He had to shout to get her to stop. 'Let's meet,' he said. 'I'll explain. Can you be at my house in half an hour?'

'What are you going to say?' Her voice trembled. He hated himself.

'Not here. I'll see you in half an hour.'

He started packing up his things. Everything else could wait. Everything else, it seemed, except Lawrence, who was lurking at the side of his desk giving off a faint, fishy smell.

'Absolutely no need to interruptitate yourself with this now,' he said, placing a sheet of paper on Rex's desk. 'Just thought it might be of interest.'

Rex found himself looking, in spite of himself, and while trying to retroactively un-hear Lawrence's use of *interruptitate*. It was a German newspaper article, topped off with a picture of a crumpled car and a mugshot of a rather pleasant-looking Turkish bloke. He waited for Lawrence to provide some interpretation.

'Seems this chap was a hitman for a number of crime groups – rumoured to have carried out the odd one for the PKK, too. You know, the Kurdish thingummy.'

'So what's happened? He crashed his car?'

'No, he's just gone on trial for making someone else crash their car. That was his speciality, you see. Death by vehicle.'

* * *

When she arrived he was looking at a map of Cyprus – in particular at a town on the northern coast, in the part now owned – or stolen – by the Turks. It had two names, as many places did on that island. The Greeks called it Lepithos. To

302

the Turks, it was Lapta. When she arrived, achingly pretty with a bit of damp blossom in her hair, she glanced at the screen and her face fell.

'It's bit like riding your bike down a hill, don't you think? That whole business – fancying someone. Liking them. Starting to feel like you're falling for them…'

He wished he hadn't asked the question because she nodded, half-eager, half-unsure.

'It's dangerous. You can end up in a heap at the bottom. Worse than that, though, you can not realise that your tyres are knackered. Broken,' he added, to her puzzled face. 'You're going so fast, that things whizz by – all these little things you ought to notice, but you don't.'

She hadn't even taken her coat off. He wondered if he should be more hospitable, offer her tea and so on, but that, surely, would be a kind of insult.

'I should have noticed that you said all your meetings here, with the Greeks, were in their church. You told me twice. And yet when I met you down Lawrence Road, near Toprak's factory, you said you were looking for the community centre.

'I should have realised that the champagne you bought me, it wasn't some special one from a Cambridge college, it's just called Trinity Hall. You can buy it in Morrison's.'

'I didn't know that either!' she said. 'I came out of the college, went over the road to a shop and there was the champagne. I thought it was the college champagne. I was in Cambridge. I didn't lie. I went to Cambridge.'

'OK. Maybe you did. But you were still lying about what you were doing, pretending you were doing your old job. Lying to everyone. Including me.' She made no response to that, so he carried on. 'I couldn't understand it – that time I suggested we go out, instead of coming here, and you accused me of trying to keep you away, of having secrets. Because you see, people often do that. I've seen it a lot, in my line of work, but I couldn't see it, when it came to you. You thought I had secrets because you did.'

She still said nothing. Her lips twitched, as if she might be about to speak, or cry, but nothing happened. He didn't want this, this long brow-beating, him angry, her silent. He'd have preferred her to throw something, slap him, shout, deny it, argue. He'd have preferred never to have met her.

'One of the other things I noticed, but didn't pay enough attention to, was how you ran away when Bilal and his father showed up at the meeting. And then how long you stared at that photograph of Kemal and his friends, on the coffee shop wall. Because they were the Siyah Tilki, weren't they? The Black Foxes. The unit that everyone feared and loathed. After the war, many of them moved to Trabzon, where the government gave them nice jobs, in the police. But during the war, they murdered Greeks, and they raped women and girls. Kemal and your parents came from the same town, didn't they? Lapta. Lepithos. And you found out that it was Kemal Toprak who murdered your mother's husband, the father of your brothers, and who raped your mother, in 1974. Kemal was your father. So you came here, to find him. Maybe you meant to kill him, but the bent council did the job for you. Then maybe you went for Bilal instead. Perhaps you only meant to talk to him but it got out of hand. I know you went to his house, to see him, on the day he died. I've seen the texts, Helena.'

She listened calmly, only that faint tremor around her lips betraying her distress. She asked him for a glass of water and drank it like a child, in one go, gasping a little for breath afterwards. She took out a packet of cigarettes – new, the cellophane still on – and asked if she could smoke. He said he didn't mind, and fetched her a saucer. She offered him one as she lit her own, her hands rock steady.

'Never got the taste for it,' he said. 'I didn't know you had either. But I suppose I don't know you, do I?'

'It was never supposed to be anything to do with the Toprak man,' she said. 'Or his son. I went to the factory next door, Spyridonidis Sons. He was the man I wanted to find – Bambos Spyridonidis. There was nobody there. I know it was stupid, but I'd planned it for so long, what I would say, what he would say... I couldn't just leave it and try again another time. I forced a window open to try and get in, find something like a home address or a phone number for him. I was climbing up to the window when this old bald man started to shout from the factory next door. Then he came down. Kemal Toprak. He was very agitated – I could see he was breathing fast, pale in the face, shaking. He frightened me, but, you know, I was worried for him. He didn't look well. I said I was a family friend trying to get in to find something. He said he knew that was a lie, because the factory had been emptied, Bambos had gone. He went back up – to call the police, he said. I wasn't even sure he'd get back up the stairs. But I ran. I ran, and then I met you. I kept wondering if he'd died, that old man.'

He'd thought it was a charming evening. In reality she must have been only a tenth with him. The rest of her panicking, going back over things, trying to keep it all in.

'What did you want with Bambos Spyridonidis?'

'Six months ago, a woman came into our office in Nicosia.

I liked her. She said she'd been working as a nurse in London. She wanted to be a doctor, but in my country, quite often you need to pay someone to help you along the way. That's why she'd been in London, trying to save up the money, you know. One night, in the hospital where she was doing the night shift, an old Greek man started to tell her about the old days. They often start talking in the night, when they're lonely and frightened,' Helena said. 'You do notice that, on the wards. Around three o' clock in the morning, when most people die and when most babies are born, then they start talking. This man was from Lepithos. The village of my parents. He told her a strange tale. About the cousin he'd hated. Not really a cousin – a second or third cousin, like a lot of people are in those villages. And you see, that was my father – his cousin – Achilles Georgiou. They'd fallen out a long time ago over a girl. They have a custom there, because there are so many brothers, and cousins: when two brothers, or two cousins, want the same girl, the younger one must defer to the older one. But it didn't happen. Achilles was the younger one, but the girl preferred him. The girl was my mother, Calysta, and they got married. They had two boys.

'Bambos hated Achilles, because Bambos was only a shopkeeper, and Achilles was a primary school teacher, and the old men would stand up when Achilles went into the coffee-shop, because they respected a teacher so much. Not just that – he hated him because he owned a thousand citrus trees, and two thousand more when he married my mother. That's a lot of income, you see. In the 1960s the village really split, between those who supported EOKA, and wanted a union with Greece, and the Communists, who wanted nothing to do with Greece and the generals running it. Even the coffee shops, where the men go in the evenings, they split, you know, according to politics. But even though Achilles was a communist, they still welcomed him in the coffee shop that was for EOKA, because he was loved. And Bambos made a stand about that, and said he wouldn't sell the coffee and the sugar and the napkins to them anymore. He just seemed to be filled with hate.

'And then the war came, and the Turks. Achilles got his wife and the two boys out, quickly, to Nicosia. He was supposed to follow on, but something happened. Bambos had a good war. Even when the Greeks were forced to retreat from the north, he enjoyed himself, he said, 'clearing' villages in the south, on the Greek side, that had been full of Turks for centuries. He got rich from all the things he found, as the Turks escaped north.

'One day, Bambos was in a village called Potamia, near to the Green Line, not far from Nicosia. Deserted in the fighting. Went into a store, to see what he could find. And he found Achilles. He was trying to get to his family in Nicosia, but he'd run into a unit of the Siyah Tilki. They'd raped *him*. Beaten him. Left him for dead. He was in the store, eating raw flour. Starving. Crazy. He didn't even seem to recognise Bambos, just begged him to help, as a Greek brother. That seemed to be the last straw for Bambos Spyridonidis – that this cousin whom he'd hated, the centre of his world for so long, didn't even remember him. He put a gun to Achilles' head. Achilles begged him, said his wife was pregnant with a third child. Bambos shot him anyway. Buried the body in a pit, set light to the store. That was the story he told the nurse. I don't know if he was sorry. Or if he just wanted to tell someone. In my job, I think sometimes it's both. Or it's neither. Sometimes, old men tell me how they took young girls. And they put words in, so that it sounds as if they are disgusted at what they did. But actually, they're just telling me how they took young girls.'

She looked at him. 'My mother wasn't raped. She was pregnant with me, but she got away without being raped. That's why everyone said she was lucky. My father wasn't. He was killed by his own people. It happened a lot.'

'The nurse told me all this. I did a lot of checking. I found out what happened to Bambos Sypridonidis and all his money. I found out where his factory was. Maybe I got too obsessed. I spent too long, listening to those stories. Doctor Lund was better at it than me – it wasn't his place, they weren't his people. But once I knew, I had to come here. Nobody was going to stop me.'

'But then Bilal and his father showed up at the community centre. So you ran.'

'I was relieved the old man was all right, but I was afraid that he remembered me. What possible reason could I have for climbing through a factory window? The whole thing could have been over before I'd had a chance to find Bambos. So I just ran. Later on I found out from the community that Spyridonidis had had money troubles, and retired. Moved to Newcastle, to be with his daughter. I went there, in the end.'

'But you sought out Bilal, too.'

'I realised he was quite an important person on the council. There was a Turkish-Cypriot Business Circle, and I was due to give a talk there, and he was on the panel. I realised I'd be seeing him again, maybe his father, too, so it was better to face up to the truth. Explain what I'd been doing at the factory.'

'So you saw him on Friday. The day he died. What happened? He didn't believe you?'

She shook her head. 'You're right. I arranged to meet him on the Friday. But I never went there that day. I saw him before. On Wednesday, when the coffee-shop collapsed. When I was helping the old man, then he recognised me. His son saw it, and most of all, Bilal saw how afraid I was. Later on that day, he got in touch with me. He was very upset, obviously, his father had just died. He sent me a text. And he said he knew my secret.'

'How?'

'On Thursday, I came back early from Cambridge, and I went to Bilal's house. But he...' She shook her head. 'He didn't know my secret at all! He'd seen me, just like you did, looking at the photograph on the wall. Kemal was one of the Black Foxes, sure. And the old man was afraid – he'd been very afraid ever since that wall collapsed after the explosion in Trabzon.'

'Because Kemal had gone to Trabzon, and joined the police, like his pals in the Foxes, and when those bodies were found...'

'Yes. Greek prisoners, abducted, taken to the mainland, imprisoned and then killed. By who? Police? Army? Prison staff? Intelligence units? And then what happened there last week – the old Chief of Police was shot dead, maybe to preserve the secret.'

'Kemal was something to do with all those murders,' Rex said. 'He thought he could be next, after the Police Chief. Or the United Nations might take an interest, put him and his cronies on trial.'

'And then what happens? A UN Investigator comes to

town. Who snoops at the factory. Takes too much of an interest in the photo at the club. Recognises Kemal Toprak, is recognised by him. And even if the old man is dead, could still bring a case, destroy his name, destroy his son's name and career with it. A whole different story. But wrong.' She swallowed. 'Just like the one you made up about me, Rex.'

He looked down, but the truth was, he wasn't embarrassed. He might have got it wrong, jumped to conclusions. But she'd lied. Their whole time together had been based on lies.

'I didn't touch Bilal. I understand – I guess you could believe anything of me. I know I have hurt you. But please believe me, I could never hurt someone like that. You know, Bilal even said, as I left him on Thursday, that he hoped I found some answers.'

'And did you?'

'Bambos Spyridonidis died a week before I flew in to the UK. A heart-attack. In Newcastle, his daughter was so pleased to meet someone who spoke Greek, she clung onto me. There were no sons. He called the business that because he wanted them. If he'd had them, they might have defended the factory, she said, from the criminals who took his money, ruined him.'

Rex nodded. This was the second person he'd come across now, ruined by criminals – extorting money. Helena rummaged for tissues in her bag.

'How could I tell her what her father had been like? It has to stay where it is. I should have realised that before. It all has to stay. But the people it has to stay with…' She looked at him, as if for help. 'What do they do?'

At the door, he asked her, meaning it, 'What will you do?'

She flashed him a sad, dull look. 'It doesn't matter to you now, does it?'

CHAPTER SEVENTEEN

Over the years he'd developed a special way of ringing the doorbell. He often visited in the night, without notice, but one short ring and then another, slightly longer one told the nuns that this was him. Sister Florence, who never seemed to sleep, usually made sure to be the one who let him in.

Rex was so used to seeing the tiny, grey-clad figure that he jumped back when a man opened the convent door instead: tall, gaunt, pale, with deep-set eyes seemingly made of amber.

'Peter.'

They shook hands. Peter wore a tool belt; behind him, in the hallway, was a ladder. He was fitting a smoke alarm. He indicated, through sign language, that this was at some crucial stage.

'I… you… talking,' he said, tapping a point on his wrist where a watch might once have been.

The boxes had all left Sybille's room now. It was bare as a cell. She had the BBC World Service on, something about Gambia's punk rock scene. This had never been her sort of thing, and he was reminded once again of how she'd changed in the last few weeks – and how that change was about to stop forever.

'So – big journey tomorrow!' he said, in a way both bright and lame. She ignored him.

'What time is Aurelie coming?'

She appeared to be ignoring him again and then inclined her head and said, in a sonorous voice, 'On the stroke of midnight.'

'Feels like that, doesn't it?' He took her hand. Today, she let it lie limp in his. Did this hurt him more than when she squeezed it? All was pain, he realised. Her absence would be as painful as her presence. So what point was there in fighting it?

'I'll ask Sister Florence and I'll be here.'

She said nothing to that. In the end, he kissed her on her cool, unmoving forehead and left. Just as he closed the door, he thought he heard her say, 'A mess,' but he wasn't sure.

Nor was Sister Florence, who could only say that Aurelie was expected sometime after midday, and would call once she hit British soil. She, like Sybille, was too gloomy to engage with him. Rex had long suspected that, however involved with the life of the house Sister Florence might be, Sybille was her only true patient. She would grieve for her.

The mercurial Peter was no longer in the hallway when he emerged, and Sister Florence had no idea where he was. Rex left, jangled and disgruntled, to find Peter, sitting on a bench among the trees, his face so white it seemed to be shining. He was encased in a huge, bright, new-looking parka, and smoking. He offered Rex his pouch. The second time he'd been offered tobacco, Rex noted, without knowing why that mattered.

'Thank you for what you did,' Rex said. 'It must feel good, to have saved a life. When you couldn't save the first one.'

A pause as it sank in. 'Yes, you were there at the shopping place,' Peter said, finally, in a soft voice. 'And I was there.' He held out his thin roll-up. 'Smoking.' He patted his chest. 'If I had good heart, I would quit, but...' He shook his head. 'I can't do it. It is my great sin.'

Rex remembered the younger Sybille and her packets of twenty, Marlboro-flavoured sins a day. Peter looked down at the ground.

'Even at work, smoking. See? Painting Sky City rail. Painting Sky City balcony. Boss – a big black boss, big hat like a Dallas hat – he says, I see you again smoking, texting on phone, that shit, you... Sack!' Peter descended into what seemed like minutes of coughing. With wet eyes and two pinpricks of colour on his cheekbones, he spoke again. 'But I am smoking still. Painting. Smoking. Hear someone coming. I think – fuck, is boss. He tells to me, that black guy, someone is coming later to fit the door. I don't know if it's them, or if it's boss back again. So I am throwing cigarette. From the rail, over door, where I am stand to paint.' He bit his knuckle, adding, huskily, 'It's not door guy, and it's not boss.'

'It was a girl.'

'A girl,' Peter nodded. 'I saw – so clear – like a photograph. My cigarette landed in... that girl's... hood. I shouted to her but she kept to run. Running from someone. She run through the doorway... and my...' He pulled his nose with his fingers. 'I smell. I smell a petrol, then...' He was silent, hands clasped, perhaps at prayer. 'That girl is on fire. Screams.'

'Where did the petrol come from?'

'I don't know. But... it's on him, as well.'

'On who?'

'I run inside after her. Too late – she falls. People looking up. You.' He tapped his forehead. 'For many day and nights I keep inside a picture of your face.'

'Me too,' Rex said, then clarified: 'I kept seeing your face.'

The pale man nodded. 'So I run away. Boss said to me, before job, anybody ask you question, you don't know English, okay? Give Council Works telephone. I don't want to be question, you know. Have to leave again. So I ran. Ran into sky.'

Rex frowned, before he worked it out. 'You ran into Sky City?'

'Sky City. Yes. I turned corner, and I crashed into a man – running, very angry. He fights with me. Smells of petrol.'

'What did he look like?'

'Short man. And a dark. Not a black. Like Tartar.'

Rex's heart was thundering. 'What was he wearing?'

'Don't remember.'

'Did he say anything?'

'He did,' Peter said, apologetically. 'But I don't remember.'

'How did it sound? What he said? Like a man from here, from London, or a man from somewhere else?'

Peter gave the question some thought, even closed his eyes again and seemed to pray for the answer, but in the end, he gave up. His cigarette was down to his fingers, but he kept on sucking at it. He seemed to want the pain, just as he wanted the cough. Rex understood the notion well.

They sat together on the bench for a while longer, each lost in the scale and the detail of what had happened. He remembered Eric Miles, who saw the hand of God, not just in things of beauty but in moments of awful fate, comings-together so perfect only the divine could have set them in motion. He understood Eric Miles now, as well.

'The nuns are paying you well,' Rex said, as Peter adjusted the hood on his new, warm coat.

'Is not nuns. My friend is give it to me.' He smiled. 'Very angry. He says, I'm not gonna do nothing else for helping you now, Peter.'

'Nothing else to help you?' Rex homed in on the comment.

'I ran to him at his University. First. After Sky City. He got a lot of money, my friend. He took me back to Minsk. Right the same day. Gave me money. He is my good friend – we know each other since Sunday School. But I couldn't stay in Belarus. I went to see my priest. Priest says to me, you cannot hide from this. You must confess. So I came back to London. To try. I haven't done it. My friend is very angry that I come back. I help you get away, he says, now why you come back? Crazy. But, still, is give me coat.'

'You've confessed now,' Rex said. 'To me. And there isn't a court in the world that would condemn you for it. It was an accident.'

Peter stared at him. 'There is no accident.' A finger pointed steeple-like, to the sky. 'God.'

'Let him judge you then,' Rex said, 'And leave the legal system alone.'

Peter made a wan face. 'It's what my friend says, too.'

'I didn't realise Jan Navitsky was so wise.' The change in Peter's eyes told him he was right. Navitsky had lied about his sudden departure. But it was to help his friend. 'Or so generous,' Rex added, patting the thick coat.

Something seemed to strike Peter – he straightened suddenly on the bench. 'The man. That man that...' He mimed a gripping hand. 'He has a one of this kinds of coat. I remember. Big, big, like balloon coat, for very cold. Yes.'

Rex wasn't sure that helped much, but he thanked Peter, and they parted soon after. He was a few yards up the hill before something struck him and he turned around. Peter was still there. Rex asked him one more question about the day at Sky City and suddenly, as if he'd triggered an avalanche, the truth was in his ears and his eyes and his mouth, taking his breath away for a while. Because he knew, then, why Mina had really died.

He went straight home, half-expecting to find the place ransacked, or to be hauled into a van along the way. Nothing happened, except that a man asked him for a light. Number three, he thought. Was he supposed to start smoking?

Inside, he filled a glass with raki, and took the stolen phone from the cushion he'd zipped it into as a precaution. It had been Sybille's, of course – what man brought cushions to a marriage? He felt it still smelt of her, sometimes, but tonight was not one of those nights. It was as if even the traces of her were going.

It wasn't a warm evening, but he felt hot, partly because the pills did that to him sometimes, but also because of his internal state: one composed of fear, elation, grief and doubt. He opened the French windows onto the front yard, just a crack. Then he went back to Mina's recording. He had a strong idea what she'd said in her closing moments, but he needed to be sure.

This file is no longer available.

Someone had deleted it from the Cloud. Very, very recently. Someone who didn't want the truth to be known.

He went into the kitchen to add some water to his drink,

lost in thought. Was it possible to hack into this storage site and find files that had been deleted? He knew a very gifted, vaguely illegal Russian by the name of Vadim who had helped him more than once before, but he'd heard Vadim was back in Vilnius, improbably, teaching HTML to ten year olds. Could he still contact him?

Then he realised there was a simpler way than that – or at least there might be, if the gods were on his side.

He hurried back into his sitting room and picked up the phone. He ran through the various menus and functions now considered essential to life, from pedometers to talking compasses, until he found the folder he needed.

He had just clicked on it when he felt something that seemed to be the opposite of an explosion – it was an implosion, a remarkable, almost human sigh which was really the drawing-in of all the air, and of every seen and heard thing into one, tiny point. It felt like the beginning of the universe. And then it was the end of the universe, as a wall of flame tore into the room, glass shattered, wood cracked and the smell of petrol blinded him.

CHAPTER EIGHTEEN

Brown, cardboard boxes stored in stacks: the abiding symbol of the weeks before and after the time it happened. At the end of 2003, the living room of the flat they shared in Camden had been packed into a tower of these cardboard containers, because Sybille had been suddenly seized by a desire for home improvement.

Rex dreaded these passing passions – dreaded them because, for all her enthusiasm and intelligence, Sybille was no good at DIY. Each task, whether it be sanding the floors or re-tiling the bathroom, began with days of careful research, but ended in tears and fury. Part of that fury reserved for him, because he wasn't there to help, or because he'd have been no use even if he had helped, or because he'd advised against it from the start.

On this occasion he'd suggested that, what with her going to a conference, her hard-drinking sister threatening to visit, and a big Press Awards do on the horizon, the painting could wait. His wife had gone ahead anyway, and in the early days of December, there'd been a tense atmosphere in the household.

That wasn't just down to the painting. She'd been tired, complaining of nausea and headaches for some time, and there'd been more than one night when he'd slept on the sofa rather than disturb her. Other nights, too, when he'd passed out, drunk, and just woken up there. Onto this strained, but not exactly unhappy landscape, had arrived Sybille's conference, and the text message, apparently Sybille's also, that Rex had never seen the like of before. *Wot u up to? Xxx*

And then Aurelie: a typhoon of vodka and tears and chaos. While Sybille was away at the conference, she'd got into their bed in the night, and while the confused Rex had sat up and stuck the light on the moment he realised whose hands and lips were on him, there'd been a moment or two before when he hadn't. Aurelie fled, very early, the next morning, but Rex had a sense, later, that she'd said something to his wife, something his wife was intending to bring up, some time. She'd been like that, Sybille: patient. She nursed things.

In addition to that, Rex had accepted a job in New York – a fact that only emerged when he and his wife were seated opposite one another at the Press Awards. This, and all the other tensions and doubts between them, seemed to billow out like poison from a gas canister as they drove home that dark rainy night, and Rex ploughed the car into some scaffolding. Their lives, as they had been lived, came to an end at that moment.

The days and weeks after were not, as people liked to say, a dream or a haze; they were an awful, pin-sharp, Reality 2.0. Rex felt every step, not least because he'd smashed three metatarsals, the cuboid and navicular bones of his left foot. He heard every sound as if he himself were some kind of oscilloscope, his own soul bunching into jagged graph-spikes each time a nurse ripped open a sterile tube package, each time someone, further down the corridor, let the lid on the metal bin slam. On the icy streets, when he hobbled out for relief from the stifling room and the machine making her breathe, he saw how people looked at him. Drunken office workers, in Santa hats, roused from their revels in the Wetherspoons to stare and whisper. Babies in the Tesco glared, as did the skull-faced women in wheelchairs in the hospital lobby, and the normally welcoming nurses.

They all knew, even if the police didn't, that the crash was his fault. He tried walking without his crutches, to see if that was causing the stares. He collapsed from the pain, on Tottenham Court Road, and the shoppers, laden with presents, just stepped over him, confirming all his fears.

It wouldn't be long before Rex ended up in hospital himself – a hospital where they nobly tried to cure his mind, then gave up, and prescribed him drugs, on top of the drugs he was already taking for the pain in his foot. They left him with a love of feeling high, but no love for himself. Before that, though, just five days after the accident, he returned to the flat, urged to by doctors and nurses and in-laws who were all sensing the sickness he carried with him to Sybille's bedside.

The place stank, and it wasn't the paint. It was something more akin to what he smelt in the corridors of the hospital where the shell of his wife lay: a sweetish, cloying, human fug. He thought perhaps it was just stuck in his clothes and hair, so, hobbling around with difficulty, he opened all the windows, despite the cold, took off his clothes, wrapped bags around his plastered-up foot and showered. But, shaving at the mirror over the sink, he could still smell it, and he looked down to the bin they kept there, normally bulging with exclusively feminine detritus. It was the same today – cotton pads, cleansing wipes, things he didn't truly grasp the purpose of. But on top of them now was a wad of some absorbent material, thick as a small loaf, which had obviously been soaked with blood, and was now dried solid. He retched into the sink. He wondered why he hadn't noticed this before.

Then he remembered: he'd been up north on assignment, pulling in a couple of all-nighters, hadn't, consequently, been in the flat for four whole days before the accident. There'd been a complex affair, involving Sybille dropping dinner jackets at the office, and posting a pair of shoes, so that he could meet her at the Press Awards without making a detour to Camden. She hadn't been happy about it.

He wondered if a person would be ill from losing so much blood. If it was Sybille's – and he couldn't see who else might have let themselves in, bled heavily and left – then she'd given no sign of physical discomfort at their final night out. She had looked a little pale, he thought, but that was because she was a redhead. She went pale when she was angry and, for one reason and another, she'd spent much of the past four months angry.

He tied up the binbag and hopped outside with it, in his boxer shorts, bagged-up foot and one slipper. He opened the bin, and the stench hit him like a blow. There were flies – even in December. And there was another bag, loosely tied, full of still more bloody material, and as he put the new one in, the first one shifted, letting some of its contents fall out onto the more usual refuse below. He let the lid slam. He couldn't work out why his wife had lost so much blood.

And then, suddenly, he could, and he just stood there, near naked in the quiet, freezing fog, rocking back and forth from his bad foot to his good one, thinking about the child she'd lost, before they lost each other. And who Sybille had found, since Rex and his wife hadn't made love in four months.

Twelve years on, Rex stood, remembering, in the trees outside the convent, wet and shivering, looking at the pile of boxes in the porch. What remained of his wife's life was in that teetering tower, waiting to be picked up. It was 7 am, and he had wandered the streets all night.

Opening the French windows had been a life-saver. The blast had come from the right, from the kitchen, and he'd almost surfed at the fringes of it right out into the front yard, tripping over a broom. As he ran, singed and scalded, on legs so useless he felt as if he was in a dream, he could see the yellow blaze raging in the kitchen, spreading, gradually, to the room he'd been sitting in. Thank God for theft, he thought, seeing that Bilal's phone was still in his hand. He rang 999 and then he limped away.

There were at least half a dozen places and people who would take him in. But if he was being watched, as it seemed, then those people would be at risk, too. Not even the deserted office would be safe. And the police? He couldn't trust them to keep him safe.

There'd been a few, blessed hours of relief on empty night buses, but eventually people had embarked to disturb his peace. They'd usually been lone, dozing shiftworkers, or gangs of giddy students, but still he'd found himself staring at them, over-alert, wondering if they'd been sent to get him. So, for the most part, he had circled the borough on his lame feet like a pilgrim, soaking in the frequent showers as he tried, in a sort of fever, to piece it all together.

So he found Mina? Concentrate! How? Why? And he poured

petrol on Mina – to set light to her? Just to frighten her? Into doing what? Out of doing what? But she ran, remember? Yes. Ran and caught Peter's cigarette in her clothes. Went up in flames. Died. Afterwards, he altered her last web post, stitching an earlier one in so her death made sense to people who wouldn't look closely, would just see the Kurdish girl and the politics and make up their minds on the spot. So is he the one who's after me? Does he only want to frighten me, or stop me for good? Or is there someone else who wants me to stop? Think! The paper... the man in the German paper. Did that happen to Mina's mother? The PKK used a hitman to kill her with his speciality – a traffic accident made to look like a hit and run. But why kill the sister of a hero? To get to the hero, maybe. So what if they came after his niece, too? And anyone else who looked too closely? Why is that van reversing so fast...

Comfortless thoughts like these rattled around his mind like ghost trains, all the night, each question only answering itself with another until he arrived, aching, exhausted, in the solace of the wooded grove. He wanted to be with his wife, before she went. But this was as close as he dared to get, hidden here, in the trees, watching her boxes in the porchway. He sat down on the wet earth, stiff twigs biting into his legs, too tired to care. He remembered the phone.

He pulled it out, uselessly pulled the collar of his sopping shirt up in search of comfort, and stared at it. He remembered what he'd been doing, just before the blast. The folder he'd found.

It was there. The killer could delete it from the cloud, but they couldn't do anything about copies already saved onto phones. Crouched in the trees, he watched Mina's true, unedited speech on the little rain-flecked screen, clamping one hand with another to stop the shaking. And at the truth, a freedom did, at last descend on him. Because he'd answered his questions now, and he knew. He looked something up. Sent a message. To Mina's killer. And he fell asleep, there, on the earth, in the rain.

He woke in darknesss. But it sounded like daytime, from the traffic noises and the shouts of the kids in the distant park. He was in a dark place, an earthy smelling tomb of sorts. He had a memory of hands pulling him, some fabric, like a towel, going over his face. Had they kidnapped him?

As his eyes caught up with the rest of him, Rex realised he was alone, in a shelter in the woods. There were hundreds of these conical structures, dotting every patch of woodland in the Borough – built by kids, or more likely, by their dads, after watching some survival show on the TV. Most were only branches grouped vertically around a tree-fork to create a draughty wigwam. This was a more serious affair – the logs lashed together, sheets of sacking or tarpaulin woven in and out to form a proper barrier against the weather. It smelt in there, smelt bad – of tobacco and feet and rotting leaves. A Bible in Cyrillic sat on a red bottle crate, next to a filthy sleeping bag. He knew who had dragged him in here.

There was no sign of Peter now, but he had left a full, unopened bottle of some Sports Energy drink on the floor, and Rex took the hint. It would be the first and only time such a thing passed his lips. As his head cleared, he heard sirens and he remembered his house. They'd have to let him put his skylights in now.

The phone had been carefully placed by his side as well, and he picked it up. No one had called on it, or replied to his message. He saw, to his alarm, that it was after 3 o'clock in the afternoon. He rushed out of the little shelter, banging his head painfully on an overhanging log. He hobbled through the trees, terrified a tubby, greying father trying to get his small son to pee in a bush, veered off in the opposite direction and arrived, panting, aching, at the doorway to the convent.

The boxes were still there. He felt a flood of relief. Sybille had not gone. Then another thought struck him. She had gone. The boxes hadn't followed yet. That would make sense – she wouldn't be travelling in a van with her boxes. The nuns had a number he knew by heart, and he rang it. A Sister – not Florence, someone younger, brusquer – said that Sybille had not been 'collected' yet. There'd been no word from Aurelie, so far.

And nothing changed, for five hours, as he stood with his clothes drying on his body, and as he sat and waited, focussing on the PAX sign and trying to steel himself for the fight to come. Two things would be happening soon, he knew that. Both promising trouble for him. He just didn't know which was coming first.

Then, around seven, he heard footsteps on the path behind him. He turned, and was shocked, momentarily, to see Rostam Sajadi.

'I should have guessed you might come instead.'

Briskly, Sajadi looked him up and down. 'There are clothes in the car. And tea. Come.'

Rex shook his head. 'I have to stay here.'

'Nobody is coming for your wife, Rex. Your sister-in-law checked into rehab this morning. Her husband has been ringing your telephone for hours.'

Sajadi handed Rex his telephone. 'It survived the blast. I sent someone to your house to take a look. Come.'

He beckoned again, briskly, a commanding officer, not used to being disobeyed. Rex was unsure. It could well be a trap. Something else in the car, besides clothes and tea. But the calls from France were true – seven listed on his phone.

Sajadi cocked his head. 'You don't trust me?' Then he chuckled. 'Actually, don't answer. I'm a man with a missing finger, standing in the woods at night and asking you if you trust me.' He rubbed his hands together. 'Look – you've got your phone. Call your friend in the police. Tell him where you're going. Record it all, if you like.'

'Where am I going?'

'Kurdistan.'

They shot down the hill, like passing royalty, pausing only in their tinted, upholstered comfort at the lights, where Wightman Road crossed Turnpike Lane. There was a big hoarding now where the doctor's surgery had once been – mock-up photos and mock-up promises, like the bullshit he'd been writing for Shopping City: *Ten, prestige dwellings in the heart of Wood Green.* Some angry lyricist had sprayed 'Wood Green Has No Heart' across the hoarding.

Rex had forgotten what Kurdistan had been called before. Halfway along Green Lanes, it was a new establishment, certainly, with a sign in the Kurdish colours, and in the window, a metal sculpture in the shape of an archer. The exposed brick interior boasted earnest-looking young men and women sipping coffee, playing backgammon, reading Kurdish newspapers. It was the sort of place Mina would have loved, Rex thought, as Sajadi led him through a door behind the counter, up some narrow, ungentrified stairs.

This was where the fathers and the grandfathers of the kids below took their pleasure – with tea instead of coffee, real cigarettes instead of vapourisers, and some kind of cash-incentivised card game. The John Major man was much in evidence on the wall. And actually, Rex realised, with an opportunity to look longer, it was John Major.

'What is it with him?' Rex asked, as he sat, damp and aching at a table, and more tea was placed at his elbow.

'The Karduchi were an ancient race of warriors. Fierce. They fought with bows and arrows.' Sajadi could not resist performing a mime of an archer, pulling back the string. 'You know? Like the statue in the window. The ancient Greeks described how every king wanted to have Karduchi in his army, but no king dared to go and recruit them. They were the Kurds. But over the centuries, you Europeans stopped being afraid of us. We became something to be used, divided up, deceived. The only politician in recent memory who has not taken that path is him.' Sajadi pointed to the bland, precise, bean-counting countenance of the former Prime Minister. 'In 1992, John Major fought for us as we died at the hands of Saddam. In the end, he could only send blankets. But he tried.'

'I didn't know.'

'No,' Sajadi replied, meaningfully. 'At school, they didn't teach about the promises the British made to the Kurds in 1926, and in 1946, the lies about ensuring them a safe homeland before leaving them to be slaughtered. The meetings, suddenly cancelled. The diplomatic correspondence, where your statesmen talk about the barbarous, feudal Kurds, who must be placated but never given real power.' He took a deep breath, seeming to master his anger. '"No friends but the mountains", that's our Kurdish saying. But even the mountains are not our friends! My mother died in the mountains, waiting for help. People are still dying on the mountains. Now can you see why I like money? You don't have to believe in it. Money just is.'

'Money only does its job because people believe in it.'

Sajadi shot him a short, shocked look and laughed. 'Horse shit. You're saying gold only exists because people believe in it?'

'I'm saying gold only matters because people believe it matters.'

'You're fucking crazy,' Sajadi said, shaking his head. Rex didn't reply. 'Money is real and it does real things. Like building towns for the refugees – bringing them down from the mountains of Syria and Iraq, out of the camps where you would leave them to rot, into the new Kurdistan. That's what money does. And the Turkish government calls me a trafficker, a people trafficker. I am not. I am the father of the Kurds.'

He made this, outwardly preposterous statement in such a calm, assured voice, that Rex didn't even smile. The man might, in some awful sense, be right.

'You don't seem to be on such good terms with your own people, though, Mr Sajadi.'

Sajadi gave him a long appraising look, as if behind those glittering eyes he was working out whether Rex was worthy of an explanation.

'In 1992, they welcomed me like a hero when I crossed into Turkey. The PKK. Sweets and flowers and photographs.' Actorly hands mimed the tributes flying in. 'Everywhere I went. Every tiny, poor, desperate village from Urfa to Kars. That's the story Keko and Mina believed. "Rostam – the lion of Kore". He spat. 'You know why every Kurdish village gave the sweets and the flowers? Because they were terrified. Terrified of Abdullah Öcalan – 'Apo', they call him, 'The Uncle' – and of the PKK thugs he controls. If the villages gave food and shelter to the guerrillas, the Turks bombed them. If they didn't give to the PKK, then the PKK set fire to them. There was no honour in what the PKK were doing.' Sajadi shook his head. Then, abruptly, slammed his hand on the table, making Rex jump. 'I decided to leave them. But before I could go, I was caught by MIT – Turkish intelligence. Sent to the prison in Van. A very bad place.' He held up the damaged hand. 'To make me talk, they beat me with wires, they burnt me, they slammed a metal door on my hand. The door of the hospital wing. And then they left me there, with my finger trapped in the door, the doctors and the nurses in the prison moving past me, around me, doing nothing, until my finger just came away like a dog's tail. Three days. Three days, during which I didn't make a sound. They got nothing. In the end, the Turks let me go and I went back to my unit in the mountains. It was snowing. My hand was very bad. I went to bed. For Mina and Keko, the story is like this: I couldn't fight any more so I left the mountains, with all the blessings of the PKK and some money, and I came to Germany to find my sister.' Sajadi laughed bitterly. 'A lovely bedtime story. In truth Öcalan's monkeys took me from my bed at the end of a gun, and said, first you tell us what you told to the Turks. I said – why would I do that, tell things to the Turks? I thought I was a hero to you. The Lion of Kore. They said, "You are not a Kurdish Lion. You are a Yezidi dog." See? See why I hate them?'

'But you never let your family know that?' Rex remembered his first meeting with Sajadi – the ornate chairs, the stuffy room, the elegant man waiting until his family had left before confiding his thoughts in a low, conspiratorial voice.

Throughout their conversation, a series of young, hard-looking lads had been coming in with cellophane-wrapped bales, the sort of thing that reminded Rex of Customs hauls on the news. They seemed to suggest the same thing to Sajadi, because he looked at them for a long time, and then cleared his throat and said: 'Behind the Marxist horse-shit, PKK were selling Afghan heroin through Turkey into Europe. So I took my war pension, Mister Tracey. One finger equals two kilograms of their pure heroin. I took from their beards, we say! I went to Germany, I sold it, I bought my shops, everything. No, I never told Keko and Mina that. They never knew.'

'And you're still selling it.'

Sajadi laughed, drily. 'Yeah? You want some? You like that shit, I've heard. Here...'

Before Rex could stop him, Sajadi had gone over to the table, removed a keyring and slashed open one of the bales. Instead of brown powder, though, it was pale blue pills that Sajadi brought back in his palm.

'Nootropics! Cognitive enhancers. The students love them. Doctors doing double shifts, restaurant workers.... Girls trying to lose some kilos. They aren't even illegal. People give them to their grandmothers, you know. Really.' He tapped his forehead. 'Helps with the memory. At some stage, of course, a stupid kid will take fifty of them with a bottle of vodka and die. His parents will make a fuss. A doctor will write a letter, maybe to a newspaper like yours, and the government will have to look busy, and make them illegal. But by the time that happens, we will be making a new kind, that is a little bit different, so it can't be illegal yet!'

Rex, who suddenly realised he hadn't taken any of his own pills for almost a day – and not missed them – picked out one of the pills and looked at it. He put it back on the table, remembering the reference to 'study aids' in the student newsletter. And Eric Miles saying he'd found some new wonder drug for his Mum.

It was remarkable, really. The old drug lords, the heroin-importing Bombacılar, had sent whole neighbourhoods to sleep, but here was this new kingpin, Rostam Sajadi, flooding the borough with things that made people work more efficiently. A manqué capitalist with a missing finger. Then he remembered something else. Sajadi interrupted him before he could bring it up.

'See? Changing. Kurdish businessmen are not moving heroin through the back of the fruit shops now. Your newspapers like to say that, but that is gone. Or laundering money. If you wanted to clean your money, you don't need a shop with one can of okra on the shelves, there is bitcoin, poker machines, money mules… Everyone is getting smarter, even the criminals. I just provide the smart pills.'

'Now you do. But you built your empire on the back of the drugs you stole. And that's why the PKK came after your sister, isn't it? In the accident that wasn't an accident?'

Sajadi nodded, his self-delight ebbing away and turning into anger. 'Just as she had started to find happiness, Meda was destroyed. Keko could never know about that side of my life, or what killed Meda. Nor Mina. So I could never tell them why I'd left the mountains, what I really knew about Öcalan and his dogs.'

'And Aran?'

Another long pause. Sajadi ordered someone to re-wrap

the opened parcel. When this had been done, he abruptly rose to his feet and asked all the men to leave. They did so, swiftly but without panic, leaving their unplayed hands of cards and their smoking cigarettes in place until Rex and Sajadi sat alone – a flashing sign from across the road bouncing regularly off John Major on the wall.

'How did you know it was him?'

'Because Aran bumped into someone that day. A friend of mine. In Sky City. That friend told me how a short, Kurdish-looking man had struggled with them in the moments after Mina died, and grabbed… my friend by the throat with his hand.' Rex was trying to reveal nothing of Peter's identity, not even his gender. 'That's what my friend said. His hand. I only had to ask what the hand was like to know it wasn't you. You still use your bad hand for everything – you'd have put it round my friend's throat if it had been you. And I knew Aran resented his sister. He certainly seemed to resent his life, and to envy hers. That's all I had to go on, really. A sense. So I sent him that message. And he passed it you, I guess.'

The flashing sign switched off, and in the same moment Sajadi seemed to change again. The Father of the Kurds left the stage, leaving a sad, bitter little man in a London café. 'Idiot. A stupid fucking idiot. When I found out where she was, in Sky City, I sent him. I told him: just do you what you have to do to stop her. Burn her passport if you have to.'

'So he tries to burn her.'

'He told me at first that, on the day she died, he went to that flat she was staying in, in Sky City, and she wasn't there. He found the place was empty and it just smelled of petrol. For a while, I wondered if he could be telling the truth.'

'So when you asked me to help – you genuinely weren't sure how she'd died?'

He nodded, distractedly. 'The day after you and I were on the marshes, the police handed back her personal effects, and there was that peacock that she wore, and there was a lighter in there, and Aran broke down then. Told me the truth.'

Sajadi lit a cigarette. 'You were right. He always hated her. From when they were kids. Mina was so quick, so alive. He was so quiet, so… locked away, with his birds and his books. To be honest she hated him, too. When he tried to talk to her, she wouldn't listen. She goaded him, about his birds, his pathetic life, doing shifts in a supermarket, odd-jobs for his uncle, a university degree but making nothing of himself. Mina had a sharp tongue,' Sajadi said, almost admiringly. 'Always did. She went, maybe, too far. Even a mouse can bite, you know?'

'But you still sent him to do the job.'

'Yes. I sent him,' Sajadi confirmed, seeming to miss Rex's point, or ignoring it. 'I had tried myself, before she ran away. She wouldn't listen. And I had to stop her from going.'

'To help the refugees, you mean?'

Sajadi nodded, slowly.

'Except Mina wasn't planning to help the refugees, was she, Mr Sajadi? She was going out there to join the *peshmerga*. To go to war, like you did.'

The Kurd sighed, nodded slowly. 'So you found out.'

'I saw the real speech Mina made. The one you deleted. Where she said she'd turned her back on politics, and the illusion of choice. I saw the kind of training she'd been doing, to prepare herself. Half in the open – pretending to her girlfriend they were just trying to get fit – half in secret.

Not even her girlfriend guessed what she was really going to do.'

Sajadi snorted. 'Don't use that word! That's how it began. When I flew back from a business trip a few months back, I went to surprise my niece, and pick her up from university after her lectures and...' He took a breath after this outburst, then seemed to relax a little, even to soften as he went on. 'We had a tradition of our own, you know. From when she was at school. A Four Seasons pizza in Pizza Express. A strawberry milkshake in McDonalds. See? She was still a child.'

Not a child, but an ordinary young woman. Stitched, without consent, into the extraordinary seams of Haringey and all its histories. Sajadi's fond look had returned to something less pleasant, as he carried on.

'From across the road, I saw them coming out of their lessons.'

'Mina and Kyretia?'

Sajadi frowned. 'Her with a boy! A Turkish boy. I didn't say anything. But after that I watched her a few times, without her knowing, and that boy was always there. So I went to visit him.'

'Haluk.' Rex remembered the black eye he'd had on their first meeting. 'I'm guessing you didn't share a Happy Meal with him.'

Sajadi smiled dangerously, and Rex wondered if he'd gone too far. There was no reason to the man, after all, no logic, only sets of contradictions. He'd rejected his traditions, but been appalled to see Mina with a Turkish boy. He spoke about honour when all he honoured was money. Financed good in one corner of the world through bad in another.

'He swore to me he wasn't Mina's boyfriend. I hit him hard enough to know he was telling me the truth,' Sajadi said, matter-of-factly, like a plumber discussing the lagging he'd used. 'He told me that she had a… a…' He shook his head, replaying the initial shock. 'That she was that way. And they were going to Turkey together. To help the refugees with their application forms! Like a man and a wife. Disgusting. But it's like I say, she was just a kid. I understand – they try something, think it's cool, make mistakes. They move on, their lives go on.'

'But if she joined the *peshmerga*, you worried her life wouldn't go on.'

'I couldn't let her go. At the best, she'd find out from the old *peshmerga* what I did, how I caused her mother's death. At worst, they would take another revenge on her. I had to stop her. We had a big argument, I tried to explain to her, for the first time, how bad those people really are. But she refused to obey or listen to reason. She knew I would try everything I could, so then she went to hide in Sky City. Full of my flats, of course.' He laughed, without mirth. 'She was even hiding in one of them.'

'Is that how you found out she was there?'

Sajadi shook his head. 'I don't go there. Nothing is connected to me. I found out because of that fat Turk.'

'Bilal?'

'Haluk! I had nothing to do with Bilal. Not his life, not his death. Who was he, to me? A clerk. A secretary. Nobody.'

'Really?'

'You saw the Inquest into that man. A stroke.'

'Maybe. I know you didn't hurt Mina, but Bilal knew how involved you were in the corruption at the council. He was dangerous to you. You killed him, didn't you? Or you had him killed.'

'Dangerous? When are you going to understand? Nothing will happen to me. This little fight in the chicken house will play out, some people will go to prison, you will get a fine, bright, new council, and I will still be here. Your police, your government, they cannot get rid of me because I am necessary to them.'

'In what way are you necessary?'

'Because of Yenişakir. Because of what I am building. You will see. In any case, I have no reason to deny something if I did it. I didn't touch Bilal. The person I mean – who told me where Mina was – it's the one I beat.' He snorted in contempt. 'Haluk is like the boys I use here. Too many gangster films on their i-Pads. He comes to me with some fantasy out of Godfather Part Two and says, you know, "Big player like you Mister Sajadi need a good lawyer-man, *naamsain innit*?"' It was a fine imitation. Rex obliged it with a smile. 'He told me the police had taken him and the girlfriend in for questioning. But he'd lied to them. To help me. To prove he was a good *soul-jah* or some horse shit of that sort.'

'So that's why he did it. Not for Kyretia. To impress you.'

'I could have told him fuck off. But I said, okay, if you got something I can use, let me know. Why not? He's got a key – this kid – master key, for the Security Guard job. When the black girl, Mina's…' Sajadi coughed, unable to say the word. 'When that black girl is in the gym, he opened the locker, looks at her phone. Sees some texts Mina has sent to her. So we found her. I knew she wouldn't listen to me any more, so I said to Aran – okay, you do it. He was getting tired of the

337

work he does for me. So I said, okay, do this instead. Talk to your sister.'

'I thought Arun just worked in the shop.'

'He works there to repay his father. And to repay me… Well. He wasted three years at Reading University, learning what? Birds. Avian… eco… biodiversity…? Horse shit. I said, all right, now something useful. I paid for him to do another degree – biopharmacology – and he works for me.' Sajadi waved towards the bales on the table.

'He's your chemist.'

'I said to him – I've had enough of the girl. Do what you have to do to stop her. Burn the passport if you need to. So he brought petrol from the shop, he said, to do that, to burn it.'

'Wouldn't a match have done the job?'

'Modern passports are too useful for identifying people, Mr Tracey. If you want to destroy one, you really need to destroy it. So he went there with petrol and Mina made him angry. So then he poured the petrol all over her, but he didn't mean to do anything else.' Sajadi leant across the table, stone-faced, as if he was accusing Rex himself. 'That's what Aran told me. He looks me in the eye, and he says that she ran away, and somehow, just out of the air, for no reason, she goes on fire. Do you believe that?'

'He didn't set light to his sister. It was a dropped cigarette.' The eyes narrowed. 'Who dropped it? Your friend? Who is your friend?'

'I'm not going to tell you. It's not relevant, is it? Where's Aran?'

There was a long pause where Sajadi seemed to be lost in thought. Eventually, he lit a cigarette and said quietly, 'I sent Aran away. He is taking a package for me, from Van to Hokkari. It's a very quiet road.'

'So?'

'If you run into some bad people out there, or you crash your car... maybe no one will ever know what happened to you. It happens a lot.'

The eyes bored into him. And the man's point eventually sunk in. 'You sent Aran away to be killed.'

'I was so sure he was lying to me about setting her on fire.' Sajadi held his head in his hands. Rex wondered if he was crying. Then, abruptly, he sat up, shook his head briefly and took a deep breath.

'That friend of yours did not do the damage. You are correct. The damage was done by the person who caused Mina to spend the last minutes of her life in terror, believing she was going to die in that awful way. The damage was done by Aran, and he deserved to die.' He banged his hand flat on the table, reminding Rex of the time he'd imitated a judge's gavel. So certain. So final. He guessed Aran had already met with his 'accident'.

'You don't think you have any responsibility for it? You knew what Aran was like.'

Sajadi stared at him, wide-eyed, as if he'd just sung a chorus. 'No. Why? I didn't tell him to do that.'

Rex was silent. Sajadi was a sharp man, yet seemingly not that clever. And this, combined with his power and his absolute self-assurance, made him frightening. He was like the parts of a man, with something missing. Like the scrawl on the sign on the housing development. *Wood Green Has No Heart*.

'Keko will never know,' Sajadi went on. Rex nodded. 'He is the only person who will miss him. And, perhaps, his sweetheart, perhaps not.'

'Did he have one?'

'I think so.' Sajadi stood up, proffered a hand towards the door. 'I see you are appalled by me. Trust me – many people in your Home Office and your Foreign Office are, too. But when I have built a new Kurdistan, then I will be to you what you failed to be to my people: a protector. Kurds from Iraq, from Syria, maybe one day from Iran, too, one family at a time, one street, one town. First, my town, Yenişakir, then another, then another, but not just towns. Factories, hospitals, laboratories, internet companies – full of people like the people you see downstairs, young people, educated, with skills and ambition. There will be no need for a war – the Turks will need my Kurdistan for what it can offer them. And you – you in the West will need it too. My country will be what protects you. A stable, moderate, democratic, burgeoning economy with gas and oil. Standing between you and the maniacs from the desert, with their black flags, and their swords and their beliefs. You know about Tawsi Melek? The Yazidi God?'

'This is the peacock?'

'One of seven angels, banished by God for his pride, then forgiven. Placed on earth to do good. And yet, to you, to Christians, to Jews, Muslims, a devil!' He laughed. 'Come here!'

Sajadi marched over to the window, beckoning Rex to follow. They looked down at the Lanes, still the place Rex loved, still that idiosyncratic crush of alphabets and languages, the garish gold and the alien root vegetables. But undoubtedly smarter now, brightly-lit windows full of people spending money. And not just on gözleme.

'Seven years ago, I told Keko to stop paying Bombacılar.

I didn't tell him why. I just said – look, I got some influence now. You don't pay them. So he stopped. And you know what happened? Nothing. You know what else happened? All these places you are looking at with me now, up and down the Lanes, they stopped paying too.'

'No magazines,' Rex said, remembering Keko's sign, remembering all the loaded, cryptic conversations he'd had. And finally understanding. Not fund-raising for the PKK, extortion by the gangsters. A protection-racket, plain and simple, run on collective fear. And useless when people stopped being afraid.

'Yes, the magazines that nobody sells and nobody buys. Well done. So you see, from being kept, just above the surviving line, by the thugs of Bombacılar, all these people began to make money. This is why you see what you see. Because your Yezidi devil brought peace here as well. Why are you looking at me like that?'

'If you bring "peace", Mr Sajadi, why did you blow up my house?'

'I didn't. Why do I need to? You want to know who bombed you, ask the bombers. Ask Bombacılar.'

'But why would they bomb me?'

'Why would I know?' Sajadi grinned. 'I am just a businessman.'

CHAPTER NINETEEN

A quirky little ska number, about a man so poor his trousers kept falling down, was playing on the speakers in the Jerk Shack, and Rex shifted uncomfortably, feeling the song could have been about him. After the explosion, HQ had authorised emergency funds for him to buy some basics – clothes and toiletries – but he'd had to get them in a hurry, from Shopping City, and he'd now spent the best part of a week in a pair of baggy Primark jeans, and a selection of shirts that seemed to have designed by someone without a basic grasp of the human form. He wondered if the sisters had played this track as a wind-up.

Brenard brought over the coffees, along with a pair of fiery curried patties. Rex envied him his neat suit. 'Still at Terry's?' the detective asked. 'Men Behaving Badly, is it?'

'Last night, Terry and I shared a fresh broccoli tagliatelle in front of "Great Continental Railway Journeys".'

'No. Really? Oh, I see… All right. Get knotted,' said Brenard, realising the wind-up. 'I was glad to hear about your missus, anyhow. Is she pleased she's staying put?'

'Who knows?' Rex said. He'd spent a lot of time up at the

convent in the past week, and the only obvious pleasure he'd observed was when he'd told his wife that Aurelie had gone back to rehab after a bout of heavy drinking. Sybille had cackled at that, as a little girl might on discovering her sister was in trouble.

'So – you want to know about Eric Miles, then?' Brenard said, changing subject as the music did. 'Magistrate bailed him. Miles says I don't want bail, I'm a very naughty boy. Magistrate says, tough, it's not requests hour, mate, you're bailed. Miles says, right, you're an effing c. Carries on like that, trying to punch the security guards, so they'll lock him up. Scared of going back to his mam, I reckon.'

'I almost feel sorry for him.'

'I don't. Listen, butt, don't swallow that line about, "ah it was just a few bits of paper". Miles was in it, long-term, up to his nose hair. Him and half a dozen of them even had some fake company going, drawing salaries out of it, all taxed, N.I. stamped, totally legit-looking, except there was no company, and the cash was all washed.'

'What kind of company?'

'Fraud Squad are having a headache over it. There was more people on the books than we've nabbed at the council, though, so one theory is they've been offering a borough-wide service to anyone wanted their funds freshened.' He took a sip of the coffee, burnt his tongue, and put the mug down again. Dizzee Rascal took over the speakers. 'Don't feel sorry for Miles. Feel sorry for the buggers who weren't having boom-time. All them little shops and that, paying through the nose.'

'What shops?'

'Looks like, while the council went on the take, Bombacılar

344

diversified too. It's always been very ethnic, round here – well, you know, don't you? Kurds only go after Kurds, Russians after Russians. You know – you shaft your own, leave everyone else alone. Seems, for whatever reason, the Bombers broke with tradition, left their own alone, started going after everyone else – Turks, Greeks, even Caribbeans. Factories, shops, newsagents, whatever. Green Lanes boomed, everyone saw that – because there are so many Kurdish businesses down there. Lots of others went under.'

Rex was silent. He knew why it had happened. Because of Sajadi's false peace. Because one lot getting a turn at the trough only meant another lot starving. That included, he now realised, the Topraks' factory, the one next door to it, Spyridonidis, so vulnerable with its non-existent sons. And Eryl Pocock's bakery. Suddenly, it hit him. He choked on his pasty – and not because of the chillies.

'I know what the fake business is,' he said. 'I know who's behind it. I know who blew up my sodding house. And I know how they're washing the cash. Come on!'

He stood up abruptly, spilling his water.

'What's got into you? Come where?'

'We're going to the bookie's.'

* * *

On a blistering hot day at the start of September, Brenda Bond finally saw her longed-for Wildlife and Wetlands Centre completed and opened to the public. A prominent local businessman had stepped into the breach, and not only completed the project, but arranged and funded a spectacular opening ceremony, complete with clowns, jugglers, steel bands and an assortment of exotic beasts and birds.

Brenda, shading herself with a parasol like a lady of yore, was torn. As a supporter of the original project, she was duty bound to be delighted. As the down-to-earth, hype-rejecting Brenda, though, she thought many elements of it were over-the-top. Especially the opening ceremonies, and their various ill-fitting elements, from helicopters and Lamborghinis, to a Bratwurst stand, a disco, and camel rides.

'What's any of that got to do with our Wetlands centre?' she grumbled. 'Is it his helicopter?'

'Probably his camel too,' said Terry.

Susan, just back from her stay in the States, rolled her eyes at Rex. She was still catching up on the major events of the past few months; catching up, Rex realised, without having said anything about where she'd been, or with whom.

Today, he realised, as he sniffed in the camel dung and the sausage fat and the sun lotion, was the first day he'd been entirely unable to recall what a burning person smelt like. All he remembered of that moment now were the colours he'd seen as Mina fell: peacock-like, iridescent, ever-shifting. His memory had done that. He didn't feel guilty about it. Memories had to wash experience like that – launder it – for their owners to endure.

A few feet away, the beaming Rostam Sajadi was standing for photos with the newly elected Labour MP, Eve Reilly, under the impressive, futuristic entrance to Mina's Place. The state-of-the-art animal refuge, wittily shaped like some Martian version of the Ark, was capable of housing every unwanted, crawling, hopping and climbing thing in Harringay and Tottenham, from jerboas to goldfish. Sajadi was just making a joke about this when his voice died in his throat and, as one, the entire party, politicians, press snappers and all, turned to gaze in wonder at the tall black girl, vaguely clad in a pale ivory sheet as she strode by, haughtily, on mighty heels. She walked past Rex and Susan, too, reserving for the former a short, intense look of undying contempt.

'She likes you,' Susan said.

'Kyretia hates me,' Rex replied. 'Mainly because I got her brother sent down for money-laundering. He was funnelling cash through his dad's moribund business, after washing it in the poker machines in the bookies.'

'Strange kind of washing,' Susan said, fanning herself with a hand. It was impossible to imagine her sweating.

'It's simple. You put a load of cash in. You bet a tiny amount. Probably lose it. Then you ask for your money back. The machine prints you a voucher that's like poker chips – take it to the lady, lady gives you cash. Then it's legally yours. In young Ashley's case, he was doing it for the bent council, then he got the idea of offering the service around. He was doing it for the Bombacılar, the same people who ruined his dad.'

'Aha. The Bombers. Who didn't like you sniffing around, so blew a big skylight in your roof for you.'

'Threatened me, then blew me up, classic Bombers business model, except I never made the connection. Shall we?'

A ribbon had been cut, a round of applause had begun, faltered and been resuscitated again. The party was now moving inside Mina's Place for the official tour, and they tacked onto the back. Rex turned round and watched Kyretia's powerful, naked back, as she strode away over the path, back to the car park. She wasn't going to stay, and he understood that, as he understood her anger. He still remembered the final, excised part of Mina's YouTube valedictory, addressed to one person alone.

"*Tatlım*, I lied. I love you and I've lied to you. They are two facts: as true as each other, *yavrum*. I didn't hide because of us. I hid because of me. Because of my blood. You can't understand. *Ben Kürdüm, sevgilim*. I'm Kurdish, darling. I'm hiding because they want to stop me fighting. And I have to fight. *Seni seviyorum*. I love you forever."

And he still wondered if he'd done the right thing, by sending it to Kyretia. It had scraped at his conscience until he did it. Then again, it still scraped now.

In the muggy, biscuity fug of the animal house, they all filed sluggishly past anacondas and sloths, who eyed them beadily back. A cheeky cub from the nationals asked about the stray dogs: after all, these were the principal abandoned species on the streets, so where were they? Sajadi, with the bluntness Rex had come to know and distrust, stared at the reporter and barked, 'We can't keep them here, can we?' before marching on.

He was in lead position here, now, the man answering the questions, doing the job Eric Miles would have expected to do. It seemed as if that was the choice: rule by the secretly bent, or the openly bent. No wonder Mina had preferred the rifle to the ballot box.

Rex wondered what she would have made of it all. She'd had some affection for animals, but clearly her main drive had been to stop people being treated like them. 'Mina's Place', with its cutesy name like a café or a bric-a-brac corner, wasn't a tribute, it was a kind of insult. He'd exchanged a couple of very basic, truncated emails with Keko – he wasn't surprised that the old man had decided to stay away. Nor was Rex surprised that Sajadi's path to glory continued unimpeded. He'd never been further away, in fact, from being shut down. As the fanatics, and their unique brand of lunacy spread, so more people fled from them and Sajadi's towns grew, a Kurdistan made by numbers rather than decree. And needed, not just to keep the Kurds safe, but also the people cowering behind them in Europe.

They'd stopped by the peacock – 'donated' by Sajadi himself, or rather, shunted off because he didn't want Aran's moody pet. The thing whined and bristled at the crowd, and then did something extraordinary, flying like a cloud of eyes to the wire and nuzzling at the fingers of one of the party, who seemed more embarrassed than pleased.

'Clever old bird,' murmured Susan. 'Knows an influential friend when he sees one.'

Outside: more milling about, terrible speeches, considerably better wine. A Kurdish Shiraz, from Sanliurfa. Glass in hand, Rex went over to the bratwurst stand, debating whether to join the long queue.

'I'd get your face painted instead,' said a curly-haired woman, standing by the next stall. 'Far less demand.'

He laughed. 'Hello, Diana.'

'Hello,' she said. She was wearing a straw hat and a pretty, 1950s-style dress. A dark-haired girl was currently on the stool, being turned, rather badly, into a lion.

'That's one of your nieces, isn't it?'

'Mm. Jessica. And this...' she said, hauling a pram-pushchair device round to display a fat, pink, chortling baby. 'Is Chaya.'

He felt an urge to squeeze one of the fat legs. Resisted it. 'Well their mum's getting a good deal out of you,' he said.

'Chaya's mine, Rex. Mine and Kjell's.'

A cork popped over by the VIPs. Sajadi telling a story, full of gestures. Acting it all out, not to make things clearer, but to make things less clear, hide who he really was. Rex looked back to Diana, then from her to the cute, blue-eyed kid, and back again. 'I thought you'd… I got the impression you'd come back on your own.'

'I came back with Chaya. Kjell is…' Diana shrugged, a silvery bra-strap emerging against brown skin. 'I don't care, really. Saving lives somewhere. He didn't want Chaya, so we don't want him.' She bent over and squeezed a fat leg.

'Tough on your own.' In his case, at least, it was more than a platitude.

'My mum helps.' She smiled. 'And Uncle Lawrence. Babies love Uncle Lawrence, you know.'

'I can imagine. The same demonic power he uses on old ladies.'

'The surgery's been really good too – letting me do odd hours. I'm going in for the late shift this afternoon. It's all okay. It's more than okay. It's good. Isn't it?' She addressed this to the baby, then looked back at him. 'Come and see us, Rex. Don't… don't not come and see us.'

'I won't. I mean – you know – I will. I'll come very soon.'

He meant that, although he didn't know if she understood that. She was just kissing him softly on the cheek when Chaya started to grumble. Diana started to tuck a sheet around the child.

'Would you believe it, this kid is cold. She was born in Cambodia. She thinks this is winter. We're going to have to get you one of those big horrible parkas…'

He was halfway back to his colleagues and the crush at the

booze table when it struck him like a sudden headache. The big, 'balloon coat' that Peter had talked about. A photograph he'd seen once on a wall. A strangely friendly peacock and its choice in friends. And the killer of Bilal Toprak.

The Personal Assistant proved unwilling to assist, until he told her to say just two words to her boss. He had to spell them out, and within less than a minute, she was back on the line, sounding very different. 'Mr Toprak?' she said, getting his name and his message mixed up, 'Sorry for the delay. Can you come to the office in an hour?'

He arrived just a little late, on account of a detour he'd made to make via Seven Sisters, and a call he'd had to make to one Vonda Paul, which had clarified things further. The office, as he'd expected, was now devoid of occupants except for one. He took the photograph right off the wall. He wasn't stopped.

'I looked up Vardo. It's in the far north of Norway. I guess that's why everyone in the photo's bundled up in huge coats. You – I can see you there. What about Aran? Where's he?'

Eve Reilly took the photograph from him and pointed, wordlessly, to a shape in a huge, blimp-shaped parka.

'Incredible biodiversity,' Rex said. 'Almost as many bird species pass through Vardo than are resident in the Amazon. Did you and Aran get it together there or later?'

'There,' she said, pale-faced and blotchy in the heat, a look of hate in her eyes.

'Not much else to do in the evenings, I guess. So for – how long was it? – ten years, you and Aran were an item. But the papers describe you as single, you've never turned up uncle said he only suspected that Aran had a girl. Why the secrecy?'

'We didn't make a secret of it at uni – no one was

interested in us. We were just a pair of geeks who held hands in lectures. But afterwards, I got into politics. And Aran's family – they never officially came here. They were illegal. I told Millbank. They just said, ditch him if you seriously want to be selected.'

'So you hid it from your bosses, too?'

'No. We parted. Until I was selected. Then, I thought the pressure would be off. But then Aran started to find about the things his uncle was involved in, and it became even more apparent. If it came out…'

'Bye-bye constituency.'

'It was about protecting each other. Because we loved each other,' she said sourly, a strange tone for a declaration of love. 'I still love him. I still want him to come back.'

Rex said nothing. He'd had enough, he thought, of telling people the awful truth. It didn't make anyone happier.

'She managed to grab Aran's phone. Mina – I mean. When I was doing the walkabout, on Newroz, he was up in Sky City, at that flat, trying to talk to her.'

'Talk to her? Drench her in petrol and threaten her, you mean.'

'You don't know what went on there. Mina grabbed his phone, while he was out of the room. He was pretending to fetch his lighter.'

'So he told you that? Aran told you what he did, how terrified he must have made his little sister, and you still love him? You weren't disgusted by that? Appalled by it?'

'Of course I was!' she shouted. 'I was horrified! I was horrified when I realised it was her, it was Mina, lying there on the floor in front of us…' Her voice died away.

'So you knew then,' he said. 'I wondered about that. You

seemed very in control – doing everything right until you looked at her.'

Eve said nothing, just nodded.

'And it was clear to you then, that Aran was part of it?'

She shook her head, several times, before the words came. 'I had no idea. I knew she was missing. I knew Aran and his uncle were looking for her. That was it. When I got out of Shopping City, and away from everyone, I rang him, and I told him. He seemed as shocked as I was. But something wasn't right. I can't explain it. I thought something wasn't right. Normally, when anything upset him, he wanted to be with me. But he was avoiding me. That's what it felt like. Until they got the last of her things back from the Police. Then he said he had to see me. And he told me.' She cleared her throat.

'And then you kept his secret for him.'

'Mina was a bitch to him,' she said, harshly. 'You think, just because she died that way, that made her good? When they were kids, she teased him about reading slowly. Told lies to get him in trouble. Mina treated Aran like dirt for their whole life together, and nobody ever tried to stop her. They let her get away with it, her dad and her uncle, all those years, because she was a girl, and because she was pretty, and he was none of those things. Tell me you'd have spent so much time on it, if it had been him on the escalator. Tell me you'd have noticed the kid in the back of the café, if it had been an ordinary-looking boy. He was there, Rex, plenty of those times you were in there, playing the Great White Explorer. You didn't notice Aran. And no one else did either.'

Silence – while he racked his brains, while she recovered her cool. She was right, of course. Life wasn't, as Eric Miles had said, full of snowflake-like perfections, it was full of ugly inequalities. The pretty girl got the attention. The wicked triumphed; the weak only became strong when someone else took their place.

'So Aran snapped,' she went on. 'Yes. He went to the flat she was hiding in to get her passport off her, and burn it. She taunted him. He lost it. But he had no intention of setting her on fire. I know that. I don't know for sure what happened to Mina. I don't care. I just know. I've seen him looking after birds. Tiny birds, feeding them with a dropper, all night, every hour, making a splint that was this big…' She held up finger and thumb, barely an inch apart. 'For a broken wing. He's not capable of killing.'

'Unlike you. Unless you're claiming someone other than yourself murdered Bilal Toprak.'

'No, it was me.' She took a deep breath. 'But it wasn't murder. I had to go to Bilal's house and see him, because she rang him. At Sky City, when Aran went out of the room, Mina grabbed his phone and she rang Bilal, but he didn't pick up. She was about to leave a message for him when Aran came back in. He says she threw the phone at him and she managed to get out of the flat. Aran ran after her and… well, you know…'

'I know,' he interrupted. 'But you don't, do you?'

'I believe Aran. That's all that matters. I haven't tried to think what happened to her after that because I…'

'Because if you did, you might doubt him,' Rex said. She said nothing, merely looked down at her hands. He could, he knew, put her out of her misery now, tell her how Mina had really come to die in flames. But Reilly's faith was as much a crime as her deceit. He'd met other women with that sort of faith: wives 'believing' in their rapist husbands, mothers not only 'believing' but providing the alibis for scumbag sons. Faith as a means of hiding. Sajadi was right about something. Belief without doubt was horse shit.

'When Aran got back to the flat, he saw she'd made that call on his phone,' she continued in a small voice. 'He didn't know whose number it was. He didn't do anything. But his phone kept ringing. It was Bilal, obviously, ringing back, trying to find out whose phone the call had come from. And every time it rang, it reminded Aran of what had happened.'

'It didn't "happen", Eve. Nothing just "happened" without your boyfriend choosing to pour petrol on his sister.'

She gave a sullen nod. 'He knew that. That's why he couldn't keep it together in the end. He broke down, and he confessed it all to me. He was lucky. He was in such a state, he might have told his uncle. I don't know what he'd have done.'

Rex looked away. She'd be finding out soon enough, he guessed, what the uncle had done.

'I told him to get rid of the SIM. So he did, and the calls stopped. But Bilal wanted to know what had happened to Mina. He knew she'd been in hiding – he'd helped her to hide. She never told him why she needed to, but he wasn't an idiot, he suspected it was to do with Sajadi. And he thought her death was, too. So he kept going to the shop, to ask Aran.'

Rex nodded. 'Like the girl in the shop said. Bilal came looking for Aran. I thought it must have happened after the social club collapsed. I thought it had something to do with that. But I was wrong. He said he was *too late*. He didn't mean too late getting to the club. He meant too late to get Mina's call.'

And he thought of that odd comment the shop-girl had

relayed, off-the-wall, an aside, really, but tellingly bitter. *People like you don't need that sign no more.* Bilal's own family had been ruined by the racketeers. Aran's had escaped them. And now Bilal must have been sure they were connected to the death of his friend, Mina.

'It made you anxious, didn't it? The last time I was here, I mentioned Bilal's visit to the supermarket. And you didn't like me knowing that.'

She gave a sullen shrug. 'It doesn't matter now, does it? Eventually Bilal caught up with him and Aran was... he was no good at lying. He let something slip about a flat. And of course, no one but Bilal and Mina was supposed to know she'd been in a flat. And now Bilal was really suspicious.'

'So you went to see him. On the Thursday morning. And, whilst doing a bit of pre-election leafleting, kill him.'

'It isn't like that.'

'You didn't kill him? Or you weren't leafleting? I know you weren't leafleting. Most of Effingham Road knows that.'

'If you'll let me answer,' she said icily. Rex fell silent. She'd have done all right on 'Newsnight', Eve Reilly. If she'd made it.

'I went to see Bilal on the Wednesday afternoon, and I told him the truth. He was working from home. He'd just got in, with a load of shopping, he was unpacking it, with the radio on. There was no point in lying. I told him what had gone on...'

'Do you get training in this? "Mistakes were made", "an event occurred". You know why I never wanted to profile you? Because I knew I'd get this bullshit. Tell the truth. Nothing had "gone on". Your boyfriend terrorised his sister, and you killed a man to cover it up!'

'Not killed!' she said, hotly, her cheeks flushing. 'We talked.

I mentioned what Aran had told me, about his uncle's empty flats, and the council scam, and I said that gave us both something on each other. But he just laughed in my face. He said he wasn't part of the stuff at the council, and he was about to bring it all crashing down. He said he'd let me fall with it. He showed me this dossier-thing. I had a look. It was like he said. He had enough to destroy them. I begged him to see reason. This wasn't like Miles and the council, this wasn't greed, this was an awful, stupid moment of anger, a family row, really, that went terribly wrong, in a way no one could have imagined.' She glanced up at him, here, for approval or condemnation. He gave her nothing.

'Bilal listened. He listened. I thought he might be seeing our side of it. But then he said it was wrong, and like it or not, the truth had to be told. So I hit him. I was so angry, I didn't think. I hit him. It was just a slap. But he fell, and he bashed his head, and he shook a bit.' Her voice trembled. 'But he was still alive.'

'So, instead of calling an ambulance, you put his shopping on the door-step, turned the music up, left his body in the bathroom with the taps running and buggered off with the front door open? What kind of First Aid course did you take?'

'I froze. I tried to run through the options. I could ring 999 and say I'd been walking past or something, but when he got better, there was no way he'd keep quiet. I could ring anonymously, but he'd still get better and shaft me. Then I thought – this is ridiculous – the guy is injured, you have to help.'

'Or, "if I save his life for him, he might keep quiet"?'

'That didn't occur to me!' she said savagely. 'I tried to move him. And that's when he stopped breathing. He died in my arms. I could have rung someone at that point – Bilal wasn't going to talk anymore, was he? But my DNA was all over him now, all over the house. I had no good reason for having been there. My only hope was to arrange it, so he could be found by someone else, and it not look like murder.'

'So you dragged him upstairs to the bathroom.'

'It kind of happened to one of my mum's friends. She had, like a mini-stroke when she was coming back in from her allotment. Sort of lost it – left all the veg on the doorstep, went upstairs and ran a bath. Collapsed in the bathroom. Luckily, someone over the road spotted the front door had been open and these bags sitting there for hours and went over. So...'

'Which you could have done when he was still alive, of course. But then he might have talked.'

'It was hard. He was a heavy man. I didn't mean to drop him against the tiles, it was just because I was exhausted, but in the end... I was sure they'd be able to tell, you know, that he'd had the bang on the head after he was dead, but I guess... maybe because of everything else, and because he was in running water, it wasn't clear... I just left him where he was, half in, half out of the bath with his clothes on, and I ran the bath taps.'

'Handily destroying the DNA, as well.'

'Then I just turned his radio up, grabbed his dossier, shoved the shopping out on the door and ran. I forgot to wipe my prints off his phone,' she added, as if this had just occurred to her.

'I've got Bilal's phone now,' Rex said. 'It'll have all my prints on it, too. But you're saying that all happened on Wednesday?'

358

'Wednesday afternoon – late. The builders had gone by the time I left. But I felt sure someone would find him. How could they not – with the door open and the shopping out there?'

'Maybe you should have known your constituency a bit better. It's not High Wycombe.'

'High Wycombe's nothing like you think,' she said, bitterly. 'There are plenty of estates. Kids like me, one eye on the meter while they do their homework, hoping the money will last. You haven't got a clue.'

'I have, actually. The difference is, I don't mention it in interviews, Eve. I don't think being poor is any more worthy of a medal than going to Eton. I reckon not killing and not lying are more important.'

'I didn't set out to do either. I kept checking the news. All night. There was nothing on your website, or anywhere else. I had to go back and see. So I grabbed some leaflets and I went back on Thursday morning. And nothing had happened. The door was open. The music was on. People couldn't even hear the music, because of all the building work.'

'So why didn't you just leg it again?'

'I couldn't bear it. And besides, this was a different day, different time. Busier. I'd seen a couple of people already. More people were recognising me after the walkabout and your piece about what happened there. Talking to me. Remembering they'd seen me, if anyone asked them. I realised it had to be me who found him. So I took the receipts out of the shopping bags and I went in.'

'And pretended you'd just found him. Whilst canvassing and leafleting on Friday. Except you made the mistake of saying you'd gone *up* Effingham Road, which made a few eagle-eyed locals wonder why they'd had neither a call nor a leaflet. You're lucky most of the road is people working three jobs and sending the cash home, or you'd have had a few more queries.'

She shrugged. 'I thought I'd covered everything.'

'No. You just thought about your seat, didn't you? It was never about saving Aran. It was about saving your job. Nothing could get in the way.'

'Well why should it?' she almost shouted, the pink patches re-blooming, like sea anemones, on her cheeks. 'Why the hell should it? None of that shit was anything to do with me. I worked fucking hard to get here. You say you know. *Do* you know? I doubt it. I doubt my journey was anything like yours.'

Her hot breath seemed to hang in the still air between them. Rex stood up.

'Aran tell you much about the Yezidis?'

She shook her head.

'They have this god, who's a peacock, who was cast out of heaven. One of their legends says he was cast out of heaven for what he did in the Garden of Eden. He tempted Eve, you see. Dragged her away from paradise.'

Eve shrugged. 'A story.'

'I lied about Bilal's phone,' he said. 'I did have it. But I handed it in to the police on my way here. It doesn't matter what's been deleted – it's all still there. Mina's frantic call to Bilal. Bilal's calls to Aran. All there, forever. So if I were you, Eve, I'd get on the blower to your Media Team.'

* * *

By five thirty, the waiting room had a saggy, sweaty look, like an airliner after a long flight. Crumpled magazines on the chairs, bits of tissue on the coffee table, a gum wrapper that hadn't made it to the bin. Even the receptionist looked like she could with a scrub.

But Rex Tracey was dapper as a daisy. Shaved, cologne on the cheeks, his hair parted, cool in a white shirt and the one suit that had survived, on account of having been abandoned at the drycleaners for six months: a biscuit-coloured linen affair. He hoped and trusted that the appointment about to begin would mark an important change for him, the beginning of a relationship that had been waiting to happen for a long, long time. And needed to, if he was ever to really live. With himself, and with others.

The previous patient left the room. After quite a while, something on the receptionist's desk trilled like some exotic bird. 'Rex Tracey?' she called out – unnecessarily, since he was the only person now waiting. 'Please go in.'

She was tapping at her computer as he walked in. She swivelled on the chair, smiled warmly.

'Glad you could make it,' she said.

'Me too, Maureen,' he said, as he lay on the therapist's couch. 'Me too.'

A NOTE FROM THE AUTHOR:

While there may be many geographical, demographic and commercial similarities between Rex's beloved borough and the real borough of Haringey, in North London, the council referred to in this story, 'Harringay and Tottenham', is as fictitious as its employees and its activities. Any similarity to real persons, events or institutions is coincidental.